PRAISE FOR IRIS JOHANSEN AND
SMOKESCREEN

"Riveting...Readers will keep guessing about the complex characters' underlying motivations as the plot races toward the stunning conclusion."

—*Publishers Weekly*, starred review

"This is dangerous, riveting, and extremely awesome—adjectives that also describe Iris Johansen to a *T*."

—*Suspense Magazine*

"In SMOKESCREEN, Johansen's Eve Duncan must outwit a vicious psychopath in the middle of the jungle. I really enjoyed this rip-roaring thriller."

—Catherine Coulter, *New York Times* bestselling author

"Every element advances the plot to a heart-pounding conclusion. This novel is sure to appeal to Eve Duncan enthusiasts as well as new readers of the series."   —*Library Journal*

"From thriller writer extraordinaire Iris Johansen comes a pulse-pounding excursion into a war-torn nation, where forensic sculptor Eve Duncan heeds a journalist's call to assist in identifying a village's dead after a horrific massacre, only to discover more sinister plots may be lurking behind the journalist's call for assistance."

—CrimeReads.com

"Propelled by a muscular narrative and elaborate subplots, Johansen's latest complex Eve Duncan thriller reliably pivots on the cerebral battle of wills among its robust characters."   —*Booklist*

SMOKESCREEN

BOOKS BY IRIS JOHANSEN
FEATURING EVE DUNCAN
(IN ORDER OF PUBLICATION)

★Starring Jane MacGuire

+Featuring Margaret Douglas

For a complete list of books by Iris Johansen, as well as previews

of upcoming books and information about the author,

visit IrisJohansen.com

SMOKESCREEN

IRIS JOHANSEN

GRAND CENTRAL
PUBLISHING

NEW YORK   BOSTON

Copyright © 2019 by IJ Development

Cover design by Flag. Cover photograph by Getty / CoffeeAndMilk.
Cover copyright © 2020 by Hachette Book Group, Inc.

Grand Central Publishing
Hachette Book Group
1290 Avenue of the Americas, New York, NY 10104
grandcentralpublishing.com
twitter.com/grandcentralpub

Originally published in hardcover and ebook by Grand Central Publishing in July 2019

First Mass Market Edition: August 2020

Grand Central Publishing is a division of Hachette Book Group, Inc. The Grand Central Publishing name and logo is a trademark of Hachette Book Group, Inc.

The publisher is not responsible for websites (or their content) that are not owned by the publisher.

The Hachette Speakers Bureau provides a wide range of authors for speaking events. To find out more, go to www.hachettespeakersbureau.com or call (866) 376-6591.

The Library of Congress has cataloged the hardcover as follows:

Names: Johansen, Iris, author.
Title: Smokescreen / Iris Johansen.
Description: First Edition. | New York: Grand Central Publishing, 2019.
Identifiers: LCCN 2018048366| ISBN 9781538713082 (hardcover) | ISBN 9781538715543 (large print) | ISBN 9781549141409 (audio book) | ISBN 9781549141416 (audio download) | ISBN 9781538762974 (ebook) ISBN 9781538713075 (U.S. trade paperback) / 9781538713068 (mass market)
Subjects: | GSAFD: Mystery fiction.
Classification: LCC PS3560.O275 S66 2019 | DDC 813/.54—dc23
LC record available at https://lccn.loc.gov/2018048366

Printed in the United States of America

OPM

10 9 8 7 6 5 4 3 2 1

PROLOGUE

Headlights!

Jill Cassidy's fingers stabbed into the mud as she saw the light spearing the darkness on the road ahead. The vehicle was going slowly, but they'd never see her on this side path. She had to get to the main road. But she had no shoes, and every muscle was aching, throbbing. She'd tried to get to her feet and walk as soon as she'd heard those bastards leave, but she was too weak. She had only managed to crawl slowly, painfully, through the jungle.

She could *do* this, she told herself desperately as she forced herself to propel her body through the mud on the path. The pain wasn't as bad as it had been when they'd first left her. Ignore it, think about the story. Always think about the story. It wasn't the pain, it was the shock that was causing her to shake and feel so weak.

The shock and this gentle, warm tropical rain that had

started to fall just as she'd finally managed to pull herself together and force herself to move. Strange that warm rain
could make her feel this cold. So gentle, she thought dazedly.
Why on earth had that word occurred to her when there
seemed to be no gentleness left in her world?

The headlights drew closer.

She had to get to the road before the car passed her.

She tried to move faster.

It was a jeep, she realized. The motor was so loud...
Would they hear her if she called out? She *had* to catch their
attention. She made a last effort and rolled out onto the road.

"Jill!" The jeep screeched to a halt. "Dammit to hell!"

Novak, Jill realized. It was Jed Novak, and he was
angry... That was okay, let him be angry. All that mattered
was that he had come, and nothing else could happen to her
as long as he was here.

He jumped out of the jeep. "Jill." He was striding toward
her. "I almost ran over you."

"You...wouldn't do...that. Spoil your...image. CIA to
the...rescue."

"Shut up." Then he was kneeling beside her, the rain
beading off the brim of his hat as he looked down at her.
"Just look at you, Jill," he said hoarsely as he wrapped his
jacket around her. "I told you to be careful. What happened?
Why wasn't someone with you?" In spite of the roughness of
his tone, his hands were gentle as he picked her up and set
her inside the jeep. "How badly are you hurt?"

"I don't know. It...feels bad. But I made it through that
jungle...so I guess it's not—" Jill struggled to keep her voice
steady. It was over. Those bastards were gone. Don't let them
do this to her. "I thought they—were going to—kill me. But
it turned out they—only wanted to teach me a lesson and
get me sent home."

"You have some nasty bruises." He stiffened as the dash-board lights fell on her torn blouse and upper body. "Blood. Shit. I shouldn't have moved you."

"Not—my blood. Hadfeld. They—wanted to show me—his head. They threw it at me . . . He's dead, Novak."

"You're not in good shape yourself. Those bruises are really bad, and they're all over you." He was carefully feeling her arms and body. "Here, too. Your head? Concussion?"

"I don't think so. I never totally blacked out." She'd wanted to black out, but she'd been afraid that if she stopped fighting, she'd never wake up. She started to shake again. Don't think about it. She'd made it this far, and she'd be fine. Just don't think about it.

But she couldn't stop *shaking*.

"Hey, it's okay. You're safe." Novak had pulled her into his arms and was holding her tight. "Breathe deep. Just take it easy. We'll talk about it later."

Safe. She lay there against him, letting his heat warm her, shut out the chill. He was so strong, and she felt as if his strength were pouring into her and shutting out that horri-ble weakness. Yet more than five minutes passed before she could stop shaking.

She finally sat up and pushed him away. "I'm sorry," she said unsteadily. "I fell apart. You asked me why—there wasn't someone—with me. I got the phone call from Hadfeld. But it was a trap. They were waiting for me."

"How many were there?"

"Four."

"Can you describe them?"

Describe the pain? Describe the smell of them? Describe the helplessness she'd felt? But she had to focus and try. She shook her head. "Scarves over the lower . . . half of their faces. One black man, three white. Two of the white men had dark hair, one was fair-haired. It felt like . . . straw. Most of the conversation was in a Maldara dialect."

She had to stop a minute before she could go on. "They . . . wanted to hurt me and . . . they did. The one who was fair-haired kept driving the others to hurt me more and more. He beat me himself, then he told the others what they had to do and how to do it. He said they'd been sent here to do a job, so do it." Say it. She had to tell him. She swallowed. "I have a little blood—down there, and I'll need a rape kit."

Silence. "They raped you?"

"Three of them did. The one with fair hair only seemed to want to beat me. He seemed . . . angry."

"Son of a *bitch*." Then Novak began to swear softly and viciously. "We'll get you to the local hospital in Jokan," he said. "Another fifteen minutes."

"No hospital. Not here," Jill said jerkily. "You're CIA, and I've seen you pull strings. You can get me anything—I need—without throwing me into the system. Do it, Novak."

"The system isn't all that bad when you've been savaged the way you've been, Jill. You're one of the best journalists I've ever come across, but not even a Pulitzer is worth this." He added harshly, "You should have done what I told you and stayed out of it. Would it have been too much to leave it up to me? You knew I'd follow up."

"Yes, I knew you would," Jill said wearily. "Because you're as obsessed as I am. But it was my story—you might have been—too late." She was getting weaker, she realized. That temporary adrenaline rush when she'd felt so safe with Novak was fading. And there was something she had to do, she remembered vaguely. "Do you have a first-aid kit in this jeep?"

"You don't have to do it yourself. I'll get you help right away, Jill."

"It's not for me. I need some medical gloves. I couldn't describe those men, but I—fought them. When they surprised me, they took away my gun, but they'll have scratches." She looked numbly down at her hands. "And I might have some DNA beneath my nails if it survived my trip—through—all that mud."

He muttered another curse, reached into the backseat for the first-aid kit, and handed it to her. The gloves were on top of the bandages, and she quickly pulled them on to protect her nails. She set the first-aid kit on the floor at her feet. Better. One more thing done to rid herself of that terrible feeling of helplessness. "You were driving slow. You were looking for me, weren't you? How did you know I was here?"

"My informant at the embassy intercepted an anonymous call to the secretary shouting about how U.S. journalists were to blame for the ruin of his country and claiming that he'd taken care of one tonight. Their directions were pretty damn accurate. They *wanted* you to be found. I was lucky to reach you before the soldiers from the embassy."

"No, I'm the lucky one." Though luck was a bittersweet concept tonight. But she could imagine how she would have felt if anyone but Novak had found her. "Now take me somewhere you can get those gloves off to a lab so I can get clean again. Then I'll try to figure out how to find out how they knew it was me Hadfeld had contacted."

He was silent. "It might be my fault."

Her gaze flew to his face. "You've got a lead?"

"Better. I think I might be able to get my hands on the skull. So go home and let me work on it," he said roughly. "You've gone through too much as it is."

"Yes, I have." Her hands clenched into fists. "And I'm not the only one. Do you actually believe I'd ever let those bastards get what they wanted? Can't you see? They knew the first thing that the embassy would do if they found out about this would be to notify my publisher. And then they'd send me back to the U.S. to some discreet hospital to go through debriefing and therapy. That's why that bastard told those other men that they had a job to do. That's why they kept beating me. That's why it was rape." Her eyes were suddenly blazing at him. "After all that's gone down here in Maldara, the last thing those diplomats would want would be to have a journalist injured and raped at this stage of the game. Six hundred thousand people were murdered here. Genocide. Now they think they've put Humpty Dumpty back together again. So they'd need to hush any disturbance and wrap me in tender loving care. Why else do you think this happened?" Her voice was shaking. "I told you, those men *knew* what they were doing. They *wanted* to hurt me. They had their orders. Well, I won't let them get away with it."

"Easy," Novak said quietly. "I'll take care of it. No one's going to let that happen."

And if he took care of it, it would mean anyone in Novak's way would be destroyed. She had seen it before. But she didn't want it to go down that way. "You bet they're not. Do you know how weak they made me feel? The pain kept coming and wouldn't stop, and I couldn't do anything about it. I'm never going to be that weak ever again." She wanted to close her eyes and just stop arguing with him. She needed to shut out the world, and maybe, for a little while, those four monsters would vanish with it. But she had to get Novak's promise first. "So this night never happened. Because you're going to let me see to it myself, aren't you? It will take a little while for me to get over this, but you're not going to let anyone sideline me. You're going to let me go after them. I *deserve* it, Novak."

"Do you think I don't know that?" he asked hoarsely. He looked away from her. "Okay, you don't go back to the U.S. I use you and let you help me take them down. And, if you get hurt again doing it, I just consider you collateral damage. Is that the plan?"

"That's the plan." She could close her eyes now. She could relax her body and attempt to block out the pain... and the memory. "Just get me fixed, and then you can tell me how you're going to get the skull."

"And just how am I supposed to fix you, Jill?"

She was getting so blurry she wasn't sure she understood. "You're right, I spoke without thinking. My responsibility... Just take me somewhere, and when I'm better, I'll take care of it."

He was cursing beneath his breath. "Never mind. You're not thinking straight enough to recognize monumental frustration when you hear it." He said slowly, clearly, "Listen. Stop trying to be strong. I know you're strong. You don't have to prove it to me. And I'm not leaving you until I know you're okay. We're in this together." He reached out, grasped her hand, and pressed it tightly. "Do you understand? I'll not let you go."

And, in spite of Novak's being one of the toughest men she'd ever met, he was having trouble with her being hurt and not being able to put her back together again. Strange...

But she couldn't help him now. Maybe later...

Right now, she could only cling desperately to his hand and take whatever comfort he could give her. Because she was starting to shake again, and he had said she didn't have to be strong. "That's very... kind. Do you mind if I—don't talk anymore, Novak?"

"Hell, no." His grip tightened. "Look, this is what we're going to do. I'm taking you to Baldar, the private airport we use near the border, and flying you to Nairobi. There's a hospital there where I send my men when I need absolute secrecy. No reports. No leaks. No one in Maldara will know where you are." He muttered a curse. "Even though I don't want to do it because it will take about an hour and a half to get you there."

"That doesn't matter." Yet she could see he was upset again, and she had to make one last effort. "None of this was your fault. Your decision. My—choice. Stop blaming yourself."

"That's right," he said bitterly. "Collateral damage."

She didn't reply. She was at the end of her strength, and she just wanted to crawl away somewhere until she could heal.

Collateral damage.

It wasn't an accurate description of her role in this nightmare. She had gone after the story with her usual drive and determination. Novak might have thought that the decision he had made caused this to happen to her, but she did not. She'd not been smart enough to read the signs of betrayal when Hadfeld had phoned her. She'd been too eager to get to him and obtain the proof she needed. Even if Novak had found a way to get the skull, things might still be on the verge of exploding.

And there might be true innocents on the horizon who could be hurt by what had happened here at Maldara.

Collateral damage . . .

CHAPTER

1

I thought you'd be finished with her by now." Michael was tilting his head and gazing in disappointment at the reconstruction of the skull on Eve's worktable. "I wanted to see Nora before I left today. Did you have trouble with her?"

"No." Eve made a face at her son as she wiped the clay off her hands with her work towel. "I had trouble with you. I was busy packing your bags and making arrangements for that summer camp your sister, Jane, is so set on taking you to. Nora had to wait."

"She won't mind." Michael wasn't taking his gaze off the skull of the six-year-old child who was Eve's current forensic sculpture. "She'll know you're trying to do what's best for her, that you're trying to bring her home, Mom."

His voice was gentle. Even as a toddler, he had never had

a horror of these skulls of the victims that had appeared in her studio through the years. Now, though he was only ten years old, that understanding and gentleness seemed to have deepened. Eve had never had to explain to him about the monsters who had killed these children, then tried to burn them, bury them, toss them away as if they had never existed. Michael just accepted that Eve was trying to fix something that was broken, that those children were lost and had to go home. Lord, she was lucky.

She gave him a quick hug. "Well, Nora may understand, but the Chicago Police Department isn't that patient. I have to finish this reconstruction and get it back to them so that they can start sending out photos to the newspapers and TV shows. We have to see if anyone can identify her." She turned him around and pushed him toward the hall. "And you have to gather all the treasures you can't bear to leave behind for the next month and pack them in your duffel. Last chance. We have to be at the airport in four hours."

"Right." He smiled at her over his shoulder, his amber eyes shining with mischief. "You're first on the list. Can I take you, Mom?"

She wished he could. She didn't know what she was going to do without him and Joe for a month. "I wouldn't fit in your duffel. But we can Skype." She made a shooing gesture. "Get going."

He laughed and ran down the hall.

She turned back to the reconstruction with a sigh. Noise. Laughter. Family. She was going to miss all of it. She reached out and gently touched the reconstruction's cheekbone. "Sorry, Nora. You're important, too. I'm just having a few issues at the moment."

"Then come with us." Joe was standing in the doorway, looking at her. "A month is a long time." He crossed the room and took her in his arms. "Or let me come back to you." He kissed her. "Screw that seminar. I'll go next time."

"Scotland Yard doesn't offer them that often. And everything is cutting-edge when they do." Joe was a detective with ATLPD and was always interested in all the bells and whistles connected with crime fighting. "And the timing is just too good to miss. Jane is taking Michael to that dig in Wales, and you'll at least be close enough to keep an eye on them."

"Come on, Jane adores Michael. And she's introducing him to digging for ancient Roman treasure at that Welsh castle. Treasure and playing in the dirt. A ten-year-old's dream. He wouldn't miss me."

"He'd miss you." She kissed him again. "Just as I will. But I'm not ten, and I'd feel better if one of us is near him. So would you." Michael had become the center of their lives since the night he'd been born, but neither of them could deny that he was...unusual and always a challenge. "And you can never tell which way he's going to jump."

"Tell me about it," Joe said dryly. "You could come and work in London."

"And then you'd feel guilty about spending all those hours at the Yard." She gave him a quick kiss. "I'll tell you what I told Michael. Skype. Go finish packing. I need to clean up before I take you to the airport." She grimaced. "And I gave in and agreed to give an interview at one this afternoon. Annoying, but it was the only time the reporter could fit me into her schedule. I'll take her out on the porch and try to get rid of her as quickly as possible. But you guys are on your own until we leave here at two."

"We'll manage." He kissed the tip of her nose. "Reluctantly. Why the interview? Does it have anything to do with Nora? She's not even finished." He frowned, puzzled. "And you don't usually give interviews anyway. You say it's a waste of your time."

"It is a waste. They tend to focus on me and not the victim."

"Imagine that," he said mildly. "The foremost forensic sculptor in the world who is both charming and beautiful. How could you possibly compare to a hideous skull that's been buried for decades?"

"Not beautiful, interesting-looking. And I'm not charming, that would require effort. I always opt for kind and intelligent. You must already be missing me if you're resorting to flattery."

"You've got that right."

She cleared her throat. "Me too."

"So why the interview?"

"It's Jill Cassidy. I liked the story she did on that DFACS scandal. She never gave up and fought those politicians who were ignoring the child abuse and fraud claims all the way."

Joe nodded slowly. "I remember. She won a Pulitzer for it." He gently touched her hair. "I should have known it would have something to do with kids. She wants to do some kind of profile on you?"

She shrugged. "I guess she does. We didn't discuss it. I said I could give her an hour if she insisted on its being today. It seemed worthwhile. I don't think she'd waste my time on trivial junk."

"You mean like telling the public how brilliant and famous you are? Heaven forbid." He was heading down the hall. "Not only trivial, but totally boring..."

Eve shook her head as she watched him disappear into the bedroom. Wry, mocking, yet as full of mischief as their son. Nothing boring about Joe. She was already missing him. Their relationship had taken them through valleys and mountains, and they had come out of both with a closeness and love that no longer faltered no matter what strain was put upon it. She frowned as she had a sudden thought. Good Lord, what if that interview involved Joe and Michael? The last thing she needed was a journalist looking for a tell-all piece that violated her privacy. She could not permit it.

Don't jump to conclusions.

If she saw that was the way the interview was heading, she'd just end it immediately. She wasn't shy about protecting her family's privacy.

And she'd taken the interview because Jill Cassidy had shown herself to be a responsible journalist. Joe had been joking about Eve's being boring, but it was true that she was not someone whom social media would find particularly fascinating. She was not only a workaholic, she was too complicated . . . and very private.

She just had to hope she wasn't getting mixed signals from Jill Cassidy . . .

———◆———

"Hello. I'm Jill Cassidy." The young woman at the door was smiling warmly at Eve as she shook her hand. "Please call me Jill. I can't tell you how eager I've been to meet you, Eve Duncan. Thank you for agreeing to see me."

"Come in. I'm sorry I can't give you very long. I have to take my husband and son to catch a flight." Eve was studying the reporter and feeling distinctly relieved. Jill Cassidy must be late twenties or early thirties, a little on the thin side, with medium-length brown hair and wide-set blue eyes. Full lips that had a touch of sensitivity and humor and clear, glowing skin. But those eyes were steady and honest, and Eve felt the honesty was also very real. She was dressed in dark slacks and a simple white blouse that made her appear businesslike yet perfectly natural and unassuming. "I expected you to be older. You won that Pulitzer two years ago."

"I got lucky. Right story. Right timing." She was looking around the open living room and kitchen. "This is wonderful."

"It's home," Eve said simply.

"That's why it's wonderful. You can feel it. I'm traveling most of the time, so my home is usually the nearest hotel." She gestured to the smiling portrait of Eve dressed in her old blue work shirt on the wall beside the window. "That's terrific. Relaxed, but there's still a sense of purpose. Your daughter, Jane MacGuire, painted it?"

Eve's eyes widened. "Yes. You're right, Jane is terrific. Her career as an artist is zooming these days. How did you know about her?"

"I do my homework." Her gaze was wandering around the room. "You have a longtime relationship with Joe Quinn, a police detective whom you married eight years ago. You have a ten-year-old son, Michael; and besides Jane MacGuire, whom you adopted when she was about Michael's age, you and Joe Quinn took in another young girl, Cara Delaney, and made her your ward. She's not with you now either, since she's a promising violinist and she's on tour." Her gaze returned to Eve's face. "Now, I found her background to be very interesting indeed."

Eve stiffened, instantly on guard. That remark had been too full of meaning to miss. "Really? But you asked to interview *me*, didn't you? I don't consider my husband or children to be fodder for the press. I believe you'd better leave."

She shook her head. "Do you think I'd have mentioned Cara Delaney if I'd meant to cause you problems? I just had to make certain you knew that I could hurt you if I chose and had no intention of doing so. Otherwise, you'd be worried all the time I was talking to you that I was going to cause some kind of scandal by revealing that your ward is the granddaughter of Sergai Kaskov, a known figure in the Russian Mafia." She gestured impatiently. "I don't care about that. All I care about is that you're brilliant and have devoted most of your career to helping children who have been murdered and abused. Evidently, somewhere along the way, you've also been able to build a life for yourself and your family that I envy with all my heart. Good for you."

"You couldn't have hurt Cara." Jill Cassidy seemed to be sincere, but Eve was still wary. "She wouldn't give a damn about scandal. All she cares about is the music. Though you'd find the rest of the family very protective and might find yourself in an extremely uncomfortable situation." Eve stared at her. "You could have just not mentioned my family at all. This was all very deliberate."

She nodded. "Because as I said, I do my homework. You're sharp and very protective. You'd start questioning what I was asking of you the minute you realized I wasn't being totally honest with you."

Eve frowned. "That's not quite clear."

"And you like everything crystal clear," Jill said brusquely. "And you said we don't have much time. Can we sit down somewhere and talk?" She smiled crookedly. "Unless I've completely misread you, and you're going to throw me out?"

"I came close a few minutes ago," Eve said slowly. "I'm still not sure about you. I believe I might have to do a little homework on you, too."

"It's a good idea," Jill said soberly. "Don't trust me. I promise I'm not trying to hurt you or your family. But you don't know me." She smiled. "And all that honesty might be intended to disarm you. But can we still sit down and talk? That won't hurt you."

Eve hesitated. And that honesty *was* disarming her, she realized. Her first wariness was fading, and she was beginning to like Jill Cassidy. "We can talk." She gestured toward the porch. "I'll give you a cup of coffee on the porch. It's our only guarantee of privacy. Joe and Michael might be all over the place while they're packing."

"Great." Jill started to turn away; and then her attention was caught by the skull reconstruction on the worktable across the room. "You work here?" She moved across the room. "I thought you'd have a separate studio." She was reaching out and touching the skull. "May I?"

"It appears that you may," Eve said dryly. "And will."

Jill looked at her. "I just wanted to see your work. She's not finished?"

Eve shook her head. "Close. But Nora will take a few more days." She gazed at her curiously. "How did you know she was female?"

"The lips. The nose. Both very feminine. The rest is blurred and incomplete, but she's there, waiting to be born."

"No, she's not. Nora was born six years before a monster decided to snatch that life away from her. Now all I can do is help her to try to find someone who loved her as much as that monster hated her and send her home." She added grimly, "And hope I can find the monster and send him to the electric chair."

"Amen," Jill murmured. "I understand you've managed to do that a number of times."

"Not enough. Never enough." She gestured to the porch door. "There are too many monsters out there."

"Yes, there are." Jill was still staring at the reconstruction. "You called her Nora. You have some idea who she was?"

"No, I always name my reconstructions. It helps me to connect with them." She started for the door. "Now I have a question for you. You appear familiar with skulls and recon-structions. You not only have a good eye, you know what to look for. Have you been taught?"

Jill shook her head. "Heavens no. Self-taught on the Internet because it's both your profession and your passion. But the key word is familiarity. I only wanted to know what I was seeing."

"Are you planning a series of articles instead of just interviewing me?"

"No." She grinned. "And that's two questions." She opened the porch door. "I'll wait on the porch while you get me that cup of coffee. But I'll give you a teaser to make you want to hurry it along." She looked back at Eve. "I don't want to interview you at all. I want to offer you a job that I hope I can convince you to take. Gross misrepresentation. If you're too pissed off to even let me try, you can toss me in that beautiful lake. Okay?"

Jill didn't wait for an answer. She closed the door behind her.

"I don't have time for this," Eve said as she handed Jill her coffee five minutes later. "You picked the wrong day, Ms. Cassidy."

"We've gone back to formality?" Jill asked. "At least you didn't choose the lake option."

"I considered it."

Jill tilted her head. "But you were curious. You have a certain amount of respect for me and were willing to risk being disappointed. But you also have an innate curiosity, which is natural considering your profession."

"That curiosity will be fading away if you don't satisfy it

soon. You don't wish to interview me." She asked bluntly, "What the hell do you want with me?"

"Basically the same thing you've done during your entire career," she said quietly. "I want you to identify a number of skulls and bring resolution and peace to their families and loved ones." She paused. "I want you to bring them home."

"I already have a waiting list of cases," Eve said impatiently. "I don't need any more. There are other forensic sculptors you can hire."

"But they're not you." Jill leaned forward. "And they won't give those children the skill and dedication you would. They were murdered, and now they're already being forgotten."

"Children? Plural? How many children?"

"Twenty-seven."

Eve felt a ripple of shock. "A mass murderer?"

"Oh, yes. Though not what you might think."

Twenty-seven children. It made Eve sick to her stomach. "Then tell me what I should think."

"Maldara."

Eve went still. "My God."

Jill slowly nodded. "Though I haven't seen any sign of God in Maldara since the moment I stepped off the plane two years ago. What do you know about Maldara?"

"What everyone knows. Two warring groups in the depths of the Congo struggling for supremacy. Civil war. Blood. Gore." She swallowed. "Another Rwanda. So many deaths. The ruling party managed to triumph about eighteen months ago." She searched for a name. "The Kiyanis I think. Their president was able to persuade the U.N. to support her."

"Yes, Zahra Kiyani is very persuasive," Jill said. "Over six hundred thousand people died in Maldara during that conflict, and only fifty thousand were laid at her door. She was Teflon."

Only fifty thousand. Eve could only vaguely remember the details of that horror she had seen on TV and the Internet two years ago. "Men, women, and children. Butchered. I didn't want Michael to watch it." She lifted her head as a sudden thought occurred to her. "Children. You want me to do reconstructions on the children of that massacre?"

"Not all of them. You'd be there for decades." Jill's lips twisted. "There are far too many. But there's a school in the village of Robaku, near Jokan on the northern border, where I've been doing volunteer work. Twenty-seven students were killed by a machete brigade led by Nils Varak, a mercenary who was hired by the Botzan faction because it was practically on the Kiyani doorstep. The children were chopped to pieces. Then the school was burned to the ground."

"Terrible," Eve said, sick. It wasn't difficult to envision the terror and pain that must have enveloped the children that day.

"Yes, every minute of it was terrible," Jill said jerkily. "Some of the children weren't dead when the fires were lit. Varak was too impatient to wait. He wanted to lure the people from the village to the school with the screams." She drew a shaky breath. "But you're in a hurry. I have to tell you why I need you. Almost half the villagers were killed that day, most of them parents. But some are left, and there are other relatives, grandparents, uncles, aunts, who also loved those children. But after the massacre, those relatives were devastated. They don't even know which of the children are their own. The damage was too great. The government of Kiyani offered a common grave, but they've refused the offer. They want to bury their own children in the village where they were born." She added softly, "It seems the feeling is universal. They want to bring their children home, Eve."

Eve nodded. The story had touched her unbearably. "Have they tried DNA?"

"It was a bloodbath. With the fires and scattered remains, only a few had enough quality DNA left to be matched. And even those parents wouldn't be satisfied. These are simple village people, Eve. They don't want to be given a piece of paper with a DNA result. They're willing to wait for the years it will take to DNA the bodies, but not the skulls. They want to see, to touch, to recognize." Her eyes were glittering with moisture. "They need *you*, Eve."

"Not necessarily me, Jill. I'm good, but I'm not the only one who could do this. Besides, it would be a massive undertaking to gather those remains and send them to me. The U.N. should hire several forensic sculptors and set up studios on-site at Robaku. That would be the quickest way to get it done."

"The quickest, not the best. Having you do it would be the best." Jill shrugged. "And U.N. funding isn't an option. They've already refused to approve anything but the least expensive methods of disposing of those children. Maldara has turned into one huge cemetery they don't want to face. If a mass grave wouldn't be such bad press, they'd probably even approve that over working with DNA."

Eve felt a ripple of shock. "That's pretty harsh."

"It's the way of the world," Jill said wearily. "The U.N. has too many fires to put out for sentimentality. They regard Maldara's fate as settled, so they want to put a period to it and move on in the most economical way possible. That's only good business. Zahra Kiyani would even like everyone to forget about that massacre and has been pushing to move the villagers to another location. I've been writing story after story about Robaku to keep the interest and sympathy high and not let the wishes of those relatives be forgotten."

"There are many charitable organizations not connected to the U.N.," Eve said. "I've worked with a few over the years. Ask for money and volunteers."

"I am," Jill said simply. "I'm asking you to volunteer. I can gather enough money together to pay you to come to Maldara and do the reconstructions on those children. You're the best one for this job, and they deserve the best."

"I'm sure they do, but there are other fine forensic sculptors." Eve had seen where this was going and had tried to offer alternatives to avoid having to refuse her. She could see that Jill Cassidy was passionately committed to helping those children. The story had touched and horrified Eve, and she could almost feel the agony of the parents who had lost their children to those butchers. "Not me, Jill," she said gently. "I have a career with commitments. I have a family who needs me. I can't go flying across the ocean to work in a country in the middle of Africa."

"I know I'm asking a lot." Jill's face was tense. "But they need help. If you could see..." She reached in her briefcase and pulled out a manila folder. "Here. You can see them." She thrust the folder at Eve. "You could put off your other commitments for a little while, couldn't you? These people have lost so much already. Someone should care enough to give them something to make—" She broke off, then said, "I can talk about your work, but there's nothing I can say that would make leaving your family any better. I don't even have a family any longer, but I know it would suck." She drew a deep breath. "But if you could give those kids just a few weeks, it would give me time to try to work something else out for them."

Eve shook her head. "I have a life, Jill. You're asking me for a major disruption. And I don't even know if it's the best thing for those village families. You're asking me to trust your judgment."

"Yes, I am. Or your own judgment after you look at

the biographies and photos in that envelope." She reached
out and grasped Eve's hand. "Look, I know it's a sacrifice.
Who wants to go to a wild, underdeveloped country and
set up shop in a jungle for those weeks? But if you agree
to do it, I know you'll come back feeling good about it.
And maybe it's not so underdeveloped any longer. It has a
U.S. embassy, there's a temporary U.N. headquarters, and
reps come in and out of Jokan, the capital city, on a regular
basis." She grimaced. "It's practically civilized compared to
when I first visited."

"You said that was two years ago." She frowned. "The
fighting was still going on then. I'm surprised they let you in
the country."

"They didn't. But I had a few friends in high places and
even more in low places who managed to smuggle me under
the radar. I had an idea it might be the story of the decade,
and I wanted to be there." Her lips tightened. "I knew it was
a second Rwanda, but I thought I was tough enough to take
it. And I did take it, I just didn't realize I'd be caught up in the
nightmare and start bleeding myself. You don't go through an
experience like that without its changing your life."

"Changing?"

"I was first on the scene, and I told the stories." Her face
was haunted. "But you can't do that in a place like Maldara
without becoming part of the story."

"Yet you want me to go and tell stories of my own when
I do those reconstructions," Eve said quietly. "And you know
that it will probably hurt me to do them. Every single one
I've ever done has hurt me, Jill. It goes with the territory. And
this time, I wouldn't even have the comfort of doing it to try
to find the butchers who murdered them. They had to have
been killed or imprisoned by now."

"I know." She nodded jerkily. "So do it for their parents

or grandparents. Nothing is perfect. Particularly in Maldara."
Her hand tightened on Eve's. "Just *do* it. I promise I'll make
it safe for you and as comfortable as I can."

"I know you would." Eve gently pulled away her hand.
"And I admire you and what you're trying to do for these
people. But I have my own commitments I have to think
about. Maldara is half a world away from them. But I promise
I'll try to find an organization that will be able to give you
the help you need."

"Thank you." Jill's voice was unsteady. "I guess I couldn't
expect anything else from you." There was desperation in
her eyes as she held Eve's gaze. "But you're the help I need.
Please. Will you promise to think about it?" She reached in
her pocket and handed Eve her card. "Just call me, and I'll
arrange everything."

"I'll think about it," Eve said. "But I'm afraid I'll disappoint you, Jill. I can't do—"

"Mom, we're ready to go!" Michael was standing in the
doorway, his eyes shining with eagerness. "Dad's grabbing
the suitcases and that present I made for Jane." His gaze was
on Jill. "But if you're still busy, I'll help Dad take the suitcases
down to the car and we'll wait for you there."

"No, I believe we're finished here." Eve got to her feet.
"It took a little longer than I thought." She held out her
hand to him. "This is my son, Michael, Jill. This is Jill Cassidy, Michael, come and shake hands with her. She's a very
famous journalist, and you'll probably be seeing her stories
in newspapers and on the Net."

"Really?" He was across the porch and smiling at Jill.
"That will be neat. I'm very glad to meet you, Ms. Cassidy."
He shook her hand and looked her straight in the eye. "I'll be
watching for them. I think you must be very smart if you're
this famous so young."

"Not so young." Jill smiled. "Compared to you, I'm ancient. I'm happy to meet you, Michael. I can see why your
mother is so proud of her family."

"We're proud of her, too." He turned away and went back
to Eve. "I think I'll go back inside and help Dad. He might
need me." He leaned forward, and whispered to Eve as he
passed her, "She's so *sad*, Mom. Be nice to her." Then he was
through the door and talking to his father.

"Sweet kid." Jill was looking after him. "You're lucky."

"Yes, I am." She shouldn't have been surprised at
Michael's instant insight, but she was. Jill had been hiding
that vulnerability very well, even from Eve, until those last
moments. But then Eve and Joe had known since the moment he was born that Michael saw deeper than other people. "But like all kids, he has a few issues." One of which was
to make her feel guilty when she agreed with what he saw,
she thought crossly. Gazing at Jill Cassidy right now, Eve was
acutely aware of the scars that had been born of the emotional battles the woman had fought over the years. "He can
be very demanding on occasion."

"I see absolutely nothing wrong with that," Jill said with
a smile. "I can be demanding myself. I believe we'd get along
fine." Her smile faded as she turned toward the porch steps.
"But I'm in your way. You said you had to take your husband
and son to the airport. Thank you for seeing me."

"You're welcome. I'm sorry I can't help you." She followed Jill to the steps. "I meant what I said, I'll get on the
phone tomorrow and try to talk to several charities."

"I'm sure you will." Jill looked back at her, and Eve was
once more aware of that hint of desperation in her expression. "Just look at the family photos and read my biographies
of the children. That's all I ask. After meeting your son, I
know that's a lot. But I have to ask it."

Eve gazed at the manila envelope on the cushions of the porch swing. "I'll look at them." She shook her hand. "But I can't let them change my mind. It was nice meeting you, Jill."

Jill nodded and made an effort to smile. "Yeah, I hope Nora turns out the way you want her."

"That depends on her," Eve said. "I never know until the last sculpting."

"Why doesn't that surprise me?" Jill waved and ran down the steps.

Eve stood there and watched her as she got into her dark blue Volvo and backed out of the driveway. Jill smiled again as she waved and drove down the lake road.

Smiles?

She's so sad, Michael had said.

"Hi." Michael was suddenly standing beside her, his gaze on the car. "Did we stay inside long enough? Did you have time to fix it?"

"No," Eve said. "Sometimes people have to fix their own problems. Though I'll make a few calls for her tomorrow." She gave him a little push to stop the protest she could see was coming. "But right now I want to spend time just being with you and your dad and not thinking of anyone else until you get on that jet. Go get your luggage."

———◆———

Jill pulled onto a side road a few miles from the lake cottage and turned off the engine of the Volvo. She realized she was shaking. Stupid. Everything had gone well, and there was no reason for her to be this upset. Yet she had felt like she had to take a few moments before she got on the freeway. She had wanted to catch a final glimpse of Eve Duncan and her family before she took the next step that would send Eve spiraling into the coming nightmare.

Maybe it would not happen. She had tried to take precautions that might keep Eve safe.

Or might not.

Either way, Jill was committed, and all the regrets in the world wouldn't alter what she'd done. So stop this nonsense and make certain that the rest of the plan was set as well. She quickly dialed Jed Novak before she could change her mind. "It's okay," she said when he picked up. "They're on their way to the airport, and Eve Duncan isn't getting on that flight with them. The only worry I had was that she might change her mind. She's very close to her family, and that could have happened."

"But you said it wasn't likely," Novak said dryly. "And I built the entire scenario around your judgment. I'm glad you didn't disappoint me."

"You would have just made me come up with something else. You don't allow failure, Novak."

Silence. "No, I don't. Not once you were committed. The stakes are too high." He paused. "Is she going to do it?"

"I think she will. She turned me down, but she'll look at the photos and the children's stories. They'll be very effective. Then she won't be able to resist going back and finding out more about Maldara. She'll allow a little time to pass, then she'll find a way to do what I asked."

"You seem certain."

"I'm as certain as I can be considering how intelligent she is. As I told her, I did my homework." Jill added curtly, "She doesn't want to do it. She wants to keep her commitments with all those law-enforcement bodies she had on her agenda. And she has family responsibilities and knows that there's always a possibility of harm when you go to a country like Maldara. That's why you have to reassure her that the risk is minimal when she starts checking. Have you set it up?"

"Of course," he said dryly. "This isn't my first rodeo, Jill."

"No, you were probably there when they built the Colosseum. I'm the one who doesn't have the experience. But I have to do this right, Novak." Her hands tightened on the steering wheel. "And the risk has to be as minimal as we're letting her think. You have to keep her safe, Novak."

"It will go right if you've read Eve Duncan right. You've told me all the things that are con, what are the pros?"

"Only two things. I'm good at what I do. I made very sure the photos of the massacre and the families will shock and touch her. And I guarantee my stories in that envelope will do the rest. They're going to haunt her, she won't be able to forget them."

"And the other thing?"

"She likes me," she said simply. "And I know it's hard for her not to trust someone she likes." She drew a shaky breath. "Because I like her, too. So make sure we don't get her butchered, Novak."

"I'll work on it."

She braced herself. "And while you're doing that, I should tell you that on that last day before I left Maldara, I thought I was being followed."

"You were. Don't worry. I'm on it. I'll get back to you."

"That's comforting," she said dryly. "Kind of you to let me know." She cut the connection.

She didn't feel as if she could talk to Novak any more right now. He was a master at the games that all those covert organizations played, and she was a rank amateur. That was fine with her; she had never wanted to be anything but a journalist and tell the story.

But not this story.

She stiffened as she glimpsed Eve Duncan's Toyota driving down the lake road. She was at the wheel, and her son and husband were smiling and talking to her. She was also smiling and looked happy as if life was good and there was no Maldara in the world.

And Jill could make certain there would be no Maldara for Eve Duncan. She could step away and take the story in another direction.

But she knew she wasn't going to do it.

She was going to let it happen.

CHAPTER

2

I'll call you from London as soon as we get in," Joe said. "Jane said that we'll be going out to breakfast after she picks us up, then drop by her apartment to rest until she and Michael leave for Wales tomorrow evening."

"And you'll be using her apartment while you're at the seminar," Eve said. "I told you it was meant to be. The timing was almost too good to be true."

"Not if you're not with us." His hand reached up to cup her cheek. "Change your mind?"

"I'm tempted." More than tempted. The idea of going back home while they flew off into the wild blue yonder was already causing her an aching sense of loss. "Maybe after I finish Nora. I'll see in a few days."

"Good." He kissed her. "I'll keep after you."

"If you have time," she said ruefully. "During that last seminar at the Yard, you were busy from dusk to dawn. And

afterward, you and the guys were cementing international re-
lations at every pub near Scotland Yard."

"Only the one on Whitehall. The others closed too early.
But I might just have time for you." He grinned. "Try me."
He slipped his arm around her waist, and they walked toward
the jetway, where Michael was waiting, playing a game on his
computer. "Though I'll have to think about it. I was a little insulted when you sent Michael in to tell me we had to sit down
and wait until you finished that interview with Jill Cassidy."

"It wasn't exactly an interview. It turned out to be something different." That was an understatement. "And that
wasn't me, that was Michael. He liked her. He was feeling
sorry for her and thought I should help her."

"Why?"

"You know Michael. He just said she was sad." She shrugged.
"And maybe she is. Journalists don't have tremendously happy
lives. They see too much. Big-time stress. But I told him sometimes people have to fix their own problems." She turned and
kissed him again, hard. "And the only problems I want to fix
right now are yours and Michael's," she said fiercely. "You take
care of yourself, and I'll expect at least one Skype a day. Even if
it has to be from a pub on Whitehall Street."

"You'll get it." His hand gently caressed her cheek. "Don't
work too hard. I don't want to come back to a haggard wife
who will send me running back to that pub to drown my
sorrows." He grinned. "Now go say good-bye to Michael.
I'm sure he wants to lecture you about your mistreatment of
Jill Cassidy."

"No, he won't. Not this close to the time he's going to
have to leave me. I'll get a break." She was moving toward
Michael. "But he might do it on our first Skype call!"

———◆———

Dammit.

Eve could feel her eyes sting with tears as she drove up the driveway to the lake cottage. The place seemed just as empty as she'd been afraid it would be without Joe and Michael. It had been bad when she'd watched the plane take off, but this was worse. This was where there were a million memories, and she'd have to fight them every single day.

She wanted to run back to the airport and jump on the next plane.

Yeah, that would be mature and responsible. It would be good for Michael to spend time with his sister. He and Jane didn't get a chance to bond that often. And she'd be in Joe's way while he was networking. Just get busy and this month would fly by and they'd all be together again.

She ran up the porch steps and threw open the door. It was getting dark, and she flicked on the light. That was more cheerful. She threw down her purse and moved to her work-table in the studio across the room. "Hi, Nora." She looked down at the reconstruction. "It's just me and you, kid. But we'll get along just fine, won't we?" She touched the clay of her cheekbone with her index finger. "And after that, we'll find someone else to help."

Nora gazed up at her from blind eyes. Eve hadn't put the glass eyes in the eye orbits yet. That was always the last touch. Usually she didn't even notice that emptiness, but she did today. Probably because she was feeling so empty herself. "Maybe we won't work right away." She turned away. "No offense. I'll just have a cup of coffee, then call Jane and tell her they're on their way. We'll get together later tonight."

But the call to Jane went straight to voice mail. Jane was always busy, and she might even have a gallery showing. Later. Everything seemed to be later today.

She took her coffee to the porch and looked out at the

lake. Beautiful as usual. But it wasn't as lit by sunlight as it had been earlier when she'd been out here with Jill Cassidy. The sun had gone down, and it was a little somber.

Jill Cassidy.

Promise you'll look at them.

Her gaze went to the manila envelope she'd left on the porch swing. She didn't want to look at those photos. She'd seen more than enough horror photos in her career in forensics. She was depressed enough today.

Promise me.

She could almost see Jill standing on those steps, pleading desperately.

She's so sad.

And Michael had ganged up on Eve.

Oh, well, just do it. She crossed to the swing, plopped down, and reached for the envelope. It might be better that her mood was as somber as that lake out there. She pulled out the photos and switched on the light. It couldn't be any worse than what she'd seen before...

———————

Wrong.

Two hours later, the tears were still running down Eve's cheeks. So much worse than anything she'd ever encountered in her career thus far. Not only the butchery and the burning of innocents, but Jill had researched and interviewed parents, relatives, friends, and siblings of each child in the village. Then she had written their stories from birth to the day of their horrible death. Each word simple but poignant until Eve had felt that every one of those children belonged to her.

She leaned her head back and closed her eyes, but the tears still flowed. She could still see that day, feel the darkness of terror as the militia had come and hacked and hacked with their machetes. Would she ever not see it? Jill Cassidy had made every moment come alive for her and anyone else who read those damnably beautiful, agonizingly human, stories.

Close it out.

Impossible.

Jill had known it would be impossible. That's why she had made Eve promise to look at them. Brilliant, wise, Jill Cassidy, who had done her homework and had no trouble reading her. She would have been resentful except for the fact that Jill could not have written those words if she hadn't been caught up in the same agony as Eve was feeling now. They were bound together by the pain of those helpless children butchered in that village.

But don't let Jill Cassidy manipulate her. Push it away. Don't give in to it. Six hundred thousand people had died in Maldara. These were only twenty-seven children.

But now, she knew every single one of them.

She opened her eyes. She would *not* cry again. Tears did no good. Find a solution or accept the pain. She reached for her computer and flipped open the lid.

Maldara...

———◆———

It wasn't Joe but Jane who called her four hours later. "I'm calling from the apartment. Michael and Joe are here and safe," she said. "But there's something missing. You. I thought I was going to be reasonable and not harass you, but then when you didn't show up at customs, I decided that was bullshit. Get on the next plane. I don't care if you smuggle that skull through customs and just work here at the apartment. Or if you decide to go with us to the dig. At least you'd be here. That's where you belong. Now do what I say, dammit."

Eve could almost see her toss her red hair as she said those last words. Jane was always passionate when it came to family, and this wasn't totally unexpected. "I'm thinking about it. Though we both know that you're all going to be so busy that you probably wouldn't know I was around."

"We'd know." She sighed. "I just thought that I'd add my two cents' worth to the guilt trip Joe has no doubt been bombarding you with. I guess I'll just have to leave it to him."

"You'll have enough on your plate with supervising Michael on that dig. He's so excited about it. I know it's going to be wonderful."

"I think it will. Most of the time, they only permit older students on these digs. I went on my first one when I was a teenager, remember? So when I ran across the information on this one in Wales that was allowing younger kids, I jumped on it." She chuckled. "And I'm not sure who's going to supervise whom. Michael is already making plans and reading all my literature on it. I'm expecting sunrise to sunset to be the time-frame agenda."

"See? You'd have to squeeze me in."

"I'm not handling this well. I'd better hand you over to Joe. He has more experience at bulldozing you. I love you."

The next moment, Joe came on the line. "As Jane said, we're here and already missing you. She insisted on trying her powers of persuasion one more time. We stopped for breakfast on the way from the airport. Did I wake you?"

"No, it's only a little after midnight here, and I've been busy," Eve said. "Good flight?"

"Passable. Michael and I played cards. He's decided that counting cards shouldn't really be considered illegal in the casinos, and he's perfecting his technique."

"Heaven help us. Don't you dare take him to a casino."

"I think he'll be content with Jane once they start working at the dig in Wales. Why weren't you sleeping? Nora?"

"No." She paused. "Just doing some research about some skulls found in Maldara. I didn't know much about it."

"Maldara? From what I remember from the news stories, you'd do better researching almost anything else. Nightmare stuff. I remember you were very careful to keep it away from Michael's eyes."

"Which meant I had to ignore a lot of it myself. I only knew it was a civil war between the Kiyanis and the Botzan factions in central Africa that tore the country and most of its people apart. It went on for almost two years before the U.N. sent in forces to stop it." Her hand tightened on the phone as she remembered the photos of what those troops had found when they'd crossed the border. "The Botzan had hired a mercenary, a guerilla leader, Nils Varak, to run rampant over the country and attack the Kiyanis. Most of the butchery and burning was done by him and his men. He used the Botzan militia machete troops on occasion, but mostly he liked the personal touch." She added harshly, "The news stories said he had more blood on his hands than Hitler before the U.N. forces managed to kill him."

"Not soon enough," Joe said grimly. "When he first started that bloodbath, every police department in the world was canvassed for information about him. When I read his rap sheet, I was tempted to volunteer to go after the son of a bitch myself. Varak was into everything from child trafficking to terrorism. Pay him enough, and he'd do anything."

Even kill twenty-seven small children who had done nothing to deserve it. "I agree, he wasn't killed soon enough. I don't remember your telling me about that query."

"It was hardly dinner conversation. Since I decided not

to do anything about it, I didn't see why I should discuss it. I was just as glad you were in Michael-protecting mode. You didn't need any more darkness hanging over you." He paused. When he next spoke, his voice was curt. "And why were you researching skulls in Maldara? Whose skulls?"

She didn't want to get into this now, but she wouldn't lie to him. "Children. I don't really know. When do I ever know, Joe? I just heard about this massacre at a school in Robaku village from Jill Cassidy and felt I had to know more about it. But I couldn't find out much. In spite of the U.N. presence, that country seems to still be in chaos."

"I can believe it," Joe said grimly. "Which is why I don't like you even thinking about it."

"Maybe if someone had thought about Maldara before that chaos started, I wouldn't have had to hear about those children's skulls today." She drew a deep breath. "Go to bed, Joe. All I did was do a little research. No big deal. I'll talk to you tomorrow. Right now, I'm going to put in an hour or so on Nora. I've been neglecting her today."

Silence. "Yes, you have. And you were so anxious to get her finished. Now I'm anxious for you to do it, too, because I want you here, Eve." He paused. "I love you. Being without you sucks. I'll talk to you when I get back here to the apartment tomorrow night."

"I love you, too. Tell Michael I'll call him before it's time for him to leave for Wales this evening. Good night, Joe." She cut the connection.

She had worried Joe, and it might be for nothing. She should have just kept her mouth shut about Maldara. No, she shouldn't. She rejected the thought immediately. Their relationship was based on total honesty, and silence could also be dishonest. Besides, they were so close, he would probably have sensed her disturbance.

Just work on Nora for a few hours and go to bed and get to sleep.
Maybe by the time she woke tomorrow, that aching unrest
would have lessened.

She picked up her ruler to check Nora's mid-philtrum
measurements one last time. That space between nose and
lips was so small, so delicate, on a child. Six years old...

There had been six-year-olds in that classroom in Maldara, too. One girl and two little boys. Robaku had been a
village school, and one teacher had taught various ages and
grades. Jill Cassidy had spent a good deal of time and effort
detailing the short lives of those six-year-olds.

Eve had to stop working and close her eyes for an instant
as the wave of horror and heartbreaking sadness overcame
her once more. Then she got control again and put the ruler
down and started to fill in the clay around the mid-philtrum.

It might be a long night.

Damn you, Jill Cassidy.

———▶———

NEXT DAY
2:35 P.M.

Do it!

Eve stabbed in the phone number on the card that Jill had
given her. She wasn't surprised when Jill answered the phone
in two rings. "Get over here. I want to talk to you."

"I thought you might," Jill said quietly. "Actually, I
thought it could be—"

"Get over here," Eve interrupted. "I'm angry, and on edge,
and I want to see your face while I'm listening to what you say
to me. You went to a hell of a lot of trouble to tear me apart,
and I have an idea why. How quick can you be here?"

"Ten minutes. I'm in a motel just off the freeway."

"I thought you'd stay close," Eve said curtly. "I'm surprised you didn't camp out in your car."

"I thought about it."

"I'm sure you did. I'll expect you in ten minutes, and don't expect either coffee or politeness. We've gone past that now." She hung up.

She got to her feet and moved toward the door to the porch. She needed air and to calm down a little before she confronted Jill. She hadn't realized until she'd actually made contact with her how the anger had been building in the last few hours. Or perhaps it had started building earlier, during all the hours she'd been working on Nora last night.

She took a deep breath and gazed out at the lake, trying to steady herself.

Sunlight. Beauty. Peace.

Everything that she wanted to surround her while she was working on Nora and others like her who had been robbed of all three.

And this was Eve's life, her *home*.

The anger was growing again.

But now she had a target.

Jill was driving down the lake road and pulling into the driveway.

Eve met her at the top of the stairs. "You're early. You must be eager to see me."

"I broke a few speed laws. I figured that you needed to vent before you exploded," she said. "You don't get angry often, but when you do, it's supposed to be impressive."

"Of course you'd know that about me, too. Research."

"Yes." Jill's gaze was studying her face. "Circles. You didn't sleep last night. I'm sorry."

"Are you? I don't believe you. I think it was all part of

your plan to manipulate me. You knew exactly how to do it. You knew which buttons to push and took time to coordinate them in the right order." Her lips tightened. "Those photos and biographies were a masterstroke. They brought me down as if I'd been run over by a fifty-ton truck. You knew they would, didn't you?"

"Yes. It was your principal weakness." She added, "And your greatest strength. I had to use it."

"You're not even denying it."

"Why should I? You'd know I was lying, and I wouldn't insult you." She paused. "Besides, I've won, haven't I?"

Eve stared at her in frustration. It was difficult to hold on to her anger as she gazed at the reporter. Jill wasn't boasting; there was only vulnerability and that sadness Michael had noticed. "Not yet. I *hate* being manipulated. Last night, I started thinking about every way you'd done that since you walked in here yesterday afternoon. It took me a little while to get it together because you were so clever and so good at what you do. Even those photos weren't close-ups of the children. Just loving family shots. Because you knew I never looked at facial photos of my reconstructions." Her lips tightened. "And then you hit me with the photos after the massacre."

"I didn't want to do it. But I had to convince you." She moistened her lips. "We need you, Eve. You don't realize how much. But I promise if you come, that you'll see how worthwhile it is."

"I can tell that you think it is. But you're asking me to put my life and career on hold while I do those reconstructions."

"Only for a few weeks. I told you, I wouldn't expect more from you."

"How generous of you," she said dryly. "It's what I expect of myself that matters. You've been playing me to get what you want, but that's over." She was silent. "I'm the only one in charge of what I do, but there are things I have to know before I commit." She stared her straight in the eyes. "Is everything you told me the truth?"

Jill's gaze didn't waver. "Absolutely. Every word."

"Even those stories you wrote about the children at the school, *their* stories?"

Jill nodded. "I swear it. You can ask their parents and grandparents. You believe me?"

Eve couldn't help but believe her. "You're so good at what you do. I had to be sure."

"I *am* good. I'm a fantastic storyteller. It's my primary talent. I have others, and I've always had to use whatever skills I have to survive. But I try to be honest, Eve."

"I had to be sure about that, too. You told me not to take you at face value. I didn't. I spent a little time this morning finding out about you."

"I thought you might. Did you discover anything interesting?"

"You spent your entire life until you were eleven years old trailing around the world with your father, who was a photographer. When he was killed in Tibet, it took the U.S. consulate over a year to get you back to the States. But you had no relatives, so you were fostered out for the next five years. Then you worked your way through a community college and started freelancing. Your gift for languages helped you to get ahead, but the first couple years must have been hard."

"Not that bad. I liked traveling around on my own again. I was a little gypsy until my father was killed." She added, "But you didn't find anything incriminating, did you? Other than being a loner, I'm pretty much what I appear on the surface."

"I *wanted* to find something."

"I know you did. It would have been an excuse to close your eyes again." She paused. "Are you going to come with me?"

"I'm close," Eve said jerkily. "Not because you want me to do it. Whether it was for a good cause or not, you tried every weapon in your arsenal to make me do what you wanted. And I could see how you'd pried and researched into who I was to make that happen. That's probably what I resent most. Talk about violation of privacy? And you did such a damn good job." She gestured impatiently. "No, it's because last night I realized those stories were like a poison inside me. I couldn't forget them. And I knew the only way I might be able to was to do something to help, to heal, those children. But you probably knew that would be my reaction?"

"I thought it was likely. You're very caring."

"And I *can't* heal them, but I might be able to heal those closest to them."

Jill nodded silently.

"So when I decided that those stories might have trapped me into doing this, I decided I had to look the situation over and explore how bad it might be. First. My family. I have a husband and a son who need me. And I need them. From what I've been able to find out, Maldara is still too unstable to be considered safe on any level. Yet you said that I'd be safe while I did those reconstructions. How?"

"I have friends at the embassy. And the U.N. staff on-site think reporters have to be given special protection. No bad press. I'll just convince them to extend that protection to you."

"From what you said, they don't even want the work done at Robaku."

Jill grimaced. "But I've been a thorn in their diplomatic asses over the last year. They'll be glad to shut me up and get rid of my nagging as long as it doesn't affect their budget." She added, "But, you know, it might be a good idea for you to call one of those charities you mentioned and tell them you're volunteering to do the job. You have tremendous name recognition, so there's no question they'll jump at sponsoring you. Just ask them if they'll contact the U.N. and advise them you're operating at their request. That way you'd get the official protection and not raise any U.N. hackles by mentioning me." She shrugged. "And the charity would get credit in the international community that might translate to donations later. Everyone wins."

"And more manipulation," Eve said.

"Would you rather I do it? I'll do anything that will make you feel more comfortable." Jill was obviously being perfectly sincere.

"No, I'll take care of it." Eve ran her hand through her hair. "If it's even possible. I just remembered I don't have a visa, no documents. That could take—"

"Twenty-four hours," Jill said. "Give me your passport, and I'll have it processed. We can stop and have the necessary shots on the way to the airport."

"Twenty-four hours?"

She smiled. "I told you that I have friends in high and low places. This is a piece of cake." She turned and strode toward the door. "And while you're getting me your passport, I'll make *you* a cup of coffee." She glanced over her shoulder. "If I'm forgiven enough to be let back into your good graces?"

"Marginally." She followed her into the house. "I'll let you know when we get to Maldara."

"Then you might never forgive me. It's hot, humid, and the poverty will break your heart." She started pouring the water into the automatic coffeemaker. "How will your husband take your decision?"

Eve was not about to deal with that now. Later. "That's not your concern."

"It is if it's going to make you unhappy." Jill was frowning. "He's a detective. Let's see...He'll be worried about your safety. I'll give you a couple of names of law-enforcement officials in the Kiyani government for him to contact. And I know a few agents with the CIA and MI6 who operate in Maldara who might reassure him."

"I wouldn't bet on it." Eve's brows rose. "Is there anyone you don't know in Maldara?"

"Not if they're useful." Jill handed her the cup of coffee. "Survival. You'll only have to be there for a few weeks. But I've been there for two years."

"Two years..." Her gaze narrowed on Jill's face. "Okay, I need to know what I'll be facing there that I couldn't find on Google. According to what I read, for decades Maldara has been torn by conflict between the Kiyanis to the north and Botzan to the south. The Kiyanis possessed most of the wealth in the country, which was based on rich farmlands and diamond mines. They even managed to develop a fairly stable republic in the last thirty years. The Botzans were poor by comparison, mostly mountain people, except for a decent fishing industry, and they changed rulers every couple years. The mountain population were principally made up of roving bands who made the majority of their living stealing from the Kiyanis, whom they hated. They'd been raiding the Kiyanis' properties for years before the Kiyanis suddenly decided to go on the attack. Civil war. The Botzan faction was finally defeated by the Kiyanis after the death of that mercenary, Nils Varak, and with the help of the U.N." She paused. "Is all of that correct? Is there anything else I should know? Is Botzan still a danger?"

Jill shook her head. "It's pretty well broken up now. The U.N. was getting too much static because of the Varak massacres, and they saw to it that the Kiyanis took over most of

Maldara." She grimaced. "And Zahra Kiyani, their president, is taking full advantage. She's even charmed the U.N. into giving her the right to speak at the next General Assembly meeting."

"I think I read something about her. She's a modern-day Madame Chiang Kai-shek?"

"Yes, that's who they're comparing her to. But you'll hear a lot more about her now that she's been able to draw a breath and start taking stock. Her father, President Akil Kiyani, was assassinated six months after the conflict started, and she tearfully accepted the presidency to honor him."

"Sarcasm?"

"I'm not a fan. When I interviewed her, she reminded me of Eva Peron. She's quite beautiful and much more flamboyant, of course. But her grateful people had just erected a statue of her in the main square of the capital city of Jokan. I found that odd after a war that had almost destroyed the country." She shrugged. "But that's politicians. She seems to have everything under control. She's built a hospital and gives to charity. The army and police seem to do their jobs. Everyone is fairly safe as long as they stay in the capital and don't go running around the countryside. She might even invite you to tea. That village where the massacre occurred is just outside Jokan. She's visited it twice and had a splendid and tearful photo op. Unfortunately, I wasn't able to attend."

"I don't believe I would either." Eve could see how that political circus would have hurt Jill. "And I'd think you'd be ready to leave Maldara. Isn't your story almost finished?"

"It's finished when it's finished. I'll know when it's done. Like your reconstructions." She'd turned away and was gazing at the reconstruction of Nora on the worktable across the room. "You've made a lot of progress on her since yesterday. She looks close to completion."

"I had a lot of time to work on her. Thanks to you, I couldn't sleep last night." She took a sip of her coffee. "And looks can be deceiving. The final will probably take me another twenty-four hours or even longer. I'm going to need this caffeine."

"But I might be able to get you out before that."

"Wrong," Eve said flatly. "I don't leave until Nora's finished and sent off to Chicago. It's bad enough I'm having to put off other commitments, I won't push *her* aside."

Jill nodded. "Sorry. I knew that, I just didn't think. If you'll give me your passport, I'll get out of your way so you can get back to her."

"Fine." Eve went to the kitchen cabinet where she and Joe kept their documents in a lockbox. "You're being amazingly cooperative." She handed her the passport. "I'll call you when I'm available to leave."

"Cooperative?" Jill's brows rose as she slipped the passport in her pocket. "I know how lucky I am that I talked you into going. I'm not about to rock the boat. Anything you need, just let me know."

"I'll do that." Eve gave her a cool glance. "And neither of us should pretend that luck had anything to do with your persuading me to commit to several weeks doing the reconstructions on those children. You were clever. You made sure you knew what would push every button. And you played me."

"Yes, I did," Jill said quietly. "But I still consider myself lucky that you allowed me to do it. If I work hard enough to make this trip easy for you, I hope you'll forgive me." She smiled with an effort. "I'll be in touch soon if you don't mind. Just to see if there's anything you need." She turned and walked quickly toward the door. "In the meantime, I'll e-mail you those names and contacts I mentioned might be useful to you." She looked back over her shoulder. "I'm sure your Nora will turn out wonderfully. Good-bye, Eve." Then she was gone.

Eve stared after her for a moment. There was no reason to feel as if she had somehow hurt Jill and should try to heal the hurt. Eve was the one who had been maneuvered into throwing her life into chaos for the next few weeks. And Jill Cassidy had not even denied it was done deliberately. Yet the emotion she felt for those children had to be genuine, and where was the line drawn in the sand where brutality toward children was concerned? Eve had never found it.

Forget Jill Cassidy. Eve had made the decision. Now she had to cope with making the best of it.

She was still drinking her coffee as she crossed the room toward the skull on her worktable. As she'd told Jill, she'd need the caffeine.

"Okay, Nora." She stopped in front of the reconstruction. "We're almost there, but now you have to help me. You're going to have to tell me who you are, show me what to do..."

———————

Jill dialed Jed Novak as she walked toward her car. "It's done," she said jerkily. "She'll be ready to leave in twenty-four hours if she finishes the current reconstruction by then. I think she will. She's driven right now."

"Putty in your hands, Jill?" Novak asked mockingly.

"Don't *say* that," Jill said fiercely. "It's stupid. She's not putty in anyone's hands. I made a situation impossible for her, and she's just trying to survive it. She's a completely private person, and she knows I probed deep to get what I wanted from her."

"Easy," Novak said. "Bad joke?"

"Very bad joke." She stopped as she reached her car and drew a deep breath. "And a very bad meeting with a woman I admire, Novak. She's smart, and nothing really gets past her. So you need to prepare very carefully. I've given her your name and a few others to pave the way. She might call you. Make her feel comfortable." She paused. "Have you heard anything from Jokan?"

"Not yet. Only a few rumbles. We still have time."

She wasn't as sure about that as Novak. "Let me know if it changes. I'm not going to let Eve go near the place if it does."

"But you'd go yourself," Novak said softly. "Who's going to stop you, Jill?" He added wearily, "It probably wouldn't be me. Never mind. I'll let you know." He cut the connection.

No, it wouldn't be Novak, Jill thought. She had never known anyone as tough or more ruthlessly motivated than Novak. He would get the job done no matter who fell by the wayside.

Yet he hadn't been ruthless after he'd taken her to that hospital in Nairobi, she suddenly remembered. He'd swept her into the ER, giving orders and making everyone snap to attention. Then he'd stayed with her, guarding her, watching that she was given the best possible attention.

And he'd been there, moving shadowlike in the background, for the entire four days she'd been forced to spend at the damn place.

But there had been nothing shadowlike about those nights he'd sat beside her bed and fought off the dragons that attacked from the darkness. There had been moments when she had hated how strong and dominant he had been during that period when she had been so weak. But there had been other times that he had seemed her only path to survival...

———

NAIROBI HOSPITAL

She screamed.

Darkness.

Pain.

She couldn't move!

She was smothering!

She sat bolt upright in the hospital bed, her hands tearing off the sheet.

"No." Novak was suddenly sitting on the bed beside her. "You're fine. Only another dream, Jill." He was holding her, rocking her back and forth. "I'm here with you. Nothing can hurt you."

She was clutching at him. Her heart was pounding so hard that she could hardly breathe. "I hate this." But she couldn't let him go yet. Another minute... Then she would be strong again.

No, she couldn't allow herself that time. It was another sign of weakness. She drew a deep breath and pushed him away from her. "Thank you. I'm okay now. I don't need you any longer." Need. How she detested that word. "In fact, I don't know why you're here anyway. As you said, it was only a nightmare. I'm not a child who can't deal with bogeymen." She leaned back against the pillows and said impatiently, "For that matter, I shouldn't even be in this hospital. It's been three days, Novak. I thought I'd be in and out of here in a matter of hours. Why won't they release me?"

"You know that besides severe bruising you had a cracked rib and a few other less obvious problems. I told them not to let you go until they could promise me that they'd done all they could for you." He got off her bed and settled back in his

chair. "I guarantee they didn't want to break that promise. I tend to get a little testy. Now go back to sleep." He paused. "Same nightmare?"

"I don't want to talk about it." She was glad of the darkness. His stare was always laser sharp, and she didn't want to face it right now. When he came to her at night, he was always only a deep, soothing voice, a strong hand that wove a barrier to keep out the weakness and the terror. "Tell them to let me leave here, Novak. I would never have come if I'd known you'd make me a prisoner. You even have a shrink coming in to talk to me every day. I don't need all this. I'm not one of your agents. Give me a week or two on my own, and I'll work it out for myself."

"No harm in getting a little therapy. The doctor says what you're going through is PTSD. I think talking to the psychiatrist is doing you good. I've noticed that you're not as tense as you were that first day." He added, "And only one nightmare so far tonight."

"I can work it out for myself," she repeated. "That's the way it has to be. It's my story, and I have to tell it."

"What?"

She hadn't meant to say that, it had just tumbled out. What did it matter? He had learned more intimate things about her during these last days. "When I was a kid, I had trouble understanding everything that was happening to me. But I loved books and reading, and the stories always made sense to me. There seemed to be a reason for everything, and I thought the writers had a kind of magic that could always make it that way if they tried hard enough." She added, "And it still makes sense to me to think of myself as writing my own story, incomplete, a work in progress, but totally in control of who I am." She shrugged. "Weird, huh?"

"Interesting. And totally logical for a premier storyteller."

*"And you're probably being polite and think that I'm nuts.
That's okay, it works for me."*

"And that's all that's important."

*"See? You're being polite. Look, you're a busy man, you
don't need to be wasting your time on me. I'm going to leave
here tomorrow and go back to Maldara."*

"We'll see." *He leaned forward and took her hand.
"Maybe if you don't have another nightmare tonight. So concentrate on keeping them all at bay."*

"I'm going to leave tomorrow." *But she found her hand
instinctively tightening in his grasp. He had been her anchor
in the storm, and she didn't want to let him go quite yet. She
could go to sleep holding his hand as she'd done for the past
three nights. She was nearly healed, but she could be with
him for these next hours. She would be strong tomorrow. "No
more nightmares, Novak..."*

And the next day Novak had taken her back to Maldara, and
she had started to make the plans and do the research that
had brought her here to Eve Duncan.

She looked back at the lake cottage as she got in her car.
Eve was probably already working on that reconstruction. In
a way, Eve reminded her of Novak as far as motivation and
steely determination were concerned. But Eve lacked the
kill gene that made Novak lethal. She didn't doubt that Eve
would kill to protect family or friend, but that was different.

But she knew others who possessed that kill gene, too.

And she and Novak were sending Eve right into their target zone.

CHAPTER

3

Her hair was just right, Zahra Kiyani thought with satisfaction as she watched her maid, Dalai, straighten the strands at her temple. Her chignon was dark and sleek and shining, with just the right touch of sophistication. It accented her high cheekbones and slightly slanted eyes and made the deep gold of her skin glow. She'd wear it like this when she went to New York next week, she decided. Then everyone would realize that she was truly a woman of style and power.

"Send her away," Edward Wyatt said roughly from her bed across the room. "You've kept me waiting long enough."

"You'll spoil my hair." She met his eyes in the mirror. The Honorable Edward Wyatt might be considered important to his cronies at the U.N., but she knew exactly how to control him. "And then I'll have to have Dalai do it again. Such a waste." He was naked and fully aroused, she noticed. She'd kept him watching her and anticipating for the last thirty minutes, and he was ready and eager for the game to begin. But she was not, and she was annoyed that he should speak to her with so little respect. Make him wait. She turned to Dalai. "I think the ruby comb tonight. Did I tell you how much I enjoy wearing it? It has such meaning for me."

"Yes, madam, you told me." She met Zahra's eyes in the mirror as she hurriedly placed the ruby comb in the chignon. Her maid was probably remembering the details of the deadly story of the comb, Zahra thought with amusement. Dalai was so easy to frighten. "It will be beautiful."

"Yes, it will." Zahra glanced back at Wyatt. "Do you think I'll look beautiful when I give my speech at the U.N. General Assembly? Will you be proud of me?"

"Stop teasing and come over here."

"But you like me to tease you. You like everything I do to you." And she had found out early in their relationship that the thing he liked most was for her to dominate him. The twisted bastard went wild when he was forced into submission. She'd seen the signs on that first night she'd seduced him and had her agent, Lon Markel, check him out. Wyatt spent a good deal of money at several specialty houses when he was in London. That information was all Zahra needed. His particular addiction suited her very well. Domination could be used in many ways other than sex. She got to her feet and came toward him. "Do you think that your wife will think I'm beautiful? Perhaps we can have a threesome when I'm in New York. Shall I call her in London and tell her to join us?" She slipped off her robe and dropped it on the floor. "But perhaps she thinks a woman's duty is only to provide pleasure to a man...and whoever else he chooses. Haven't you taught her?" She slipped naked into bed. "I'll teach her for you."

He started to reach for her, and she pushed him away. "No, my rules. Always my rules."

"Bitch," he said through his teeth. "I'm going crazy. Let me *in* you."

"I told you, you'll mess my hair." She ran her fingers down his belly. "But I might allow you to persuade me. But you'll have to give me something that will please me to make up for it."

"What a whore you are."

"No, I'm a queen. I've told you that before."

"You keep saying that. Being president isn't enough for you?"

"No, presidents rely on elections. A queen has power because she is what she is. That's why it hurts my feelings that you don't believe me. You should feel honored that I let you have my body."

"Stop playing this game, Zahra. Just let me—" He gasped as her hand closed on him. "What . . . do you want?"

"I want you to tell me that you know I'm a queen, and you'll do everything you can to make sure that's how I'm treated in New York."

"You—know—I—will."

"How do I know it?" Her hand tightened around him. "Prove it to me. I haven't noticed you doing anything to make my position here in Maldara stronger lately."

"I do everything you ask." He gasped again as her nails dug into him. *"Shit."*

"I don't appreciate how unfriendly the newspapers have been to me. You have influence. Do something about it."

"I told you, interfering with the free press would be a mistake. It would shine too bright a light on me and my office here in Jokan. I can't do it."

"All I wish is for you to get rid of just one journalist. Jill Cassidy. That's not too much to ask."

"She's very well regarded, and it might cause a stir. You said you'd take care of it yourself."

And she would have, if only those fools had been a little rougher with the bitch that night in the jungle. She'd given explicit instructions, and it should have worked beautifully. But Jill had disappeared for only a few days after the attack; and then she was back in Jokan and still very much in the way. "It didn't work out. I want you to do it."

Wyatt was silent. "I'll do it. You know I'll do anything you wish. But you should know they will probably recall me. Is that what you want?"

No, it wasn't what she wanted. Wyatt was still useful, and it would take her time to develop a relationship with a replacement. "You know it's not," she said curtly. "Very well, I'll find another way. But you will be sure and block anything she tries to do here?"

"Of course." He looked relieved. "Whatever you want. That's a much better—"

He gasped. She was suddenly above him and he was deep inside her. *"Yes."*

She reached up and took the ruby comb from her hair and held it in front of his eyes. "Isn't it beautiful? Full of glitter and power. But there's always danger with power. What if I'd coated these prongs with a deadly poison?" She brought the prongs closer to his throat. "Then you'd really know how powerful I am, wouldn't you?"

He was staring in fear and fascination at the comb. "Yes."

"But it excites you, doesn't it?" She brought the comb still closer to his throat. "I can see it does." Then she was taking the comb away and putting it back in her hair. "Whatever I want?" She was moving fast, controlling him, not letting him touch her, totally dominating. "Stay still. Don't move. You have to be punished for not giving me everything I need tonight. I'll permit you to have this, but then I'll tell Dalai to use the quirt on you. You'll like that, won't you?"

His cheeks were flushed, his mouth open to take air. "Yes. But I—want you—to do it."

"Why should I care what you want? You're only my slave, and so is Dalai. I'll lie here as a queen should and watch the two of you perform for me." She leaned over him, her dark eyes glittering. Her sharp white teeth sank deep into his shoulder. "Say it."

"Whatever pleases you." He shuddered as the blood ran from the wound. "Yes . . . watch us . . . as a queen should . . ."

———◆———

LAKE COTTAGE

"It's crazy," Joe said curtly when Eve finished telling him why she was going to Maldara. "I knew that there was something going on last night. I just didn't know I wasn't going to get a chance to talk you out of it."

"You have a chance now," Eve said. "I called you as soon as I was positive I was going. I won't be leaving until tomorrow afternoon at three." She added sarcastically, "It seems Jill has arranged with one of her friends in high places to lend her his jet and pilot to give us a lift to Maldara. For all I know, she might have even set it up before she came to see me. But at least that will eliminate a lot of red tape and give me more time to send Nora off and postpone my other commitments." She paused. "Please don't give me a hard time, Joe. It won't do you any good. I've decided I have to go."

"You *don't* have to go, dammit. You told me yourself that Jill Cassidy played you. Why should you let her have her way?"

"Because she made sure that I'd know her way was my way this time. I can't do anything else." She added wearily, "I'll e-mail those photos and biographies Jill gave me to you. Then I think you'll understand."

"Oh, I'll understand," Joe said. "But it won't make me want to keep from boiling her in oil at the earliest opportunity. I did a little more research after I hung up with you last night. I could see this coming. Granted, Maldara isn't the powder keg it was two years ago. But between Zahra Kiyani's power grab and all the other ex-mercenaries and crooks who are trying to line their pockets with what's left of that country, it could still be lethal. I don't want you there."

"Three weeks. A month tops. It's all I promised Jill." Then she realized what she'd just said. "No, to hell with Jill. It's what I promised myself. And I may not be able to do reconstructions on more than a portion of those children. I'll have to examine the skulls and make a decision. I may be done sooner. But if I'm successful with only a few, it will show what can be done and might encourage the U.N. to hire someone else to complete the job." She paused. "Remember when I said the timing was just right for you to go to Scotland Yard and Michael to take his trip with Jane? Well, maybe this timing is right, too. Maybe if I can help the relatives of those children, then it was meant to be."

"I'm not in the mood for you to bring up fate at this particular time." Joe was silent another moment. "I'm going with you."

Just what she'd expected. "No, you are not," she said firmly. "I wouldn't get anything done with you floating around like a drone ready to strike. You're going to stay at Scotland Yard, keep an eye on Michael, and call me on Skype as you'd planned to do. If I get nervous about anything, I'll let you know."

He didn't reply.

"Look, Joe, I gave you the names of those officials at the embassy and the U.N. that Jill sent me. She even supplied you with a CIA operative and someone from MI6 to call. Check them out. They should be able to tell you anything you need to know."

"Maybe. I recognized one of the names. I ran into Jed Novak two years ago when I was over here picking up a counterfeiter in Paris." He was silent again, thinking. "They'd given Novak a team and sent him to go after a terrorist ring in southern France. He has a reputation that's . . . impressive. I wonder what he's doing in Maldara . . ."

"Discuss it with him and find out." Jill had been right, Eve thought. A detective like Joe would feel more secure about her if he knew she was going to be surrounded by law enforcement he knew and understood. "I'll call you when I get there. I'm sure by that time, you'll have all the information you need."

"Are you trying to get rid of me, Eve?"

"Lord, no." The sound of his voice, the knowledge that he cared, was a comfort even when she had to argue with him. "I just have to get back to Nora if I'm going to finish her tonight. So just do all the things that will make you feel better about my going because it's going to happen."

He didn't speak for a moment. "I think it is, dammit. So by all means I'll do everything I can to prepare for it. Count on it. Good night, Eve."

Eve put down the phone after he'd disconnected. There had been a tinge of grimness in that last sentence. He was already planning what he could do, whom he could use to protect her. She wished she was like Joe and could prepare and make plans for the weeks ahead. There was no way she could do that this time. She just had to go with what she felt.

Because she couldn't see anything but the pitiful photos of those slain children and the siren call of the tales Jill had woven about each one of them.

———◆———

JOKAN, MALDARA
THIRTY-SIX HOURS LATER

"We'll be landing at Jokan in forty-five minutes." Jill had come out of the cockpit and dropped into the passenger seat next to Eve. "I wanted to let you rest as long as possible, but now there are things I have to talk to you about." She grimaced. "You'll notice I've tried to stay out of your way during the flight."

"I could hardly miss it," Eve said dryly. From the moment the Gulf Stream had taken off, Jill had either been in her own luxurious leather seat across the aisle or in the cockpit with their pilot, Sam Gideon. She had been polite, seen that Eve had drinks and food, given her updates on their progress, but other than that, she had worked on her computer and allowed Eve total privacy. "I appreciate the effort, but you didn't have to treat me as if I had Ebola."

Jill smiled. "I didn't want to push my luck. I know you resent me. No one has a better right. You'll meet a lot of people here who have problems with me, so you won't feel alone."

"You mentioned that the U.N. officials here weren't your fans. The Children for Peace charity had no problem dealing with them. They found the undersecretary, the Honorable Edward Wyatt, both charming and cooperative when they called him and told him they were sending me."

"Because I wasn't involved." Jill shrugged. "If they'd

known I'd convinced you to come, they would have stonewalled you. Lately, it's been a solid wall whenever I need something from them." She made an impatient gesture. "And that's okay, I can work around them. I just have to warn you that I'm going to have to do that. It will be easier and safer for you if no one knows that I had anything to do with bringing you here."

She raised her brows. "You're abandoning me?"

"No, I'd never do that." She made a face. "Though you'd probably prefer if I did. But this is a country that's not like Main Street U.S.A. I know people, you might need me."

"If they don't hate you?"

She nodded wryly. "There is that to consider." She leaned forward, and said urgently, "You won't be alone. I'll surround you with people you can trust. And I'll be able to be on hand for you in a few days. I've had Sam Gideon set up an interview with the press on Thursday, to which I'll be invited. We'll have a nice meeting and find we have everything in common. Everyone knows I've been trying to convince the government to give the villagers what they want for their children. They just can't know that I brought you here."

"Why not?"

Jill hesitated. "Zahra Kiyani didn't like me any more than I did her. I told you, Robaku is a village practically on her doorstep. She was born and raised as Kiyani royalty, and now she's the president of the country. Her father gave up the throne to become president, which I don't believe pleased her. She also has more control than I'd like and is the prime mover in the effort to get the village moved to another location. I don't want her to influence anyone against what you're doing."

"You didn't mention that the deck was already stacked against me," Eve said dryly.

"It's not. I just have to deal around a possible bad hand," Jill said. "And I'm doing it. And I'm telling you about it."

"And letting me know the possibility that this Zahra Kiyani might get me ousted from the country before I can start doing one reconstruction. After a very long trip and a good deal of inconvenience." She shook her head. "And now you tell me?"

"You won't be ousted. We're working around it." She smiled. "And I thought this was the best time to tell you. You won't be likely to give up easily after traveling all this distance. And it's not as if I'll force you to stay. Gideon will take you directly to Robaku after you get off the plane, and you'll meet Hajif, the head of the village. He'll take you to the school and show you where you'll work if you choose to help them. President Zahra ordered the place be made into a sort of memorial, and you'll have to do the reconstructions on-site." She paused. "If you don't want to do it, just tell Gideon. He'll bring you back here, and you'll be on your way to your lake cottage within the hour."

"But you're confident that's not going to happen." Her eyes were narrowed on Jill's face. "You think you know me so well. I might surprise you."

Jill shook her head. "I'm not confident. I know you can surprise me. You're very complicated, and bad things can happen to any plan. I'm just hoping I'm not wrong about you in this instance." She got to her feet. "I'll go back to the cockpit. I'll stay on the plane until I'm sure I won't be seen getting off. After Gideon lands, he'll take care of you from then until we stage our meeting at the press interview."

"Gideon," Eve repeated. "You've dropped that name through the entire conversation. You're talking about Sam Gideon, our pilot, whom you introduced me to at the beginning of the trip?" She vaguely remembered a good-looking, dark-haired young man with a flashing smile. "I'm to put myself in his hands? I take it he's another friend of yours who is a bit more than a pilot?"

Jill nodded. "Well, he does own this Gulf Stream. And flying would be his career of choice if it were up to him." She made a face. "But he owns mega stocks and diamond mines and other boring stuff here in Maldara that tend to get in his way."

"Poor guy."

"Don't be sarcastic," she said quietly. "He's my friend, and he did me this favor. He's helped me before, and I trust him. The fact that he inherited a good portion of the entire wealth of this country made that a hell of a lot easier. I've known Sam Gideon ever since I first came to Maldara. He was born here and lived on a family plantation near Jokan before he graduated from Oxford and moved to London. He knows everybody who's anybody in the country. He won't let you get in trouble. And if he does, he has the man who can get you out of it on speed dial." She stopped at the door of the cockpit to look soberly back at her. "You might find him a little unusual, but you can trust him, too, Eve. I'd never turn you over to someone you couldn't trust." Then she was opening the cockpit door. "I'll see you Thursday if you're still here."

Eve watched the door shut behind Jill. That last sentence had probably been said to convince her that she wasn't being taken for granted. Yet every word Jill spoke sounded sincere. But the fact that she'd let her get here to Maldara before she'd told her that she happened to be having trouble with the ruling head of the damn country was both frustrating and suspicious. Trust her? Trust this Sam Gideon?

Eve shouldn't even get off the damn plane.

But she was already here in this place where savages had

thought nothing of killing children as they studied in their classroom.

And she knew she was going to go to Robaku.

———————◆———————

"Jill says you're very important to her and I'm to be polite and respectful." Sam Gideon's dark eyes were twinkling with mischief as he came out of the cockpit after he'd landed the Gulf Stream. He had just a hint of an English accent that made the mockery in his tone take on an additional slyness. In his thirties, he was very good-looking, with olive skin, dark hair cut close to tame a tendency to curl, and that smile that was definitely reckless. "I told her that I'd been so polite to you when we were introduced that I'd never be able to do a repeat. So what you see is what you get." He shook her hand. "But I did promise her not to try to seduce you. Though it was a sacrifice since I do have a thing for intense, stormy women."

"Stormy?" Eve studied him. Jill had warned her that he was unusual, but it was clear there was much more to Gideon than what he seemed on the surface. He had chosen that remark deliberately because sex was blatantly inappropriate in this situation and definitely would have been forbidden by Jill. That opening could have been meant to either put her at ease or shock her. "Then it's lucky you're wrong about me. I have a very calm nature and avoid turbulence at all costs. Besides being married to a man who makes every effort to keep me from having to deal with the storms of life."

He chuckled. "And you've firmly put me in my place and given just a hint of a threat in case I step out of it. But I notice you don't deny the intensity, which means the storms probably come to you. Jill didn't really need to try to protect you from me, did she? But she tends to go the extra mile." He took her elbow and nudged her toward the door. "Now we've taken each other's measure and can get down to what's important to you." He threw open the door. "Welcome to Maldara, Eve."

A wild study of contrasts...

She stood on the steps, her gaze taking in the sleek commercial jets and military planes that occupied the hangars and runways of the small airport. Everything was new and modern and shining. In the distance, she could see a few skyscrapers on the horizon that contrasted sharply with the dense jungles surrounding the city. On either side of the road leading to Jokan, she could see ragged men, women, and children who had put up their booths of fruits and vegetables and brought their animals to sell at market.

"It's very... different," she murmured as she went down the steps. She was suddenly assaulted by heat, humidity, and the smell of gasoline from the planes on the tarmac. "Though I guess I expected more damage from the fighting."

"Jokan had less destruction than Botzan," Gideon said. "Amazing, since Varak's ghouls were hired by Botzan to decimate it. Our magnificent President Zahra claims her advisors and loyal people managed to hold them at bay by the grace of God." He was leading Eve toward the wire enclosure that she assumed was the parking lot. "The presidential palace wasn't touched. She was able to welcome all the diplomats with her usual grace and style when they liberated Maldara."

"Do I sense a little antagonism?" Eve glanced sideways at him as he opened the passenger door of a tan Land Rover for her. "Yet I don't believe Jill would refer to her as being magnificent in any sense of the word."

"Well, that's where we differ. I've had a closer relationship with Zahra than Jill has. I had an opportunity to assess her qualities." He tilted his head, considering. "I think she has a magnificent opinion of her own worth. I think she's not brilliant but has a magnificent talent for self-preservation." He paused, thinking. "Physically, she has magnificent breasts and possibly interesting, but not magnificent, sexual abilities. So Jill is not being entirely fair."

Her gaze narrowed on his face. "Yet you don't have any use for her."

"Not any more than I would have a use for a spitting mamba I ran across in the jungle." He smiled gently. "Except to sell the venom—and then the snake would have to be alive to milk it. Much too much trouble." He was driving out of the airport onto the road. "But fair is fair. One has to be accurate. How else can you be allowed to make your own judgments?"

"I hope I won't even have to meet her," Eve said. "I intend to keep a low profile while I'm here."

"It will be difficult for you to do that. You're very famous, and you're in Zahra's kingdom. If she doesn't know that now, she will soon. And she's possessive of Robaku. Didn't Jill tell you?"

"Zahra's *kingdom*? But she's the president of Maldara."

"Zahra has a few bizarre ideas of her own regarding that." He shrugged. "Which are entirely in keeping with her opinion of her own magnificence. But I won't go into that since you're going to make the attempt to avoid her."

"You do know her very well, don't you?" Eve asked curiously.

"You mean, were we lovers? Oh yes. When I came back to spend the summer with my parents after graduating from Oxford, I was ready for a great passion. Zahra was the president's daughter, but she considered me deserving of her attention. I'm very rich, and she automatically associates wealth with royal entitlement. She thought she might be able to mold me into the prince she felt was her due. We had an interesting summer."

"A great passion?"

"No, but erotic and fascinating, until I saw the mamba raising its head. Then I left her and went back to London." His lips twisted. "She wasn't pleased. She'd thought she'd found someone who could survive her bite; and then she had to start over." He gestured to the curve of the road ahead. "Robaku is just ahead. I called from the cockpit and asked the headman, Hajif, to come to meet you at the school. Jill said you had a decision to make and to give you the information you needed to make it."

"And then you'll take me back to Atlanta immediately if I decide I don't want to stay?"

"Of course. Jill always keeps her word. Even if it means I have to bear the brunt of it." He gave her a keen glance. "But I think I'll probably get a good night's sleep tonight here in Maldara. I'd wager that intensity usually wins out when it comes to children. Why else are you here?"

"Your friend, Jill, conned me," she said flatly.

"Then she had her reasons," Gideon said. "And it probably hurt her more than it did you. Jill is one of those rare people who take honor seriously. She'd agonize over it." He paused. "And I bet she made it as painless for you as possible."

"The hell she did," Eve said curtly. "She wrote me a biography on each of those children that would tear your heart out."

Gideon gave a low whistle. "Ah, that pen of hers can be a lethal weapon. She's a great wordsmith. But she is usually responsible about how she wields it. Maybe you'll find that she was this time, too." He'd negotiated the turn in the road, and they'd suddenly left all semblance of the modern world and were in the jungle. He drove on a bumpy dirt road for another few minutes, then pulled to a stop and gestured to a large, square structure several yards away. "Robaku."

Eve stared in shock. Destruction. Chaos.

It was a burnt-out shell of a building. No roof. Only blackened, jagged openings that had once been windows. There was a wide, gaping opening that must have been a door, which vines and shrubs were trying to devour.

Eve could almost smell the acrid scent of the smoke from the flames that had destroyed the school. It had been a long time, but she could swear the smell lingered. She had thought it would at least have been cleaned up, perhaps flowers planted. Some attempt made to have the painfulness of the scene erased.

"Nothing...has been done." She got out of the Land Rover and stood looking at that gaping mouth of a door. "Jill said Zahra...some kind of memorial."

"This is Zahra's concept of a memorial. She ordered the villagers not to touch the school." Gideon got out of the car. "She said that everyone should see the horrible destruction that the war brought to her country so that they would never be tempted to repeat it. Unusual, but it sounded vaguely patriotic when she was quoted in the newspapers." He was striding toward the door. "Step into Robaku's pride and joy, Eve."

No hint of either pride or joy here, she thought, sick. She followed him slowly until she reached the doorway and stood staring into the half darkness. It was worse inside than it was outside.

The desks...

Most of them were blackened and destroyed, but a few of them had escaped the fires and sat there on the burnt-out floors as if they were waiting for the children who came to occupy them every day.

Eve could feel her eyes sting. "Oh, shit."

She moved into the huge room. The blackboard... broken and melted.

Something dark streaking the floor that was neither ash, nor dirt, nor burnt-out boards.

"Jill was told that's not blood on the floor," Gideon said. "That Zahra had given permission for the blood to be cleansed when the body parts were taken from here." His lips curled. "But since Zahra's own people extracted the bodies, I wouldn't give odds that they were careful about cleaning up the blood."

She couldn't take her eyes from those dark streaks.

He was looking at her face. "You don't look well. Maybe I'd better get you out of here."

She paid no attention to him. She was being bombarded by visions of what must have happened here that morning. The children at their desks... The teacher at the blackboard... probably chatter and smiles filling the room. Everything normal and right, as it should be for children in a classroom. As it was in her son Michael's classroom.

"Did... they have any warning? Why didn't they run away?"

"No warning. The school is located on this hill at the far end of the village. It's about a ten-minute walk to the village itself. Varak's militia struck the school first, then went on to burn the village. Hajif said they heard the screams from the children and ran toward the school to save them. But it had already been torched by the time they got there. A few of the bodies found inside were parents who ran into the flames to try to save their children. But most of the villagers were hacked to pieces by the militia, who were waiting for them. The children were only bait." He took her arm and was moving her toward the door. "And now I'm getting you out of here. Jill won't be pleased that I let you get this upset. You're done. You've seen it, you won't forget it."

No, she'd never forget it, Eve thought. It wasn't just the terrible ruins, it was as if the spirits of those children were still here . . . still waiting.

She pulled her arm away. "It's not as if I'm going to break down or anything, Gideon." She concentrated on keeping her voice steady. "I've seen terrible things before in my career. It's just that this is . . . overwhelming. I feel if I look over my shoulder, I might see them there." She did not look over her shoulder, but at him. "I thought this Hajif was going to meet us here."

"He always asks if he can meet us at the museum a little down the road. It's only a few yards away, and he finds this place pretty hard to take." He was leading her farther into the jungle. They were passing a beautiful brook surrounded by tall boulders. It seemed odd that anything beautiful could exist this close to that atrocity, Eve thought dully. And Gideon was saying quietly, "Hajif's grandson was killed in the massacre at the school."

Hajif. Eve thought for a moment, then made the connection with the biography Jill had written. "Hajif, grandfather of Amari, nine years old. Amari liked building model airplanes with his father. He wanted to be a pilot when he grew up . . ."

"You have a good memory. His father was also killed in the massacre. Now there's just Hajif and his wife, Leta, left."

"It doesn't take a good memory to remember what Jill wrote about Robaku." She changed the subject. "Museum? Jill never mentioned a museum."

"It's part of Zahra's memorial. Not that there are many

museum artifacts there. Just a few trinkets and photos. She just wanted a place to entertain dignitaries and news media that would show her off to advantage and keep her designer outfits from being contaminated by the soot of the schoolhouse." He lifted his head as a small black man with grizzled hair and lined face, dressed in flowing trousers and a loose white shirt, appeared, coming toward them. "Hajif." He moved quickly toward the man and bowed. Then he rattled off something in an African dialect and turned to Eve. "Eve Duncan, Hajif. She came to see Amari and his friends and hopes she can be of service."

"Jill Cassidy told me of her." The old man's English was broken but his expression was desperately eager as he turned to Eve. "It's we who should strive to serve you. Ask us, and it will be given."

"I don't know if I can help you," Eve said gently. "I'll have to examine the skulls and see if the damage will prevent me from being able to measure and do the sculpting. I understand there was considerable . . ." She hesitated. She didn't want to say that during fires, the brain often exploded and shattered the skull. "The fire might be a problem . . ."

"But Jill said you are wonderful and can work with such problems. Is that not true?"

"If there are no other elements that cannot be overcome."

Hajif was silent. "Please." His dark eyes were glittering with moisture. "We need to see him at least one more time as he was. My wife, Leta, keeps hoping that Amari escaped into the jungle and is afraid to come home to the village. She will not listen to me. She said that head in the box is not her Amari."

Eve frowned. "Head in the box?"

Gideon said quickly: "The remains of the children were sent to the American embassy to be kept at the medical lab there until they could be ID'd. But the villagers made such a fuss about the skulls being taken that they were allowed to keep them on-site until it was decided how to dispose of them."

"*She* kept them," Hajif said. "It should not be. They belong to us."

"Zahra stepped in and took over the preservation of the skulls until the decision could be made," Gideon said. "She put the skulls in her museum."

Eve stiffened. "What?"

"With all due respect, of course," he said ironically. "Blessed by the church. Properly preserved in specially crafted boxes." He gestured to a sleek, modern, one-story, gray-stucco building. "Would you like to see them?"

"Yes, I would." She was already striding toward the museum. "Now!"

The first thing she saw as she approached the building was the huge glass-enclosed gold-framed portrait of Zahra Kiyani beside the front door. Dressed in a white designer suit, she looked beautiful, sad, and dignified. Her arms were outstretched as if in welcome.

Eve ignored it, threw open the glass door, and went inside. Clean, bright, beautifully tiled green-and-beige floors. Several glass cases with very few artifacts, as Gideon had said. "Where are those boxes?"

Gideon nodded at a row of rust-colored leather boxes with elaborate gold lettering on the front. No names, just numerals. Not simple, dignified numerals, they were scrolled, then encircled with a fanciful design.

Hajif came to stand beside Eve. "Her soldiers told us that Amari is probably in the fourth box. And if we would consent to have the DNA test, Madam President's experts would be able to tell for certain."

And, until he consented, his grandson's skull would remain in that beautifully crafted box like a forgotten library book on a shelf only yards from their village. Or even worse, a macabre reminder of his death at the hands of Varak and his butchers. Jill had told Eve that the U.N. officials wanted those children to be buried and forgotten, and it was clear Zahra Kiyani was also systematically working to make that happen. Why? It could only be that as the surviving ruler of the conflict, she wanted everyone to forget the details of that brutal struggle to secure her new image. Children were so often used as pawns.

Eve could feel the anger begin to rise within her. It was all *wrong*. No one should forget those children. It was even worse than what had happened to Nora. At least the police were trying to find out what had happened to her. It didn't matter that those butchers who had killed the children of Robaku were known and probably ended up butchered themselves. Their victims needed to come home to the people who had loved them.

"Four?" Eve went behind the counter and looked at the glossy Roman numerals. "They said your grandson was numeral four?" She found the box and pulled it out. "And he was nine years old?" She laid the box on the counter and carefully opened it. The skull was blackened by fire but as carefully preserved as Gideon had said. "Let's take a look…"

"May I ask what you're doing, Eve?" Gideon was gazing over her shoulder with interest.

"Just checking to see how competent Zahra's experts are. It's not all that difficult to establish approximate age if you have the experience." She took the skull out of the box and set it on the glass counter. She carefully went over the skull, paying particular attention to the teeth. "It's a male, but the age is wrong. And the long bones of the face indicate he's at least twelve. One of the older boys in the class." She was trying to remember Jill's notes. "There were two older boys... one was... Maha?"

"Or Shaka," Hajif said eagerly. "Shaka was thirteen, Maha twelve."

"I'd have to examine him more closely to determine which one he is." Eve carefully replaced the skull in the box. "But he's *not* your grandson, and that 'expert' who said he was is no expert." She took the box to the back shelf and slipped it back in its place. "Your wife was right, Hajif. Your grandson might be in one of these boxes, but it's not that one."

"But you will find him?" Hajif asked. "You will bring him back to us?"

She stared helplessly at him. He wanted promises, and there were so many pitfalls that could get in the way of her giving him what he wanted. She wasn't even sure if these were the skulls from Robaku. That had been a stupidly careless mistake about Amari's age.

"My wife needs to know," Hajif said. "She... hurts."

And so was he hurting.

And, dammit, there should be some way to ease that pain. They had lost enough, they had a right to *know*.

She reached out and touched his shoulder. "Then we'd better do something to help her," she said gently. "But I'll need your help first, Hajif."

A brilliant smile lit his face. "You will do it? Anything. I will do anything."

"Will you get some men from the village to come here and take out all these display cases and shove them outside the building? Then I'll need a level table put in the center of the room. I'll show you how high it will have to be. And I'll need a stool of some sort."

"Right away." Hajif turned and moved quickly out of the museum.

"Any orders for me?" Gideon was smiling faintly. "Am I to assume that you're going to be delving into those boxes in the near future?"

"Yes," she said curtly. "Jill is going to feel very satisfied, isn't she? I don't give a damn. Those neat little boxes crafted of the finest leather with all those pretty gold letters made me go ballistic. They look like fashion accessories. I use boxes myself for transport. But this is pure showmanship, no dignity, no feeling. Zahra Kiyani made them part of her personal scenario. I want those kids out of those boxes."

"Obviously. You didn't answer me. What can I do?"

"Get me a cot to set up in here. I'll probably be spending most of my nights in this blasted museum."

"That's not necessary. And unless you're into communal bathing, the hygiene arrangements will be awkward for you in the village. I've made reservations for you at the one decent hotel in Jokan. I can run you back and forth."

"Keep the reservations. I'll need to use the room to shower occasionally. Otherwise, I can wash up in the bathroom here."

"How do you know there is one?"

"Of course there's a bathroom. You said that Zahra used this place to receive the media." She was looking around the room. "And I bet it has a lovely mirror for touching up her makeup." She saw a door across the room and strode toward it. She opened the door and glanced inside. "Yes, a great mirror with her traditional gold frame. I think I'm beginning to know Zahra Kiyani."

"Then heaven help you," Gideon said softly.

"I won't need divine intervention. I'll just stay out of her way and rely on Hajif and his people. I'll work hard and fast and get through this job as quickly as possible."

"Twenty-seven children, Eve," Gideon reminded her.

"I'll do as many as I can in the next month. I'll arrange for the others to be done by someone competent after I have to leave." She gave a last appraising glance at the bathroom and started to close the door. "Make certain I have towels, shampoo, and soap. That's all I need for the time being. Bring in my duffel from the car, will you? How many people in the village speak English?"

"Probably only a handful. But you have Hajif if you need a translator. He said he'd do anything as I recall." He paused. "And I'll stay within ten minutes' distance from you in case of emergencies."

"I'm not expecting any emergencies," Eve said. "This is what I do. I'm in control here. I can handle anything that comes along."

"I can see that." Gideon's gaze was on her flushed cheeks and glittering eyes. "And you can't wait, can you? Well, just know that I'm available." He turned toward the door. "I'll go get your duffel and find you a cot somewhere. You're really staying here tonight? Why don't you let me take you out to dinner and start tomorrow?"

"Because tonight I'll be going through all those skulls until I find one that fits Amari's age and description. Then I'll have to examine it and see if I can do what Hajif wants me to do."

"So Amari is going to be first?"

"He *has* to be first. His grandparents want it so much that I couldn't do anything else. After that, I'll be able to try to be more selective."

"Then I'll tell Jill that you have the initial process going at full speed." He looked back over his shoulder. "Anything else?"

"Bring in my computer and make sure I'll have no problem with Internet while I'm here. That's essential."

"You'll need it for your work?"

"Possibly for the final. But it's principally because I planned on using it to Skype. I prefer it to my smartphone to contact family, and I won't be stranded out here in the jungle and lose contact with my husband and son. That's *not* acceptable."

"Ah, yes, the protective husband in the background? Dedication and total devotion on both sides of the coin. You're an interesting woman, Eve Duncan. I believe I'm going to enjoy you."

"Interesting? You haven't seen anything, Gideon. And I couldn't care less if you enjoy me. Just get me what I tell you I need."

He chuckled. "I'll definitely get you what you need. It will be my goal in life while we're together." He mockingly flipped his hand to his head in a half salute. "I'll be back in a flash with the first installment."

He was gone.

Eve gazed after him with impatience and frustration. She still didn't know what to think of him after these hours in his company. He had smoothed her way seamlessly with Hajif and furnished her with both information and a subtle challenge. She hadn't the faintest doubt he would continue to do so until she could wrap up her work here. But he had almost casually admitted to having an affair with a woman about whom she was beginning to be very wary. And he was clearly loyal to Jill Cassidy and her agenda. And that agenda was aimed at using her to do whatever Jill wished here at Robaku.

Forget it. None of this is important right now, Eve thought impatiently. Jill Cassidy wanted to use her? Good luck to her. Since she had told Gideon that she was committed to doing these re-constructions, it meant that she automatically took charge of everything to do with those children. It was how she worked, and she would have it no other way. If Jill interfered, Eve would have to roll right over her if necessary. Jill had started this, but that didn't mean that Eve couldn't finish it...

CHAPTER

4

S he's a powerhouse," Gideon said when Jill picked up his call.
"Eve listened. She questioned. She let me see the horror she
felt. Then she took over. She's setting up shop even as we speak.
She's even ordering *me* around. Doesn't she realize what a blow
to my ego that is? You might have trouble with her."

Jill had known that from the beginning. The moment she
had chosen Eve Duncan, she'd been aware that manipulation could only go so far and felt fortunate that she'd at least
gotten Eve here. "Your ego will survive. I believe the only
trouble we'll have right away is that she's a workaholic, and
we'll have to keep her supplied with materials. Hajif is coop-
erating with helping her?"

"She's going to do the reconstruction of his grandson
first. He thinks she's an angel from heaven." He paused. "She
wanted to make certain that her computer and phone would
operate at top efficiency. What do I do?"

The phone. Jill could see problems looming on the horizon. "Stall. It might be fine. I'll check with Novak. He's supposed to be here in five or ten minutes to smuggle me off this plane. I'll get back to you." She cut the connection.

She sat there staring out the window of the plane. It was starting. The first step. Eve had now committed, and she'd be working on the skulls. Jill just hoped that they could move to the next step with more speed, and—

She tensed and whirled to the door as she heard the steps come down outside. She dived to press back against the wall as she saw a strong, brown hand open the door.

"Easy, Jill," Novak said dryly as he came into the cabin. He was hauling a broom and a large, stainless-steel waste-disposal container behind him. "I'd appreciate it if you'd neither shoot me nor hit me in the head with your object of choice." His skin was stained chocolate brown, his contact lenses were the same color, and he was dressed in red coveralls and hat with a cleaning-company logo on the brim. "It would spoil any chance of getting you out of here without being noticed. I'm supposed to tuck you in this waste-disposal container, and who would tote you out of here if you dispose of me instead?"

She let her breath out in relief. "I don't know why you're here anyway. I'm hardly important, and you could have sent one of your men to get me."

"Yes, I could have done that." He paused. "Just as you could have come back into the country alone without going near Eve Duncan and causing me this trouble."

"I had to make sure she'd get here safely. She's my responsibility." She held up her hand as he started to speak. "I know that Gideon could have taken care of her, but she's mine now. It was my plan, and I have to own it."

"That's right," he said mockingly. "She's an important

figure in what you call 'your' story. It has to be as you dictate it."

Nairobi. She'd revealed too much to him that last night. "I'm surprised you remember I said that," she said lightly. "It must have been the sedatives."

"I could hardly forget it. I believe it defined your philosophy of life. I'm always on the lookout for clues to understand you."

"You're always on the lookout for clues, period. You take everything apart, then put it back together again." She dropped down in her chair again. "What about Eve's computer? She'll be Skyping her family and telling them everything that's going on. That means anyone who is hacking her will get a complete report via Joe Quinn."

He nodded. "I can't see that would be a problem right away. There's no reason why anyone would believe Eve's here for anything but the obvious. Besides, interfering would send up a red flag to Quinn. I'd rather not do that until the last minute. I've met him, and he'd be a son of a bitch to get rid of if he decided he had to step into the picture." He frowned thoughtfully. "And I've monitored her telephone conversations to him, and I think we'll let her take care of it. She's as protective of him as he is of her. She doesn't want him here either."

She gazed at him in surprise. She had never seen Novak this wary of anyone. He was always cool, always totally in control, and the smartest man she'd ever met. Even sitting here in those ridiculous red overalls and tennis shoes, he didn't appear anything but assured and able to conquer his particular world. She tried to smother the tingle of tension as she gazed at him. After their time together in Nairobi, she should have gotten over that edginess. But he'd always had that effect on her, a combination of wariness and fascination. The lean face, the intelligent, deep-set eyes that always seemed to see too much, the firm lips. There might be handsomer men than Jed Novak, but Jill had always found his super intelligence and quiet strength to be mesmerizing from the moment she had met him over a year ago. "I never actually got to meet Quinn. Have I missed something?" She smiled. "You're being very cautious."

"And so should you. Quinn respects her. He'll stay out of her business as long as he believes she's safe. The minute that changes, he'll go into overdrive."

"I would, too. That's why she has to stay safe." She tensed. "And when is that going to change, Novak? When do we get the skull?"

"Soon. I'm hoping not too soon. When I get word it's a go, we'll have to move fast." He met her eyes. "Whether or not you think Eve is ready for it. You'll have to go in and convince her."

"I know that," she said jerkily. "I'll do what I have to do. It might even be a relief." She got to her feet. "And now you should get me out of here. You've taken long enough to clean this plane. I need to get to the embassy, check in, and annoy the ambassador's secretary to give me any story that he has available on a dull news day."

Novak lifted a brow. "And make sure that no one makes the connection between Eve's arrival and you?"

"No one should if you've done your job. You said you'd arrange it so no one would realize I'd left Maldara."

"No one will. Your tail only caught glimpses of a look-alike as she moved through the streets or visited a friend or restaurant."

She smiled with an effort. "And now Eve appears here courtesy of a notable charity while I've been here all the time and obviously had nothing to do with it." She moistened her lips. "Did you, by any chance, manage to identify the man who's been following me?"

"Not 'by chance.' You insult me." His lips tightened. "We knew the day you showed up in Jokan a week after the attack. I had my own men on you, and he was spotted immediately. His name is Ken Bogani, and he's one of Zahra Kiyani's agents." He paused. "But I don't think he's one of the men who attacked you. We checked DNA, and there was no match for the specimen under your fingernails or the trace evidence on your clothes."

Not under her nails.

Think of the words, don't let the ugly pictures bombard you.

Novak's voice was cool and without expression, and she must be equally calm and composed. She'd already revealed too much to him when he had stayed with her while she was recovering in that hospital in Nairobi. She knew it was dangerous that she had become so dependent on him. But the situation was different now. She was a professional, and she mustn't show him any more weakness.

"But that doesn't mean he's not on the backup team, does it? It's odd you haven't been able to locate any of those men when you're so good at what you do. It's as if they dropped off the face of the earth."

"I'll find them, Jill."

"I know you will. But that shouldn't be a high priority anyway right now." Then she wearily shook her head. "And there's probably no connection between this Bogani and Hadfeld's death, or what happened to me. It wouldn't make sense. Zahra wouldn't have anything to do with Varak, a man who nearly destroyed her country. It has to be something as simple as the fact that I got in Zahra's way at the Robaku school, and I'm suddenly on her watch list."

"Not necessarily. I don't believe in simple answers when it comes to Zahra Kiyani."

Her gaze flew to his face. "You do think she's involved?"

"I didn't say that. You're right, it's not logical, considering who she is. It would be at odds with both Zahra's past and everything she stands for. I just don't discard the possibility because it might be complex."

"And she *is* complex." Jill was thinking quickly. "If you'd heard the bizarre stories Gideon told me about her...But if you think there's even a possibility, we need to pursue it. It's not that I'm afraid. It's not about me. We just have to look at everything, and—"

"It *is* about you." Novak's hands were suddenly hard on her shoulders. His eyes glittered down at her. He muttered a low oath. "I can see you thinking, trying to find a way to go after them. Are you crazy? It's *all* about you. They hurt you. Do you want it to happen again?"

"I believe you know the answer to that," she said unsteadily. "I didn't behave with a great amount of courage that night, did I? And I wasn't any better after you flew me to Nairobi. You had to...help me and I—" She broke off. "And now you're feeling guilty because you think it happened because you wouldn't give me what I asked you. I could see it coming that night you picked me up on that road. *I* made the decision. It was a big story, and I went after it. You had nothing to do with it."

"The hell I didn't."

"Okay, you want to feel guilty, go ahead." She pulled away from his grasp. "Though you don't have that reputation, and I don't know why on earth you're focused on me."

"Neither do I." He gave her a push toward the stainless-steel disposal cart. His voice was rough, but his hands were gentle as he lifted her into the cart and closed the lid. "Now shut up until I get you out of here and into the work van."

The waste container was hot, small, stuffy, and she had to curl pretzel-like inside. She could hear him open the door, and the sunlight pouring on the stainless steel made it even hotter. She knew she should be silent now. But he had been angry with her, and she had to make sure it wouldn't make a difference. She whispered, "You made me a promise. I won't let you break it, Novak."

"Don't you ever give up?" His voice was no longer angry but weary. "I can't break it. We're too close, and you have Eve Duncan, the only wild card in the deck." He started to maneuver the cart down the steps. "Let's hope I can keep her alive for you."

———

"It's about time," Joe said as he answered Eve's Skype. "I know you asked me to wait until you called me, but you didn't say it would be at three in the morning."

"Sorry." She leaned back on her stool and took a swallow of coffee. Bless caffeine, she just might make it through the night. "It took me longer than I thought to set up my lab; and then I had to go through the skulls to see if I could find Amari."

"Amari?"

"Hajif's grandson. He has to be the first reconstruction." She started to go into the reasons for the selection, but he cut her off.

"Later," he said grimly. "All I want to know right now is that you've definitely decided to do the reconstructions. You said it wouldn't be a done deal until you got there and looked the situation over. If you've set up your lab, it means that you're committed. Right?"

"I have to do it, Joe," she said quietly. "I'll get them finished as quickly as I can."

"I know you will. I'll admit I was hoping it would go the other way." He paused. "You look tired. Don't work yourself into a nervous breakdown because you think I'm pressuring you. I'm behind you whatever you do."

"You're not the only one who's pressuring me," she said ruefully.

"Jill Cassidy? Tell her to go to hell."

"She's being very subtle. It's hard to have a confrontation when she dumped me on this Sam Gideon the minute the plane's wheels hit the tarmac here. I think she's designated him to do the pressuring for the time being."

"Sam Gideon?"

"Our pilot. I imagine he's several other interesting things as well. He mentioned casually that he'd been Zahra Kiyani's lover at one time. But Jill said I could trust him."

"Providing you can trust her."

"Neither really matters. I'm back at work. I'm the only one I have to trust now."

"Wrong. You have to trust me. You might have gone into your cocoon, but I have to make certain that no one messes around and tries to break into it."

"From long-distance," she said pointedly.

"For the time being."

She tried to change the subject. "Tell me what you're doing. Do you like the guest instructors at the Yard?"

"They're superb. I'll tell you all about them after you finish telling me about Robaku." He paused. "I want every detail, Eve. Every impression."

She laughed. "Joe, are you debriefing me?"

"In a way. Partly. But I've already been away from you too long. I *need* you. It will help if you just let everything flow out and share with me."

"It's been quite a day. I don't even know if I'll remember everything. It's sad here. Some things will hurt talking about..." But she suddenly knew she needed to share them anyway. She always needed to share with Joe. It kept the bond firm, doubts at a minimum, and the love shiny and new. Do as he asked and let it flow. "I guess it started on the plane when Jill came to tell me that everything wasn't quite as I thought it was going to be..."

———

An hour later, Eve turned off the computer, sat there, and gazed around the room. For that short hour she'd been with Joe, it had faded away, and she wanted to keep it at a distance. She didn't want to face that schoolroom only yards away, nor the memory of those children who had died so terribly. She wanted Joe and Michael and the life she'd had only days before. She wanted to close her eyes and forget about anything else.

But there was always a price to pay if you allowed yourself to forget the madness and the horror.

It could come again.

She took a deep breath and pushed her computer aside. Then she took the skull she'd mounted on the dais and started to examine it. First, she'd have to repair the damage. Next, she'd start to measure. She was very tired, and she'd probably have to catch a nap on that cot before she actually started. Her hands tended to shake if she was too exhausted.

But she needed a little time with this young boy now that they had come together.

She looked down at the hideous, blackened skull and gently touched the cheekbone. "Hi. You've been through a nightmare, but you're not the nightmare," she whispered. "I think you probably know that by now, but we have to make certain everyone else does, too. We're going to make you as handsome as you were before that day, and that will make your grandmother very happy. Okay? And I usually give my sculptures names, but I believe I know yours, Amari. So we'll go from there. Are you ready?" She began to check for breaks in the orbital socket. "Let's clean you up a bit, then we'll get you started on your road home . . ."

———

"You're a fool, Wyatt," Zahra said savagely. "I don't *want* Eve Duncan at Robaku. Why would you permit her to come to my city and work on those children? I've worked hard to try to filter all publicity about them through me, and now you let some charity send a world-class forensic sculptor here? She's bound to attract attention."

"They went through the London office. I was told to accommodate them. What could I do?"

"What I want you to do." She drew a deep breath and tried to smother her anger. This was not the time to alienate Wyatt when everything must go smoothly over the next few weeks. "You said Duncan has already arrived? Did Jill Cassidy have anything to do with bringing her here?"

"The home office didn't mention her. But you know that her stories about the massacre did stir up a good deal of sympathy. It might have influenced the charity to act."

"Tell me about it. That's why you should have gotten rid of her. But she had no direct connection with Duncan?"

"No, I believe Duncan called the charity and volunteered

her services. Though I was told she arrived on Sam Gideon's plane. Perhaps he had something to do with it."

Gideon. Zahra's hand tightened on the phone. Son of a *bitch*. Yes, he could have done it, just to annoy her. She'd made no secret of her views about Robaku. He was constantly getting in her way, and it was dangerous for her to do anything to put a stop to it. His plantation might have been burned to the ground during the conflict, but he still had enormous economic influence in Maldara. She wished he'd been burned up with the damn place, she thought savagely. "That doesn't mean she isn't involved." But her temporary chief agent, Bogani, had told her that Jill Cassidy had been in Jokan for the weeks since the attack. If she was involved, it had not been directly, and Gideon was quite capable of raising enough hell on his own. "I'm going to meet this Eve Duncan. I'll be able to tell if she's just a do-gooder or if she'll get in my way."

"Let it go, Zahra," Wyatt said. "What harm can she do? I'll keep an eye on her, and in a few weeks she'll be gone. She's probably doing it for the publicity and working on a few of those burnt-out skulls will be enough to discourage her."

"I want her gone now. Robaku is mine, and it's time all these arguments about the DNA ended." She was done talking to him. "Let me know if you find out anything else." She cut the connection.

She sat there for a moment. She didn't like this. She needed to talk to Lon Markel, her primary agent, and discuss how far she could go to discourage it happening. She started to dial her cell again, then stopped. Markel had been involved in the attack on the Cassidy woman, and she'd been told not to call on him again unless it was an emergency.

Screw it. No one could tell her what to do. Markel was

her agent, her employee, and she trusted him more than she did the others in her service. He'd been with her for years before he'd been yanked away from her these past months. She'd only tolerated Bogani since she'd been told she couldn't have Lon Markel for the time being. But she would *not* have him hijacked and permanently taken away from her. She paid his salary, and she would do what she liked with him. She began to dial again.

She stopped and put the phone down.

It wasn't fear, she told herself. She was never afraid. It was just that perhaps it wasn't wise to use Markel again so soon. There was a slight chance he might have been recognized by Jill Cassidy that night. Of course, it was entirely her own decision. It would be better to handle this herself.

It was entirely her own decision...

———◆———

"How is it going?"

Eve looked up from her reconstruction to see Sam Gideon standing in the doorway. "Well enough." She arched her back to ease the stiffness. "Amari isn't easy. Just reconstructing the damaged bones of the right temple took me almost a day. It must have been a machete blow to be that shattered. But the measuring isn't causing me too much trouble. I'm almost done with it." She tilted her head. "I haven't seen you for two days. Weren't you supposed to stay around and be at my beck and call?"

"I was around. I peeked in a couple times, but you were so absorbed that I decided to let Hajif handle everything. He seemed to be doing a good job, and I'm always tempted to ask questions." He was looking at the reconstruction. "What are those red flags all over his face?"

"Depth-measurement markers."

"Not flattering. But the rest of him is looking a hell of a lot better than that first night, when you pulled him out of his box."

"Thank you for your critique. Now go away, Gideon. I'm busy."

"Presently. I just thought I'd drop by and give you fair warning. I just got word that Zahra Kiyani is on her way to pay you a visit. I thought you'd want to be prepared."

Eve frowned with annoyance. "I don't need this. Can't you get rid of her?"

"No, you'll have to do it. Zahra doesn't listen to me. She'd prefer that I didn't exist. I actually thought she'd be here before this. She obviously took a long time to make up her mind whether you were worthy of her personal attention." He paused. "It would be best if you didn't mention Jill. Zahra can't hurt me, but she'll try her best to hurt Jill. And Zahra has enough power in Jokan to make it . . . uncomfortable for her."

"You want me to lie?"

"That's up to you." He smiled. "No one is going to stop you from saying anything you wish to say. If you think what you're doing here isn't worth doing and that Jill should be punished for being involved, by all means have a chat with Zahra about it." He turned and headed for the door. "I'll just hang around outside until her entourage shows up and greet her." His smile was a combination of both mischief and malice. "That should make her day . . ."

She gazed after him with exasperation. She didn't want to deal with Zahra Kiyani, and she didn't want to have Gideon telling her how to handle the woman. She just wanted to go back to work and finish Amari.

But it was too late. She heard the roar of several automobiles exiting the road, then the slam of car doors as they reached the museum. Eve got to her feet and wiped her hands on her work towel. Then the door was being opened ceremoniously by a uniformed soldier, and Zahra Kiyani was sweeping into the museum. She did not look pleased, Eve thought. Evidently, seeing Gideon had definitely *not* made her day.

She was dressed in a designer gold-paisley suit and was just as beautiful as she appeared in her photos. Her frown disappeared, and she gave Eve a flashing smile. "How happy I am that you're here in my country." Her English was faultless, with just a hint of an accent. "And doing such good work. I thought I'd drop by and personally welcome you." She looked Eve up and down. "But I should have let you know. You're obviously working so hard that I might be in the way..." She trailed off and shrugged. "You do look so tired. I hope you'll forgive me."

The needle was faint but definitely there. Eve was annoyed enough about the interruption not to let it get a pass. "I'm not at all tired. When I become this involved in my work, I forget everything else. I'm looking forward to many engrossing hours spent here at Robaku," she said. "Thank you for coming to welcome me. But I know how busy you must be, so I won't keep you." She gestured to the skull. "And I'm busy as well. He's one of your own people, so I know you'll want me to finish as soon as possible."

"Yes, of course." She gazed at the skull. "One of the children..." Her glance shifted back to Eve. "I understand you have a child. Aren't you worried about leaving him to take care of my problems here? Children can be so very fragile."

Eve went still as she looked at her. Zahra's voice had been soft, and her expression was serene, but Eve had felt a chill.

Could that have been a threat? "My son is always safe even when I'm not with him. And my work is too important to leave it undone when a charity says I'm needed."

Zahra nodded. "You appear to be very talented." She forced a smile. "Though I do prefer the certainty of DNA over a pretty sculpture. I suppose Jill Cassidy told you that we disagreed on that score?"

"Jill Cassidy? Isn't she a reporter or something? I believe I've heard of her. But it was Sam Gideon who told me about you."

She stiffened. "Really?" she said warily. "What did he say?"

"He used the word 'magnificent' quite a bit. I can see why he thought it applied to you." She inclined her head. "Now if you'll excuse me?"

But Zahra Kiyani was still looking around the room. "I can't say I like what you've done to my beautiful museum. It's in shambles. I'll tolerate it for now because I don't wish to be unfair. However, if I find that your work isn't what it should be, I'll have to ask you to leave. I'll be back next week to see if that charity that sent you has made a mistake." She moved toward the door. "I'll see you then, Ms. Duncan."

Then she was gone. A few minutes later, Eve heard the low roar of the cars as they departed Robaku.

Gideon came back into the museum a moment later. "That was very short. She didn't waste much time on you."

"No, *I* didn't waste much time on *her*," she corrected. "She only came to threaten and find out who had sent me here. I said enough to satisfy her so that she'd get out and let me work."

"Satisfy?" he repeated. "She looked almost triumphant when she glanced at me when she left."

"That's because I told her you thought she was magnificent. She probably thinks that if she made the effort, she could have you worshipping at her feet again."

He flinched. "That was wicked of you, Eve. When she has time to think it over, she'll realize I must have been lying to you." He tilted his head. "But you must have been doing a little prevaricating yourself if you let her believe it."

"I didn't lie. She asked what you'd told me about her, and I told her the truth. I just didn't elaborate."

"And were you equally truthful when she asked you about Jill?"

"I might have been a little less open. She had a perfectly good target in you, and bringing in Jill would have confused things and wasted more time."

"And you wouldn't have wanted that to happen," he said softly. "It was all for the benefit of Amari and friends."

She was silent. "I didn't like her." She was remembering that instant when Zahra had mentioned her son. She was still feeling that chill. "I've met women before who are antagonistic toward other women. I've never understood it. She was trying to be subtle, but underneath, she was practically bristling."

"She believes she has no need for them, and they might prove competitive. Not that she'd admit the latter." He smiled. "After all, she is magnificent."

Eve smiled back at him. "You left out one descriptive noun. Magnificently arrogant." She waved her hand. "Now get out of here and let me work. If I'm lucky, I'll get Amari finished tonight or early morning and reward myself by letting you take me to that hotel so I can shower."

"And sleep in a real bed?"

"That's too much luxury. The cot is fine. I'm usually so tired I have no trouble sleeping. Out, Gideon."

"I'm going." He hesitated at the door. "But I should tell

you that Zahra wanted to leave one of her soldiers on guard here. I'm sure she'd say it was for your protection, but I still sent him on his way."

"Does she think that I'm going to steal one of these skulls?"

"No, I'm sure she's checked you out thoroughly. She just likes to be in control, and you didn't fall into line. It probably wouldn't have done any harm to let the guard stay as long as I knew he was around. I just didn't want you to stumble over him if you went to get a breath of air." He grimaced. "As if you would bother." He lifted his hand in a wave. "I'll be back around midnight to see Amari in all his glory."

"No glory." Eve was already sitting back down on her stool. "Just a little boy spruced up and ready to go home to see his grandparents..."

Then she closed everything out as she settled down to spend the next hours working on completing and checking the measuring. It was undeniably the most important if least satisfying part of the sculpting process. It was the precise building block of features and contours that made Amari who he was. But it was only the final stage of sculpting that revealed the details that gave him the personality and presence that brought him to life for Eve.

So do the hard, gritty work and make sure that she made no mistakes. Then she'd do the initial smoothing and make ready for that final step. She felt her fingers tingling at the thought.

Stop it. Not yet. This boy deserved care and certainty.

The measuring...

———

It had not gone as well as she'd hoped with Eve Duncan, Zahra thought impatiently as she gazed out the window of her limo. She'd hoped to impress her enough so that she would be able to oust her during the next visit. But Eve Duncan was one of those women who thought so much of themselves that they didn't realize how far above them she was. Station and beauty meant nothing to them because they had some idiotic skill and thought they could compete. It was not only laughable, it was an annoyance. Now she would have to spend more time than she'd planned on getting rid of her. It would probably mean trying to influence that charity to—"

Her phone was buzzing.

She stiffened as she saw there was no ID.

Dammit! She had been afraid of this.

She punched in the access code and typed rapidly.

IT DIDN'T GO WELL. DUNCAN IS STUPID AND I CAN SEE SHE WON'T COOPERATE. IT WILL TAKE ME A LITTLE LONGER THAN I PLANNED.

A pause, then the answer.

WE BOTH KNOW THAT'S NOT ACCEPTABLE. I TOLD YOU I NEED HER GONE. MAKE IT HAPPEN.

Orders? She tried to smother the bolt of sheer rage that shot through her.

I'LL DO IT AS QUICKLY AS I CAN. HOW DARE YOU TELL ME WHAT TO DO. YOU HAVE NO IDEA HOW COMPLICATED IT IS TO KEEP ALL THE BALLS IN THE AIR.

Another pause.

HOW DO I DARE? YOU KNOW HOW I DARE, ZAHRA. NOW STOP STALLING AND GIVE ME WHAT I WANT.

She should have been more cautious. She might have made a mistake. She typed in quickly. AS SOON AS POS-SIBLE.

The answer came back instantly.
MAKE IT HAPPEN!

———————

Eve finished the initial smoothing of the clay just after midnight.

She leaned back and gazed at the reconstruction as she wiped her hands. Everything was there, and smooth, and presumably correct. But he was like a baby asleep in the cradle, waiting to be roused. It was time to wake him up and bring him back to those who loved him.

Her hands were tingling again. But that was okay now. The blood flow usually helped the process and kept her from becoming exhausted.

"It's time for you to get to work, Amari," she said softly. "We're almost at the end, and I need a little help here. I'll be with you all the way, but there are so many tiny things I could miss that would make them sad if I didn't catch them. We don't want that to happen, so let's make sure it doesn't. Okay?"

She reached out and delicately touched the place on his skull that she'd repaired. "Let's do this, first. Let's make it go away forever..."

Smooth.

Careful.

Delicacy.

Don't hurry. It has to be perfect.

Don't let anyone know the pain that caused that wound.

See? It's gone now, Amari.

Perfect.

Smooth.

Mold.

Go on to the cheekbone.

It's going faster now.

Smooth.

Mold.

Hollow the left cheekbone a little more.

The clay was cool beneath her fingers.

Ears. Make them generic. Hajif could tell her if she'd gotten it right.

Smooth.

Mold.

Fill in.

The clay felt warmer now as her fingers moved faster.

Eyes.

No, not yet. There was something troubling about the eyes...

Go on to the nose.

Pay attention to the measurements of the space between the nose and upper lip.

Smooth.

Fill in.

Mouth.

So difficult.

Just go with what seemed right.

Eyes?

No, not yet. What was wrong with the eyes?

Go back to the cheekbones.

Not full enough, he'd not reached puberty and was still a child.

Smooth.

Mold.

Fill in.

Her fingers were flying now.

What's wrong with the eyes?

Check the measurements.

Measurements correct.

But something was wrong.

Not with the right eye, she realized.

Left eye. Outer corner of the left eye.

Too smooth.

Indent.

No, build up.

It didn't matter if she didn't know the reason.

Just do it.

Now it was right.

Go on to the curve of the lips.

Something was missing.

Mold.

A deeper crease.

Her fingers were hot, fast, mindless.

Let it all come together.

Smooth.

Fill in.

Mold...

CHAPTER

5

"Finished?" Gideon said behind her from the doorway. "It's almost three. I gave you an extra—"

"Almost," she interrupted. "I just need to put in his eyes. Go get Hajif and his wife."

"It's three in the morning. You want me to wake them up?"

"Yes, by the time they throw on some clothes, I'll be finished. And they're not going to care if it's three in the morning. They deserve to be the first to see him. Go!"

"You're continuing to order me about," he complained. "I can't say I'm accustomed to such treatment..."

He was gone.

And she was reaching for her eye case. There was no question about the color, they would be the same rich brown as Hajif's. She carefully inserted the glass eyes in the orbital sockets and sat back to look at him.

Yes.

Only Hajif and his wife, Leta, could tell her if this was Amari, but the skull had come alive as she'd wanted it to. She'd put the hint of a smile at the corners of his lips, and the shining brown of his eyes appeared oddly eager as he stared up at her. She'd engraved gentle curves that mimicked short curls or waves framing that face. It had just seemed right.

"Are you ready for them?" she whispered. "They're ready for you, Amari."

She stood up as she heard them coming. She stood to one side as she saw Gideon open the door and Hajif and his wife appear in the doorway. "I thought you wouldn't mind getting up a bit early, Hajif." She gestured to the reconstruction. "Is this what you wanted from me?"

Hajif stood stock-still in shock.

He was silent, staring dazedly at the sculpture. "I . . . did not expect this. It . . . is magic." He drew his wife, Leta, toward the worktable. His eyes were shimmering with moisture as he slipped his arm around her waist. "You see, Leta, he has returned to us." He reached out, and his index finger gingerly touched the raised scar at the corner of his left eye. "Remember how upset you were when the propeller flew off his toy plane? You kept saying one more inch, and he would have been blind. But he was fine, wasn't he?" He looked at Eve. "How did you know?"

"I didn't. Some things just seem right. Is it Amari, Hajif?"

He nodded. "It is my grandson." He turned to his wife, whose eyes had never left the face of the reconstruction. "Is it Amari, Leta?" he asked gently. "Has she brought our Amari back to us?"

"Yes." The tears were suddenly running down her cheeks. "He is not alive. He's not hiding in the jungle waiting to come home to us because he's afraid. They killed him, Hajif." She was sobbing. "They *killed* him."

"You knew that." He pulled her into his arms. "But does he look sad and afraid now? He is our Amari, and there is no fear."

"No fear," his wife said brokenly. "I have nightmares about how afraid he was when those butchers came."

"I know. I know." He held her close. He looked over her head at Eve. "Words cannot—I thank you. May we come and visit him here in the museum?"

She shook her head. "I don't believe he'd like staying here. Why don't you take him home?"

His eyes widened. "But he belongs to—"

"He belongs to you now." She grimaced. "As long as you promise not to ever put him in that box again." She took a step closer to Leta. "Leave him here for the time being," she told her gently. "Go home and make a place for him. No fancy shelves. Just a place where he'll be safe, and you can see him every day. Use his favorite colors, put things he loved around him. If you see something you think he'd like, give that to him, too. See him as he is now and let him become part of your life." She paused. "And maybe that will make the nightmares go away."

"I hope that is true." Leta suddenly launched herself into Eve's arms and was embracing her. "But if it's not, when I wake, I will have him with me." She awkwardly backed away, embarrassed. "Come along, Hajif. We must go home and find this place for him. It will not be as easy as she makes it out to be."

"But I'm sure you will be back in just a few hours with the perfect place." Hajif smiled again at Eve as his wife pushed him toward the door. "There is nothing I will not do for you," he said quietly. "You have only to ask."

"Oh, I'll ask," Eve said. "I have twenty-six other skulls to deal with after this. I'll need help."

"Skulls," he murmured, his wondering gaze on Amari. "It does not seem possible. He is . . . alive." He smiled brilliantly. "Magic."

"No, skill and experience," she called after him, as Leta pulled him from the room. She made a face, and said to Gideon, who was still leaning against the wall beside the door, "I don't think Hajif believes in witch doctors, but this is Africa. You can never tell."

"He may not be far wrong." Gideon straightened and strolled across the room toward the reconstruction. "This is pretty incredible."

"It's hard work and making sure every measurement is correct." She moved toward her duffel beside her cot. "And now you can take me to that hotel and let me spend the next hour under a hot shower." She slipped the strap of the duffel over her shoulder. "I need it."

"Give me a minute." Gideon was closely examining the reconstruction. "You're selling yourself short. Probably intentionally. I've never seen anything like this. It's superb."

"Yes, I'm very good. I want to go, Gideon."

"Hmm." His index finger was tracing the scar at the corner of Amari's left eye. "I just wanted to get a closer look at this. Hajif was impressed. I agree." Then he gave her a slanting glance that held pure mischief. "Magic . . ."

She ignored him, already on her way toward the door. "Bullshit. Haven't you ever heard of inspiration? Get me to that hotel."

She heard him laugh as he followed her from the museum.

———◆———

The Soran Hotel was one of the few skyscrapers in Jokan, and it looked like a luxurious Ritz-Carlton, Eve thought. It even had a uniformed doorman who rushed to open her door. "You said it was a decent hotel," she said to Gideon. "This is several steps up from that. Zahra's intervention?"

"No, my father had it built when he still thought Zahra's father could make a difference here in Maldara. Once Zahra took power, she couldn't bear to give up a quality hotel when she could use it to her advantage. Though it irritates her that I prevented her from nationalizing it and still have major control. She tries to exert her influence whenever she gets the chance." He walked with Eve into the lobby and handed her a key. "Suite 735. It's the room I keep on reserve for myself. You'll find it comfortable. Enjoy your shower. I'll give you an hour, then have them bring you your meal. I'd guess you haven't eaten for hours."

She couldn't remember when she'd grabbed that bowl of soup yesterday. "No, but I think I'm getting hungry."

"Then I'll call Pierre Gaillon, the chef, and get him out of bed. I hired him from the George V in Paris, and he does miracles with coq au vin. You won't be disappointed."

"I'm sure I won't. But I'm not accustomed to gourmet cuisine, Gideon. I'd be satisfied with a sandwich."

"I wouldn't. I told you that I'd take care of you." He walked her to the elevator. "I'm tempted to join you for dinner, but this is the time for you to relax, and I'm much too stimulating."

"I didn't notice," she murmured.

"Of course you did." He punched the elevator button. "You're just dedicated to keeping me humble. So I'll stay here in the lobby and talk to the manager and wait for you to call me and tell me how much you enjoyed that coq au vin. Try to get a nap if you can afterward. Call me if you need me."

"No nap." The doors of the elevator opened, and she

stepped inside. "And I'll be ready to go back to Robaku as soon as I've eaten. I need to start the next reconstruction. I think I'm going to do one of the six-year-olds. But I'll call you as soon as I've finished that gourmet meal you're ordering for me." She said quietly, "Thanks, Gideon. I appreciate your making everything easier for me."

"My pleasure." He smiled. "It's been an interesting few days. If you don't mind, while I'm waiting around, I'll give Jill a call and tell her about Amari. She'll want to know."

"I don't mind." Being able to help Hajif had caused her resentment toward Jill to lessen, she found. There was no doubt that so far her work here had been worthwhile and caused a major difference in Hajif's and Leta's lives. "Tell her if she wants to see it, she should visit Hajif's home."

"And not get in your way?"

She found herself smiling as the elevator door started to close. "And not get in my way."

"I won't get in her way," Jill said. "In fact, I'll wait until the press meeting day after tomorrow to even show up at Robaku. Do I detect a little softening?"

"A little." He paused. "She's got a different mind-set. Doing that reconstruction meant something to her. She's pretty fantastic, you know, Jill. You chose the right person."

"I'm well aware of that, Gideon. There wasn't a choice when I realized how amazing she was."

"But I like her," Gideon said. "And I'm not cut out for all this secretive bullshit." He returned to Eve. "And she covered for you with Zahra. But that isn't because she was fond of you but because she didn't like Zahra or the way she'd used the kids as a display for her museum."

"I thought that would push her buttons," Jill said. "It did mine. I deliberately left it as a surprise." She'd be glad when all this manipulation ended, she thought wearily. "But if she's so involved with the kids, it might make it more difficult when I try to move her away from them."

"No word about the skull?"

"Anytime now," Jill said. She was as impatient as Gideon. "Novak said he'd let me know as soon as he does. It has to happen, Gideon." She changed the subject to Eve. "Take care of her. I don't like that Zahra wanted a guard stationed at Robaku."

"She didn't get it. I'll be there for Eve," he said quietly. "The worst thing that will happen is that she'll drop from exhaustion. I don't seem to be able to control that possibility. Now let me go and order her dinner. The other possibility is that she might forget to eat and starve to death." He cut the connection.

Gideon seemed almost big brotherly, Jill thought as she hung up, and that was never Gideon's style. He was cool, sometimes amusing, sometimes sensual, and always wary these days. He tended to keep everyone at a distance. But he had said he liked Eve, and that might have made the difference.

They had both developed feelings for Eve since they had brought her to Maldara. It was becoming more and more difficult to face drawing her even deeper into the quagmire.

Novak, get that damn skull!

———

"I'm clean at last." Eve stopped drying her hair and tossed aside the towel as she grinned at Joe on the Skype. "Sorry you have to put up with my soggy hair, but I wanted to catch you before you went to the Yard. I didn't get a chance to call you yesterday. Did you get my message that I was finishing Amari?"

"I got it," he said dryly. "Or I would have been on the next plane to Jokan. I take it that it went well? You're practically floating."

"I am floating. It was so *different*, Joe. You know I usually have to just send the reconstructions back to a police department and they do the follow-up to find who the child is and the killer. This time I was able to see that boy go home to the people who loved him five minutes after I finished. I got to see their *faces*, Joe."

"And it meant the world to you," he said gently. "That's wonderful, Eve."

"Everything's wonderful tonight." She chuckled. "I sent Amari home, Gideon brought me to this five-star hotel so that I could dine in style and shower, and I got to share it all with you. It can't get any better."

"Until next time." He smiled. "I'm not going to be able to get you away from that place, am I?"

"I'm needed here, Joe. But I'll leave when you and Michael are finished there. I promised you. Besides, I couldn't stand being away from you any longer than that." She heard a knock on the door. "That must be my room service. Gideon said that the chef was preparing me coq au vin, and it was guaranteed to be delicious."

"Evidently, I'll have to trust your opinion of this Gideon," Joe said. "Though I'm not certain how I feel about his being able to whisk you to five-star hotels and ply you with gourmet meals. I'll have to tell you when I meet him. But as long as you're not sharing that meal with him, soggy hair and all, I guess I'll be able to tolerate it."

"You're joking," she said as she got to her feet. "I have to answer the door. I'll tell you tonight if it's as good as Gideon said. I love you. Have a good day."

"Only half joking. My humor is suffering drastically since I've been limited to Skype to see you. You'll remember I don't like sharing you. But I'm glad you've already had a wonderful day. I love you, too. Be safe."

Eve headed for the door as she disconnected the call. Those last remarks had had an edge, she thought. Joe had been very patient, but she knew he was worried. She had to be careful to reassure him that though everything was strange, and there were annoying elements like Zahra Kiyani, there had not been anything obviously threatening during these days.

A smiling waiter wheeling a white-draped cart with several silver-domed serving dishes bowed as she opened the door. "The chef sends his regards and hopes his offering will please you."

"I'm sure it will." She was suddenly ravenously hungry. She stood aside as he rolled the cart into the room. She would have to tell Joe about the elegant presentation when she talked to him tonight. It would amuse him. Or maybe it wouldn't. She'd have to think about it. But it would certainly emphasize that everything surrounding her at the moment was ultracivilized and completely without threat...

———————

Eve pushed back her chair and sighed with contentment.

The meal had been as fantastic as the presentation, and this coffee she was drinking was excellent as well. She was tempted to call Gideon to tell him how well he'd done, but she decided against it. She'd call him after she got dressed and was ready to leave. That would be time enough. She was eager to get back to Robaku and start the new reconstruction.

She quickly dressed in slacks and a work shirt and brushed her hair. She did feel fresher and able to cope now. She'd been right to take this little break between reconstructions. She'd be able to attack the new work with a clear head, and that would make it go faster than—

Pain!

She bent double as agony knifed through her stomach.

She felt so sick.

Then her stomach was suddenly heaving.

She had to hold on to the vanity to make it to the toilet.

Then she was throwing up . . .

Time after time, trying to hold herself upright, fighting the violence of the vomiting.

Her head was throbbing, pounding . . .

And then the cramping attacked her stomach.

Hideous cramping.

Her legs gave way, and she fell to the floor.

Her head was on fire.

Her phone . . . She had to get to her phone. She reached blindly toward the vanity where she'd laid it.

No strength . . .

Only the pain and the terrible nausea.

She felt as if she must be dying.

Because everything was going dark . . .

◆

"I don't have much time, Jill," Gideon said curtly when Jill picked up his call. "I'm in an ambulance heading to the embassy hospital. I found Eve unconscious in her suite, and I couldn't bring her around. I have to get her to the ER right away."

Jill stiffened. "Gideon, what happened? You said she was fine when I talked to you before."

"I don't know what happened, dammit. No obvious wounds. She'd obviously been throwing up, but I don't know if it was drug-induced. All I know is she's damn sick."

Panic seared through her. "I'll meet you at the hospital."

"No, I'll call you when I know more. You can't do anything I can't do. Novak doesn't want you near her."

"That's too bad. I don't *care*. I figure all bets are off now. She could *die*, Gideon. She wasn't supposed to get hurt. There's no reason. Not for what she's doing at Robaku."

"Evidently, someone disagreed. And she might not be that sick. Let me find out." As she started to protest, he cut in harshly: "I told you I'd be responsible for her, and I screwed up. Do you know how that makes me feel? Now let me take care of her. I won't let you blow everything we've worked for because you're panicking. There's too much at stake. Now call Novak and tell him to check her suite and see if he can find out who or what brought her down. I ordered dinner for her, and she'd finished it. But you stay away from the hospital unless I call you, Jill." He cut the connection.

Jill *was* panicking. She was terrified. And there was no way she wasn't going to go to the hospital to see Eve. Gideon said he was responsible, but he was wrong. She was the one who was responsible for everything that had happened to Eve. She had chosen her, then done everything possible to make her come here.

Yet if she did show up at the hospital, it would make Eve more of a target than ever. Any association with Jill might draw attention to Eve. But this couldn't go on. She had to *do* something.

One step at a time.

First, do as Gideon suggested and phone Novak.

She quickly dialed Novak's number. "I suppose you already know what happened," she said unevenly. "Gideon asked me to call you. But you always know what's going on before anyone else does."

"I know an ambulance just took Eve to the embassy hospital," Novak said. "Stay away from there, Jill."

"I've already heard that song, and I'm trying to do it. Because if Eve manages to live through this, I don't want to make it any more dangerous for her than it is already."

"I know you're upset, Jill. But we don't know what her condition is right now. We'll do everything we can to—"

"Upset?" Her voice was shaking. "You bet I'm upset. I can't take this any longer. You go find out exactly what happened to her. And you make certain that Gideon lets me know as soon as possible whether I've killed her or not."

"It isn't your fault that—"

"Don't tell me that," she said fiercely. "I am to blame. I'm going to pray that I didn't hurt her too badly, but I won't try to escape the fact that if I did, the fault was mine." She drew a deep, shaky breath. "But it's not going to happen again. We thought she was safe, but she wasn't. And we let her walk right into it. It's got to change."

"I don't like the sound of that."

"And I didn't like it when Gideon said he couldn't wake Eve up." Those words were still chilling her. "It's got to change, Novak."

She hung up the phone.

———◆———

EMBASSY HOSPITAL
12:40 P.M.

"Eve? Open your eyes. I have to talk to you."

Gideon, Eve realized dazedly. It was good he was

here . . . She'd been trying to phone him when she'd been so sick.

"Eve. Open your eyes, dammit. This might be my only chance to talk to you."

He sounded so urgent that she forced herself to open her lids. His face above her was as strained and urgent as his voice had been. He was frowning, and Gideon seldom frowned. Then he was smiling at her. "That's right. Now stay awake. These hospitals suck, and I have to try to get you out of here."

Hospitals? Green walls. The smell of antiseptics and cleanliness. Definitely a hospital. Eve had been around enough of them to recognize one when she saw it.

And Gideon's face above her was sober again. A hospital face . . .

"I was sick . . . " she whispered. Her throat was sore, and she could barely speak. She was sore all over, she realized vaguely. "Fast . . . it happened so fast. What happened to me, Gideon?"

"I don't know. They're calling it food poisoning." He was putting a straw between her lips, and she was sipping ice water. "But it was a damn violent strain if that was what it was. Besides the nausea, it caused unconsciousness. When you didn't answer your phone, I went up to your suite and found you crumpled on the floor. I couldn't wake you." He took her hand. "It scared me. So I called the American hospital that the embassy uses and had them send an ambulance. You still weren't awake when you got to their ER. They diagnosed it as food poisoning and pumped your stomach."

That was why the muscles of her stomach felt this sore . . . "Food poisoning . . . not such good coq au vin after all."

"Maybe. But I'll swear that chef would never give you anything contaminated. I know him."

"I might argue with you about that." She swallowed to ease the soreness of her throat. "I felt so sick. But I'm going to be okay?"

He nodded. "Very nasty case, and it's going to leave you weak for a few days. They say you'll have to rest. But you'll be fine eventually."

"That's good." She closed her eyes again. Then they flew open. "No, it's not. I can't stay here in the hospital. I have too much to do. I have to get back to Robaku."

"I thought that would be your reaction. That's why I wanted to get to you before anyone else had a chance to try to brainwash you." He smiled. "I prefer to do it myself."

"Go to hell, Gideon." She lifted her hand to her aching head. "Just tell me what you want, and I'll see if I want the same thing."

"I want you out of this hospital. I want you back at Robaku. I'll pull all the strings I have to in order to get you there. But you'll have to put up a fight to do it. All those nice kind people who want only what's best for you are going to go on the attack in about fifteen minutes. And then, if you don't cave, they'll bring in the big guns."

"Don't be ridiculous. No one can keep me here if I want to walk out of this place. I'm already feeling better. I'll just take a couple more hours to rest, then I'll leave." Not totally the truth. She was still feeling terribly weak, and her head was throbbing again. "I can't just lie around. It would drive me crazy. I always feel better if I'm working."

"I'm not arguing with you. I'm on your side. But I can't be the one to force the issue this time. I'll just tell you that when I get you to Robaku, I'll take care of you, and you'll be better off." He got to his feet. "Now the first one to see you will be Dr. Jeremy Santiago. He'll be comforting and re-assuring but will tell you that you should rest here for a few days and let the ambassador send you home to the U.S. for a longer rest. When you refuse, you may even get a visit from Ambassador Sandow himself. The message will be the same. And that may only be the beginning. Your phone is on that nightstand. When you get through running the gauntlet they set for you, give me a call, and I'll whisk you out of here." He touched her hand gently. "I'm sorry, Eve. I wish I could do more for you, but that's not possible right now."

"It's okay." She only wanted to close her eyes and rest. "You didn't cook that damn coq au vin. But you should really hire a different chef for that fancy hotel."

"I'll try to do that." He was on his way toward the door. "As soon as I locate him. He seems to have disappeared..."

Disappeared. That sounded all wrong, she thought wearily. But she was too tired to work out why right now. She'd get a little rest, then she'd think about it.

"Ms. Duncan, how glad I am that we were able to help you. I'm Dr. Santiago." A tall, plump man in a white coat was entering the room. "You were a very sick woman." He was beaming at her. "But you're going to be fine, and we're going to make you comfortable for the rest of the time you're in Maldara. But we do have to talk about plans for your recovery..."

"Get me *out* of here, Gideon," Eve said in exasperation when he answered the phone two hours later. "I can't take much more of this. I've talked to two doctors, the head nurse, and I just had a telephone call from the ambassador. They want to keep me in this hospital for another week, then send me back to Atlanta."

"Told you so," Gideon said. "I'm just surprised the ambassador didn't visit you in person. Did you feel slighted?"

"Stop it. No one is listening to me. I tried to explain that I'm fine and need to get back to work, but they said they don't want to take the responsibility for my recovery since the attack was so severe."

"It was very bad, Eve," he said soberly. "You have to know that was true."

"*Get me out of here.*" She pronounced every word with emphasis. "Everyone agrees I'm not on the critical list. There's no reason why I can't go back to work."

"You're certain that's what you want to do? I don't mind persuading you, but I won't coerce you."

"You listen to me, Gideon. The last thing the ambassador said when I turned him down was that he thought it might be a good idea if I talk to President Kiyani, who had expressed concern I'd become this ill in her country. My head is already aching. I won't sit here and get a migraine from having to deal with her."

"I'll be there in thirty minutes." He cut the connection.

Eve put down her phone, leaned back on her pillows, and closed her eyes. She felt totally exhausted. She should probably have told him to bring her something to wear, she thought wearily. The clothes she had worn when the ambulance had brought her here must have been a total disaster. Oh, well, let Gideon worry about it. She had found him quite capable of producing anything she wanted while she was here in Maldara. Except maybe that coq au vin, she thought wryly. He hadn't done such a great job at that particular—

There was some sort of bustle in the hall...

Oh, shit.

Her door was being ceremoniously opened by the same uniformed guard she had seen at Robaku yesterday.

Zahra Kiyani entered the next moment. "What a terrible

thing to have happened to you," she said sweetly. She motioned to the leather chair beside Eve's bed. "Dalai, do something with that chair. You know how careful I have to be to avoid germs in places like this." A young, pretty maid in an ankle-length tan sarong scurried forward and put a gold-silk shawl on the chair before fading into the background. "This hospital is truly deplorable," Zahra said. "You should have been brought to my hospital when you were taken ill. I had it built this year." She gracefully sat down on the silk-draped chair. She wore an exquisitely draped scarlet dress that contrasted boldly with the gold shawl. "It's like a wonderful palace but with all the modern facilities."

"This hospital seems entirely adequate," Eve said. "And I'm not certain patients who are as ill as I was would appreciate being treated in a palace. It's a little over the top."

"It's all what you become accustomed to." Zahra studied Eve. "And you still appear to be quite pale. Would you like me to have Dalai do a makeover to give you a bit of color? She's quite clever about all sorts of different things."

And one of them was evidently how to please Zahra at any cost, Eve thought. The girl had seemed almost frightened as she'd scurried around at her command. "No, thank you. All I need now is a nap. I'm planning on checking out of this hospital soon."

"So I've been told. I've come to try to dissuade you. We don't want someone of your stature to take any chances with your health. What if you had a terrible relapse? It would look very bad for my government when I'm trying so hard to show the world that we are not savages after that terrible war." She smiled. "Why don't you transfer to my hospital, and we'll take great care of you? Then when you're well, I'll either send home or you can return to Robaku."

"I intend to return to Robaku today," Eve said. "And I

don't need to remain in your hospital or any other. My work is going very well."

Zahra's flashing smile remained, but it was now fixed. "As I said, I'll have to visit you again and make that judgment. It would be unfortunate for you to go through so much when we might have to send you home anyway."

"I'll take my chances," Eve said. "You'd have to have cause, and, as I said, I have proof that my work is going very well. And I'll have more proof when I finish the new reconstruction."

Zahra's smile was now a mere baring of teeth. "I hate the idea of your being so stubborn. Look what's already happened to you. That horrible bout of food poisoning. Did they tell you there was a possibility you might die? Wouldn't that have been terrible? It's really too bad they don't have food tasters in this day and age."

Eve's eyes widened in shock. There had been a thread of intimidation in those words, and that last remark had been totally bizarre. "Food taster? I'm sure that my food poisoning was accidental, and I'm glad we have no use for food tasters."

"Yes, of course. But I admit that I've often thought that they did have their uses. When one is of a certain importance, naturally there are people who wish to take that stature away from them in any way possible." She met Eve's gaze with defiance. "I'm sure my own ancestors must have felt bound to protect themselves by such means. After all, the food tasters at court were only slaves and considered of no importance. The royal line had to be preserved."

"Why? The idea is totally barbaric." Then something Zahra had said caught her attention. "Court? I don't know anything about your family background except that your father was the president of Maldara before you, and it was a republic." She added dryly, "But I doubt if he appointed any food tasters to his cabinet."

"No, of course not." She was smiling again. "But we're a very old family, and our traditions go back over two thousand years. Did you think that we'd emerged from the same jungle as those crude Botzans?" Her lips curled. "When he was president, it suited my father to pretend that we were one with all these people, but I would never be so stupid as to give up my heritage. We did not make the Great Journey from the north and struggle all through the years to keep our lineage pure just to sacrifice it to those uncivilized barbarians. I told my father that he couldn't do it." She drew a deep breath. "And I was right, the Botzans killed him. So you can see why I believe that one must protect oneself in any way possible. When death comes near, you should take it as a sign to stop and consider all the consequences."

There was that hint of a threat again. "I don't believe in signs and portents," Eve said. "And I do believe in doing what I think is right in spite of consequences."

"Too bad." Zahra shrugged as she rose to her feet. "I do hope you'll change your mind. Let me know, and I'll send someone to make accommodations for you." She snapped her fingers at the servant girl. "Dalai!"

The young woman jumped forward and snatched up the gold shawl on the chair. Her subservience annoyed Eve. In that moment, she could imagine Zahra indulging herself in any cruel arrogance she chose with those she considered beneath her. She found she wanted to strike out. "Thank you for coming." She paused. "Oh dear, I just had a thought. How do you know that all those stories about your so-called pure lineage weren't a fairy tale? You said yourself that it was a long time ago that your family came to Maldara." She smiled gently. "Who knows? Maybe the Botzans were really your first cousins."

Zahra stopped and whirled to face her. "You insult me," she hissed. "It was no fairy tale. *Look* at me." Her eyes were blazing. "I am everything she was and more." Her voice was shaking with anger. "She made mistakes I will never make. And some-day, I will have the world she lost to her own stupidity."

She turned on her heel and left the room.

What was that all about? Eve wondered. She had clearly opened up a nasty can of worms when she had taken that pot-shot at Zahra's august family tree. And who the hell was *she*?

Later. Gideon should be arriving at any moment, and she needed these few moments to pull herself together. At least she had gotten rid of Zahra before she had to confront Gideon. She was in no mood to referee the explosiveness she sensed between them. She glanced at the clock on the night table. It was almost five in the evening. It seemed like days had passed since she'd talked to Joe early this morning. She'd promised him she'd call him back tonight and what was she going to say to him? He'd be worried and immediately on the attack.

Think about it on the way back to Robaku.

Too many questions. Too many decisions.

And where the hell is Gideon?

———

"That bitch!" Zahra's lips were tight with rage as the chauffeur opened the door of her limousine outside the hospital. "How dare she? Did you hear her, Dalai?"

Dalai knew that Zahra didn't want an answer, only an audience, but she nodded as she slipped into the backseat beside her. One could never tell what would offend Zahra and cause her to take that rage out on the nearest target. Her anger with Eve Duncan was so intense that Dalai had to be extremely careful.

"She *insulted* me." Zahra leaned back in the seat, fuming. "And she doesn't even realize how lucky she is to be alive. Stupid. Incredibly stupid."

Agree. Then try to distract her. "Yes, madam," Dalai said. "And very rude. She doesn't have any idea how wrong she is. She's just a peasant, and you're a queen. You should pay no attention to her."

"Are you telling me what to do?" Zahra asked sharply. "You were stupid, too, today. You weren't quick enough when I told you to fetch that shawl."

The distraction hadn't worked. It had only served to transfer the anger from Eve Duncan to Dalai. She had been expecting it. Eve Duncan could not be touched right now. But Dalai was always available as an outlet. Be humble. Show Zahra fear. She liked the fear. "I know, madam. Forgive me."

"Why should I?" Zahra's smile was malicious. "You should be punished. You're obviously getting lazy. I'll think about it on the way back to the palace."

So that Dalai would have time to anticipate what was to come, she thought wearily. It was all part of the fear Zahra liked to make her feel. Dalai would almost certainly be beaten if she didn't think of some other way to distract Zahra once she got back to the palace. But it would be easier to distract her there, where Zahra had decisions to make and Dalai could make herself useful in helping her. If she was beaten, it would probably not be severely.

"What are you thinking about?" Zahra asked suspiciously. "You're very quiet."

"Nothing, madam." Dalai's eyes widened with fear. "Nothing at all."

It was a lie. She was thinking that it was worth a beating to have seen Eve Duncan cause that look of outrage and indignation on Zahra Kiyani's face.

And that someone should warn the woman what a dangerous thing it was to do.

CHAPTER

6

Gideon arrived ten minutes later, and he was a whirl-wind of activity for the next hour. Somehow he managed to persuade one of the nurses to help Eve dress in the slacks and shirt he'd brought with him. Then he ignored all the protests of the doctors and nurses, negotiated a miraculously fast exit, and whisked her to his Land Rover, parked in front of the hospital.

"Now lean back and relax. I'll have you at Robaku in forty-five minutes." He buckled her seat belt. "You did good, Eve."

"So did you." She closed her eyes and took a deep breath. "I wasn't sure that they wouldn't call security. They were very determined, weren't they?"

"Very." He started the Land Rover. "I could see it on the horizon once they got you settled in that room. It seemed to be a concerted effort."

"It was annoying, but it's hard to be angry. After all, it's the job of a hospital staff to do whatever they think best to get their patients well. The only one I had problems with was Madam President. But then, that was a given."

"Sorry I didn't get there in time to spare you."

"So am I. You might have been able to keep me from insulting her." She shook her head. "No, I doubt it. I rather enjoyed it. She was so ugly to that young maid, and all that arrogant bullshit about royal tasters and such..."

Gideon went still. "Tasters?"

"It was almost a threat." She looked at him. "Some nonsense about her family having had poison tasters in the past and that it wasn't a bad idea. I found it peculiar she'd mention it in the same breath as telling me how sad she was that I'd become so ill. Is there any reason why I should consider it a threat?"

"There's always a reason to suspect Zahra of any effort at intimidation. She doesn't want you here, and she'd take advantage of any opportunity to make you feel afraid and uncertain."

"But there's no reason to think that my food poisoning was anything but an accident?"

Gideon was silent. "Not as far as I know. The food was examined, and it contained mushrooms that could have made you very ill. And we haven't been able to talk to the chef yet. We're still trying to locate him."

"And it would have been crazy for Zahra to slip me anything that would make me that ill just because I wouldn't get on the next plane and take off for home," Eve said. "She's the president of the damn country. She must have more important things to worry about." She made a face. "Though tonight I wasn't sure if she wasn't a little off base when she started talking about her Kiyani ancestors. That's when I lost it and told her that her ancient history could all be bullshit."

"What?" Gideon burst out laughing. "You do like to live dangerously. You couldn't have said anything to make her more angry."

"It didn't seem to matter at the time. She was talking something about the Great Journey and how much better she was than *her*. Whoever that was." She rubbed her temple. "It got pretty confusing."

"Not for Zahra," he said quietly. "It means everything to her. And I guarantee she doesn't think it's bullshit."

She nodded as she looked at him. "That's right, you'd know, wouldn't you? You were . . . intimate."

"Not exactly. But we had sex, and that was entirely different from intimacy." His lips twisted. "But she enjoyed me enough to consider me a candidate. It was amusing to watch her. If I'd stuck around, I might have gone from candidate to consort. Pity I didn't find her that exciting."

"Consort?"

"Yes, Zahra always considered herself a queen, and naturally, she needed a consort. Her ancestress had taken many important men as consorts, and she eagerly followed in her footsteps. I had enough power in Maldara to be fairly impressive, and she thought I'd be a good enough match."

Eve frowned. "Ancestress?"

"Oh, you didn't get that much in depth? Zahra only acknowledges two of her ancestresses, and only one earns her reluctant respect. One is Kiya, the founder of the Kiyani family. The other is Kiya's mother." He smiled. "But to get to the answers, you have to travel on the Great Journey. I can't tell you how often Zahra bored me with looking at her map of that journey." He took out his phone and pulled up a Google map of Maldara and the rest of northern Africa. "We sit right here above the Congo and directly northeast is Ethiopia, then South Sudan, Sudan, and Egypt." His index finger touched a destination on the Mediterranean coast of Egypt. "And here is the city of splendor that is no more. At least in its original state. Don't you think it's a fine birthplace for our Queen Zahra's ancestors?" He smiled. "Now reverse it, and we have the Great Journey that's now Kiyani history, whether or not it's true."

Eve looked at the city. "Alexandria? Zahra is claiming Egyptian heritage?"

"She will be soon. It serves her purpose right now to please the nationalists here in Maldara, but there's a certain glamour to the stories connected to the Great Journey, and Zahra will want to take advantage of them. Maldara is a small fish compared to Egypt. I'd bet Zahra will start climbing as soon as she makes her position unassailable here."

"The Great Journey." Eve was frowning. "I don't understand any of this, and you're making my headache worse. Tell me what you're talking about."

"I'm getting there. I told you that you'd have to go back to Zahra's favorite ancestress for clarity. Work it out for yourself. Who would Zahra accept as an acceptable predecessor?"

"I'm not ready to play games. You're enjoying this too much." But she was intrigued and thinking in spite of herself. "An ancestress who started her journey in Alexandria and traveled south to the jungle country of Maldara."

"Go on."

"Why would she do that? Alexandria was a queen city for thousands of years. It had the greatest library in the civilized world and the Pharos lighthouse, which was one of the seven wonders of the world. It had famous scholars and scientists."

"Which Zahra would not appreciate as you do, Eve. What would make that city acceptable as a place of origin for her? You said it in that first sentence."

Her eyes widened. "Queen city. The Pharaohs had their

palaces on the bank of the Mediterranean." She took the next giant step. "And the most famous queen was Cleopatra. Zahra actually thinks she's related to Cleopatra?"

"By George, I believe you've got it. Not thinks, knows. She couldn't be more certain."

"She's got to be nuts," Eve said flatly.

"Perhaps. But you have to accept that she believes it, so you'll understand who she is. All her life, she's identified with the royalty of Egypt and particularly with Cleopatra VII. You can either call it bullshit or you can use it to manipulate her."

"Which did you do?"

He smiled. "I did what I had to do at any given moment. But I'm afraid you're too honest to follow my lead. Jill had problems doing it. Though she did become interested in the literary aspects of Zahra's fantasy. But then, Jill's a storyteller."

"So I've discovered," Eve said dryly. But she couldn't deny that her curiosity had been aroused. "What literary aspects?"

"The Great Journey wasn't only a map, it was a journal. It was passed down from generation to generation in the Kiyani family."

Her gaze flew to his face. "Whose journal?"

He chuckled. "Not Cleopatra. Gotcha."

"No, you didn't. I'm not that gullible. Everyone knows how Cleopatra died. And it wasn't on a Great Journey to this steaming jungle in the middle of Africa. Whose journal?"

"Does everyone know how she died? Zahra would disagree."

"Gideon."

"Just a little food for thought." He grinned. "And a warning not to take anything for granted in this world. You're right, it isn't Cleopatra's journal. But it was written by an ancestor of Zahra's whom she viewed with a certain respect and tolerance. Her name was Kiya."

"Kiya? That's right, you mentioned Zahra respected her. You're saying a woman made her way from Alexandria to Maldara and founded the Kiyani dynasty?"

"I didn't say she was alone. She had slaves and at least one consort. That was in a day when a woman had to be able to use a man to get what she wanted. That was why Zahra had respect for her in spite of her many flaws. But Kiya was powerful enough to pull things together and set up her household and family to suit herself." He paused. "And it was her name that remained on all the record books from the time she crossed the Maldara border." He smiled. "Kiya, beloved daughter of Cleopatra VII."

"What? It was actually true?"

"Perhaps. If it wasn't, Kiya told a good story."

"You said record books. Not just her journal?"

"Come on, what do you think? It was over two thousand years ago. The records were only vague references other than Kiya's accounts. And the Kiyanis became almost as savage as the natives who attacked them when they invaded their territory. But they were smarter, and they had more civilized methods of torture and murder than the tribes had seen before. So they beat them back and started to build their empire."

"Which evidently was no Alexandria. It's pretty much as undeveloped now as when they came here."

"They had several obstacles to overcome. A few Zahras and similar male counterparts appeared over the centuries. They were low on family values and high on world domination." He was driving off the highway and onto the bumpy dirt road that led to Robaku. "Like most families, good and bad. But with the Kiyanis, it just seems to be exaggerated. They go up and down like a roller coaster." He pulled up to the museum and shut off the car. "Here you are." He got out and ran around to open the door for her. "See? What else could you want? Chauffeur service, and I even provided you with entertainment to keep you amused." He was unlocking the door to the museum. "Now I'll get you settled and make sure that it's okay to leave you."

"Of course it's okay." She got out of the car and joined him as he opened the door. "I only have a little headache now." And her knees were still damnably weak. But she ignored both because she was still fascinated by the story with which Gideon had been regaling her. "Did Zahra ever show you this journal?"

"Of course." He nodded. "Not the original. But it had been copied multiple times over the centuries." He smiled mockingly. "It was at a time when she was still enthralled with the idea of me as a consort and wanted to impress me."

"And were you impressed?"

"It was…interesting. But her take on it was even more interesting." He stepped aside for her to enter. "Now story time is over. Sit down. You're not as steady on your feet as I'd like."

"I'll get a cup of coffee and an aspirin and I'll be fine."

"I'm sure you will." He turned on the lights. "Go sit down," he said again. "I'll make the coffee. I could use one myself. I seem to have been telling you tales like some male Scheherazade all the way from Jokan. Do you suppose Scheherazade got hoarse from talking all night?"

"She had motivation. She was under a death sentence if she didn't keep the sultan entertained." She dropped down on her stool. "And you're no Scheherazade, Gideon." She suddenly chuckled. "Sorry, I just had a vision of you dressed up in a veil and harem outfit. I may never be able to look at you again without seeing it."

He flinched. "You really know how to hurt a guy." He

was pouring water into the coffeemaker. "Oh, well, I have enough confidence in my manly vigor to be able to suffer through it." His gaze went to the reconstruction of Amari, which was still on the dais on her worktable. "He's still here. It seems a long time since I brought Hajif and Leta here last night."

"It was a long time." Her gaze shifted to Amari. "A lot happened..." She suddenly straightened on the stool. "And Hajif must have wanted to get in here to get Amari. They were so eager to take him home. But the door was locked, and we weren't here. I thought I'd be back before they were ready for him."

"And then you were so rude as to develop food poisoning and kept them out. I believe they'll forgive you."

"But I'm back now, and there's no reason why they have to wait any longer." She got to her feet and steadied herself on the worktable for a minute as that blasted weakness swept over her. "I'll go down and tell them that they can—"

"No," Gideon said firmly. "I'll go down and get them if you don't think they can make it through the night." He pushed her back down on the stool. "Rest."

He was out the door before she could protest.

Gideon was being a little too protective, she thought with exasperation. It wasn't as if she were tottering on the edge of death. She might as well have had Joe here. No, Joe would not have been that obvious. He would have been subtle and warm and...Joe.

Damn she missed him.

She looked at the clock. Eight-ten. No, it wasn't time to call him yet. She usually waited until she was sure he wasn't at an evening session at the Yard. That was about ten or eleven Maldara time.

And she needed that coffee if she was going to keep alert

until it was time for her to make that call. She got to her feet and went to the cabinet where the coffee was brewing.

She'd just poured herself a coffee when Gideon came back into the museum.

"Caught you," he said. "What didn't you understand about the word *rest*?"

She was frowning. "Where are Hajif and Leta?"

"They weren't quite ready for him. They said they'd see you in the morning." He came to the coffeemaker and poured himself a cup of coffee. "So sit down. You don't have to be hostess to me. We're way beyond that, aren't we?"

"Yes." She was still staring at Amari. "I don't understand. They were so eager and Leta said only a few hours…" She shifted her gaze back to Gideon. "Unless you gave them the impression they wouldn't be welcome?"

He grimaced. "I wouldn't do that when I know you'd have my head. I was charming and caring, I just explained that the reason we didn't show up earlier was that you'd been very ill and had to go to the hospital." He held up his hands. "All very truthful."

"And you knew Hajif and his family probably wouldn't go to a hospital unless they were dying."

"It did occur to me that might be the effect."

"But you knew I wanted them to come."

He nodded. "People make their own decisions, Eve. I just gave them the facts."

And he was so clever that he knew just how to shade them. "I could go down to the village and bring them back with me," she said coolly. "I don't appreciate manipulation, Gideon."

"I know. Even if I didn't realize it, Jill told me. She was afraid that it might be the one thing that would keep you from coming here." He said quietly, "But I told you that if you left the hospital and came back to Robaku, I'd take care of you and you wouldn't suffer for it. I was acting instinctively with Hajif to keep that promise."

"Because you want me to rest?"

"Partly." He smiled. "I imagine it's difficult for the people around you to take care of you without a little manipulation and sleight of hand. Admit it. Doesn't your family have to resort to it on occasion? What about your husband?"

"Joe and I are honest with each other. Besides, that's different."

"Which means that you *try* to be honest with each other."

"Which means that you don't have the same rights and privileges."

"Unfortunately." He chuckled as her eyes widened. "I told you I liked intense women." He shook his head. "I'll back down now. You left yourself open, and I couldn't resist. I know you're as faithful as Penelope was to Odysseus."

He was impossible. "Now you're delving into *The Odyssey*? First, it was that wild tale about Kiyani, and now you're into mythology?"

"Well, I did minor in English Lit when I was at Oxford. And there was a two-headed female monster in *The Odyssey*. When you think about it, there might be some connection with Zahra Kiyani." His smile faded and he added soberly, "But I'm really still trying to distract you as I've been attempting to do since we left the hospital. That's not being fair. You've had a rough day, and some of it was my fault. You like honesty, and I should give it to you."

Eve frowned. "Distract me?" She didn't understand any of this, and it was beginning to frustrate her. "Distract me from what?"

"Any number of things." His lips twisted. "That's been my main duty since Jill called me into this with you. Protect and distract. I'm very good at both though you'd never know it by today. But Jill says she can't take any more, so evidently there's a change coming. I might as well begin again now. Yes, I did want you to rest, but only because you're going to have enough with which to contend when Jill gets here. That should be in about ten minutes. You're going to get all the honesty and absence of manipulation you can stand." He grimaced. "Which is completely wrong for the situation. I'm surprised Novak is letting her do it. I guess he thinks she deserves it. She paid the price."

"Who is Novak?" Then she remembered. "CIA. Jill gave me his name to pass on to Joe. What has he got to do with this?"

"You can ask Jill. I don't know how honest she's going to be. If she tells you about Novak, then you'll probably have the entire picture." He moved toward the door. "Now it's time I went into protection mode again. This time for Jill. She wants to make sure that Robaku isn't being watched. She doesn't want anyone to know that she's coming to see you tonight. I'll see you later, Eve."

He left the museum.

What the hell?

Eve put her coffee cup down and leaned back against the cabinet. Her knees were still shaky, and she hadn't needed those enigmatic words from Gideon to make her any dizzier. She hadn't understood what he was talking about, but she didn't like the sound of it.

Well, she would soon find out and handle it. She just wished that Jill Cassidy hadn't picked a night when she was feeling this weak and vulnerable to spring something of which even Gideon seemed to disapprove.

Forget it. Stop dwelling on something she couldn't change until she was confronted with it. She went back to her stool and began to prepare Amari for his final trip to Hajif and Leta tomorrow.

Then she stopped as she realized what she was doing. Not questioning, just accepting what was happening to her no matter how strange she thought it. Meekly going back to this work she had chosen to do.

Or that had been chosen for her to do.

And Jill would be coming in that door soon, and, in spite of what Gideon had said, the reporter might try to manipulate her once again.

No way.

Clear your head and get ready for her, dammit.

———

"It's wonderful," Jill said quietly from the doorway behind Eve, her gaze on the Amari reconstruction. "Or should I say *he's* wonderful. Your Amari seems almost alive again."

Eve looked over her shoulder. "That's what you wanted, isn't it? You wanted him to come alive so that Hajif and Leta would have something besides a DNA report to file away? That's what I wanted, too." She turned on the stool to face her. "And I did it. But that isn't all you wanted, is it, Jill? That isn't why Gideon is outside cruising around in his 'protective mode' to be sure no one will know you're here. By the way, you're twenty minutes late. He must have been worried. Or maybe he isn't as efficient as he told me he was." She added coolly, "But what can you expect when you choose an errand boy who was born with a silver spoon in his mouth?"

Jill went still as she studied Eve's expression. "Gideon did his job. It was my fault. I had to make sure I wasn't followed." She crossed the room toward her. "I didn't want to ruin everything because I was having an attack of conscience.

There was still a possibility that I could salvage bits and pieces even if you socked me, then threw up your hands and took the next flight out."

"You seem to think that a possibility. I probably will, too. Particularly since Gideon was talking about honesty, which was clearly lacking, and manipulation, which was obviously present. Though I'm not surprised he brought them up. I've known since the day I met you that you were very good at luring people into doing what you wish." Her lips tightened. "And yet I didn't realize that you were lying to me. I consider myself a good judge of character, and when you answered my questions, I would have sworn that you were telling me the truth."

"I was telling you the truth. I just couldn't tell you everything." Jill shook her head. "Otherwise, you wouldn't have come, and we had to have you here." She continued in a desperate rush: "And I thought it would be okay. I was sure we could keep you safe. I didn't expect this to happen. There was no reason."

"You mean that the food poisoning was no accident? I tried to tell myself that it didn't make sense that anyone would want to hurt me. But I've been sitting here waiting for you and trying to put everything together from what Gideon said, and that stuck out in living color. He was very tentative, but he didn't really deny it. I might have been too woozy to figure out the whys and wherefores, but the fact that it was intentional became crystal clear as I thought about it. Evidently someone believed they had reason not to want me here. Zahra?"

"I'm not . . . sure. I knew Zahra wouldn't want you here, but I didn't believe she'd feel strongly enough to actually strike out at you. She just wants control of Robaku. She's very careful of her image, and there's no way she'd want even a suspicion touching her."

"Yet Zahra Kiyani was in my hospital room this afternoon expressing her sympathy and her opinion that I should get the hell out of Dodge. Diplomatically, of course. Well, as diplomatically as she was capable of. But I was having trouble appreciating anything but the fact that she'd come running when there was a chance to get rid of me." Now Eve was having trouble suppressing her anger. "I was so sick, and I was told I could have died. When I woke up, the entire world seemed only to want to get rid of me. It pissed me off, and I didn't even know then that it had been a deliberate attempt. Then I got Gideon's 'distractions' laid on me and his irritation that you weren't behaving as everyone wanted you to." She glared at Jill. "That about topped off my day. If you hadn't come tonight, I was going to go after you. I'm mad as hell. I want answers, Jill."

"That's why I'm here." She looked for a place to sit down, saw only the cot across the room. She shrugged, dropped to the floor, and crossed her legs tailor-fashion. "That's what I've been trying to tell you. There are still things I don't know, but you'll know what I know."

"How refreshing. You're not denying that someone tried to kill me?"

"I'm not denying it could have happened. But Novak said that the poisoning was done by an expert, and you weren't meant to die. The mushrooms were blended with an additive from Egypt that altered the toxicity. They just meant to discourage you, just like they did me. It was meant to make you a little ill to encourage you to leave. That's the only reason why I think there was even a possibility that Zahra might have anything to do with it. This was more of a threat than an attempt on your life. She'd use every threat before she'd endanger her position."

"That threat was very painful. I thought I was dying. I

couldn't tell the difference at the time." Eve went on to the next item on her agenda. "Novak. Jed Novak is the name of the CIA operative you gave me to reassure Joe. Gideon said he didn't think Novak would let you talk to me. Do you work for the CIA?"

"No." She grimaced. "Though Novak did do his best to keep me from coming here tonight. I told him I couldn't do anything else, and we'd have to make other plans if you blew up. I've only known Novak since I came here to Maldara, but I'd heard enough about him to reach out when I needed him."

"One of your friends in high places?"

"Novak operates on both levels. That's why he's so valuable." She added wearily, "He's gone to a lot of trouble and expense to set up the switch. He's got a right to be angry with me. But I'm not like him, and I can't go by his rules. Please believe me. I knew there might be some danger to you, but I thought we could get you out of here before it—"

"Became fatal?" Eve interrupted. "You're not making your position any more sympathetic. And you're certainly not making this situation less muddled. Now, I'm going to ask you questions, and you're going to answer me clearly and concisely."

"Whatever you say," Jill said quietly.

"You said that doing these reconstructions was important to you, but that's not the real reason why you put all your time and effort into luring me here. What was that reason?"

"I needed the best forensic sculptor in the world to come here to Maldara. I had a job that had to be done by the very best."

"What job? Not the children?"

She shook her head. "But I knew that would bring you. I hoped that once you were here, I could persuade you to do the other reconstruction."

"The honorable thing to do when offering a job is to give terms and let me decide."

"I couldn't take a chance. It was too important. We didn't even have the skull, and to get it might have made you—" She stopped.

"Made me what?" Eve said impatiently.

"An accomplice." Jill didn't let her absorb that but went on quickly: "We wanted to switch a skull that's being held in the vault at the U.N. headquarters in Jokan for a counterfeit so that you could do a reconstruction to verify the identity."

Eve stared at her, openmouthed. "What?"

"I know. It's not the kind of… You would never have done it."

"That's quite correct."

"That's why I wanted you to be here. I wanted you to see that schoolroom." Her voice was shaking. "I wanted you to see what he'd done to this village. I wanted you to see what he'd done to this *country*."

She stiffened. "He? Who are you talking about?"

"Nils Varak. You know it was his men who butchered those children."

"Of course I do. He was a monster. What does that have to do with anything? Varak was killed right after the U.N. forces invaded Maldara. Some kind of helicopter explosion."

Jill was shaking her head. "That's what I thought." Her voice was unsteady. "And, after what I'd seen while I traveled around the country writing my stories, I wanted to send up fireworks when I heard it had happened. I'd interviewed people who told *hideous* stories about him that I couldn't write about, that I didn't even want to remember." Her voice was jerky. "Robaku wasn't the first school he'd destroyed. He *liked* to kill the children. He told his men that it made their parents more likely to cave when they saw the remains of their children. Besides, it brought him a particular pleasure to take their lives before they'd barely started to live. And he didn't want to make it quick…he liked the machetes…"

"Stop," Eve said. Jill's face was tense, pale, her words hoarse and feverish. Eve could see that she was reliving those stories, and she suddenly couldn't stand for it to go on. "Okay, so he was a monster. Monsters should be destroyed, and that's what they did. The French forces said there was absolute proof that they'd cut the head off the snake."

Jill nodded. "Absolute. That's what they said."

Eve's eyes narrowed on her face. "You're saying it's not true?"

"I'm saying that I hope it's true. But I'm afraid it's not." She moistened her lips. "And what if it's not true, Eve? What if he's out there somewhere, waiting until all the smoke clears so that he can come out and start all over again? If not here, then somewhere else. Six hundred thousand people dead, and he killed a hell of a lot of them. And he'd do it again, he wouldn't stop. He liked it too much."

"I can't believe this. Why do you think Varak might still be alive?" She was trying to remember all the details of the account she'd read on Google. "He was killed in a helicopter explosion in the mountains in the south Botzan area. The French blew him out of the sky as he was trying to escape. But they immediately retrieved his skull from the wreckage, and he'd been positively identified by DNA." She went still, her eyes widening. "The skull? I can't believe you'd want me to do a reconstruction on Varak. Are you crazy? Absolute DNA ID. Everyone knows it."

"That doesn't mean it's true."

"It means that it will be accepted in any court in the world. And any reconstruction I do would not have a chance over DNA results. Even if I showed the skull didn't resemble Varak, it wouldn't make a difference. DNA rules."

"But it would insert an element of doubt with people who would go after Varak full throttle if they thought he was still alive." She paused. "One of them is Novak. The director of the CIA accepted the proof that Varak was dead. Novak would have to have some credible reason for them to reopen the investigation. But regardless, he'd never stop if he was sure that Varak was still alive. He almost caught him twice while he was on the hunt for him in the mountains. He was the one who notified the French he'd be on that helicopter."

"And he thinks that Varak slipped away?"

"He doesn't know, but he wouldn't put it past Varak. But he has to be sure. When I came to him, he promised me he wouldn't stop until he was certain Varak hadn't played him and everyone else for fools."

"*You* came to him? And he believed you with no proof?"

"No. Novak is a cynical bastard who doesn't believe in much of anything but himself. But I had a shred of information that caught his attention . . . as it caught mine."

"What information?"

"I had an informant with the Botzan faction, Ralph Hadfeld, a mercenary. After the war ended, he wanted to get out of Maldara with enough money to start again in another country before he ended up being caught and tried. He called me and tried to sell me the story of the century. He said that he had been in the hills with Varak that last day, and Varak didn't get on that helicopter. The last Hadfeld had seen of him he was in a jeep heading north."

"How reliable was this informant?"

"He'd never steered me wrong." She paused. "He said he'd taken a photo of Varak in the jeep when the helicopter was taking off. And the price he asked for the story and the photo was over a million dollars. I think he knew I'd put that info under a microscope. He said he'd give me two weeks but no longer. He wasn't sure if any of Varak's men had seen him take that photo, and he wanted out of the country."

"And you went to Novak for the money?"

She nodded. "I knew the CIA would authorize any amount to Novak. He's their golden boy." She drew a deep breath. "But he wouldn't give it to me. He listened, then he said that Hadfeld could be playing me. He said he'd go after him himself, and he even had an idea how the info could be verified. He said that I should keep out of it."

"And you didn't do it."

"It was *my* story, my informant, and I had to know if it was the truth. But if Novak wouldn't give me the money, I had to go somewhere else. So I called Sam Gideon. I knew I had a chance with him. There was no way he'd want Varak to slip away after what he'd done here. Gideon agreed to make the buy, and I called Hadfeld."

"You got the story and the photo?"

"No, he said he'd call me later with arrangements. And he did call me one night a few weeks ago and set up a place in the jungle to meet him." She looked away. "Emphasis on *set up*. It was a trap. When I got there, Hadfeld was dead, a very bloody death. He'd been tortured. Evidently, Varak's men had been tracking him and forced him to make the call. They wanted to make sure that I saw what they'd done to him."

"But you got away?"

There was the faintest hesitation. "Yes, I got away." She looked back at Eve. "But if they did that to Hadfeld, I didn't need much more to convince me that what he was going to sell me was the real McCoy and that Varak was still out there. Wouldn't you feel the same?"

Varak *alive*? Eve felt a ripple of shock. She had been so involved with listening to the horrific details of Jill's story that the idea that Varak had not been killed in that helicopter crash had not actually gotten through to her. But as she stared at Jill, a chill went through her. How could she not consider it? Because Jill Cassidy thought it was true and had gone to this extreme to prove it. "I might feel there was a chance except for the DNA."

"Novak says that DNA can be faked if you know the right experts. Particularly in an explosion, when only minute amounts can be extracted."

"I've never heard of its being done with complete success. Particularly not in a circumstance where the scrutiny is so intense."

"Novak says it can be done. I believe him. But he wants to be sure that skull isn't Varak's before he goes to the people who matter. It's a scenario that will have everyone from politicians, to noted scientists, to Novak's own CIA director, ready to tear it apart. And in the furor, Varak could disappear."

"And you want me to be caught in the middle."

"No. But you might be anyway," Jill said. "I don't know what's happening. No one should have targeted you just for doing these children's reconstructions. I could see it if they thought you were working on trying to prove Varak is still alive."

"Which you want me to do at the earliest possible opportunity." Eve shook her head. "I can almost see why you decided to set up this elaborate charade. You needed to hold all the cards possible to even think I might do it."

"And even then I knew you might tell me to go to hell," she said soberly. "I only hoped that you'd remember that Varak had created all this carnage. He should pay for it, Eve. And he shouldn't get a chance to do it again." She looked at the reconstruction of Amari. "Those villages were helpless before his militia. They were savage. Varak even hung some of the body parts in the trees..."

Eve flinched. "Shock value, Jill?"

"Anything I can do." She got to her feet. "I'm sorry I wasn't completely honest with you. You know everything now. I'm praying that you won't let my duplicity affect your decision. Let me know what you're going to do, and I'll make it easy for you." She grimaced. "Unless a miracle happens, and you decide to help us. Then I can't promise it will be easy, only that we'll try to keep you safe." She headed for the door, then stopped before she opened it. "No, I still wasn't totally honest. I'd better tell you all of it. Even though it's going to make you even angrier. After I decided it had to be you who did Varak's reconstruction, I told Novak what he had to do. We had to get rid of Joe Quinn, so Novak pulled strings with some bigwigs in London and got the Scotland Yard seminar pushed up so that it would fit in with our plans."

"What?" Eve's eyes widened. "You went to those lengths?"

"You love Quinn," she said soberly. "You were right when you said I'd probed every facet of your life. That was a very big part. The chances were very slim that you'd leave him unless the circumstances were right."

"You're damn right."

"Your Michael was easier. Novak just had to find a conveniently located dig in the U.K. and send Jane MacGuire folders that described it with glowing references to how healthy and fun it was for children. Jane doesn't see your son that often. She grabbed at the chance to give him a treat like that."

"And you did your research and knew that Jane had gone on digs before."

She nodded jerkily. "I had to make sure that if I took you away, it would be worthwhile for them. You had to be certain they were safe and happy."

"How very kind," Eve said sarcastically.

"No, completely selfish. I interfered in your life. I had to do it in the most painless way possible. You have a right to be furious about that, too." She paused. "I'm sorry," she whispered. "I wouldn't have done it if I hadn't thought that it was necessary. We can't let a Robaku happen ever again."

Then she was gone.

Leaving Eve alone with her confusion and anger...and terror. She didn't know how long she sat there just trying to comprehend all that she had been told. At least ten, fifteen minutes passed while she struggled to understand both the horror of the possibility Jill had shown her and this feeling of betrayal and being used.

She closed her eyes and let the emotions flow over her, not trying to sort them out yet. She could still see Jill's face before her. She'd looked like a little girl sitting on the floor at Eve's feet, her blue eyes big and so full of fear yet terribly earnest as she tried to do what she'd thought was honorable and right.

She would *not* feel sorry for her, Eve thought fiercely. Jill had been totally manipulative and moved them all around like chess pieces to get what she wanted. It didn't matter that she'd thought she was doing it to keep that monster from getting away to strike again.

But how could it not matter? It was what Eve did every day of her life. Bring the children home so that monsters would be punished and not be free to kill again.

But she did not lie or cheat or use anyone else to do what had to be done. There was no question what she should do now that she knew why Jill had brought her here.

"Are you okay?"

Her eyes flew open, and she saw a tall man wearing a black-leather jacket standing in the doorway. She had never seen him before. "Who are you?"

"Jed Novak." He held up his hand. "Sorry to startle you. I'm no threat."

That was a lie. Novak might not be a threat to her at this moment, but she had been around dangerous men for most of her life. She was married to one. She knew she was facing one now. "You're CIA. Jill told me about you. Did she send you to try to convince me that everything she did was fine and for the greater good? Go away, Novak."

"No, she didn't send me. She told me not to come." He smiled faintly. "She was afraid I might attempt to intimidate you. She wanted to be sure to be fair to you. She's having a major guilt trip. She was scared to death when she thought you might die this morning."

"She should feel guilty. I can see you're not similarly prone to it. What a surprise."

"I have my moments. But I've learned that guilt has no place once I've made a decision. I'd end up in a psych ward with all the blame that can be laid at my door. Jill, on the other hand, has a conscience that constantly gets in her way."

"Not so I'd notice."

"You should have noticed. Jill fought me and Gideon and herself to come to you tonight. She knew it was the wrong thing to do."

"Then why are you here, too?"

"Because I need to try to save the mission." His lips tightened. "If you won't help us, Jill will go off in another direction and might get herself killed. She's vulnerable, they know her name, they know her face." He paused. "And they know she'll never stop. So that's why I'm here to repair the damage and ask you to forget everything but why she did it. I know that it was a shock, but you're tough. I can see you're okay."

"No, I'm not okay." Her voice was cold. "I'm angry, and I feel as if I've been treated like a marionette in a puppet show. How did you think I'd feel?"

"Just like that." He walked toward her. "That's why Gideon and I both tried to talk her out of it. She knew it was a risk, too. She told you everything?"

"Yes," she said tersely. "Even down to how she pulled the strings with Joe and Michael."

"I was hoping she'd leave that out." He made a face. "That must have struck a little too close to home."

"It was an invasion," she said harshly. "And I can't believe that she'd be able to talk Gideon into helping her do this. He's not even CIA. It's crazy."

He nodded. "And it was crazy that his home was burned to the ground and his parents butchered by Varak. Did he mention that?"

"No," she said, shocked. "And neither did Jill."

"He doesn't like to talk about it." His lips tightened. "I was with him in the mountains when he heard about it. He knew those mountains like the back of his hand, and he was trying to help the farmers who had fled their villages to find safe havens. The killing of his parents was particularly brutal even for Varak. It was clear that Gideon had been targeted to discourage him from throwing in more help and money to fight that son of a bitch." He added softly, "And then to find out that we might not have killed him after all? He has to know, Eve."

"Well, I don't. Not if it means risking my freedom and my life with my family because I became involved with this madness. Stealing a skull, doing a reconstruction, when it could mean absolutely nothing?"

"You wouldn't have to steal the skull. The skull is being held in the main vault at the U.N. headquarters in Jokan. I've arranged a bribe to one of the guards to switch the skulls. It would be brought to you, and you'd do the work in total privacy here at the museum. Then, when we have an answer, you document it, and your work is over. If the skull is really Varak's, then we return the skull to the U.N. headquarters and make another switch. And that would be the end of it."

"No, it wouldn't. I'd have to undo the reconstruction and bring it back to the way I started. And what if it's not Varak?"

"Yes," Novak said softly. "What if it's not, Eve?"

Eve couldn't answer. It was a question that frightened her more than anything else. What if her work uncovered a horrible truth about the man who had killed those children here at Robaku and all those other children slain in this bloody land?

"It's something to think about," Novak said. "I promised Jill that I wouldn't reveal you as a source, but there would probably be suspicions."

"Of course there would be," she said impatiently. "She brought me here because I have a reputation. I'd be the first one anyone would suspect. There would be so much uproar, I could lose that reputation, and the entire world would think I'm some kind of radical crackpot."

"Or a brave woman out to save that world," he said quietly. "It could go either way, but in the end it would depend on how much it means to you. No matter how we try to protect you, you'll probably go through a firestorm. I'll try to move fast enough to get my hands on Varak right away, but no guarantees."

"There are too many ifs and mights in this scenario. And I seem to be the one who's bearing the brunt of all this violence and ugliness that's going on. I was *poisoned* today," she said through set teeth. "It's easy for Jill to wring her hands and talk about how Varak has to be stopped when she's not taking the punishment."

"None of it's easy for Jill," he said roughly. His coolness had suddenly become ice. "You don't know what you're talking about. I gave her every chance to get out of this, and she still went after them. And if you bail on us, she'll still do it. No matter what they do to her. And there are worse things than a bout of food poisoning, Eve."

His violence had caught Eve off guard. All the smoothness and persuasiveness had disappeared in a heartbeat when she'd attacked Jill. And it had been triggered by that one comment Eve had made. Why? Then she was suddenly remembering two sentences that Jill had spoken that had been lost in the bombardment of information she had been throwing at Eve.

They meant to hurt you and discourage you as they did me.

And that tiny hesitation, *Yes, I got away.*

She met his eyes across the room. "She said she got away after she found Hadfeld. It wasn't true?"

"Oh, they let her get away afterward. They wanted to teach her a lesson first. There were four of them. They beat her and they raped her and left her to crawl out of that jungle to find her way back to the road. So don't tell me about her not paying her dues. The only thing she asked me when I found her on that road was to let her be the one to go after them."

"And you agreed?"

His lips twisted. "At that point I would have given her anything she asked. She believed that Hadfeld was telling the truth, and she'd paid the price. I could have negotiated that payment and handled the transaction. I didn't do it. I wanted to go after him my way. So she did it on her own."

And Jed Novak was not as cynical as Jill had said, Eve

thought as she gazed at him. She didn't know what he felt for Jill, but she could tell that what had happened to her that night had struck a deep chord. And it had struck a deep chord in Eve as well. The mere fact that Jill had not tried to arouse Eve's sympathy by letting her know about the attack made the feeling even more poignant.

But that didn't change the situation. It merely made it more painful. "Do you believe that skull is Varak's, Novak?"

"Maybe. I was convinced he was dead at the time, and I tend toward doubting everything that comes my way. The attack on Jill made it seem less likely. I do believe that skull could be a phony. I've been sending agents into the mountains asking questions of the people who were there the day of the explosion. There are a few who have doubts that Varak was on that helicopter. The others are afraid to admit to anything that would disturb the status quo." He shrugged. "And I've already started to trace a few scientists who could possibly fake that DNA. But I can't make a move on them until I'm sure I know what I'm doing. Varak would be quick to get rid of any witness."

"If he hasn't done it already," Eve said. "You're not being at all reassuring."

"Jill made me promise not to lie to you. The decision is yours. I'd appreciate it if you'd make it quickly. The switch is supposed to be made tomorrow night. It would be foolish for me to spend a fortune in bribe money if I have no forensic sculptor of your caliber to do the work. By the way, I'll have to ask you not to talk to Quinn on your Skype about any of this. It was safe to let you contact him before, but not now. There's the possibility that you might be hacked." He met her eyes. "This would take only a few days, and you might be able to keep a monster from coming back out of the shadows. Jill thinks that it's worth it. Let me know if you agree."

He turned on his heel and left the museum.

CHAPTER

7

There was no decision to be made, Eve thought. Particularly after that last remark about her not talking to Joe about it.

She shouldn't even think of doing that reconstruction. There were so many reasons why it was a bad idea.

And there was only one reason why she should do it.

To stop a monster from coming out of the shadows and striking again.

Someone had killed Hadfeld to keep Jill from getting evidence that the monster was still out there, waiting.

And that violence and horror done to Jill. Eve's own pain and sickness. Maybe Varak was no longer hiding but was on the move.

Her gaze went to Amari on the dais in front of her.

"I don't know what to do," she murmured. "But that was a terrible thing he did to you. We have to be sure that he paid for it, don't we?"

He gazed back at her with those big brown eyes and the eager expectancy that she had unknowingly sculpted in his expression. Eagerness to go home, to end the sadness of that final parting.

But could that sadness be ended if those shadows remained?

"In my court?" Eve nodded slowly. "Yeah, I know. You've had enough to deal with." She got to her feet. "Okay. I'll think about it and get back to you." But not here, where she was surrounded by those lavishly trimmed boxes, and Amari, who was both her triumph and despair. She headed for the door. She needed *air*.

She stood outside and breathed deep, her gaze on the night sky. There was moonlight, the bright orb barely visible over the canopy of trees. Just stand here and look and listen to the night sounds and don't think about anything that Jill had told her earlier.

She had come here for a specific purpose, to help Amari and all the other children who had been so terribly mutilated and destroyed. It wasn't right to put that aside and go on a wild-goose chase that could be a senseless waste of time.

It wasn't right.

Then why was she walking through the overgrown brush down the path toward that schoolroom she'd never wanted to see again?

Go back.

There's no one there.

No way she could help what had happened in that room. Those lonely desks, the dark streaks on the floor...

She stood in the gaping opening and gazed at that broken blackboard. Had the teacher been standing there when the school had been overrun? Had the children had time to scream before the machetes began to tear into them? They must have been so afraid...

"Eve." It was Gideon standing beside her. He asked gently, "What are you doing here?"

"I don't know." That desk couldn't have been Amari's. It was too small. Maybe one of the six-year-olds... "I'm just... They were used to kindness... They wouldn't have known why..."

"No, they wouldn't." He touched her wet cheek. "We have to hope it was very quick. Come on, I'll take you back to the museum." He was propelling her away from the schoolroom and down the path. "It's been a bad day for you. You need to get some rest. We all ganged up on you, didn't we? We should have waited until you'd had time to heal at least."

"Yes, you should." Now that she was no longer looking at the schoolhouse, she was beginning to function again. Though she was unutterably sad and weary. "And you'll hear from me about it later. Right now, I have to take it all in and start thinking instead of feeling." They had reached the museum, and she turned to face him. "How did you know I was down there?"

"Jill told me to keep an eye on you." He smiled. "Though I would have done it anyway. I care about you, Eve. You may think that we all just wanted to use you, but it's not true. Yes, we had to do what we had to do, but that didn't change how we feel, who we are."

"And what you had to do dominated your life," she said soberly. "You didn't tell me about your parents, Gideon."

His smile vanished. "They were good people. I loved them. What else was there to say? Except that I have to be certain Varak died in that helicopter." He held the door open for her. "So many people died here in Maldara. After I went back to our plantation, which Varak had burned to the ground, I thought it was only one more graveyard out of thousands."

She shook her head. "I'm so sorry that you lost them, Gideon."

His brows rose. "But not sorry enough to forgive me?"

"No. I have to understand it first, and I'm not nearly there yet." She grimaced. "Particularly since I'm feeling so alone right now. Your friend, Novak, asked me not to call and talk to Joe about this. Do you know how difficult that is for me?"

He nodded. "But you're not as angry as you were, or you'd want to do it anyway and to hell with whether or not your phone was being tapped."

"No, that isn't an option, whatever I decide." She moistened her lips. "Because I can't be sure you're not right. I told you before that I felt that if I looked over my shoulder, I'd see one of those children? What if I looked over my shoulder and saw Varak in that classroom? What if he's out there somewhere?"

"Welcome to our nightmare," he said quietly.

"I have enough of my own." She turned and went into the museum. "Good night, Gideon. I'll see you in the morning."

"Night. Try to sleep."

She might actually manage to sleep, she thought as she locked the door. She had thought she might start to work, but she was too exhausted. Tomorrow would have to do.

She went to the bathroom, washed, then brushed her teeth. Then she went to her cot and sat down with her computer.

How she wanted to Skype Joe, to see his face, to release all the tension and share everything with him. But Novak had said there might be someone listening, spying, and even the idea of that intrusion made her angry. It was as if she were being robbed. Hell, she *was* being robbed.

Don't think about it now.

Just make sure that Joe wouldn't worry without totally lying to him.

And she hated the idea of that half-truth, too.

She texted.

WILL CALL YOU TOMORROW EVENING. HAD A BIT OF FOOD POISONING AND I'M HITTING THE SACK EARLY. I'M FINE, BUT YOU KNOW HOW THAT KIND OF THING TAKES IT OUT OF YOU. A GOOD NIGHT'S SLEEP WILL FIX ME RIGHT UP. I LOVE YOU.

EVE

———————◆———————

LONDON

Son of a bitch!

Joe clicked off Eve's text message and leaned back in his chair. He didn't like this at all. Knowing Eve was ill was bad enough. But the fact that she'd played down the severity of her illness and hadn't Skyped tonight made it worse. She either didn't want to answer questions, or she didn't want him to see the toll that food poisoning had taken. Or it could be both.

She had been so happy when she'd called him from that hotel early this morning. He'd even felt a little of the uneasiness he'd had about her being in Maldara fade.

Now it was back in full force.

He wasn't going to be able to take much more of this.

Eve did not like him hovering, but then she shouldn't have taken off for a country like Maldara. Even food poisoning could be dangerous if not properly treated, and he wasn't sure what kind of medical facilities were available. And how had she gotten food poisoning anyway? She knew all the rules about not eating fresh products in foreign countries.

It wouldn't be a bad idea if he took a flight to Jokan and checked out what—

His phone was ringing.

Michael.

"Shouldn't you be in bed by this time?" Joe asked when he answered Michael's call. "Jane was telling me that you were up before daylight, and they were working you like slaves at that old castle."

"Yeah, but it's fun. Every time I find something, I go look in Jane's archaeology book and see if it's anything that could be interesting." He paused. "But I was wondering if maybe it would be more fun if we went over to that Maldara place where Mom is right now. You said that it was in the middle of the jungle, where there are all kinds of wild animals and stuff. What do you think?"

Joe stiffened. This coming out of the blue from Michael was weird as hell. Particularly since he'd been raving enthusiastically about his work on the dig since he'd arrived there. "I think that your mom would tell you that she's not there to have fun and that she wouldn't have time for either one of us. She's doing the same kind of work she does at home, and it has nothing to do with jungles or wild animals." He paused. "But I believe you knew that, Michael. I don't remember discussing the wild animals when I was telling you about Maldara."

"No, you just said it had jungles. I looked the rest up on the Internet."

And what else had he found on the Internet about that war-torn country that would have sent up red flares? "Well, you don't have to worry about your mom hiking around the jungle and getting eaten by tigers. She's working in a museum doing her work, and you know how boring museums can be."

"Not all museums are boring," Michael said. "Remember that movie *Night at the Museum*? That was cool, wasn't it?"

"In a crazy kind of way." Michael was being entirely too persistent, Joe thought. Which meant he was genuinely worried. Time to cut to the chase and get to the bottom of this. "So why are you calling me now when you should be sleeping? Did your mom say something the last time she phoned you?"

"No, she's only called me a couple times, and she was asking about what Jane and I were doing. She seemed okay." He was frowning. "But I was just thinking today that maybe we should go be with her. I don't like her there alone."

"She's not alone. She was very careful to give me an entire list of people she could call on if she ran into trouble."

"But they're not us."

"No, they're not us." And Joe felt exactly the same as his son about that. He wanted to be the one who was there for her. But something Michael had just said was making him uneasy. Michael had always had an almost psychic bond with Eve, even before he was born. She might not have said anything to him, but that didn't mean he hadn't sensed something. "Today? Why would you suddenly feel like that today, Michael?"

Silence. Then Michael said simply, "Something was wrong. I got scared."

"Why?"

"I don't know. It was really bad, then it was gone. She's okay now. I just don't want her to be alone anymore."

"Neither do I," he said gruffly. "I'm working on it." He had to try to reassure Michael even though his son's words had done the opposite to him. "It might be nothing. Your mom had a touch of food poisoning today. But, as you said, she's fine now."

He shook his head. "It was . . . really bad, Dad. Can we go, please?"

"Not right now. You know your mom, she wouldn't like it if we showed up on her doorstep without an invitation. I'll work it out." He added brusquely: "In the meantime, stop worrying. Enjoy the dig and take care of Jane. She went to a lot of trouble to give you a good time."

"I know she did." He paused. "You probably won't take me with you if you go, and that's okay. I know you'll take care of her. She'll be safe." He paused. "She's *got* to be safe."

"I believe I know how to do that," Joe said dryly. "I've been taking care of your mom for a long time, since long before you were born. Now get to bed. Let me keep an eye on her for both of us."

Michael was silent. "Sometimes it seems to be easier for me to keep an eye on her. But, okay, whatever you say. Good night, Dad." He cut the connection.

She's got to be safe.

And Michael had been very worried that Eve *wasn't* safe.

So was Joe supposed to rush out and take the next plane to Jokan because his son was getting some kind of psychic vibes that all was not well with Eve's world?

Why not? It was what Joe wanted to do anyway, and Michael's instincts had been almost a hundred percent correct in the past.

But that meant trusting Michael's instincts over Eve's explanation. Which would definitely not please her.

Okay, he didn't like it, but he'd give Eve the twenty-four hours she'd requested and talk to her tomorrow night. She'd be honest with him. If something was wrong, she'd tell him then.

Or he'd be able to know just by looking at her face. As he would have tonight if she hadn't sent him that damn text instead of Skyping.

It was really bad, Dad.

———◆———

ROBAKU
3:40 A.M.

Machete!

Varak liked killing children, Jill had said.

And he was there in the schoolroom waiting for Eve to come so that he could show her that bloody machete.

She didn't have to look over her shoulder, she could see him now, smiling, waiting . . .

But she couldn't see him clearly because she didn't know his face. She could see the evil, but how could she stop him if she didn't know his face?

And he was raising that machete . . .

———◆———

Eve jerked wide-awake, her heart pounding. She was panting, unable to get her breath. She sat upright on her cot.

Only a nightmare. Only? She felt as if she'd been there that day and been helpless to stop that carnage. She got sluggishly out of bed and went to the bathroom. She drank a glass of water and stood there looking in the mirror. She was pale, and the hand holding the glass was shaking. She looked as helpless as she'd felt when she'd faced Varak in that nightmare.

She *wasn't* helpless. She couldn't be helpless. She steadied her hand as she put the glass down on the vanity. And she wouldn't let herself spend her life looking over her shoulder, wondering if he was still there, waiting with that bloody machete.

Eve grabbed her phone and punched in Jill's number the

minute she left the bathroom. "I want you over here. I want Novak, too. Right now. If I can't sleep, I'm not going to let either one of you sleep, either."

"Twenty minutes," Jill said. "And I'll find a way to get Novak there."

"I know you will. I'll make the coffee."

Silence. "That sounds promising."

"Not necessarily. I desperately need the caffeine, and I want both of you to be awake enough to give me answers." She cut the connection.

———

Jill arrived fifteen minutes later. "Novak is right behind me." She went over to the cot and pulled it into the center of the room. "If you don't mind, I'll try to avoid sitting on the floor at your feet this time. I don't mind being humbled, but I have an idea I might need all the dignity I can gather together for this session. You really should have Hajif find you a few more chairs."

"You do it." She gave Jill her coffee. "I like the idea of your being humble, considering what you've put me through." Her lips twisted. "Though I can't see Novak being humbled in any situation."

"He pretends well." Jill sat down on the cot. "But you're right, he knows what he wants and goes after it." She glanced at Novak as he walked into the room. "I've saved you from groveling, Novak. Come and share my cot."

"How can I resist? I've never had that invitation from you, Jill." He strolled toward Eve. "But I think we should get down to business before pleasure. Since you summoned both of us, I assume you do mean business?"

"*My* business," Eve said. "I had one hell of a night. I have to be sure that Varak won't ever come back. And the only way I can do that is to do a reconstruction and see for my-self that I don't have to worry about it." She added, "Which could get me into all kinds of trouble. You're going to go af-ter that skull tonight?"

"That's the plan," Novak said. "We'll try to keep you from being hurt by this. All you'll have to do is perform the recon-struction and the computer measurements and photos. We'll keep your identity confidential."

"Which will be fine if this skull is Varak's. It will be bull-shit if it's not," Eve said. "We all know that my identity will be secret only if we return that skull to the U.N. vault before the switch is discovered. You won't do that if you think that I've proved Varak is alive. You'll want to take the next step and find the person who falsified the DNA." She looked him in the eye. "And then you'll try to hunt down Varak and trap or kill him. Isn't that right?"

He nodded slowly. "I've told you that I would."

"And that's why it's a miracle she's even considering doing it," Jill said.

"More than considering," Novak said softly, his gaze studying Eve's face. "She's going for it. She only wants us to tell her the best way to do it."

"Wrong. I want to tell you how *I'm* going to do it," Eve said. "When you leave here, I'm going to start on the re-construction of the six-year-old girl who's next on my list. I'll get as much done as possible today and tonight before you give me the Varak skull. I hope to get past the measur-ing to the initial sculpting. At that stage, a layman can't tell how much is being accomplished. Then I'll start work on Varak. That will be slower; depending on condition, it may take me up to three days. If I'm interrupted or have to leave the museum for any reason, I'll hide Varak away and put the six-year-old on the dais in his place."

"Only three days?" Jill leaned forward, tense. "Are you certain?"

"No, not if the damage from the explosion is more extensive than I think. But they would have had to have found some kind of basic bone structure to even begin to identify Varak and start to search for DNA. You said there were five passengers on that helicopter?"

"Including the pilot," Novak said. "But according to my interrogation of Varak's men we captured after the explosion, Varak was wearing a leather jacket that day. There was melted leather in the rubble near the remains of the body." He grimaced. "Which was basically the skull."

"And the jacket led you to the right victim," Eve said. "How convenient that they didn't have to waste time beginning their search for the DNA. Particularly since the whole world was so very eager to know that Varak was dead."

"Do you think that didn't occur to me?" Novak asked. "But the French forces had made the kill and were in charge of the investigation. The U.N. told us to back off. Why do you think I even listened to Jill when she came to me with that story about Hadfeld?"

"Because you're not an idiot," Jill said. "Though you should have—" She broke off and turned back to Eve. "If the skull isn't too degraded, it will only be three days. That would be enough time. Novak said that the safe is only opened for a visual check every five days."

"Only? You appear to like that word. I'm glad you think it's going to be so easy," Eve said dryly. "It doesn't seem like that much time to me to do the reconstruction, determine if it's Varak, then erase all signs I'd even done the work so that you can slip it back into the safe as if it had never been touched." She added grimly, "And, if it's *not* Varak, then everything will probably blow up in my face."

"Our faces," Jill said quietly. "You're not alone in this. Anything that happens to you happens to me from now on." She smiled faintly. "If you get tossed into jail, they'll have to give me the next cell."

"I'd prefer to avoid that possibility," Eve said. "I have a son to raise, and I don't want to leave it up to Joe." She glanced at Novak. "Which brings me to what I have to do to keep Joe from going ballistic about this. Joe told me that you'd met him. Did you actually think you could keep him out of it?"

"I was hopeful. But I was considering options. Unfortunately, developments are escalating."

"You mean because I was poisoned yesterday? You mean because no one told me what had happened to Jill before she drew me into this nightmare? Yes, I think either one of those events might have caused Joe to believe the situation here had escalated out of control." She added, "And I haven't told Joe any of the details about either one, but I'm going to have to do it. Jill gave me your name to reassure Joe, but he's not going to be reassured by the fact that I almost died and you can't find the chef who was responsible for the poison. Has that changed?"

"No, Gaillon hasn't shown up back at the hotel. I suspect he might have taken a bribe and skipped the country, or he might have proved embarrassing to whoever hired him and was taken out. I'm exploring both possibilities. I'll let you know as soon as I know."

Eve was shaken for a moment by Novak's coolness and complete lack of expression. But then she should have expected it. Jill had told her he was ruthless, but she found she wanted to disturb that coolness. "How nice of you. But you can see how Joe wouldn't believe you're particularly efficient." She glanced at Jill. "Look what you let happen to her."

His lips tightened, but there was only a flicker of expression in his eyes. "That's true. So what's your remedy for the situation? How do we keep him out of this?"

"We can't. It's too late. If there were any way that I thought I could keep him in London, I'd do it. But the minute I ended up in that hospital yesterday morning, I knew it was the end. Even if I left this place, he'd be back here checking out that hotel and why it happened to me. Joe never lets go, it's not his nature."

"I repeat, do you have a remedy?"

"I can't keep him out, so I tell him the truth." She paused. "And we invite him to help clean up this mess. He'll be here anyway the minute he hears what's been happening." She shrugged. "And he can be a great help, he's a superb detective. Give him all the facts and turn him loose. You'll be surprised how good he is."

"I don't doubt it. He has that reputation. I would have ordinarily welcomed his help. But I remembered that when I met him, I thought he'd probably be a difficult man to control, that he'd always go his own path." He was searching her face. "And you don't want him here, do you?"

"You're damn right I don't. But I can't go away until I know about Varak. And Joe will come regardless when he knows I was targeted." She added curtly, "And I might still be targeted. You can't deny that, can you?"

"Not as long as you're working on the skull. After that, you might be safe."

"Might?" She shook her head. "Then your job is to keep Joe so busy that he's nowhere near me while I'm working on that reconstruction. Otherwise, you can forget about my doing it. I won't risk him. Do you understand?"

"I understand. Anything else?"

"Evidently you don't trust me to Skype him. Get me a satellite smartphone that's virtually impossible to hack. And make sure my security is good enough that Joe will feel comfortable about leaving me alone here."

"I would have done that regardless."

"I had to be certain. Joe would notice."

"I imagine he would," he said. "But you should know that Gideon is fully capable. After his parents were killed, he came to me and asked to be sent to a training camp the CIA runs in Afghanistan. He did very well."

"You mean he's fairly lethal." She nodded. "I can see he'd be motivated. But he just doesn't give off those vibes."

"He's complicated," Jill said. "He adapts to the situation. I think you've found that out."

"Yes, I have." She added, "But then so do you, Jill. But I don't think you persuaded Novak to send you to a training camp to increase your kill quotient."

"I was tempted to blackmail her into it at one time," Novak said grimly. "I still might decide to do it. She's damn vulnerable."

"Back off, Novak," Jill said. "I'm not that vulnerable. I made one mistake. You keep coming back to it."

"Because I can't forget it," he said grimly. "Though you appear to have managed."

"Do I?" Jill asked. "No, I haven't forgotten. Though I try very hard."

Novak muttered a curse as he turned back to Eve. "I'm supposed to take possession of the skull at eleven tonight. Can you put off talking to Joe Quinn until I'm certain the switch has gone through? You might not have to bring him here. That guard, Swanson, is very edgy, and even the prospect of retiring with a fortune may not overcome his nerves. I might have to start all over if he panics."

"I can't believe you'd let that happen," she said caustically. "Joe said you were the CIA's go-to man."

"Which only means in situations like this I can't delegate, I'll have to be there tonight when the switch is made."

"Then you won't let this Swanson change his mind." She shrugged. "I'll wait, but the result will probably be the same. Once I let Joe know how sick I was, it will be all over. If I don't tell him I'm on my way to him, he'll be coming here." She stared him in the eye. "So handle it, Novak. Having Joe hovering over me while I complete that reconstruction would be suspicious to say the least. Joe's reputation is remarkable, and no one would believe he'd fly here from Scotland Yard just for a conjugal visit."

"I'll handle it," Novak said. "Just stall him. Okay?"

"No, it's not okay. And it won't work for long. Get me that phone so I can talk freely to him, or it won't work at all." She made an impatient gesture with her hand. "Now both of you get out of here. I have to start to work." She got to her feet and strode over to the row of leather boxes on the shelf. "Did I tell you how much I hate these boxes? But no more than I hate everything else that happened here." She took down the box with the skull of the six-year-old girl that she'd set aside in preparation. "Her name is Mila. She has a right to expect my full attention, but instead I'm making her part of this charade."

"You'll make it up to her," Jill said quietly as she got to her feet. "And I believe she wouldn't mind that she has a role in catching the man who did this to her and her friends. Do you, Eve?"

"No." Eve opened the box and gazed down at the small, blackened skull. "Very clever, Jill. Just the right thing to say."

"Not clever. It's what I feel. From now on, that's what you'll get from me." She headed for the door. "Now I have to get back to my apartment and change. I'm supposed to be back here for that press interview Gideon has set up for this morning." She smiled as she stopped at the door. "It's good that you'll be in the midst of working on a new reconstruction. I'll be able to be admiring and ask dozens of questions."

"Not dozens." Eve was frowning with exasperation. "And I completely forgot about that damn press interview." Too much had been going on that was more important. "I have to *work*. Tell Gideon to get everyone in and out within an hour."

"Don't worry. It will be just long enough to make me appear to be only another journalist out to get a feature story. Along with trying to convince Zahra that it was Gideon and not me who was behind bringing you here."

"Zahra's going to be at the interview?"

"It would surprise me if she wasn't," Novak said as he joined Jill at the door. "She seems to be ever present. She'll want to take some of the media attention away from you and focus it on herself." He glanced at Jill. "And her agent, Bogani, is still following Jill everywhere she goes."

"She's being followed?" Eve frowned. "Why? Just because she's trying to keep Zahra from swallowing up this village?"

"Interesting question," Novak said. "I'm looking into it. I'll see you this evening, Eve."

Eve turned to Jill as he left the museum. "Why?" she repeated. "Novak may be 'looking' into Zahra Kiyani, but I think she's weird as hell, and I want more than a look. I wouldn't put anything past her and her 'food tasters.'"

"Gideon told me about that conversation." Jill shrugged. "Novak's 'looks' are very thorough. But I agree she's a piece of work. It seems to run in the family. Remind me to tell you about Kiya and her journal. It's enlightening." She lifted her hand in farewell. "I'll see you at the press interview. You won't have to suffer through it for too long. Gideon is a master at this kind of bullshit. He was trained from childhood to be head of the Gideon financial empire. This is nothing."

"No wonder Zahra wanted him as prince consort," Eve murmured. "Well, all I want is for him to get those reporters and Zahra out of here and let me keep on working."

"He'll do it." Jill turned to leave. "One hour. No more."

———

One hour.

Jill had kept her word, Eve realized, as she watched Gideon whisk the six reporters he'd invited out the door. He'd managed to get them all individual interviews with her that were at least five minutes long, and he hadn't allowed them to take control or ask her any awkward questions. More important, he'd made Jill just one of the crowd with no special privileges, and Jill had played her part to perfection. She'd been eager, intelligent, and no one would have been able to guess she'd ever met Eve before today.

Then he'd turned the spotlight on Zahra Kiyani and switched the reporters' focus to her. Thirty minutes of Zahra's exuding charm, and he'd started herding the reporters toward the exit.

"He's very good, isn't he?" Zahra was suddenly at Eve's elbow. Then she frowned. "Though I could have used a few more minutes with the media before he decided to get rid of them. But it's difficult to control Gideon."

"I thought the timing was just right," Eve said. "I have to get back to work. It was kind of you to take the time to come."

"I couldn't do anything else." Zahra's flashing smile illuminated her beautiful face. "I had to make sure that you were all right after that horrible food poisoning yesterday. You're a little pale, but better than I thought. But, of course, you'll have to worry about a relapse. These things do happen." She didn't wait for a reply but gestured at Jill, who was now being ushered out the door by Gideon. "What did you think of Jill Cassidy? She and Gideon know each other, but I notice he didn't give her any more time for her interview than the other reporters. I was expecting...more."

"That wouldn't have been fair, would it? What did I think of her? She seems very competent and appears to know quite a bit about the village. She said I could ask her anything I needed to know, but I don't believe it will be necessary. I'm only interested in working."

"And besides, you can ask me," Zahra said softly. "I'm the only one you should consult. Robaku is really my property. My father allowed these villagers to live here, but now it's time for them to settle somewhere else. Keeping this village alive only keeps the memories of the war fresh to everyone. I've been trying to make that clear to you. It's just as well you stay away from busybodies like Jill Cassidy, who can only cause trouble."

"I'll keep it in mind." But she found she was too annoyed to leave it at that and be diplomatic with Zahra at the moment. The woman always managed to push her buttons. That comment about evicting the villagers from their homes had been a jab too deep to ignore. "But I did enjoy reading her stories. Now that I think of it, I might want to discuss them with her. It's always wise to get a few viewpoints." She turned and moved toward her worktable. "Thank you for coming, but you really didn't have to check on me. I'm doing very well. Not a hint of a relapse."

"It's early days," Zahra said. "Dalai!" Before she swept toward the door, Zahra gestured imperiously to the young servant girl who had been hovering in the background. "You might keep that in mind as well." She brushed past Gideon as if he weren't there. "And you might have given those reporters their story for the day, but you saw how eagerly they turned to me. You mustn't feel bad about that. In the end, they'll always come back to me. I have a certain glamour that you'll never possess." She lifted her chin. "I'm a Kiyani."

Then she was gone.

Gideon gave a low whistle as he gazed after her. "Her ego is flying high today." He turned to Eve. "Did she do you any damage?"

"Only a not-so-subtle hint that I could have a relapse if I wasn't careful." Now that Zahra was gone, Eve found she felt chilled. "I don't like it. There's something very savage about Zahra Kiyani. And I'm tired of threats, subtle or not. She might have had something to do with my getting ill, right?"

"It's possible."

"Then I want to know if it's more than possible. I want to know why. I want to know everything about her."

"Then we'll have to accommodate you. But I assume that's not first on your list? You appear to have a full agenda."

"Yes." And her agenda tonight included looking at a skull that might be that of Nils Varak.

Another chill.

"You might say that." She quickly looked down at the measurements she'd started on Mila. "Not first, but Zahra is definitely on the list."

———◆———

Zahra braced herself as soon as she got in her limousine. She'd like to wait until she got back to the palace, but she'd found that wasn't an option. Now she seldom had a choice, and nothing she did was private any longer.

Not from him.

She typed the text.

DUNCAN'S WORKING ON ANOTHER DAMN SKULL. SHE'S NOT PAYING ANY ATTENTION TO ME. IT'S NOT MY FAULT.

The return text came immediately.

OF COURSE IT'S YOUR FAULT. I TOLD YOU TO GET RID OF HER. YOU DIDN'T DO IT. YOU WERE TOO FRIGHTENED. NOW I MIGHT HAVE TO HANDLE IT.

She'd known she'd get the blame. It made her furious.

YOU DON'T UNDERSTAND. I WON'T GIVE UP WHAT I'VE WORKED FOR ALL MY LIFE BECAUSE YOU'RE IMPATIENT. IT COULD HAVE WORKED. FEAR AND PAIN ARE WEAPONS TOO. THEY JUST DIDN'T WORK ON DUNCAN. I'LL TRY SOMETHING ELSE.

The reply came explosively:

YOU'RE RIGHT, I AM IMPATIENT. YOU MADE ME PROMISES. YOU'RE NOT KEEPING THEM.

She couldn't let him get away with that bullshit.

YOU MADE ME A PROMISE TOO. YOU SAID YOU'D GET IT BACK FOR ME AND YOU DIDN'T DO IT. IT'S MINE. I WANT IT BACK.

He didn't answer, and Zahra began to get nervous. It was all very well to defend herself, but the result could be unpredictable.

STOP WHINING. IT'S ALREADY IN THE WORKS. BUT THAT HAS NOTHING TO DO WITH YOUR NOT GETTING RID OF DUNCAN. I'LL GIVE YOU A FEW DAYS BUT AFTER THAT I'LL TAKE OVER. DO YOU WANT THAT TO HAPPEN, ZAHRA?

The threat terrified her.

I'LL MAKE IT WORK. I'LL GET HER OUT OF THERE. JUST A LITTLE MORE TIME.

She had to wait for a full moment.

FOUR DAYS. SHOW ME YOU'RE NOT A COWARD AND WE'LL COME TO TERMS. OTHERWISE IT WILL BE MY TERMS.

The text conversation was clearly ended.

She drew a deep breath and tried to keep control. She had expected anger, not an ultimatum. But she could work with it. She would try to fix Duncan her way, but if necessary, she'd do whatever she had to do. The alternative was too dangerous to accept.

Four days . . .

CHAPTER

8

I've brought you dinner," Jill announced from the doorway of the museum. Her arms were full of takeout sacks. "I'd bet you haven't eaten today."

"You'd lose," Eve said. "I had a sandwich before that ghastly interview. I know I have to take care of myself when I'm working."

"Well, this Chinese takeout is much better. It's the only restaurant in Jokan that I'd trust to have genuine ingredients that have nothing to do with monkeys or reptiles." She was taking cartons out of the bag and putting them on the work-table. "Sweet and sour soup and a bland beef lo mein. I figured your stomach might still be tender."

"Good guess." Eve was looking at the cartons. "But this isn't necessary. I shouldn't take the time."

"Yes, you should. There's no telling when you'll allow yourself to eat after Novak dumps that skull in your lap. You know that's true." She smiled. "Besides, I hate to eat alone." She set her own cartons on the desk. "So eat, and if you want an excuse while you're doing it, so you won't feel you're wasting your time, ask me any questions you wish about Zahra Kiyani. Gideon told me that you were becoming very wary about Madam President. Since he let me read the Kiya journal, he thought that I'd be less likely to be biased."

Eve gazed at her for a moment and reached for a carton and utensils. "You're sure about the reptiles and monkeys?"

"I have a friend in their kitchen. He wouldn't steer me wrong. Trust me." Then she made a face. "You really can trust me, Eve. About everything."

"Really?" Eve said noncommittally. Then she changed the subject. "Why didn't you bring another meal for Gideon? Isn't he still drifting around the village?"

"I didn't see him. I think Novak sent him off to do something or other after he finished staging that interview." She handed her a handful of paper napkins. "But don't worry, Novak would have sent a man here to replace him."

"I'm not worried. Though I'm sure Gideon would say that no one could replace him." She tried the soup. "Excellent. Now tell me about Zahra. Gideon said that there was a possibility that she was to blame for my very painful morning yesterday. Do you agree?"

"I agree it's a possibility. Zahra is capable of anything. How far would she go? I'd judge to the limit if she thought it safe. But she's cautious, and she'd make certain that the end result would be worth any action she takes." She was gazing thoughtfully down into her soup. "She's into power, and she believes it's her due. It's all part of that royal bullshit she's embraced since childhood." She looked up at Eve. "Gideon told you she believes that she's descended from Cleopatra?"

"Are we back to this Kiya again?" Eve asked impatiently.

"I ask about Zahra, and I get a tall tale about Cleopatra's daughter."

"Because when I first came to Maldara and was trying to get a handle on how to keep Zahra from kicking all those villagers out of their homes, I had to understand her. I didn't even come close until Gideon told me about Kiya. Then it started to come together. In many ways, Zahra *is* Kiya. With a generous sprinkling of Cleopatra thrown in."

"How?"

"You take a psychotic personality and throw in the idea that nothing is forbidden and everything is your right to take. The final result you come up with is a very dangerous woman. Zahra really admires Cleopatra, you know. If you look deeper into who Cleopatra really was, you can see the similarities. She wasn't the gorgeous, tragic queen that the movies portrayed. Intelligent, yes. And she possessed a kind of glamour that had its own attraction. But she killed her brother and sister. There were even rumors that she might have killed her own father. No one counts how many of her slaves bit the dust. Food tasters were a way of life, and any cruel indulgence was allowed with slaves. According to Kiya's journal, Cleopatra even threatened her with death and torture innumerable times when she was angry with her. It didn't matter that Kiya was her daughter."

"Gideon said that you appreciated the literary aspects of her journal," Eve said. "Do you think it was fact or fiction?"

"It . . . was persuasive."

"But Cleopatra only had one daughter, Selene, who later became Queen of Mauretania."

"Only one acknowledged daughter," Jill said. "According to Kiya, she was the result of a sexual liaison between Cleopatra and a soldier in her army while Caesar was away. She gave Kiya to her slaves to raise, and later, Kiya herself served as a slave to Cleopatra. Evidently, she wasn't treated too badly. Cleopatra ordered her named Kiya after Queen Kiya, who was a queen to Akhenaten during the Eighteenth Dynasty. She was one of Cleopatra's favorite ancestors because she was known as the Beloved Wife. Other of his queens were called royal and powerful, and Nefertiti was famous for her beauty, but Cleopatra thought Akhenaten probably loved Kiya more. Wherever her name was inscribed, it was followed by Beloved Wife. Anyway, maybe Cleopatra wanted to tell her daughter she loved her even though she'd made her a slave. At times, Cleopatra actually did show her affection." She added ironically, "Providing Kiya kept in mind her lowly place in the scheme of things."

"Which would have been very painful considering that she knew she was Cleopatra's daughter."

"True. But she seemed to have inherited Cleopatra's toughness because she adapted and played her mother's game while she waited for her chance."

"Chance?"

"To be a queen herself." Jill finished her lo mein and pushed the carton away. "I wonder if she actually managed to outthink Cleopatra, or if she took advantage of circumstances."

"What are you talking about?"

"The Great Journey." Jill leaned back. "What do you know about how Cleopatra died?"

"What everyone knows. When she knew Octavian was on his way to capture her, she locked herself in her mausoleum and committed suicide by letting an asp bite her."

Jill nodded. "Partially right, according to what Kiya related in her journal. Not complete enough. No one gives more than a mention to the slaves she took with her into the mausoleum to die with her. They were the maids Eiras and Charmion. But there was one more slave who went with her."

Eve stiffened. "Kiya?"

"According to Kiya's journal, she went there with her mother by her own choice. She makes a point of saying she felt it her duty to do whatever her mother wished her to do. Or whatever seemed wisest." She paused. "Do you know what else is seldom mentioned? Cleopatra's burial treasure that was in the mausoleum. One of the greatest treasures ever compiled. That was why Octavian was rushing to reach her—he needed that treasure."

Eve stared at Jill, guessing where this was going. "And did he get it?"

"Oh, yes, it was a vast treasure, and he was very pleased with it." She smiled. "And, according to Kiya's journal, there was so much that Octavian never even missed the wagonload of treasure that was taken out of the mausoleum during the time before Cleopatra actually got around to committing suicide."

"My, my," Eve murmured. "Kiya, again?"

Jill nodded. "Remember her line about whatever was wisest to do? It seems that what was wisest for Kiya to do was not to kill herself with Cleopatra. Her mother had sent Caesarion, her son and heir, away to hide from Octavian. Kiya convinced Cleopatra that she should spare a little of her treasure to make certain her heir was safe and had enough funds to fight Rome. Then Kiya magnanimously volunteered to risk her own life to take the treasure to Caesarion." She sighed. "But unfortunately, Octavian found Caesarion and murdered him before she was able to get to him. What a pity. The only good thing was that Cleopatra had already killed herself and didn't have to hear the sad news." She shook her head. "But what could Kiya do with this huge fortune in the back of her wagon? What a conundrum."

"The Great Journey," Eve said.

"Well, she obviously had to leave Alexandria or Octavian would kill her. The only solution was to go somewhere far away, a wild, mysterious place that she had been hearing about in the market." She nodded. "The Great Journey."

Eve chuckled. "You're a much better Scheherazade than Gideon. How much do we believe?"

"As much as you like. It's a great story, so I prefer to believe it all. Particularly since Kiya was such a scheming bitch that she reminds me of Zahra. If she was that clever, couldn't she have found a way out for Cleopatra? Was this her master plan from the beginning, or was she making it up as she went along?"

"Probably a little of both."

"I believe you're right." Jill got to her feet and went over to the coffeemaker. "She had been waiting for a long time, but when the opportunity came, she was ready. She even knew where she was going." She made the coffee and leaned back against the cabinet. "But after that first journal about the Great Journey, the treasure isn't mentioned. I found that interesting."

"Dispersed by her heirs through the centuries?"

"Not much to buy in primitive Maldara. It seemed to disappear when they reached the border." She shrugged. "A mystery to solve. But, then, the entire story is something of a mystery all bound up in True or False." She suddenly smiled. "And, speaking of True or False, that story about the way Cleopatra died wasn't entirely true, according to Kiya. She didn't die of the poisonous bite of an asp though she wanted everyone to think she did. The snake was a symbol for royalty, and Cleopatra liked the idea for that reason. But she wanted her death to be as perfect as her life, so she wasn't going to take any chances. Kiya said that she did extensive research by having several slaves bitten by asps so that she could study the effects before she made her decision."

"Charming."

"Entirely practical from Cleopatra's viewpoint. When a goddess dies, it must be with glory and dignity. But she found when an asp bites, it causes swelling and ugly discharge and intense pain that lasts up to six hours or longer. It's a horrible death. There was no way she was going to put up with that agony and loss of dignity. So she opted to have the snake brought to the mausoleum for effect, but she arranged to have her jeweled hair comb coated with a fast-acting poison. She pressed the prongs of the comb into her arm when the time was right."

Eve's brows rose skeptically. "Definitely another True or False."

"But think about it. Consider what we know about the era and Cleopatra herself. It's possible." Jill shrugged. "And, if you believe in Kiya, then it's more than possible." She smiled quizzically. "Anyway, did I manage to help you to get a glimpse of Zahra's character by studying Kiya?"

"With a few major differences. Kiya was a survivor. Everything she did was because she had to fight or die. Zahra doesn't have that excuse. It's pure ambition."

"How very perceptive." Jill poured coffee into a cup and took it back to Eve. She mockingly inclined her head. "Your after-dinner coffee, madam." She looked at the scant remains of the food. "And you managed to get most of your dinner down. That's good." She took the sacks, plastic plates and utensils and tossed them into the trash can in the corner. "That should hold you until I get back. I have to go now. I'll see you about midnight."

Eve stiffened, her eyes widening. "You're going with Novak? Neither of you mentioned it."

"It's my story," she said simply. "In more ways than one. Novak would have just argued with me. It's better if I just present him with a fait accompli." She headed for the door. "Get back to work on Mila. With any luck, we'll have a replacement for her within a few hours."

If they weren't caught and killed by those guards at the U.N., Eve thought. The soldiers guarding that vault might shoot first and ask questions later. This would be considered robbery on an international scale. She was sure Varak's skull must be the principal prize being held there. Villains on the mega scale of Varak were rare, and proof of his demise was even more rare. Trying to steal Varak's skull would have been like trying to steal Bin Laden's corpse. Eve had not been worried about Novak. He was a professional, and Joe said a good one. But Jill was different. Novak had said she was vulnerable, and she'd already been terribly hurt. She said impulsively, "Jill."

Jill looked back over her shoulder and grinned. "What's the matter? Going soft on me? I'm the bad guy, remember? I'm the one who got you into this mess."

"I remember." But she still had to say it. "But it won't hurt you to be careful, Jill. You're...valuable." She turned back to Mila's reconstruction, and said lightly, "Who else knows where to get Chinese food with no serpents or monkeys?"

———◆———

U.N. HEADQUARTERS
JOKAN

No Novak.

And it was only fifteen minutes until he had to meet with Swanson, Jill thought tensely. She'd gotten here twenty minutes ago and expected to see some sign of him before this.

Her gaze narrowed on the huge mansion on Wabona Street that had formerly belonged to the owner of a diamond mine before it was taken over by the U.N. The house and grounds were enclosed by a twelve-foot stone fence that the U.N. said was necessary for their employees' security. Though she knew most of the employees had been given quarters in the city after Edward Wyatt had taken residence in the mansion. The house itself was dark now, and there was only one uniformed guard at the gate.

And there was a camera mounted on that gate.

Jill's hands tensed on the steering wheel of her Volvo. She was parked some distance down the street from that front gate, but she'd be in view of that camera the minute she walked within several yards of it.

But Novak would have taken care of that camera, wouldn't he?

And how had he been planning to get rid of the guard?

No way to be sure without checking. She would have had to call him anyway, but now the need was imperative. It was getting very close to that eleven o'clock deadline.

She dialed his number. "Where are you, Novak?" she asked when he picked up. "I need to know if you've taken out this damned camera."

He muttered a curse. "I knew it. I was hoping that you wouldn't do this. Why couldn't you leave it up to me?"

"Where are you?" she repeated.

"In the garden behind the building. Swanson is going to meet me here with the skull."

"How do I get back there?"

"You don't. Stay where you are, and I'll call you after I've left the garden."

"That won't work for me. I started this, I need to take my share of the risk. Tell me a safe way I can get to you."

Silence. "There's an unlocked gate on the north side of the block. No guard. Camera is disabled. Get here quick. I only have five minutes to make the switch and get out after Swanson shows." He cut the connection.

Yes!

Jill was out of the Volvo and running down the street.

North side of the block...

Where was the gate?

There!

She was inside.

She paused for a minute, breathing hard, leaning against the gate, her gaze searching the darkness.

A large fountain. A courtyard... Paths leading toward the main house. The windows were dark here, too.

Where the hell was Novak?

"Keep quiet and follow me." She hadn't heard him approach and could barely make him out in his dark garb. He was carrying one of the gaudy paper totes sold in the marketplace. He added curtly, "The courtyard."

She had to almost run to keep up with him as he moved toward the courtyard. She skidded to a stop as he put out his arm when they reached it. No one was there. "Shouldn't he be here by now?" she whispered.

"If he hasn't gotten nervous." He glanced at his watch. "And turned me over to his captain. Be quiet, Jill. I need to—" He stopped, his gaze on the doors at the far end of the courtyard. "Okay..."

A young soldier in a British private's uniform was hurrying toward them. He was pale, obviously nervous, and carrying a medium-size brown-leather suitcase. It had to be Swanson, Jill thought with relief.

He stopped short as he reached Novak, his gaze fixed warily on Jill. "Who is she? You were supposed to be alone."

"Yes, I was," Novak said dryly. "Plans changed. You're not compromised. She's just an expert to make sure that you're not trying to pass off bogus merchandise."

"I couldn't do that. The imprint of the ID on the skull can't be counterfeited."

"She'll verify it." He handed Swanson an envelope, then the shopping bag. "The replacement. And if anything is wrong, I'll be back for you."

"Nothing will be wrong." Swanson stuffed the envelope in his jacket pocket. "But you have to have it back by Monday. When the inspectors come, I can't cover for you."

"I know that. Get out of here and get that replacement skull in the vault."

Swanson turned away. "I'm going. You have only three minutes before that guard will be back at the gate after his smoke. You'd better hope he doesn't come back early."

He was gone.

And Novak was grasping Jill's arm and running with her toward the gate. He pushed her through it and was locking the gate behind them. "Run! South to the end of the block and around the corner."

Jill ran.

She didn't look back.

Three minutes.

But it must be less than that now . . .

Then Novak was passing her, and the next moment pulling her around the corner.

She pressed back against the high stone wall, breathing hard.

"Don't stop. Keep moving." Novak jerked her back into motion. He was still running, holding tight to the suitcase. "My jeep's a half block down."

She saw it, the black jeep he usually drove. She dived into the passenger seat as soon as he pressed the lock release.

Novak shoved the suitcase onto her lap and slammed the driver's door. The next instant he was starting the car and pulling away from the curb.

Jill's heartbeat didn't slow until they were three blocks away from the U.N. headquarters. "So I'm an expert?" she asked after she got her breath.

"What else was I supposed to say? It was as good a lie as any. I would have been ready with a better one if I'd known you'd do this to me."

He was angry, she realized. It wasn't unexpected. He liked to be in control. He probably thought he had a right to be angry with her for interfering with his plans. Too bad. She hadn't been about to let him do this without her.

"I think you did know. You even said it when I called you. So stop growling about it. You know I had to be here."

"The hell I did. If I hadn't thought that you might do something to blow the switch if I didn't monitor you, I'd have hung up when you called."

"I would have been careful. I wouldn't have done anything to put you in danger. That's what this was about." Why couldn't he understand that? "We've been together since the beginning. I wasn't going to let you be alone. You might be CIA's golden boy, but stealing this skull could cause you big trouble if anything went wrong."

"I can take care of myself." He was gazing at her incredulously. "What could you have done to save my ass anyway?"

She shrugged. "I'd just say that I was the one who was going after the skull because of the story potential. Everyone would believe me. Reporters have the reputation of doing anything for a story." She added quietly, "And I'd tell them that you were trying to stop me. But I had to be there at the switch tonight or it wouldn't have worked. Swanson had to see me."

Silence. "Oh, he saw you all right." He looked straight ahead. "And he'll remember you. You're crazy, you know."

"Maybe. And it might have all been for nothing. Everything seems to have gone smoothly. But I had to do it."

"Why, dammit?"

"I owed you," she said jerkily. "The night I was...hurt, you came after me. You didn't have to do it. You'd already told me to stay out of it. But you found me, and you took care of me." She moistened her lips. "It was a bad time for me. I've been alone most of my life. I wasn't alone that night."

"Your thinking is wonky as hell," he said hoarsely. "That's not how I remember it."

She shook her head. "And then you did everything you could to let me help, to let me find them. I *need* to do that." Her hand touched the suitcase he had thrown on her lap. "And it's brought us to this. One step closer." She had a strange, tingling feeling in her palm. The skull was here, separated from her only by the sleek hardcover leather of the case. Was it the head of the monster? "How could I not be here, Novak?"

His glance shifted back to her face. "*You* couldn't," he said. "Because you don't see things like other people. But do me a favor and don't try to save me again. Okay?"

"You didn't listen to me." She changed the subject. "Swanson was nervous tonight. Do you think he'll be able to hold himself together until we can get the skull back to him on Monday? What's to keep him from going on the run before that? That would trigger instant suspicion."

"I only gave him half of his money. He'll be motivated to keep cool and do everything right until he gets the other half Monday. After that, I don't care what he does. One way or the other, we'll have our answer by then." He paused. "Provided Eve comes through for us."

"Yes." Her hand tightened on the case. "After tonight it will all be up to Eve."

———————

"Everything went well?" Eve carefully moved her reconstruction of Mila to the cabinet she'd cleared in readiness. "No problem?"

"It depends on how you look at it," Novak said as he placed the case on her worktable and opened the snaps. "And also how you look at this skull. I don't think Swanson had the guts to double-cross me, but you'll have to tell me." He opened the lid of the suitcase. "Check the ID number on the skull interior below the left-ear cavity before you go any further. It should be 1066." He gave her a small vial. "One drop should bring it out."

She carefully took out the skull and put it on the dais. "This is like something from a James Bond movie," she grumbled. "Ridiculous, Novak."

"The CIA is much more advanced than 007 these days," he said dryly. "But the Brits did work out a way to guarantee the authenticity of this skull. It's foolproof." He watched as Eve put a minute drop of liquid on the back of the ear bone. It fizzed, and four tiny numbers appeared—1066.

"Though it's a bit showy," Novak said. "I could have done without the sound effects."

"But you're always understated." Jill took a step closer. "This is the skull they took from the helicopter? We're certain?"

"The Brits would be insulted. The skull had almost a guard of honor before the French forces turned it over to the scientists the Brits flew in to tag it," Novak said. "And I was there in the lab watching as they did it. I'm naturally suspicious, and I wanted to be sure. I stayed with it through the entire ID process until they put the skull in the vault." He turned to Eve. "This is the skull taken out of that helicopter. Now can you find out if it's Varak's?"

"I can find out what this man looks like. If it's a strong resemblance to Varak, then it should be fairly simple," Eve said. "If it's not, you'll have to prove whether or not he's Varak to your satisfaction. But I told you, the DNA specimen taken from that back molar was judged absolute proof." She frowned as she examined the skull. It was badly burned, and it was no wonder that other DNA was not available. It was going to be very difficult to do the reconstruction. "I can't promise anything else."

"We can't expect you to do anything but your best," Jill said. "I'm grateful you're going to do it at all." She grimaced. "Particularly since you have a perfect right to tell me to go to hell."

"Yes, I do." Eve was securing the skull to the dais. "But then I'd never know if Varak is down there ready to greet you." She shrugged. "So I guess I'll have to forgive and forget until I find out for sure. After that, we'll go into it again."

"Works for me," Jill said. "I suppose you're going to start on him tonight? A little rest would do you good."

"I'll get some sleep tonight. I'm going to need it. But I'll work on repairs for a few hours before I go to bed." She turned to Novak. "But now I talk to Joe. Did you get my phone?"

"Yes." He took a sleek, small gray phone out of his jacket pocket and handed it to her. "Very safe."

"I'm glad something is safe around here," Eve said. "I guarantee Joe isn't going to be impressed by it. Alarms are going to go off the minute the call doesn't come in on my computer Skype." Her gaze shifted back to the blackened skull.

It seemed to be staring malevolently back at her. Foolishness. Those stories that Jill had told her about Varak were causing her imagination to run riot. "Why don't you both get out of here? You've done your part. Don't worry. Nothing Joe says will change my mind. I've agreed to do this. Now I'm committed."

"I'm not quite finished here." Jill put up her hand as Eve started to speak. "I'm not hanging out to eavesdrop on your conversation. It's time we trusted each other." She glanced at Novak. "I speak for myself. Novak has been playing in the shadows for so long it comes natural to him. Most of the time, he can't help himself. But he won't do anything to hurt you."

Novak's eyes narrowed on her. "What are you up to?"

"I'm just trying to tell her that she has to put up with having me bunk here at the museum from now on until the reconstruction is finished."

"What!" Eve said. "No way."

"My thought exactly," Novak said to Jill. "After all you've gone through to make sure that no one was aware of the connection between you?"

"The press interview already established that, and you'll just have to make certain there's no one snooping around here. You'll do that anyway."

"Why?" Eve's lips twisted. "Because we trust each other so much?"

"I want you to have someone here to protect you. I think that has to be me."

"I have her guarded, Jill," Novak said. "You know that."

Jill shook her head. "How quickly could they get to her? It might not be soon enough." She turned back to Eve. "I won't bother you. You won't know I'm here. Unless you need me."

"I don't want you here."

"I'm sorry," Jill said sincerely. "It has to be this way. I got you into this, and I have to be responsible for you."

"The hell you do."

Jill smiled slightly. "Then we'll have to be responsible for each other. Earlier today, I told Hajif to have a cot ready for me. I'll go down and tell him to bring it up now." She headed for the door. "It will be fine, Eve."

"It's not *necessary*, Jill," Novak said.

"Yes, it is." Jill looked at him over her shoulder. "I don't want her to be alone."

"That seems to be her mantra these days," Novak said to Eve between set teeth, as they watched her walk out of the museum.

Eve repeated, "I don't want her here, Novak. I can take care of myself."

"I'm sure you can. Quinn would make sure that you would never be helpless. It doesn't seem to make any difference to Jill." He looked back at Eve. "Oh, she can take care of herself, too. She survived here in Maldara for two years. And she might not have gone to one of our training camps like Gideon, but she knows karate and is an excellent shot."

"You said she was vulnerable."

"Because she does things like this," he said harshly, his eyes glittering in his taut face. "Because she knows that no matter how good anyone is, there's always a situation where being good isn't enough. She was hurt in one of those damned situations recently. She doesn't want anyone else to be hurt." He gestured impatiently. "You might as well give in to her. You're not going to win. She'll make it work for you. But she won't let you go through this alone." He turned and headed for the door. "I'll go help her. First I have to send someone to pick up her car at the U.N. building, then talk to the guards so that we can get her settled. Go ahead and call Quinn."

Eve shook her head ruefully. So much for privacy and being in total control of the reconstruction process. She supposed it didn't really matter if Jill stayed. If Jill annoyed her, then she would just toss her out.

She doesn't want anyone else to be hurt.

Those poignant words had touched Eve in spite of her resistance to this invasion of her privacy. That memory of Jill's attack must be a constant battle to overcome. But she was dealing with it and not trying to hide away.

Courage...

And, dammit, Eve's own admiration for the blasted woman that had flowed in and out like a tide was back again.

Until Jill did something else to infuriate her.

She looked back at the skull.

She shivered again.

It might not be entirely unwelcome to have someone else in this place while she worked on the skull.

Think about it later.

Joe.

She reached for the phone Novak had given her.

<hr />

"What the hell is happening?" Joe said the instant he picked up the call. "Why aren't you using your computer? I want to *see* you."

"Well, I don't want to see you right now. Later we'll arrange face time on this smartphone," she said wearily. "But now you're going to be pissed off, and it's enough that I'll have to hear you. But I would have bitten the bullet and continued on the Skype if Novak hadn't said this phone he gave me was guaranteed not to be hacked. That was important."

Silence. "Why? No, don't answer that. First I want to know exactly how ill you were yesterday. That's what's important and was driving me crazy. What the hell happened to you?"

"And that will go back to why the new phone is necessary. I'll tell you everything. Just don't say anything until I've finished. Okay?"

"I'm listening," he said grimly. "But I don't think there's going to be anything okay about it."

And it wouldn't get any better, she thought. *Just go for it.* She dived in, and started, "It was right after I hung up from talking to you when I was at the hotel..."

He was ominously quiet as she related the entire story of the last twenty-four hours. When she stopped, he only asked, "That's all? Nothing else?"

"That's not enough? Say something."

"Give me a minute. Right now, anything I'd say would be obscene."

"I went down that road, too. But here I am, sitting here staring at this ugly skull that I hope is Nils Varak's." She added quietly, "Because I don't think I could bear it if I find out that it's not, and he's still out there. Yes, I was drawn into this by deceit and subterfuge, but in the end, that's the bottom line. I can't let a monster who almost butchered an entire nation walk away."

"You told me that you could have died," he said harshly. "I can't think of anything else right now."

"But I didn't." She had to batter through that protective side of him, which was always present and paramount and make him start looking at the entire picture. "But the fact that I came close makes me wonder if Hadfeld wasn't telling the truth as Jill thought. Even Jill can't figure out why anyone would try to hurt me just for doing those children's reconstructions here at Robaku. It was the perfect red herring."

"It certainly lured you," he said curtly. He didn't speak for a moment. Eve could almost hear the volatile storminess in that silence. "I want you out of there. But I'm not going to be able to persuade you to come, am I?"

"Not now. I have to be certain."

"Eve."

"I know. But I can't leave until I know the man who killed those children is dead, Joe." She said with sudden passion, "You told me yourself what a monster he was. Since I've been here, I've seen it with my own eyes. If you could have seen that schoolroom, you'd understand."

"Yes, he was a monster, and that monster is making you go through hell even now that he's dead."

"*If* he's dead."

"You wouldn't question those DNA results if Jill Cassidy hadn't conned you."

"She conned me to get me here. She's not conning me about her belief that Varak is still alive. Neither is Gideon or Novak. They're all very smart and taking big risks because they think Varak might not have been on that helicopter."

"They *should* be the ones to take the risks and not drag you into it."

"All I'm doing is the reconstruction, Joe."

"And you won't give that up," he said. "Okay. Then do the damn reconstruction. But I'm not going to trust anyone else to keep the heat off you while you're working on it. I'll take the next plane out."

"I didn't expect anything else," she said. "But it's not what I want, Joe. I believe that Novak will see that I'm safe. I don't want you involved in this."

"And I don't want you working on that reconstruction that could either get you thrown into jail or murdered. It's a standoff." He paused. "I'm involved in everything you do. It will always be that way. And prepare to see me involved up to my neck in this fiasco. I'll make a few preparations, call Jane and Michael, then I'll be leaving."

"Michael," Eve repeated. "Don't say anything to him that would worry—"

"He's already ahead of you. He called me yesterday and wanted us to take a trip to Maldara. I stalled him, but he won't be surprised that I'm leaving. It was almost a direct order that I go and take care of you."

"Shit."

"Exactly. That's why I have to call Jane and make sure she'll see that he won't try to find a way to join me."

"Heaven forbid."

"And why I have to wrap this up as quickly as possible. No doubts, no strings. Finished. I'll call you when I know when I'll arrive in Jokan. Bye, Eve." He cut the connection.

Michael.

Eve had realized that he might be a problem since they'd always had that special sensitivity to each other. But recently he had also been reaching out to Joe in a similar manner. She should have been just as worried about that as Joe's reaction. The mere idea of Michael's being here in Maldara frightened her. Her gaze flew back to the skull on the dais in front of her.

He liked to kill children.

She didn't want Michael anywhere *near* this place where so many children had died. Even if there proved to be no physical danger, he might sense that overpowering aura of death.

"How did it go with Quinn?" Novak had come in and was standing behind her. "As expected?"

She nodded. "He'll be on his way soon. He's not happy with any of us. He says this has to be wrapped up quickly. No doubts. No strings. Finished. That's the way Joe always works his cases." She stared into the skull's gaping, empty eyes. Evil. Death. Terror. Had those eyes looked out with pleasure at the bloody savagery he had created? That's what Jill had said, that's what Eve had felt, when she had stared into the darkness of that schoolroom. "Joe's right, Novak," she whispered. "No matter what I find, I can't stop until it's finished."

CHAPTER

9

Two hours later, Joe left Jane's apartment and headed for the taxi stand on the corner of the block.

"Could I give you a lift, Quinn?"

Joe tensed, then he whirled to see a dark-haired man standing beside the door of the apartment building. Joe's gaze raked his features with one quick glance. "You're Sam Gideon. What the hell are you doing here?"

"Easy." Gideon put up his hands. "Just offering you a lift as I said. I expected you to be a bit edgy but not on the attack. And how did you know who I was, anyway?"

"Did you think I wouldn't find out every detail about everyone Eve was connected with at Robaku?" he asked coldly. "I could tell that she was beginning to trust you. That made you dangerous. And now she tells me that you were responsible for getting her poisoned. That might make you dead."

"I don't blame you," Gideon said. "I screwed up. I was supposed to take care of her, and I didn't do it. I thought she was safe." He made a face. "I really don't want you to attack and make me defend myself. I'm pretty good these days, but you were a SEAL and can probably cause me intense bodily pain or death. Besides, I think Eve has forgiven me and might get pissed off if I end up seriously damaged. Wouldn't it be better to just put up with me and let me help you to get to her as soon as possible?"

"I'd have to think about it," Joe said. "The other option is much more tempting."

"I was afraid of that." Gideon sighed. "Novak warned me that you'd probably be major pissed off. But he also said you were smart and that might make a difference. How long is it going to take for you to think about it before I prepare for personal Armageddon?"

"I repeat, what are you doing here? The last thing I heard from Eve was that you were in Maldara." He was quickly processing the information he'd acquired about Sam Gideon. "You're the rich guy who was banging Zahra Kiyani. Not a good recommendation. I don't like what I hear about her." He added, "But you also pilot a Gulf Stream, and I assume the lift you offered wasn't just to the airport. How quickly can you get me to Maldara?"

"Shall I go down the list? One, yes, I am rich, and I did have an interlude with Zahra that might prove beneficial to us. Two, the reason I'm here is that Novak knew that when Eve agreed to do the reconstruction, it wasn't going to work unless we brought you into the mix ASAP. So he immediately sent me here to put myself at your disposal. Three, it took me seven hours and thirty minutes to get here from Maldara today, and I believe I can guarantee to get you back in the same time. Anything else?"

"Novak sent you? Then he owns you?"

"Was that meant to insult me?" Gideon smiled. "I have many talents, but I'm new to this game Novak knows so well. Yes, I let Novak own me because he's an expert at what he does. I'd let you own me if you show me you're better than Novak." His smile faded. "I'd let the devil himself own me if it meant that he could deliver Varak to me. Is that clear?"

Joe studied him. "It seems to be. I'll have to give it time to verify whether you're being honest or just telling me what I'd consider acceptable." He turned on his heel. "In the meantime, get me to Maldara. And seven hours and thirty minutes is not what I wanted to hear. So be prepared to spend that time filling me in on every phase of what you and Novak have been doing regarding that damn skull. Eve might be a major part of this, but I know Novak isn't waiting for verification or permission from his director. He's already on the move, isn't he?"

"You'd have to ask him."

"No, I'm asking you." Joe's smile was tiger bright. "And by the time we reach Maldara, I'll have answers. I believe we'll start with the DNA..."

———————◆———————

ROBAKU

"Hey, you said you were going to nap for a while. Isn't it time you stopped working?"

Eve looked up from the reconstruction to see Jill standing beside her. She realized she hadn't heard her leave her cot on the other side of the room. But then she had been so absorbed that she hadn't been aware of anything but the reconstruction in front of her. "Soon." She stretched her stiff neck around in a circle. "I got carried away with doing Varak's repairs. It took awhile. But I have a clean slate now. I can start with the measuring."

"He doesn't look clean to me." Jill was gazing at the blackened skull. "He still looks like something from a horror film." Her glance shifted to Eve. "And you're calling him Varak. I know you told me that you always have to name your reconstructions so that you can connect, but this is different, isn't it? You're assuming he *is* Varak?"

"No." Eve shrugged. "I didn't know what to name him, so I decided to give him the benefit of the doubt. If he is Varak, then I'll have it right; if he's not, then I still might be close." Her lips tightened. "Because it would be almost certain that he's a Varak victim, maybe even one of his butchers who was on that helicopter. Either way, this is a Varak entity."

"Complicated. Sort of a reconstruction with a split personality. But what else could we expect from Varak?" She asked curiously, "How does that affect you in making a connection with him?"

Eve felt herself stiffening. She quickly looked back at the skull. "I won't have to worry about that yet. There's a lot to do first. The measuring, the initial sculpting."

"And you'd prefer not to dwell on it," Jill said softly, reading her expression. "Have you ever done a reconstruction before on someone . . . like Varak?"

"You mean an evil son of a bitch who scared the hell out of me?" She moistened her lips. "Once. Several years ago. I hoped I'd never have to do it again. Call me crazy. But when a soul is that evil . . . it seems to linger . . . And I imagine Varak would be a million times worse." She straightened her shoulders. "I'll face that when it comes. Now I have work to do."

"After you sleep a few hours," Jill said. "You said soon."

"This isn't soon," Eve said flatly. "I let you stay with me, but I won't have you ordering me around."

"I'll back off. I just didn't want you to get too tired." Jill paused. "I was wondering after Joe Quinn called back and told you that he was on his way whether you might be waiting up for him. It will be a few hours yet before he gets here."

"I know that, Jill." She found her lips curving with amusement. "It's not as if I'm pining away and burning a candle to light his way."

"I wasn't certain," Jill said quietly. "You love him. I wasn't sure how that worked. I've heard it's different for different people."

Eve's brows lifted. "You've heard?"

She shrugged. "I had a major crush on a guy in college, but that went away fairly soon. And, though I'm usually too busy, I do love sex. But I've been around long enough to realize that it's more than that to some people. It would be for you."

"Yes, it is," Eve said. "But Joe and I have been together long enough that we don't need burning beacons to find each other in the darkness. We know who we are and where we are, and there's no question that we would ever lose each other. Burning beacons are fine, but they tend to be a little wistful." She chuckled. "We just go straight for the heart of the flames."

"Which is very difficult to research," Jill said. "Sorry that I misunderstood. But you have to admit I've been very good about keeping out of your way. You didn't even know I was here all night."

Eve couldn't deny it. Once Jill had set up her cot on the far side of the room and settled down, she had been totally silent. "The reality might have been better."

"Maybe. But you wouldn't have had anyone to keep you

company in warding off the monster." She smiled. "I know about monsters, too, Eve. Company can be a help." She turned away. "Could I get you a cup of coffee?"

Yes, Jill knew about monsters, Eve thought. They were unlike in so many ways, but in that one way, they were sisters. Sisters... That thought had come out of nowhere. They had both grown up fending for themselves and fighting for survival. It would have been nice to have someone like Jill there to share that struggle. She felt a sudden rush of warmth. "Coffee? No thanks. I've had too much caffeine tonight as it is." She leaned back on her stool. "For that matter, I've had more coffee since I met you than I've had in the last six months. I seem to need it to survive. Does that tell you anything?"

"Sorry. But you can't blame me entirely. You're a workaholic, and you do like your coffee. Can I get you a water?" She was going over to the ice chest. "If you're going back to work, I'll stay with you in case you need a reminder that you promised you'd nap. Is it okay if I drag up one of those chairs I got Hajif to bring up and sit and watch you? I promise I'll be quiet and won't ask questions." She took out two bottles of water from the chest and brought them back to the worktable. "Though it will be torture." She wrinkled her nose. "You know how curious I am."

Eve shrugged as she took the bottle of water. "I don't mind questions while I'm doing the basic measuring. It's almost automatic since I've done it so many times. And it's so important that I recheck it several times anyway. It's when I get into the layers that I have to concentrate."

"Good." Jill was dragging a chair over to the worktable. "I only had time for an overview of your work process while I was researching you, and I've been frustrated ever since. When I'm interested, I have to know everything." She plopped down on the chair. "Now tell me where we're going with this."

Eve laughed. "We? I wish it could be a joint operation. I could use a little help on this one." She paused. "Okay, I'll answer your questions, but then at some point you have to answer mine. You're not the only one who is curious. All I got was a thumbnail sketch about Jill Cassidy." She added mockingly, "And I have to know *everything*."

Jill was silent, wary. "That's not . . . easy."

"Take it or leave it."

"I'll take it. You have a right. But maybe not tonight." She smiled with an effort. "Now tell me why you have to concentrate on 'layers.'"

"Because it tells me what I need to know." She started to measure. "There are more than twenty points of the skull for which there are known tissue depths. Facial-tissue depth has been found to be fairly consistent in people the same age, race, sex, and weight. There are anthropological charts that give specific measurements for each point. For instance, in a Caucasian male like Varak, the tissue-depth thickness between the mid-philtrum point, which is the space between the nose and the top lip, is ten millimeters. The architecture of the bone beneath the tissue determines whether he has bulging eyes or jutting chin or whatever."

"What happens next?"

"I insert the depth markers and take strips of plasticine and apply them between the markers, then build up all of the tissue-depth points. Kind of like a connect the dots game in three dimensions."

"Only that's an enormous simplification," Jill said quietly.

Eve glanced at her. "Enormous," she agreed. "But that's the basic step. Then you worry about being absolutely true to your measurements and keeping track of the placement of facial muscles and how they influence the facial contour. And so on and so forth. Are you bored yet?"

"No way. I want to know about noses and mouths." Her gaze was narrowed on Eve's face. "But you're getting tired. You're fading. I can see it. I don't want to be an extra stress on you. I'll just sit here and watch quietly until you give up and go to bed."

She was right, Eve realized. She was suddenly feeling drained. She had thought she'd be fine for another hour or so, but if she wanted to finish these basic measurements, she needed to gather her strength and concentration. "Whatever." She shrugged. "Later."

She closed Jill out and focused entirely on the hideous skull before her. Strange, she never considered skulls hideous. It must be the thought of Varak . . .

Whatever it was, she wanted to be done with him for a while.

But the last measurements, which should have taken her another thirty minutes, stretched out to an hour. She was totally exhausted when she pushed back her chair. "Enough," she told Jill as she headed for her cot. "Now I need a nap."

"At last," Jill murmured as she flicked off the overhead light and followed Eve. "Can I get you anything? Another glass of water?"

"No . . . too tired." She crawled onto the cot. She was yawning as she pulled up the sheet. "You wanted to know about mouths and noses? They can be difficult. I'll tell you about it some other time . . ."

"You do that. Don't worry about it. That's another story. I can wait."

"Another story . . . Sounds like you. But sometimes the story turns out to be a mystery and has to be guesswork that you have . . ."

———

Eve was asleep.

Jill shook her head as she gazed down at her before she gently tucked the sheet higher around Eve's shoulders. She was glad that Eve had finally given in, but she wished it had been before she was this exhausted. Yet she'd known it had to be Eve who made the call. She turned and glided away from Eve's cot.

She should probably go back to her own cot across the room and try to get a few hours sleep herself, but she knew she was too wired to relax. Too much had been going on in the last twenty-four hours, and she hadn't had Eve's nonstop work to burn off adrenaline and energy.

And these nights, she had to be as exhausted as Eve had been before she could sleep without the nightmares coming.

Don't think about them. It was only a matter of time before she'd overcome that damn weakness.

Fresh air.

Clear her head and listen to the soothing night sounds.

She quickly moved past the worktable, avoiding looking at the Varak reconstruction as she headed for the door. Not now. She'd face that battle again later. He was part of this village's nightmare as well as her own personal nightmare. She needed to get away from him for a little while.

She drew a deep breath as the cool night air hit her face.

Bright moonlight.

Night sounds. Jungle sounds. Birds. Animals . . . Was that a monkey?

That was better. She could feel some of the tension leaving her. She sank down and leaned back against the stucco wall of the museum. Twenty minutes, and she'd be ready to go back inside and try to sleep . . .

"Is everything okay?"

She jumped.

Novak was a dark silhouette a few yards away.

"It would be if you didn't move like a damn panther," she said wryly. "I didn't hear you. What are you doing here?"

"Making phone calls. Checking on the sentries I set up. Waiting for Quinn to show up and raise hell. According to Gideon, he's as pissed off as we thought he'd be." He dropped down beside her. "I didn't think that you should be the only one to take the flak."

"I was prepared for it." She leaned her head back against the wall and gazed up at the night sky. "After all, it was my plan. When will Quinn be here?"

"Three or four hours. He would have gotten here sooner, but he's having Gideon drop him off at our private airfield at Baldar and will make his way here on his own."

She frowned. "Why?"

He shrugged. "He was a SEAL. His instincts are to go in and make that first strike before anyone knows he's hit the ground running. He'll want to slip in and look the situation over. Particularly where Eve is concerned, and he trusts no one in Jokan." He grimaced. "And that includes us."

She studied his expression. "And you'd do the same?"

"Certainly. I have a few problems with trust myself." He was suddenly bending toward her, his eyes narrowed on her face. "You didn't answer me. Is everything okay? I saw the lights go out in the museum, and I thought you'd both be going to sleep."

"Eve's asleep. I thought I'd get some air before I tried to settle down."

His gaze was still searching her face. "Why?"

She was suddenly aware of something different about him tonight, a tension, a recklessness, and that tough ruthlessness that was such a part of him seemed more obvious than usual. It was making her uneasy. "For goodness sake, because I wanted some air. Stop interrogating me, Novak."

"But I do it so well," he said mockingly. "Check my credentials. Though I'm better with Al-Qaeda and Isis. You're really not worth my expertise." He changed the subject. "You didn't think Quinn would go easy on you?"

"Why should he? I think Eve is beginning to forgive me, but I knew her family might never do that. I can take any flak Quinn hands out."

"Yeah, you're just collateral damage," Novak said bitterly. "How could I forget?"

"I don't know. I guess because it seems to bother you." She was trying to keep her tone light. "We've discussed this before. In your job, you usually accept it as a fact of life. Yet you seem to be making some kind of exception for me." Her gaze shifted to his face. "You were even kind to me those days in Nairobi. Extraordinarily kind."

"Imagine that," he said dryly. "Since I'm sure you didn't deserve it. You've caused me nothing but trouble since the day you came to me with that wild tale about Hadfeld. And when you showed up at the U.N., I was ready to break your neck."

"I know." She moistened her lips. "But I had to do it."

"You made that clear. No debt left unpaid." He added harshly, "What did you say? You'd been alone all your life, but I hadn't left you alone when you needed someone that night. So I had to have my payoff, too."

"I was grateful. I don't understand why it upset you."

"Then you should have thought about it," he said curtly. "I *know* you, Jill. You forget that I was there with you after those therapy sessions that shrink put you through in Nairobi before he'd release you. I know what kind of life you've led."

His words were suddenly spitting like bullets. "Talk about collateral damage. You trailed all over the world behind your father from the time you were four, and he paid more attention to his camera than he did to you. It's no wonder that you were so confused you had to develop your own concept of who you are and how to survive. You had to fend for yourself."

"I never said that," she said quickly.

"No, but you made a few slips, and after I left Nairobi, I did a check to fill in the blanks. Your father never even made provisions for you if anything happened to him. When he was killed in Tibet, you ended up in an orphanage in Hong Kong for over a year until you managed to convince the local U.S. ambassador that you were a U.S. citizen. You were only eleven years old, and you had to do it yourself."

"My father never intentionally hurt me," she said quietly. "I just wasn't high on his list of priorities. Some men aren't meant to be parents. I'm not a victim, Novak."

"No, you didn't let yourself be a victim even when you were bouncing through five foster homes, who accepted you only for the paycheck and treated you less decently than that orphanage in Hong Kong."

Novak was really on the attack, she realized in bewilderment. His intensity was overpowering, and she could almost feel the electricity he was generating. What was happening with him? Suddenly, she didn't care. He had no right to bring back the memories she kept firmly tucked away. She sat up straight. "You're damned right I didn't let myself be a victim," she said fiercely. "You're only a victim if you don't learn from a bad experience. It was one of the first things I found out when I was a kid. Do you know how I won that Pulitzer?"

"You wrote a series on the corruptions in the DFAC system," Novak said. "I made the connection. But it wasn't enough. Not unless it ended with your own foster parents ending up in jail."

"Maybe they did. I don't know. I wrote the series years later. I was past any desire to punish individuals. I just wanted to punish the system, so it couldn't happen again to someone else."

"I wouldn't be so forgiving." His smile was suddenly savage. "As a matter of fact, I have to admit to taking down their names for future reference."

"What?" she said, shocked. "You're joking?"

"If you want jokes, call on Gideon. As you've said, I don't tend to be soft and easy. I grew up on the streets of Detroit, and I guarantee that everyone who ever caused me problems ended up regretting it."

"I can believe it. But these are *my* problems, Novak."

He shrugged. "I've decided you're entirely too philosophical and I should take over the handling of this type of difficulty myself."

She gazed at him in disbelief. "Are you crazy? Not if it's my business."

"It's all how you view it. That doesn't seem to make any difference to me." He added through set teeth, "Which really is beginning to piss me off."

"I'm the one who should be pissed off. You're not making sense. Why are you being like this?"

"It was bound to come out sooner or later. I've been holding it in too long." His lips twisted. "I don't *want* this. I want it to be like it was when I first met you over a year ago." His light eyes were glittering. "You were smart and gutsy, and I wanted to go to bed with you three minutes after I met you. That was all I wanted, very simple and clean, with no complications. That's what should have happened."

"What?" She inhaled sharply. "You never said anything. You never made a move."

"We were both busy and at opposite ends of the country most of the time." He smiled sardonically. "But tell me you didn't know it was there waiting to happen."

She was silent. The words had shocked her, but she couldn't deny that what he'd said was true. Yes, she had known, but she had refused to acknowledge it. She had instinctively blocked even thinking about him sexually. She was still doing it. Because along with that instant explosive sexual attraction had come the realization that he would demand too much of her. She had a career she was passionate about, and he wasn't like anyone else she had ever met. He . . . disturbed her. Novak was too difficult, and she had not wanted to have to deal with him. She swallowed. "Well, then it was a good thing that it never got past that first three minutes."

"The hell it is," he said roughly. "If we'd just gone to bed together, then it might have been over by this time. It wouldn't be like this. I don't like feeling what I'm feeling now. It's too damn complicated. And I don't have any way to control it."

"I don't know what you're talking about. All I'm getting out of it is that you're angry and it's somehow my fault that we didn't jump into the sack together. That's not complicated, it's plain nuts. And it's bullshit that you're not in control. You're always in control of yourself and everyone around you."

"If I were in control, we wouldn't even be having this conversation. After Nairobi, I swore to myself that it wasn't going to happen, that you were off-limits, that you were walking wounded, and that's how I had to treat you."

She stiffened. "Walking wounded?"

"What do you think? It *killed* me to see you like that. I didn't expect to feel that way."

"Walking wounded," she repeated. "You son of a bitch. How do you have the nerve to say that?"

"With extreme trepidation. You don't want anyone to know you're not invulnerable. It doesn't go along with the story you've created to always keep your personal world in order. But I was there with you when you woke from those nightmares. You're still having them, aren't you? I think I might have held on if you hadn't lied to me tonight." His eyes were blazing. "That's why you came out here, not because you wanted a breath of air."

She didn't answer him. "I'm *not* walking wounded. So you can stuff your pity, Novak."

"You're not listening. Don't worry. There wasn't pity even when I was there with you in that hospital. I don't know what it was. I was just...aching and wanting to kill someone, anyone." He added fiercely: "And there's sure as hell no pity now, or I wouldn't have decided to toss out all that crap about going through this by myself. I don't know what I was thinking. So I'm going to be my usual selfish self and take what I want any way I can get it."

"Going through what by yourself?"

"I *feel* something for you, dammit." He added fiercely, "It's that same sexual attraction multiplied about a thousand times, all mixed up with what I felt in that hospital and what I've learned to feel about you since then. You don't want pity? Great. Because sex was my first choice anyway. Though I doubt if we can go back to square one. It probably wouldn't be enough for me." He was suddenly on his feet, looking down at her. "I just had to give you warning that if you really are walking wounded, you should get away from me. Run, not walk. Because these days, whenever I look at you, I want to take you to bed. If I can talk you into it, that's where we'll end up. And I don't know where we'll go from there because I'm not sure I'll be able to let you go after that." He reached out his hand and pulled her to her feet. "And now you'd better go in and get to bed. You shouldn't have to worry about having nightmares unless they're about me. I've given you enough to think about to distract you." His voice was suddenly low and intense. "But remember that I'd never hurt you, and it would always be your choice."

Electricity. Intimacy. His hand grasping hers was warm, vital, and she could feel her pulse pounding in her wrist. He must feel it, too, because his thumb was rubbing back and forth on the pulse point. She was shaking, her breasts firming, tightening. He was too close... No, he wasn't close enough.

She needed to pull away from him. Why didn't she do it? Because her emotions were in such a shambles that her responses were purely physical. She couldn't think, she could only feel. Don't let him see it. She had sworn she'd never be weak again, and no one was more dominant than Novak. She nodded jerkily. "Of course it's my choice. And you won't hurt me because if you did, I'd pull out the Beretta in my jacket pocket and shoot your nuts off."

He blinked. "Point taken." Then he threw back his head and laughed. "And that side of you is another reason why I'm finding handling you so complicated."

"Then don't try to handle me." She turned toward the door. She had to get away from him. Because she wanted his hands on her again, dammit. He had only touched her hand and wrist, yet her pulse was still pounding crazily. "I was right, the first time. It was good that it never really started. It would never have worked out."

"Maybe." Then he was smiling recklessly. "But this is a

new game with new rules. And we can change those rules as we go along. Anything you want to do." He reached out and gently touched her cheek with his index finger. "Go to sleep. I had to be honest with you, but I'm not going to let it get in the way of what we have to do. Good night, Jill. If I can deter Quinn, I'll try to do it."

Her skin was warming, throbbing beneath that gossamer-light touch. She moved her head to avoid it. She had an idea that "honesty" couldn't help but get in the way. It was as if he had ripped down a safe, sheltering barrier between them and left only heat, electricity, and vibrant awareness. "I told you I didn't need your help." She opened the door. "Good night, Novak."

"Jill."

She looked over her shoulder.

He was standing there, lean, muscular, infinitely male. "I just wanted to tell you that you've convinced me." His smile was both intimate and knowing. "After careful observation, I can see you're no victim and definitely not walking wounded. What a relief." He turned away. "Let the games begin…"

Games? Jill's pulse was pounding, and her breath was uneven as she closed the door behind her. This wasn't any game she wanted to play. No, that was a lie. It was obviously one that she wanted passionately to play in every single physical way possible. She just couldn't permit it to happen.

If she could stop it. Because Novak had decided that wasn't the way he wanted it. Screw it. It was only sex, dammit. Why didn't she just go back outside to him and find somewhere to make it happen?

Because it was never only sex to her, and she couldn't risk its being anything more to her with Novak.

I wanted to go to bed with you three minutes after I met you.

That had been an exaggeration. He'd been too angry with her during those first three minutes on that mountain in Botzan. And she'd only been concerned with persuading him to get out of her way so that she could get to that bandit, Abdi Zolak, and keep him from getting killed...

BOTZAN MOUNTAINS
ELEVEN MONTHS AGO

"What the hell are you doing here?" Jed Novak was skidding down the hill toward Jill. His blue eyes were glittering with fury in his taut face as he pulled her down behind a banyan tree. "Do you want to get killed? There's a band of roving bandits camped up on that hill. I gave orders that this area was to be cleared."

"I know you did, Novak," Jill said impatiently. "You didn't make any secret about it in any of the villages I had to go through to get here." She jerked her arm away from him. "You wanted to send a message to Zolak that the big, bad CIA were on their way and that he'd better not throw in his lot with those Botzan mercenaries. He was just to meekly give up his weapons and let you take him down." Her eyes went back to the top of the hill. No movement. But there probably wasn't much time before Zolak would get edgy that she hadn't shown up yet. "Only he won't do that, and you're stupid if you think he will. He's too scared of not dying a brave death that will make his sons proud of him." But Jill knew that Novak's reputation was that he was far from stupid. She had only seen him from a distance since he'd arrived in Maldara, but she'd made it her business to research him. He was superintelligent, and the word was that he'd been sent here to Maldara by Langley to try to find a way to stop this hideous war. So reason with him. Persuade him. It was her only hope to get Abdi Zolak home to his

village. Her gaze shifted back to Novak's face. "He'll fight you. He has fifty-two men in this band he's gathered. There would be deaths on both sides." She leaned forward, her voice urgent. "But I can keep that from happening, Novak. The only reason he's here at all is that he agreed to come down from his hideout and meet with me. Wouldn't it be better to let me go up there and talk to him?" She wasn't getting a response. Okay, try harder. "Look, I'm Jill Cassidy, and I'm a reporter, not some missionary out to save Zolak's soul. I know he's been a thief and a bandit most of his adult life. But he's always taken care of his family and his village. And he's not a murderer . . . yet. But if he joins those mercenaries, he'll become what they want him to be. Here in Maldara, that means butchery. And the only people who can stop him are his wife and family. He cares about them. I might be able to talk him into going back to them so they'll have a chance to do it."

"I know exactly who you are, Jill Cassidy." Novak's eyes were fixed on her face. "I had reports on you from my men watching that village down the road. I'm used to handling reporters getting in my way, but I didn't think I'd have to deal with one who seems ready to get herself killed for the damn story." He looked up at the hill, then turned back to her. "I have credible info that Zolak is up there, and I'm going to go get him. I have orders to find any way I can to keep those mercenaries from recruiting any more local people to add fuel to the fire that's burning up this country. Zolak's an experienced fighter, he's exactly what they're looking for." His voice hardened. "And I don't give a damn about Zolak's soul or the story you're hoping to get from him. I'd prefer you stay alive, but that's up to you."

"I'm not going to get myself killed. Not if you stay out of my way." She had to get through to him. In spite of his coldness, she could tell that Novak was listening, his face was very intent. She had an idea he always listened, was always thinking, trying to put everything together. "Zolak only became involved in this war because he thought that it would be just like the raids he'd been doing most of his life here in the mountains. From the time he was a young boy, that was what he was taught. But he didn't count on all the deaths, and the slaughter of children all around him when this country exploded. He told his wife it made him sick. There's no way he wants to join those cutthroat mercenaries Botzan hired. He wants out if we can find a way to bring him home honorably." She reached out, and her hand closed on his arm. "Help me to do that, Novak. I've heard you're smart and have enough influence to pull it off. Or just let me do it on my own."

He was silent, gazing down at her hand on his arm. Then he looked up at the top of the hill. "You said he agreed to meet with you?"

She drew a relieved breath. "Yes, but he said I'd have to come alone. I've been writing my stories from his home village for the last month. I've grown to know his wife and children. They're the ones who told me how he felt about the war. I talked to him on the phone myself last week. He wants to go home to protect his own village from all the Varaks of the world. I believe him." She added: "But he's very proud, he could be forced to go the other way if we don't let him keep his dignity."

Novak's eyes were narrowed on her face. "You think you know him that well?"

"Some stories are easier than others to read. Will you stay here and let me go up there?"

His lips indented in the faintest smile. "What would you do if I didn't?"

"Find a way to go around you. But I don't think I'll have to do that. You have a job to do, and you'll do it. What do you care if some egotistical reporter thinks she can do it better?" She paused. "As long as you think I'll get Zolak to go home, you're going to let me go up that hill." She took her gun from her pocket and handed it to him. "Will you keep this until I get back? Zolak said I can't be armed."

Novak looked down at the gun for an instant. "Then of course you have to obey his rules." He put the Beretta in his jacket pocket. *"Go on. You don't want Zolak to get nervous. You can tell him that I'll work out something for him once he's back at his village if you think it will help."*

"It will help."

"Good." Then he reached for his automatic rifle and settled down on his stomach, sighting down the scope before lifting his head to look at her. *"But you'll have to put up with me covering you for the entire time you're up there with Zolak. I'd find explaining away the death of a reporter much too awkward."*

"Don't interfere, Novak."

"Did I say I'd interfere? I'll give you your chance. But we've just met, and how do I know whether or not I'd regret it if Zolak decided to kill you? I do hate regrets." He smiled. *"But you'll learn what I hate most is to lose an opportunity."*

She inhaled sharply. She wasn't sure what he meant. Yet she found she couldn't look away from him. The intensity, the force, the intelligence that was far more interesting than just good looks. She wanted to stay and see what else was there . . .

He nodded at the hill. *"Get going. It will be fine. I've got your back."*

She hesitated for only a second, then she was turning and swiftly climbing the hill. She could see the bushes move as Zolak's sentries spotted her. She felt she was safe from Zolak, but she didn't know how nervous those sentries would be.

Forget it. Think of what she had to say to Zolak. How to persuade him to save his life and that of his family. How to keep him from joining those butchers. She couldn't worry about anything else right now.

Not even that strange, intimate moment before she had left Novak.

Besides, she found that anxiety was ebbing away. She could

almost feel Novak down there, watching her, aiming that rifle, protecting her. With every step she took, she was beginning to have a feeling that everything was going to be okay. She was going to pull this off. She was going to be able to convince Zolak to change his story or start a new one.

And somehow it all had something to do with the fact that this time she wasn't alone and that Novak had been there for her. Strange. When she was almost always alone.

You'll learn what I hate most is to lose an opportunity, Novak had said.

Well, so do I.

But at this moment, my opportunity is with Zolak waiting for me on that hill. I don't have time for you.

But I do admit it does feel good that right now you have my back, Novak.

———◆———

And that day Jill had talked Abdi Zolak out of going to join the mercenaries and gone with him back to his village to get him settled with his family. But the next week she'd been sent to Jokan to cover an attack. Novak was right, they'd been at opposite ends of the country for almost a year, only seeing each other casually.

But there had been nothing casual about him tonight, nor the way she was feeling. Which was an indication she should regard it as even more dangerous. Damn right, they couldn't let it affect the work they had to do.

So forget everything but getting rid of the monster who might already be knocking on their door.

———◆———

DAWN

The first pearl shading of dawn was lighting the sky as Joe punched in Jed Novak's number. He'd just done an initial reconnoitering of Robaku. "Your security sucks, Novak," he said curtly. "Two sentries? And they were deaf and blind. I could have taken them down in my sleep. Is this how you're supposedly keeping Eve safe?"

"No," Novak said. "There's another sentry nearer to the museum that you didn't see who informed me that you were near the village. Plus there's another guard down the road furnishing surveillance on anyone approaching from Jokan. I'm also using a drone that's equipped with an infrared monitor to make a pass over the village every ten minutes. It just identified you as an unknown object and will notify those three sentries immediately."

"Two of whom would already be dead," Joe said. "But the drone is a decent idea if you increase the number of flyovers."

"I'll consider it." He paused. "And those sentries are good men, you're just better. If you're through critiquing my arrangements, would you like to come and have a civilized discussion? Where are you?"

"In the palmettos behind you." Joe moved out of the trees. "And I'm not feeling particularly civilized at the moment." He swiftly covered the yards that separated him from Novak. "But we might as well get this over with before I go to see Eve." His gaze went to the stucco building behind Novak. "That's the museum?"

"Yes, but you probably already know that. I imagine you had Gideon draw you a map of the village or you wouldn't have been so familiar with it. And you have plenty of time. Eve's asleep, and Jill said she's been pushing too hard and really needs it."

"That should make you both very happy," Joe said bitterly.

"It doesn't. We don't want to drive her to exhaustion," Novak said. "But the sooner we get this over with and have an answer, the better for all of us. We can't do that without Eve." He met Joe's eyes. "I realize you want her out of here, but you don't have a chance until she finds out if that skull she's working on is Varak's. I believe you know that."

"Oh, I do. Because you have her caught in your net. So by all means let's move fast. Tell me what else you're doing other than depending on my wife. You wouldn't be able to stand in the background any more than I would. You'd go straight to find the scientist who could have created the DNA evidence. Gideon said he knew you'd been investigating, but no details." His lips twisted. "He said you were a very secretive man. Imagine that."

"Wouldn't it only be practical to wait for Eve to give us some evidence of proof?"

"But that's not your style. I'm surprised you didn't ask for the money to pay off Hadfeld in the beginning. Politics in the director's office?"

Novak nodded. "The U.N. was being difficult. And I'd already been accused of being something of a fanatic about Varak." His lips tightened. "But Jill wouldn't wait. She went for it herself. Which ended with her going after Eve."

"Big mistake," Joe said. "I still haven't decided what I'm going to do about that. But I do know that if that reconstruction is not Varak, I'm not going to stand around and wait for politicians to decide what to do. I've got to be ready. So go back to the DNA evidence. Who do you believe to be responsible?"

Novak gazed speculatively at him. "No questions about the possibility of even being able to defeat the mighty DNA? What do you know about falsifying DNA evidence?"

"Enough," Joe said curtly. "I had a murder case two years

ago in which I was positive I knew who the murderer was but couldn't prove it. I *knew* that Richard Sander had killed his wife. But the DNA blood evidence seemed infallible. So I assumed that it was a big lie and went out to prove it."

"And you did it? Interesting. How?"

"Followed the money. I traced a bank draft from Sander to Tel Aviv to a dummy company. Then, when I started digging, I found out that one of the scientists, Sol Goldfarb, who had set up the company, had previously worked for an Israeli think tank that created a way of proving whether or not DNA evidence had been falsified." He shrugged. "And if you know how to prove that, then it's the next step to be able to create a better way to do it yourself."

"And did you get your killer convicted?"

"No, I had an extradition problem getting Goldfarb out of Israel. But I'm still watching him. I'll do it someday." His expression became more serious. "And then I'll hang them both out to dry."

"I'm sure you will," Novak said. "And Israel did do some groundbreaking work in that direction. You must have learned a lot while you were trying to gather in Goldfarb. But I don't think that the person who falsified the DNA on Varak is in Israel. I'm betting on Egypt."

"Why?"

"Because Yusef Dobran is the most talented scientist I've ever run across in that line of work. His execution is nearly foolproof. He's also the most expensive, and it would take big money to hire him. He's got money to burn these days, and he can afford to be picky. Besides, anyone undertaking a replication of Varak's DNA would think twice about doing it. Not only would it be dangerous because of the conse- quences of being caught, but the first thing Varak would do is eliminate the witnesses."

"Then why would Dobran do it?"

"I have no idea. Fear? Blackmail? A staggering amount of money that he just couldn't refuse? We'll have to find out."

"If he's still alive."

Novak nodded. "He's alive. He's rich enough to be able to afford excellent protection and lives in an exclusive area just outside Cairo, with a bevy of bodyguards." He paused. "But everyone has an Achilles heel. He has an assistant, Hassan Sebak, who's willing to cooperate for the right price."

"And he's already told you Dobran did the job?"

"No, he's very cautious. But he did tell us that Dobran had recently done a very big job. For a price, he's willing to find a way to bypass Dobran's guards and get me in to see him. After that, it's up to me to find out if he did the job and who hired him." He paused. "Or up to you, Quinn."

"You'd rather risk my neck than your own?"

"Any day of the week." He smiled faintly. "But I realize it's your decision. We'll play it your way. My highest priority is keeping Eve working, and I'll do that any way I can. I don't want you to persuade her to do anything else."

"You must realize that's bullshit," Joe said impatiently. "Jill Cassidy researched her, and you know exactly what Eve will do. I've done all the persuading I can, and now I have to jump in and help her try to stay afloat."

"She thought that would be your plan, so I'm offering you the opportunity. I'll send Gideon with you to Cairo along with any backup you need. Find out what you can about Dobran and everything he knows. It's not many men I'd trust to go after him, but you'll be able to do it. I'll stay with Eve and protect her while she's finishing the reconstruction." He paused. "Or you can stay here and hold her hand, and I'll go to Cairo."

"And that remark is obviously aimed at sending me down

the road. I'll think about it." He started toward the museum. "But right now, I want to see Eve."

"Not yet." Novak was suddenly moving past him. "Give me ten minutes. Jill insisted on staying with Eve to protect her, and I don't want her shooting you. I'll go and get her out of there." He disappeared into the museum.

Joe muttered a curse. Patience. But he was not feeling patient. Ten minutes? He didn't want to stand here twiddling his thumbs. He wanted to see Eve *now*. He wanted to talk to her, see her face, and he wanted to know why she was willing to risk everything for this madness.

If you could have seen that schoolroom, you'd understand.

The schoolroom. The place that had horrified and captured Eve in a way that Novak and Jill Cassidy would never have been able to do.

The schoolroom...

He turned on his heel and started down the path.

———

"Joe..."

He was near her. The familiar scent of him surrounded her. Eve could feel his warmth, sense the strength...

"Shh," he said softly. "It's not time to wake up yet. Just let me hold you..."

He was here, gently sliding onto the cot and turning her into his arms. Safety...Love...Home...

Her arms slid around him, and she nestled closer. "Not much room on this...cot, Joe."

"We'll manage." His lips brushed her temple. "We always manage. Though I agree it's not conducive to doing what I've been wanting to do since I left you in Atlanta. So just rest a little longer and let me hold you. That will be good, too."

Yes, they always managed to be together. And it was wonderful just having him here beside her.

She relaxed against him and lay still, listening to his heartbeat. "Jill was . . . here. Where is she?"

"I have no idea. Nor do I care." He kissed her ear. "I believe Novak removed her from the premises to avoid conflict."

"She meant well."

"And she's won you over," he said grimly. "She won't find me that easy."

"I wasn't easy. She just proved to me that I wouldn't be able to live with myself if I didn't do the reconstruction." She rubbed her cheek against his shoulder. "I have to do it, Joe."

"I know." He was silent a moment. "I saw the schoolhouse. I could see the effect it would have on you." Then he burst out, "Hell, it tore *me* apart."

"It's the children," she whispered. "I keep thinking about Michael. Outside of the home, a schoolroom is where a child feels safest. What if Michael had been in that classroom facing Varak with those other children? You wouldn't be able to keep from trying to stand between them either, Joe."

"No, I wouldn't." Joe was silent again. "Then let's get moving and make sure no one else will ever have to face him." He brushed a strand of hair away from her forehead and gave her a kiss on the tip of her nose. "So much for you getting a little extra rest." He carefully released her and moved off the cot. "That wasn't going to happen, was it? Lights?"

"Wall switch beside the door." She was already missing the *feel* of him. She saw him silhouetted against the faint light pouring into the glass of the windows as he lithely crossed the room. It must be almost dawn. "I slept longer than I intended anyway." She sat up and swung her legs to the floor. "I've got to get back to work."

The lights flashed on, and Joe's gaze immediately zeroed in on the skull on her dais. "This is him?" He went to the workbench and examined the reconstruction. "You've only done the basic measuring..." he murmured. "You have a long way to go."

"Not so long," she said defensively. "I had repairs. It will go faster now."

"I'm not on the attack," he said. "I'm just trying to gauge the time frame I have to work with." He paused. "Novak wants me to go and check out a scientist who might have been capable of doing the DNA substitution. Did you know anything about that?"

"Not about the DNA." She had to be honest with him. "But I told him I didn't want you hovering over me while I did the reconstruction. I would have trouble concentrating. Is what he wants you to do something that would be helpful?"

He nodded slowly. "It would have been my first move anyway. I just don't like leaving you again." He was still looking down at the skull, thinking. "But Novak seems to have your security well in hand." His lips twisted. "And your friend, Jill, is apparently ready to stand guard over you. Which is only right considering that she got you into this."

"I don't think I could call her a friend, but she will protect me as much as she's able." She met his gaze. "I'll be okay here, Joe. Don't worry about me."

"Of course I'll worry about you," he said roughly. "You're barely recovered from being poisoned. You look exhausted and pale, and you'll drive yourself until you get this finished." He tapped the skull. "But I can't help you do it, so I'll have to go and find another way to reach the same goal. I suppose I'll head for Cairo."

"Cairo?" Eve repeated. "Egypt? That's where you're going to find this scientist?"

He nodded. "Yusef Dobran. Why the surprise?"

"Not surprise really. But Egypt has been turning up in the conversation ever since I got here. Zahra Kiyani has a passion for it. But it had nothing to do with Cairo."

"One can never tell where a passion will take you." He turned away from the reconstruction. "I'll go tell Novak I'll head to Cairo to talk to his scientist. I'll be back before I leave."

"You'd better. Otherwise, I'll track you down."

"Promises. Promises." He smiled at her over his shoulder. "It's going to be okay, Eve. And that's another promise."

She watched him walk out the door. She wanted to go running after him, to touch him again... Instead, she got to her feet and headed for the bathroom to wash up and change her clothes. They both had their jobs to do, and the sooner they were done, the sooner they could be together.

It was best that Joe was leaving, she told herself. Best that he wasn't going to stay here in the center of the hurricane, where she had to be with the reconstruction. After all, it was what she had wanted.

But Joe never stayed out of the eye of the hurricane for long. How did she know there wasn't a worse storm waiting for him in Cairo?

CHAPTER

10

Joe saw Novak standing by the path the moment he left the museum. "I'm going to Cairo."

"I thought you might. I'll call Gideon unless you prefer someone else to accompany you. He's been involved with investigating Dobran from the beginning. He's very good, and he has advantages that my other men don't have."

"Money and contacts?"

Novak nodded. "Those, too. But I was thinking that he learns from every situation and adapts to find a way to win the next one. Didn't you find that to be true?"

Joe nodded. "Gideon will do." He looked him in the eye. "As long as you make it clear that he obeys my orders instead of yours. And as long as I find him valuable. The minute I find he fails me in either category, I'll send him back to you and work on my own." He paused. "He wouldn't tell me anything on the way here. He lies very well, but he's obviously clever, and I realized he'd know more about you than what he told me."

"I'm glad you didn't force the issue with him. I like Gideon, I might have had to address it with you." He added, "Yes, he knew. As you say, he's clever, and I needed him. But he's his own man, and I'll let him know that he can trust you. You'll have to forge your own relationship with him."

Joe nodded. "Whatever. And I'll need to know everything there is to know about Yusef Dobran and his assistant, Hassan Sebak. Right away."

"What Gideon doesn't know, he'll find out for you. When do you leave?"

"In the next hour or so."

"I'll assign someone to take you back to the airport and let Gideon know you're coming. Backup?"

"Get someone local to Cairo that Gideon can call if needed. I'll let him know when I think—"

"Hello. You're Joe Quinn?" It was a woman's voice from the path behind him. "I'm Jill Cassidy. We've never officially met." She was coming out of the brush from the direction of the village. She slanted a cool look at Novak. "You lied to me, Novak. Hajif didn't need to see me. I told you I wasn't going to hide from Quinn." She turned back to Joe. "You deserve to meet the person who hurt Eve and manipulated your family." She lifted her chin. "Is there anything you'd like to say to me? Whatever it is, I'll listen and agree with every word. There's no apology I can make that will make what I did any better." She held his gaze, and said quietly, "But I owe you, and I promise I'll find a way to make it right."

"Believe me, she will, Quinn," Novak said dryly. "Which isn't always a good thing."

"You're right." Joe was gazing straight in her eyes. "Your apology sucks. What you did to Eve is unforgiveable. Eve may have come up with some way to find excuses for you, but I won't. If you need to kill a snake, then cut its head off. Don't make Eve do it for you. You could have gotten her killed."

"I know that," Jill said steadily. "It's all my fault. And even if I wanted to stop her now, I couldn't do it. It's too late. All I can promise is that I'll take care of her."

"Yes, you will," Joe said fiercely. His hands clenched into fists as the rage tore through him. His gaze went from her to Novak and back again. "Because you're right, it is too late. So Eve is going to do what you asked her, and I'm going to find where the snake is hiding. And you will both make certain that nothing happens to Eve. Not a scratch, do you hear? If anything does, then I'll come after you, and I'll never stop until I kill you." He whirled back toward the museum. "Call Gideon, Novak. I need to get out of here."

Eve was coming out of the bathroom when Joe walked into the museum. "That was quick," she said warily as she studied his expression. "What's wrong?"

"Nothing. It's just time that I left." He took her into his arms. "No, that's a lie. I just ran into Jill Cassidy and blew my cool." He held her close. "And uttered dire threats if she and Novak didn't take care of you." His arms tightened. "And meant every one of them."

"I'm sure you did." She looked up at him. "They both want to keep me safe, Joe. Just take care of yourself."

"Always." He kissed her. "I'll call you when I can. Try not to work too hard." He cupped her face in his two hands. "Yeah, that's not likely. I'll see you soon, love."

She nodded and blinked to keep back the tears. "I'm sorry that I pulled you into this, Joe."

"I'm not. I just wish it had happened sooner." He pulled her close again for a long moment, then he was turning away.

"I'll call Michael on the way to Cairo and reassure him that you're doing well."

"I'll have to call him again myself soon. It was just difficult..." She made a face. "He'd see right through me and worry."

He nodded. "He does that anyway even long-distance." He suddenly whirled back and was across the room again. He kissed her, long, hot, passionately, then he let her go. "Change your mind. Let me take you out of here. I'll find another way to do this."

Her arms tightened around him. "What if you can't? I have that skull here, now. Give me the time, and I can do this. You know I can."

He muttered a curse and pushed her away from him. "Yes, you can do it. I thought I'd try one more time." He turned away again. "Hell, I would have tried sex if it wasn't for that damn cot and a whole roomful of skulls glaring down at us."

Eve shook her head with a smile. "The cot was a problem, but the kids wouldn't have been glaring; children usually think sex is funny." Her smile faded as her gaze fell on the Varak reconstruction on the dais. She suddenly shivered. "But I think he might have been a challenge."

"No, he wouldn't. We wouldn't let him," Joe said. "But I prefer you not have the distraction. He bothers you. So get rid of him, and when I come back, we'll discuss the other hurdles to overcome." He paused at the door and looked back at the reconstruction. He smiled, then deliberately gave the Varak skull the finger. "Get rid of him," he repeated. "He's no threat to you. Alive or dead, we won't let him touch you."

Then he was gone.

———

Jill opened the door of the museum ten minutes later. "Quinn is on his way," she said. "Novak got him out of the village as soon as he could. I think he was afraid he'd have to protect me from him and that would have caused all kinds of trouble with you." She hadn't moved from the doorway. "Am I allowed to come in? I have to do it anyway because I have to be near you. But I hope that you'll still permit me to do it. I know that Quinn was terribly angry with me."

"For heaven's sake, come in." Eve shook her head with exasperation. "And you should have expected him to be angry. Your research should have told you that Joe can be very cool most of the time, but he has his limits."

"And you're definitely one of those limits." Jill shook her head. "No, you're the supreme limit. I did realize it, I just hadn't experienced it." She came into the room. "It's going to take me a long time to find a way to get him to forgive me."

"No question." She sat down at her worktable. "Does it matter?"

"Yes. Making amends is always important. I'll just have to do something very good that will make up for the bad. It's all a question of balance. The monks taught me that when I was a kid."

"Monks?"

"In Tibet. They were cool dudes." She looked at Eve with a frown. "You haven't had breakfast yet, have you?"

"I'll eat later."

She shook her head. "You'll get involved and put it off. I'll go down and get some fruit from Hajif, then send someone to Jokan for something more substantial." She frowned. "Tea or coffee? I can make you decaf."

"Tea will be fine. And now isn't the time for decaf."

"No, it isn't." She started to turn away. "Thank you for not letting him turn you against me. I know that I'm nothing to you, and he's everything. But you won't be sorry. I'll keep you safe."

"Just don't let anyone disturb me until Varak is finished. That's all I need from you." She grimaced. "And that's all Joe will want also. To have this over."

Jill shook her head. "But he wants something else more. He told Novak and me he'd kill both of us if you got even a scratch while we were taking care of you." She smiled. "So I have to make certain to pay attention to his priorities even if they conflict with yours." She headed for the door. "I'll be right back. Please don't acquire any scratches while I'm gone."

Eve shook her head ruefully as Jill disappeared. She had known Joe was in a fury when he'd come back to the museum, but she'd hoped he'd been exaggerating when he'd said he'd been threatening dire things. She should have known better. Well, Novak and Jill would have to learn to accept Joe as he was and be damn glad to have him on their side.

She forced herself to turn back to the Varak reconstruction. Blank gaping holes for eyes stared at her from that scorched, blackened face. Joe had realized that she had been nervous about doing this reconstruction. And though he hadn't wanted her to do it, he had offered her his support in typical Joe fashion. She smiled as she remembered that scornful, insulting finger Joe had given Varak before he left.

Lord, she loved him.

"He's right, I can do this," she murmured as she gazed into those gaping eyes. "Screw you, Varak."

She leaned closer, her gaze intent, as she started to measure again.

Gideon was standing beside the steps of the plane when Joe was dropped off at the airfield. "I hear we're going to Cairo," he said as he turned and went up the steps. "I thought that's where we'd end up after you talked to Novak."

"But you still didn't tell me anything about Yusef Dobran on the way here," Joe said as he followed him into the plane. "That could have been dangerous. I was frustrated as hell."

He shrugged. "It was the chance I took. You were an unknown quantity." He grinned. "And what I did know was explosive. I had orders to bring you here. I wasn't certain that you wouldn't make a detour to Cairo on your way if you thought you had a chance to bring this to a close a bit faster." He headed for the cockpit. "And after all the effort I put in setting up Hassan Sebak, I wasn't going to let it all go down the tubes because you were in a hurry."

"You set up the deal with Sebak?"

"Novak can't do everything." He dropped down in the pilot's seat. "Though he'd prefer to try. But I convinced him that I could handle this better than he could. It was quite an accomplishment, since Novak thinks very highly of himself." He was doing the checklist. "Rightly, of course. But I'm a bit impatient. He has too much on his plate, and I *want* Varak." He looked at Joe. "So sit down, buckle up, and we'll get out of here. I'll tell you everything I know about Cairo on the way."

Joe slowly sat down in the copilot's seat. "You think Dobran did the DNA. You believe Varak is alive? Why?"

"Because Jill does, and I trust her. Nothing has changed that since the day she came to me and asked for the money to give to Hadfeld." His lips twisted. "Besides, I can't do anything else. It's a puzzle I have to solve. I'll use you or anyone else to help me do that." He started the Gulf Stream checkdown. "But I'll let you use me as well, Quinn. When I get this baby in the air, I'll be at your disposal."

"Yes, you will," Joe said grimly as he buckled his seat belt. "And I'm pretty good at puzzles, Gideon, but I don't intend to spend much time on this one. I want an answer before Eve gets finished with that damn reconstruction." He leaned back in his seat as Gideon started to taxi. "And you don't know what impatient means yet."

"Five minutes," Gideon said, as the plane left the ground. "Just five minutes..."

It was only four minutes before he gained the altitude he needed and turned to face Joe. "What do you want to know?"

"Dobran. Everything."

"He was born in Cairo to an upper-middle-class family, his parents were both prestigious professors of arts and antiquities at the Cairo University. But Yusef chose to go for a medical degree at the Sorbonne in Paris and went on to get both a medical and chemistry degree there. He was totally brilliant, but when he was at the Sorbonne, he developed a drug habit that required he make more money than he could earn in medicine. That led him to explore other alternatives that took him into the DNA netherworld, and he found his niche. He spent six years in Paris, and by the time he returned to open his own lab in Cairo, he had developed a stellar reputation among the criminal underworld. For the last fifteen years, he's built on that reputation, and I'm sure Novak told you that Dobran is probably our man."

"And what do you think?"

"That Dobran is an arrogant asshole who will do anything to prove how clever he is. He likes money, but he also considers himself one of the elite intelligentsia like his parents. Unfortunately, both his parents and his social set don't agree and have ostracized him."

"What a pity. Does he have a wife? A mistress?"

"He changes mistresses every few months, but he always visits them in town and never permits them to come to his Asarti estate." He glanced at Joe. "He's very careful. Only his guards and his drug dealer and Hassan Sebak are permitted on the property. That's all."

"And what does Sebak do for him? What kind of assistant? Does he help in the lab?"

"Sometimes. But he's more of a gofer. He runs interference and errands for Dobran." He smiled faintly. "And he makes sure that all is secure and well in his gallery. That may be his most important task as far as Dobran is concerned."

"Gallery?"

"Dobran is a collector. Paintings, sculptures, antiquities. He has a fabulous collection that he's acquired since he came back to Cairo. It's what he spends those fat fees that he gets for his work on." He shrugged. "It's almost as much an addiction as his drug habit. Though it could be that he just wants to stick it to his father and all those other people who don't recognize how superior he is."

Joe's gaze narrowed on his face. "But you don't believe that."

"No, but I'm giving you both sides of the coin. Though it could be a little of both. He was exposed to fine art and antiquities from childhood, so the appreciation has to be bred into him. But he's shown himself to be vengeful and selfish all of his adult life. I'm certain that adds to the pleasure enormously. Hence, the addiction."

Sharp. Very sharp, Joe thought. Gideon was impressive. "Two addictions. Drugs and his art collection. Which can we use?"

"That's up to you," Gideon said solemnly. "Novak said that I'm to let you lead the way. I gave you possible weapons, so now I'll meekly let you take charge."

"Meekly?" Joe's brows rose. "Is that supposed to be amusing? You're like a chameleon adapting to your surroundings to get what you want. That's a dangerous talent."

"Only if you don't want the same thing." He handed his phone to Joe. "Check out the photos of Dobran and Sebak. You'll want to know them on sight."

"That goes without saying." Joe glanced at the two photos. Dobran was in his early forties, hollow-cheeked, thick, dark eyebrows. Sebak, older, receding hairline, a little plump. "What else do you have?"

"Shots of his estate, Asarti, outside Cairo. It's a château he bought from a French businessman five years ago and had renovated. You'll notice the placement of his exterior sentries are clearly indicated." He gave Joe a glance. "Just in case you don't want to rely on Hassan Sebak to get us in to see Dobran. I dangled the money, and he snapped at it, but he's a little too comfortable with Dobran. He tends to be nervous. He's still tempted, but it's possible he could change his mind before the deal is struck. He might decide that trapping us is a safer option for him."

Joe flipped through the photos. "No interior shots?"

"No, but you'll find a copy of the original renovation plans filed by his architect when he bought the château. That should do it."

Joe examined the plans. "Yes, that should do it."

"So do we ignore Sebak and go for his boss?"

Joe thought about it. "Not immediately. There are things Sebak can tell us that might help us. And you've already proved that he can be tapped." He held up his hand as Gideon opened his lips to protest. "You haven't set the deal in place, so he won't have a decision to make that will impact us. Where are Sebak's quarters? Is he in the house?"

Gideon nodded. "Dobran assigned him quarters near the

gallery. I told you that was his main duty to Dobran. Care and security for his treasures."

"Yes, you did." His gaze was raking the house plans. "And yet there's something missing..."

"What?"

Joe didn't answer, his gaze still on the plans. "You can get us to the house, but after that, we're on our own?"

"I can do better than that. I hijacked the Internet info of the company who installed his security system and got one of Novak's experts to figure out the codes to both the exterior and interior. I can disable the alarms, video cameras, and the motion sensors to everything but the gallery. That's on a separate circuit and code. The security there is foolproof against fire, theft, earthquake, and acts of God or Satan. Dobran doesn't want anyone touching his treasures."

"But we can get to Sebak's quarters?"

"If we can get past the guard stationed near the French doors in the library." Gideon's eyes were narrowed with interest on Joe's face. "Look, we can have Herb Nassem, the operator Novak set up as backup, drop us off and pick us up at the château. And I can manage to get us into the place. But all this would be difficult. If you still want Sebak, why not let me set up a meeting with him in the city instead?"

"I don't want to waste the time," Joe said curtly. "I want it all. I want Sebak. I want Dobran. I want answers. And I want it all to go down tonight." His lips tightened. "And since you've done such good prep work, we might be able to pull it off."

Gideon blinked. "If we don't get killed. You were right, I don't understand the word impatience as you define it." Then he smiled slowly. "Go for the entire jackpot? It's very appealing. Providing you have a plan?" When Joe just looked at him, he said, "You don't have a plan."

"Not yet." Joe went back to flipping through the photos on Gideon's phone. He added absently, "I'll get there. We have all day. But the first order of business is that we've both got to memorize this floor plan. Now tell me about Dobran and his drug addiction. He obviously has to keep it under control, or he wouldn't be this successful. What does he use?"

"Opium pipe. He started off on pills, but after he came back to Cairo, he found himself an antique pipe that I'm sure made him feel like a caliph. But you're right, he keeps control. He likes money too much to do anything else. Sebak said he locks himself in his suite at night and goes into never-never land. But during business hours, he's not a user."

"That could be bad or good. Do you know his typical schedule? We need him coherent but not troublesome . . ."

———

ROBAKU
2:45 P.M.

"You've got your red voodoo markers in place," Jill said as she handed Eve a bottle of water. "Don't argue. Drink it and take a deep breath. You've been racing nonstop all day." She tilted her head critically as she gazed back at the reconstruction. "Now he looks more like a ghoul than ever. Does it bother you?"

"No." Eve took a drink of water and leaned back. "That's a necessary process that leads to a successful conclusion. Why should it bother me?"

"You said you weren't looking forward to working on a man like Varak. Just checking." She made a face. "And I suppose I shouldn't have even mentioned it. It's my damned curiosity again. I'm glad that he's not putting his mojo on you."

"If he were, it would be because I let him. If evil lingers, it could be because we invite it into our minds." She took another drink of water and looked directly into the skull's gaping eyes. She hadn't realized until this moment that she had not done that since she had started working. Well, why should she? she thought defensively. She'd been doing depth measurements. It wasn't because she'd been afraid. "The trick is to concentrate on the work and not give in to imagination." She was speaking as much to herself as to Jill. "I've probably blown Varak's mystique out of all proportion because of what I've learned from reading and hearing about him." And the horrible nightmares. The machete glittering in the darkness of the schoolroom. She forced herself to keep her gaze on the skull. "Do you realize I don't even know what he looks like? That's not a bad thing since I avoid it anyway. But I only saw a couple photos of him on Google, and none of them were close-ups. I wasn't interested in him, only the children. I just got a vague impression that he was very big and had dark hair. Then when I came here and saw what he'd done in that schoolroom, I didn't want to look at him. He's not even a human being to me any longer. He's a Hitler or Bin Laden."

"Close," Jill said. "But you have to add a little Jeffrey Dahmer to be exact."

"You should know." She tore her gaze from the skull. "I'm sure you've researched him ad nauseam, just as you did me."

"As much as I could. He was a big part of the story of what happened here in Maldara, and I had to try to understand him." Her lips twisted. "I never succeeded. I felt like one of those FBI profilers trying to see into the mind of a serial killer. There has to come a time when there is no answer but the fact that Varak was a monster." She paused. "But I think you should know about Varak. Because he didn't look like a monster. He was quite good-looking in a Slavic kind of way, and he's over six-five and very powerfully built. Strong. Exceptionally strong, and he liked to break things...and people." She moistened her lips. "And everyone around him sensed that he did, and it gave him power over them. He loved power from the day he was born. He searched for it in violence, sex, money, or anything else that gave him the same thrill."

"You seem to know him better than you thought you did," Eve said slowly.

"Maybe I wanted to be like you and close my eyes to the monster. But I'm not allowed to do that because I have to tell the story. And now you don't get to do it either because I brought you into this. You have to get to know him. I'll try to make it as brief as possible." She paused. "Varak grew up in the slums of Johannesburg and was the first of three children born to Marta Varak, a worker in a local clothing factory. His father was a soldier who deserted Marta after eight years, and she became a whore to support her children. She treated them all well enough, but she was besotted with Nils. She spoiled him rotten, and he might have been the reason her husband deserted her. Nils didn't like the competition, and there's no telling what he did to push his father out the door. There was no doubt he was the perfect sociopath and was as smart as he had to be in every category. He had temper tantrums until he learned it didn't get him what he wanted, then he became devious. But he had all the signs of a psychopath from the time he was a toddler. There were rumors that were never proved that he killed small neighborhood animals. Then, when he was nine years old, his eleven-month-old baby sister suffocated in her crib when he was supposed to be taking care of her. It was said to be accidental. His mother said the poor boy was devastated even though he always complained about her crying. The only family member Nils got along with was his younger brother, Oscar, because he let Nils totally dominate him. When he was fifteen, he took Oscar with him to Venezuela when he joined a rebel group as a mercenary. But when Nils formed his own army two years later, Oscar took off and went back to Johannesburg. He was evidently tired of being his brother's punching bag." Jill paused a moment. "You know the rest. Varak has been building his reputation country by country and one massacre at a time. Only the massacres and the butchery kept getting worse and worse. Maldara was just the last in the line of his bloodbaths."

Eve looked back at the skull. "I hope this *is* Varak. Somehow we have to put an end to him, Jill."

Jill nodded, her gaze on the reconstruction. "You're working very quickly, aren't you? As I said, you're on fire. But you said three days..."

"I said *maybe* three days, he's going very fast." She took another drink of water. "But it may slow down as I do the fill-in. I have to be very careful."

Jill was studying her expression. "But you don't believe it will slow down, do you?"

Eve didn't answer for a moment. "No, sometimes a work just takes off and leaves me far behind. I can't seem to do anything wrong. This could be one of them."

"So how long?"

Eve shook her head. "I have no idea. Right now it's a fever. But sometimes a fever breaks." She finished her water. "And I won't know if I don't get back to work."

"I'm dismissed?" Jill asked. "When am I allowed to disturb you again?"

Eve started to put on another depth marker.

"When?" Jill persisted. "Next on my list is a cup of beef soup. I have to keep you strong. Give in, and the interruption will go faster. Tell me when it will be convenient."

Jill obviously wasn't going to surrender, Eve thought resignedly. "Before I begin the final sculpting."

Jill's eyes widened. "Shit. You're going to finish tonight."

"I didn't say that."

"But you are, aren't you?"

"Perhaps. More likely tomorrow."

"I think...tonight." Jill's gaze went to the reconstruction. "What did you say about sometimes a work's just taking off?" She murmured, "Maybe we're not the only ones who are impatient..."

━━━━━━━━▶

ASARTI
1:40 A.M.

"You're sure the kitchen entrance is the safest?" Joe asked as he went down the path after Gideon. "I've always found less obvious—"

"Have I been wrong yet?" Gideon interrupted. "Face it, I've been bloody perfect. After Nassem dropped us off down the road, I led us right past those sentries, didn't I? You shouldn't mess with perfection, Quinn." He'd reached the kitchen alcove, and his fingers were racing over the security panel. "Particularly since I'm not at all sure that I'm not the only perfect thing about this venture."

"Perfection is overrated," Joe said. "It doesn't leave room for innovation." Yet he couldn't argue that Gideon had fulfilled every need. He had been a constant surprise to Joe.

And this door was opening silently with no alarm. "Okay, you're awe-inspiring. Meet me at Sebak's quarters. I'll go take out the guard in the library."

"I'll do it," Gideon said as he moved down the hall. "The guard will be easy. I'll let you handle Sebak. You want him alive, and my impression is that he's very edgy. I bet he has a gun in his bedside table."

He probably knew Sebak did, Joe thought as he turned in the opposite direction and made his way through the darkness toward Sebak's suite.

Sebak's door was locked. Definitely edgy.

It took Joe two minutes to silently pick the lock. Then he was inside.

More darkness.

But Joe's eyes were accustomed to it now, and he could make out a bed across the large room.

Joe moved silently toward it.

Movement!

The bedcovers were suddenly thrown aside, and the man who had done it was lunging toward the bedside table.

Joe was across the room in seconds, and his hand came down in a karate chop on Sebak's wrist as he fumbled to get the drawer open.

Sebak cursed in pain as he turned and launched himself upward at Joe. "Son of a bitch. What are you doing? One scream, and I'll have guards all over the place." He struck out blindly and hit Joe in the chin. "They'll *kill* you."

Enough.

Joe's hand cut down on Sebak's neck in a karate chop and put him out.

He went limp.

Three or four minutes maximum before he'd regain consciousness, Joe thought. Get ready.

He flicked on the bedside light, checked to make sure the man was indeed Sebak, and removed the .38 revolver from the drawer of the bedside table. Then he took out his handcuffs and snapped them on Sebak's wrists.

"No trouble at all?" Gideon was at the doorway, his gaze on Sebak. "I admit I'm disappointed. I wasn't aiming for serious, but a few minor problems would have made me feel better about having to be so wary around you. I don't like not feeling totally in control of the situation."

"Then you shouldn't have told me that he'd go for that gun." Joe took a small roll of duct tape out of his jacket pocket. "Did you take down the guard?"

Gideon nodded as he watched him tape Sebak's mouth. "Complete with the duct tape. I did a neater job than you." He closed the door and walked toward him. "I think he's coming around. Maybe you'd better be the first one he sees. You're more threatening. I concentrated on being intelligent and charming when I was trying to lure him to our side. That's not the impression we need right now." He stepped out of Sebak's field of vision. "So be intimidating, Quinn."

"I will," Joe said grimly as he moved forward and jerked Sebak's head back. Sebak's eyes flew open, and he gazed up at Joe in alarm. He tried desperately to open his lips and speak.

"I'll let you talk soon," Joe said harshly, "when I'm sure you understand what will happen to you if you scream or cause me any trouble. Nod if you understand."

Sebak nodded but then tried to lift his arms and strike out. When he saw the handcuffs, he began to struggle frantically.

"Helpless," Joe said. "I can do anything I wish to you, and you won't be able to stop me. And you might be able to get out of this alive if you don't make me angry." His voice lowered. "But it's going to be very easy to make me angry.

I need information, and you've been playing games with my friend. Do you know there's a pressure point I can press here on your neck that can make you very sorry that you did that?" He reached down, and his thumb and forefinger found the exact place. "Ah, there it is."

Sebak opened his lips, trying to scream as pain jagged through him.

"But I never play games, Sebak. I just make certain the pain keeps coming and coming until I get what I want. I want this information very much because without it, someone I care about is going to suffer." He pressed the cord again and watched Sebak's face as it twisted in agony. "I won't permit that to happen. I'll do anything I have to do to keep it from happening. But I don't care if you suffer at all. I believe you understand that now, don't you?"

Sebak nodded frantically.

"Good. Then you won't try to escape, and you'll cooperate with everything I ask of you. Is that true?"

Sebak nodded again.

Joe leaned forward. "Then I'm going to take off the tape, and we'll begin." He stared deep into his eyes. "But you'll have to remember that if I see any sign of trickery, I won't hesitate. You're expendable, Sebak. And, if I don't get what I want, then I'll have no hesitation about showing you that." His fingers moved gently on Sebak's neck, and he could feel the muscles tense. "You're in my way. It's up to you to prove that I should keep you alive." He suddenly reached up and ripped off the tape with one motion. "Are you going to scream, Sebak?"

"No!" His gaze was holding Joe's. "I promise. I won't—" He stopped. "I want to live. Tell me how I can do that."

"I fully intend to do that." He said over his shoulder to Gideon, "It's over. Come out, come out, wherever you are.

Sebak isn't going to have any trouble believing that I'll do anything I have to do now."

"I can see that." Gideon moved forward. "Intimidating, indeed. Is that how you treat the prisoners at your precinct when you're interrogating them?"

"No, that's my job, and there are rules. This is Eve, and there are no rules." He looked back at Sebak and gestured to Gideon. "You'll remember him, he was going to give you a great deal of money. But now you've decided that's not necessary, haven't you?"

"I remember him." Sebak's tone was surly. "We can still deal. I'll get you in to see Dobran. You didn't have to hurt me."

"Yes, I did," Joe said. "I don't have time to do anything else tonight. But I could learn to enjoy it if you don't cooperate." He took a step closer to Sebak. "And we will pay a visit to your boss, but I think you know a good deal, and that will save me time. Gideon tells me that he indulges in his favorite opium pipe in the evening and might be a bit bleary when I wake him."

Sebak hesitated. "Gideon said that he wanted info about some DNA project Dobran was doing. I don't know anything about his business." He looked suddenly alarmed as he met Joe's eyes. "Well, maybe a little. But you'd do better to talk to him."

"I think you'd know about this," Joe said softly. "It was a very big job, perhaps the biggest Dobran has ever done. It would have been very difficult for him not to call in all the help he could get to keep himself safe and the work secret. You're his errand boy, and he trusts you. You might not know anything about the lab work, but you'd be drawn into the job itself."

"He doesn't trust anyone that much."

"I thought we had an understanding," Joe said. "Now I'm going to ask questions, and you're going to answer quickly and fully. Or we go back to the moment before I ripped off that tape. Do you want that, Sebak?"

"No! I just—" He was breathing hard. "He knows bad people. He could have them kill me."

"That's your problem, but you have a bigger one with me." Joe smiled. "Don't you?"

"Yes."

"Then we go forward. What do you know about that DNA job Dobran took on several months ago?"

He was silent, then said reluctantly, "He didn't want to do it. From what I overheard when he was talking on the phone, the money was more than he'd ever been offered before, but he said it was too dangerous. He said that he had plenty of money and didn't need to run that kind of risk to get more."

"And who was on the phone?"

Sebak shrugged. "I don't know. Somebody important. Dobran said something about not caring how big they were, it was nothing to him. He had enough business, and he wasn't going to run the risk."

"But evidently he did run it."

Sebak's lips twisted as he nodded. "Dobran was offered a price he couldn't refuse. A box was delivered here a few days later, and he sent me to take it to Caladon that same day."

"Caladon?"

"Kalid Caladon. He's Dobran's favorite art expert. He's expert *and* discreet. Dobran has all his artifacts appraised by him."

"And this was an artifact that Dobran sent to him for appraisal? What kind?"

"A gold statue. Dobran was excited about it. He was even more excited when I brought the report back from Caladon.

He had me set up a special glass case in the gallery for the statue and arranged maximum security for it." He added, "And he started work on the new DNA project the next day."

"How? Did he meet with someone? Did he go to the lab?"

"He didn't go to the lab. But he must have met with the client because he flew out that morning." He added quickly, "And that's all I know. I did what Dobran told me to do, then I was out of it. Dobran spent the next three weeks at the lab before the job was finished."

"You know nothing else?" Joe asked.

"Only that Dobran is crazy about that statue and spends time with it every day." He thought of something else. "Oh, and he told me to put two more guards on the property." He added sourly, "But they didn't keep you out, did they?"

"Names," Joe said. "I need client names."

"I don't have any names. I've told you all I know." Sebak's voice was shaking. "You'll have to get it from Dobran."

Joe was afraid that was true. Sebak was still too frightened not to tell him if there was anything left to confess. "Then that's what we'll do." He pulled Sebak to his feet. "Let's go."

"And am I to be allowed to interrogate Dobran?" Gideon asked. "I'm getting very bored, Quinn."

"Maybe." He pushed Sebak across the room and out the door. "But we're going to make a stop before we go to see him. I want to take a look at that statue."

"I told you that I don't have the code for the gallery. You'll have to rely on Sebak."

"I'm certain he'll cooperate," Joe said as he nudged Sebak toward the gallery. "Isn't that right?"

"I don't know why you want to see it," Sebak said. "It's just a statue."

"Maybe I'm an art lover. Besides, I want to see what Dobran sees in it and why he wanted it so badly." He stopped before the ornate carved doors of the gallery and gestured to the panel. "Do your thing. If you set off an alarm, I don't have to tell you that you'll regret it."

"No." Sebak was quickly putting in the code. "I wouldn't do that. Haven't I done everything you've told me to do?" The carved door opened to reveal steel panels that slid silently to each side. "You see?"

"Yes," Joe said. "You've made a good start. But it's all in the follow-up. Where's the statue?"

"At the end of the second row." He hurried on ahead. "I'll show you."

Gideon gave a low whistle as he fell into step with Joe. "I've seen rooms at the Louvre that don't have this many treasures." His gaze was on the rows of glass cases on either side of them containing Egyptian artifacts of every description. "No mummies? I half expect to see King Tut in one of those cases. I bet there are artifacts in here that the government would never permit to be owned in a private collection."

"No bet." The gallery was very heavy on Egyptian artifacts, but there were also priceless originals on the walls by Cezanne, Rembrandt, Titian... "It's clear he sometimes took his fee in fine art. That Titian is worth far more than this château."

"You have a good eye," Gideon said. "And whoever sent Dobran that artifact must have known that it would be irresistible to him."

"Here it is." Sebak had stopped before a softly lit case at the end of the row. He gestured impatiently. "I told you, it's just a statue."

Joe inhaled sharply as he gazed at the superb artistry of

the work. It was no more than eighteen inches but was made of pure gold, and every complicated detail of the slim Egyptian woman it represented was done to perfection, from her crown headpiece to her sandals. "Yes, you did. Only a statue." He bent closer. "Take it out of the case. I want to examine it."

"I'm not allowed to do—" He met Joe's eyes and reached out to press the coded release on the top of the case. "Be careful. He'll kill me if it's damaged."

"It's gold. I'm sure it's already very old, and gold isn't that fragile." He took the statue and looked at it. It was just as magnificent as he'd first thought. "But I can see why he was impressed by her."

"I can't," Sebak said sourly. "I don't know why he wanted it. He has others, you know." Sebak nodded at the row of cases across the room. "Probably older than this one. Age is everything to value according to Caladon. This one is only 44 B.C. But Dobran couldn't wait to get his hands on it."

"Why?" Joe murmured. "It's exquisite, but why would it mean that much to him?"

Sebak shrugged. "He told me to make sure Caladon cleaned the base carefully so that every engraved hieroglyph was clear. I think he hoped it would be a name, but it wasn't. Yet he didn't seem disappointed. When he got the statue back from Caladon, he even had a gold plaque made for the case itself with the same words inscribed." He gestured to the small rectangular gold plaque inside the case. "And that wasn't even done in hieroglyphics."

"No." Gideon was suddenly pushing forward to shine the beam of his flashlight down on the gold plaque. "It's ordinary, modern Egyptian script, and it only shows that Dobran is a true collector. He wanted to see the proof, know what he had, every time he came to see her. It was his way of claiming her as his property, bringing her into his world where she didn't belong." His gaze was narrowed, focused on the delicate script. Then he abruptly went still. "Shit." He muttered an oath beneath his breath. "Let's get to Dobran fast, Quinn. No wonder he put on extra guards. I'm surprised that he's still alive. We have to get the hell out of here. I think we've found out all we need to know."

"In a minute. I don't want Sebak around when I'm talking to Dobran." He pushed Sebak down on the floor and fastened his manacles to the leg of the case. When Sebak started to protest, Joe taped his lips shut again. "And you might have found out all you want, Gideon. But evidently I haven't," he said. "I don't speak Egyptian, much less read it. What does it say? Is it a name?"

"No, Sebak is right, no name." Gideon turned toward the door. "Just a kind of title."

"What title?"

"Three words." He threw open the door. *"Great Beloved Wife."*

CHAPTER

11

"Take it away." Eve pushed the bowl of beef soup to one side. "I can't eat any more, Jill. And if you argue with me, I'll throw this bowl at you."

"I'm not arguing." Jill took the bowl and turned away. "I'm lucky I got that much down you. But you had to eat something, you've been on fire all day." She glanced over her shoulder at the skull. "I can tell he's waiting for you. Or that you're waiting for him. Or something..." She shook her head. "He's blurred. I look at him, and I can't tell anything about him. Can you?"

Eve nodded. "Like you, I can tell he's ready and waiting."

"Are you nervous?" Jill asked.

"No. Yes. I'm a little sick to my stomach, but I need this. I have to know." She drew a deep breath. "Now be still and let me get back to work. I don't want to hear from you until I've finished."

"You won't." Jill sat down in a chair across the room. "Promise. I won't even watch what you're doing. But I do have to be here to watch your back. Okay?"

"Okay," Eve said absently, as her fingers reached out to tentatively touch the brow bone on the reconstruction. "You have that photo of Varak?"

"In my briefcase under my cot. It's waiting for you, Eve."

Waiting.

She sat there gazing at the smooth clay before her. Everything had been waiting for this moment. The measurements had been taken and checked. The initial sculpting done, the part that told her basically nothing but laid the groundwork. Now it was time to make him come alive.

She shuddered. No, she couldn't think of it like she did other reconstructions. She didn't want him to come alive. Ever since she'd put that skull on the dais, she had been fighting not to think of the person he could be, so that she could block out all the evil and think only of the work itself.

But now she could no longer do that, she had to accept who and what he was so that she could sculpt that face. Was it her imagination, or did she feel something dark and angry stirring?

She moved her shoulders to release the tension, her gaze never leaving the skull. "Okay, are you ready?" she whispered. "I'm not afraid of you. Be as angry and ugly as you like. I'll still get what I want from you. You took so much from so many. Now you have to give at least some of it back."

Her fingers moved down to his right cheek.

Come to me.

Smooth.

Mold.

Fill in.

Darkness.

Anger.

Pay no attention to it. Keep working.

Go to the ears. That should be easier. They had to be generic. She had no idea whether they stuck out or had longer lobes. Just let it flow and do what seemed right.

Anger.

I don't *care.* I'm doing this.

She could no longer even attempt to block him out, but she could keep to the flow and work through that anger and do what she had to do.

Smooth.

Mold.

Fill in.

Hatred.

Work faster. Go to the mouth.

Generic again. She knew the width but not the shape. Better to make the lips closed and without expression. Because the only expression she'd be able to put would be anger and hatred.

Concentrate.

Her fingers were flying now, hot and facile on the clay.

She could do this.

Lips done.

She was moving too fast.

Check the measurements. They were still important.

Nose width, 31 mm. Correct

Nose projection, 18 mm. Okay.

Now concentrate and do the job.

Anger.

Go away!

More shaping to the nostrils.

Mold.

Smooth.

Creasing on either side of the nose.

Good.

Smooth.

Mold.

Fill in.

It was better now. She could still feel the darkness dragging at her like a huge lodestone, but it was only exhausting, not frightening.

She was working feverishly.

Start the creases beneath the orbital cavities.

Fill in.

Mold.

Smooth . . .

———————

ASARTI

"Great Beloved Wife?" Joe repeated as he followed Gideon down the hall toward Dobran's suite. "What the hell is that supposed to mean?"

"Trouble." He glanced over his shoulder at the statue Joe was still carrying. "And very revealing. Plus as dangerous as a flesh-eating parasite for Dobran to possess. That's why we've got to get out of here ASAP. There's no way that Zahra would let that statue out of her hands if she hadn't intended to get it back. She probably has her own version of a SWAT team watching the house, ready to take Dobran out."

"Zahra Kiyani?" Joe said. "You're saying she hired Dobran. Why would she want to fake Varak's death? He worked for the Botzans, her enemy. She had every reason to want him dead. He almost destroyed her country."

"You'll have to ask Dobran. All I know for sure is that she almost certainly did the hiring."

"Because of the statue." Joe looked down at the statue. "It belonged to her? You've seen it before?"

"No, but it's a statue of Kiya, one of Akhenaten's queens during his reign in the Eighteenth Dynasty. On every artifact bearing her name, it was followed or preceded by *The Great Beloved Wife*. That's what's engraved on that statue you're holding. Zahra has always had an obsession about her. Kiya, Zahra's ancestor who founded the Kiyanis, was named for Akhenaten's wife by her mother, Cleopatra. Even in Kiya's journal, she mentioned that the reason that Cleopatra gave her the same name was because of the stories, passed down through the centuries, of how Queen Kiya was so loved by Akhenaten. Didn't Eve mention any of this to you?"

"Probably. It's vaguely familiar. But I guarantee I wasn't paying much attention to any tall tales about Cleopatra. I had other things to think about. As I do right now." He added grimly, "And there could have been other people who had access to a statue of Akhenaten's queen."

"But maybe not one sculpted between 50 and 30 B.C., when Cleopatra and her daughter were alive. That's unusual in itself when Akhenaten and his wives died back in the Eighteenth Dynasty." He slowed and gestured ahead. "Dobran's suite is the second door on the left. Let's see if he can give us a few answers, provided he can focus through his usual haze. Though it might not be possible. Either way, we have to get out of here. Agreed?"

"Agreed." Joe moved quickly down the hall and unlocked the door.

The heavy scent of opium.

A man dressed in loose trousers and an open white shirt was lying sprawled on the couch with an opium pipe in his lips. He appeared to be asleep.

Shit.

"Not much chance of getting answers," Gideon said. "Still want to try?"

"Hell, yes," Joe said. "I don't like the alternative of having to take him with us and get answers later."

"You didn't mention that alternative," Gideon said. "I don't like it either."

"Hold this." Joe thrust the statue at Gideon. Then he was across the room and yanking the pipe out of Dobran's mouth.

No response.

He shook him. "Wake up, Dobran."

Dobran opened his eyes. "Go away." His voice was slurred. "You have no...right to be here. Son of a bitch...I'll have you...castrated."

"Oh, now that does make me mad. Wake up." Joe slapped him. No response. Once again. "Keep your eyes open, dammit."

"Tired..."

"Give me the statue, Gideon." He dug his hand in Dobran's hair and jerked his head back. He held the statue squarely in front of his face. "If you don't keep your eyes open, I'm going to hammer this statue into a pile of rubble."

"No!" Dobran's lids flew open. "Mine. I'll kill you..."

"Is it yours? Who gave it to you?"

"Bitch. Arrogant bitch...Only a down payment. She promised she'd give me more. She said she had lots more..."

"Who?"

"But she never gave me anything else...and she even wanted that statue back. Bitch." He reached out and tried to grasp the statue. "So beautiful...Mine."

"Who?" Joe repeated.

"Did I tell you I was going to castrate you?"

"Who?"

"Maldara...Kiyani..."

"Why?"

"How do I know? She wanted it done..." His eyes closed. "They pay me, I do it. But he was too dangerous. She shouldn't have cheated me."

"Who was he?"

"You know who he is. Everyone knows him..." He was dozing off to sleep again. "But she shouldn't have tried to take the statue back..."

And no matter how Joe shook him, he only got mumbles and complaints. Joe was cursing low and vehemently beneath his breath as he released Dobran's hair and let his head fall back on the pillow of the couch. "Dammit, it's not *enough*."

"What do you mean? You know it was Zahra. He said as much."

"Yes, but I'm going to have to squeeze more out of him. I can't risk his going on the run or ending up a corpse if Zahra decides he has to be taken out." He put the statue in his backpack. "And Eve may need him to testify if all this shit comes tumbling down around her." He slipped on the backpack. "Come on. Help me. We've got to take him with us."

"That was the scenario I wasn't looking forward to facing." Gideon helped him get Dobran onto his feet, and they half carried, half pulled him toward the door. "How do you intend we do it? Go right through all those sentries, lugging him along behind us?"

"No, we go back to the gallery, pick up Sebak again, and let him show us the other way out."

"What other way out? We have the house-renovation plans. Every exit leads out front or to the side gardens protected by sentries."

"But there was something missing." They'd reached the

grand staircase and were having to balance Dobran's weight to keep him from falling down the stairs. "I told you that it wasn't right."

"But you didn't tell me why."

"The gallery. You said everything was built around keeping the gallery safe. But there was only one door, and it led to the hall and the front doors. Dobran would have wanted another way to get his treasures out of the château in an emergency. Only he wouldn't have wanted it put in the house plans for everyone to see."

"You're guessing."

"Of course." They were on the staircase landing. "But it's a good guess, and I'm banking on it. It's better than trying to yank Dobran through that garden and having to deal with—"

An explosion rocked the house.

Fire!

Flames were suddenly ripping through the foyer below them.

Then another explosion.

"The gallery." Joe and Gideon were dragging Dobran down the rest of the steps. "Get him to the gallery."

Smoke.

Another explosion. This time from the kitchen.

It was hard to see now.

It took them twice as long as it should have to reach the gallery.

A minute more to punch in the code he'd watched Sebak enter.

Then they were inside.

The heavy steel door slid closed behind them.

Joe released his hold on Dobran and pressed the lock on the door. "Bring him. I've got to get to Sebak." He was running down the aisle. "We've got to get out of here before the local fire department shows up with the police and an antiterrorist unit. And those grounds out front will be teeming with Dobran's sentries by now." He'd reached Sebak and knelt to free him from the handcuffs and rip off his tape.

"What did you do?" Sebak screeched. Tears were streaming down his chalk-white face. "I heard the explosions. Are you trying to kill me? I did everything you told me to do." Then he saw Gideon and Dobran. "I thought you were only going to question him. He's the one who will kill me."

"Not if you get us out of here," Joe said as he jerked him to his feet. "You'll never see Dobran again if you help me get him away from here before anyone breaks in and tosses another bomb. I didn't set off those explosions."

"You're lying," he said uncertainly.

"Have it your way. I don't have time to argue. I have to find a way out." He pushed him down to his knees again. "I'll put the manacles back on you and you can wait for someone to come . . . or not."

"No." He struggled back to his feet. "I'll show you. But then you'll let me go?"

"We'll talk about it. I'm still not sure you don't know more. But we're not going to let Dobran go, I need him. So he won't be around to go looking for you. Move!" He was gazing around the gallery. "No doors. But there's another way out, right? Show me. Hurry!"

"I will. I'm hurrying." Sebak was running toward the back of the gallery. "The mummy . . ."

"Mummy?" Joe was helping Gideon move faster with Dobran. "What are you talking about?"

Sebak was standing before an upright ornate mummy sarcophagus whose top was a huge, carved hawk. "It's a passageway that leads out of the back of the house and down a tunnel toward the road." He was opening the lid, then swinging the five-foot shelf containing the wrapped mummy to one side. "Dobran liked the idea of using the mummy to hide the door." He ducked inside. "Follow me."

"Wait a minute." Joe had a thought. "Gideon said that everything in the gallery was on a separate control. Does that include video cameras?"

"Of course," Sebak said. "Everything."

"Then where can I pull the tapes?"

"They have a special code to release each section of the display areas. There are six kiosks."

"Six!"

"Sirens, Quinn," Gideon said quietly.

Joe heard them, too.

"Shit." *No time to stay and grab the videos. Worry about it later.* "Get going, Sebak."

Sebak disappeared into the darkness.

"Macabre," Gideon said dryly as he dragged Dobran farther into the sarcophagus. "This decision must have been made during one of his more bizarre narcotic episodes."

"Whatever." Joe was negotiating the entrance to the tunnel while still trying to help Gideon with Dobran. "Pull that lid shut behind you, then call Nassem and tell him to meet us at the road in back of the château."

"I'm sure it's bad luck to close the lid of a coffin on oneself." Gideon slammed the lid behind him. "Oh, well, I look to you to protect me."

"Don't count on it."

"But I most certainly do, Quinn. Otherwise, I'll drop Dobran and let you lug him out yourself." Gideon reached for his phone. "And I think those sirens are closer..."

ROBAKU

It was done.

Eve was breathing heavily, as if she'd been running.

She was shaking from exhaustion.

But you didn't beat me, you son of a bitch.

No, he wasn't quite done. But only the eyes were left to insert. The eyes were always the last step in completing a reconstruction.

Her hands were trembling as she reached for her eye case.

"Eve?" Jill was beside her. "Can I help you now? You don't look so good."

"Tired..." Eye case. "I have to get the eye case. We can't look at him until I put in the eyes."

"I won't look at him. I know this choice is as important to you as the sculpting itself." She gave Eve the eye case and opened the lid. "Which ones?"

"Brown. We'll try brown first. Brown eyes always predominate." She took out the right eye and carefully put it into the socket. She didn't look at the face, her gaze fixed only on that dark, shiny eye. "I think it's time you got that photo, Jill."

"I do, too." Jill squeezed Eve's shoulder. "I'll be right back. Put in the other eye."

Eve was already doing it. She carefully inserted the left eye.

Anger.

Screw you. I've *done* it.

"Here it is." Jill handed her the blown-up photo. "May I look now? I don't need the photo. I know what the son of a bitch looks like."

"Go ahead." She forced herself to look down at the features of the man in the photo. She felt a ripple of shock as she gazed into those dark eyes so much like the ones she'd just inserted. The shape of the orbital cavities were identical to the ones she had just created. Varak? It must be Varak. What other features were the same? She identified the curve of the cheekbone immediately. She remembered those bold, Slavic cheekbones. She couldn't take her eyes from the photo, caught by the sheer power of that face. Dominance. Power. Intensity. And darkness, so much darkness.

"Eve," Jill said gently.

Eve glanced up from the photo. "You should be relieved. It has to be him. It was lucky that I was able to repair those orbital—"

"Eve. Look at him."

Eve's gaze followed Jill's to the reconstruction.

She stiffened. Her hand was shaking as she reached for her phone. "I've got to call Joe."

ASARTI

Joe's phone was vibrating in his pocket.

Not now. Later.

He couldn't answer it. He was almost at the end of the tunnel. He could see Sebak ahead, rolling aside a large boulder.

"No!" Joe called. "Don't go out there yet. We don't know what's happening. This might be too easy. It doesn't take a mental giant to figure out that there might be a back way out of that gallery. Explosives. Fire. Then someone waits to see who goes running. Let me take a look." He pushed Dobran at Gideon and strode to the opening. Shrubs. A thin stand of trees. A stretch of lawn that led to the road several yards away.

As he watched, he saw their driver, Nassem, pull to a stop at the curb of that road.

No sentries. No police. No fire trucks. They all seemed to be at the front of the house, where he could hear sirens, shouts, breaking windows.

"Safe?" Gideon was beside him.

"How the hell do I know? Probably not." Joe's gaze was scanning the trees. "But it's safer than any other option."

"What are you doing to me?" Dobran had raised his head and was staring blearily at Joe. His voice was slurred. "You won't get away with this." He saw Sebak a few feet away. "Call the guards. Why are you just standing there?"

"You said you'd keep him away from me," Sebak said to Joe. "He saw me with you. Knock him out or something."

"Sorry," Gideon said. "With the drugs, he's handicapped enough. Yes or no, Quinn?"

"Yes. But you head for the car and let me follow. Zigzag. Don't give anyone a good shot. I'll cover you." He unlocked Sebak's manacles, then pulled out his gun and pointed it at him. "Help him get Dobran to the road. If you cause us any trouble, I'll put a bullet in you, Sebak." His gaze was scanning the trees. "Go!"

Gideon moved. Joe stood in the shadows for an instant, letting his vision become accustomed to the dark as Gideon and Sebak streaked toward the car. No one on the grounds or behind the trees. What about those upper branches? If he were a sniper, that's where he would be.

But a sniper would now have to change positions because he had a prey constantly moving in a zigzag pattern.

Watch.

Look for any motion.

Which tree?

A rustle in the leaves of the oak tree.

Joe swung his gun to cover it.

An owl flew out of the branches.

But something nearby might have startled it.

The pine next to the oak.

A rifle barrel aiming, then leveling.

Shit!

Joe was aiming even as he ran toward the tree.

His shot was only a second behind that of the sniper.

That second was enough, dammit. He heard Sebak scream with terror as he watched the sniper plummet from the tree to the ground.

Joe barely glanced at the man's bloody skull as he tore across the grass toward Gideon, who was kneeling beside Dobran.

Gideon looked up at him and shook his head. "Head shot. Dead. Either the shooter was good, or I wasn't zigzagging at my top potential."

Joe muttered a curse. "He was good, and there's no doubt Dobran was the target. It was no random shot. He was being slow and careful, or I would have seen him before I did. And I went for the head. So I can't even question him."

"Then may I suggest we get out of here?" Gideon asked. "With all that noise going on in the front, I doubt if anyone heard the shots, but it's best not to risk it." He glanced at Sebak, who was curled up, frozen, a few yards away. "What do we do with him?"

"Take him with us," Joe said curtly as he turned and ran toward the car. "You're right, we have to get back to Robaku. We came up almost empty with Dobran. I'll let Novak question Sebak and see what else he can drag out of him. And as soon as we get back to the plane, I want you to call Novak and tell him to find a way to get those security videos out of the gallery museum before the police yank them and get around to scanning them. The last thing we need is for anyone to know we were here if they didn't know already. There has to be a reason why there was only one sniper waiting here for the rats to run out of the trap. We've got to have time to put everything together."

"You're calling me a rat?" Gideon jerked Sebak to his feet and pushed him toward the car. "Most unkind and inaccurate, Quinn. I've been more a beast of burden tonight..."

———————

Joe glanced at his phone the moment they were a few miles away from Asarti.

Eve.

He muttered a curse as he punched in the return. "What's wrong?"

"That's what I was about to ask you. Why didn't you answer me?"

"I was involved. Things didn't go as expected. Are you all right?"

"No." She went on quickly: "I'm okay. It just doesn't seem as if anything is all right at the moment. I just finished the reconstruction. I thought it was going to be fine, that we'd gotten lucky." She paused, then said shakily, "I was wrong. It isn't Varak."

"No, it isn't," Joe said. "Look, I have to get off the line, you stay where you are until I get back there. We'll be boarding Gideon's plane in another fifteen minutes. Let me talk to Jill."

"Why?"

"Because I don't want to relay a message through you. I have a few orders to give, and you might phrase them as requests. They are *not* requests."

Silence.

"You weren't surprised about Varak, were you? Why not?"

"Not now. You'll know everything I do as soon as I get back there. Until then, all I want is to make certain you're safe. Let me talk to Jill."

Silence.

Then Jill's voice on the line. "What's happening? Eve is upset enough without having you worry her."

"Does Novak know about the reconstruction yet?"

"No, Eve wanted you to know first. I'll call him when she hangs up from you."

"No, you will not. Novak doesn't know until I'm there to control him."

"Control? Novak? And he deserves to know. He's been in this from the beginning."

"The only one who deserves to know is Eve. But I'll probably need the two of you to get her out of this nightmare, so you'll both know as much as I do once I'm certain that I can trust Novak. He's entirely too accustomed to running the entire show, and I won't risk Eve because he has some plan I don't know about."

"He wouldn't risk her."

"And I don't trust either of you, so how would I know? We'll discuss it when I get back. Until then, no one finds out that the reconstruction is done. Eve is still working on it. As long as no one knows there's a weapon to be wielded, then no choices will be made that might put a bull's-eye on her chest."

"I won't lie to him."

"That's up to you, but if you ever want me to trust you as Eve appears to do, you'll handle it so that only you will have the responsibility. You *will* do this, Jill."

Silence. "I'll consider it."

"No, you'll keep her *safe,* and when I get there, we'll let Novak join the party. I'll see you in a couple hours, Jill." He cut the connection.

He glanced at Gideon. "Any comment?"

He shrugged. "Not unless you expect a vote of approval. I'm playing this straight down the middle. From your point of view, you might even be right about Novak. He does have an obsession about Varak that might lead him to be a little impetuous." Gideon looked him in the eye. "But then so do I. That doesn't mean I'd do anything that would hurt Eve. I don't believe he would either. But you'll have to make up your own mind. I won't get in your way as long as you don't put obstacles in my path." He smiled faintly. "It was an interesting evening. You do keep things moving, Quinn..."

———

"He knew that it wasn't Varak," Eve said, as Jill handed her phone back to her. "Something happened there tonight."

"Well, we obviously won't know what it was until he gets here," Jill said sharply. "He could have spent the time he used trying to intimidate me on telling us. But evidently he didn't want to do that. And something pretty important happened tonight with us, too." She shook her head. "Sorry. I'm a little annoyed with him."

"He told you that you couldn't tell Novak," Eve said.

"Novak has a right to know. He's not going to run out and start some kind of bizarre offensive just because we're certain."

"We might be certain, but proving it is a different matter. We always knew that would be true, Jill." She looked at the reconstruction. Why could she still not shake this feeling of darkness and hate as she gazed at the skull? "And I can see why Joe might not want to jeopardize either my life or freedom."

"Do you think I can't?" Jill grimaced. "But he's put me on the spot by not letting me tell Novak. We've been on the same team, and now I'm not supposed to trust him? At least he said that it would only be until he got back here."

"You're going to do it?" Eve gazed at her in disbelief. Then she smiled faintly. "I don't believe it. You're angry with him. Why are you doing it?"

"He offered me a price I couldn't refuse. The bastard said it would help him to trust me." She got to her feet. "But I don't intend to lie to Novak. It will only take Gideon a couple hours to get Quinn here, and you're not going to be finished with this reconstruction until he walks in that door." She took out Eve's computer and opened it. "You said there were all kinds of computer details and comparisons to complete a reconstruction job. Sit down and start doing them."

Eve slowly dropped back down on her stool. To her amazement, she couldn't smother her smile. Only moments before, she had been swirling downward through confusion and terror, yet now she was feeling an instant of welcome humor. "And what if I finish before Joe shows up?"

"I've got it covered. I'll be nagging you and asking questions to make certain that computer reconstruction will have so many minute details that it will take you twice as long as it usually does." She opened her own computer. "Though I might annoy you a little."

Eve brought up her forensic programming. "And all to keep from lying to Novak?"

"And to stop your idiotically stubborn husband from saying I didn't obey his damn orders. He said to keep you safe and not tell Novak." She was focusing on the photo. "It's up

to me if I do it in a way that may please both of them..."
She suddenly looked up at Eve. "Do you think I'm being manipulative again?"

"Perhaps. But I can see it's sheer self-defense." And it would keep Eve busier until Joe did walk in that door. She had been frightened when he hadn't called her back, and she didn't want to think about what he'd been doing during those minutes. "I'll permit myself to be manipulated as long as I'm aware it's happening."

"It just seemed easier."

"You sound like my son, Michael. He's always certain everything would be easier if he did it."

"I'll take that. You love the kid." Jill looked down at the photo again. "Now I'll get back to doing a facial analysis, while you get busy with the victim."

Victim.

Eve felt a ripple of shock at the word.

All the time she had been working on this reconstruction, she had never consciously thought of this skull as that of a victim. The possibility had always been there, of course. But she had only felt the darkness, the antagonism, the hate. Even now, it was difficult to feel sympathy for this man who had died in Varak's place. Split personality, Jill had called it, when Eve had given the name Varak to the reconstruction. Was it the reason that lingering darkness remained?

Or was it the ferocious anger that his identity had been stolen as well as his life taken from him in this horrible way?

Either way, she had to change how she thought about him.

Not a monster but a victim.

CHAPTER

12

Joe and Gideon walked into the museum two hours and fifteen minutes later, followed closely by a very grim Novak.

"Surprise. Surprise," Novak said sarcastically as he glanced at the completed reconstruction, then at Jill. "At least a surprise for me until Quinn showed up here fifteen minutes ago and told me. But I appear to be the only one who wasn't on the need-to-know list."

"I really just finished his computer input ten minutes ago," Eve found herself saying quickly. "Stop glaring at Jill, Novak."

"But you knew two hours ago it wasn't Varak." He made an impatient gesture. "I'll deal with that later."

"No, you won't," Eve said. "My job. My decision." She turned to Joe. "How are you? I was worried. What happened in Cairo?"

"Not much that was good," Joe said. "Except that we might have acquired some valuable information to coordinate with what you found out about the ID of the reconstruction."

"But you got Dobran killed," Novak said bitterly. "He's the only witness we knew about, and he's dead. And we needed his information. I'll interrogate Sebak, but from what Gideon told me, I doubt if I'll get anything. By all means, tell them what happened at Asarti. It will be interesting to have all the cards on the table for a change."

"I'm sure it would be a great change for you," Joe said coolly. "That's why I didn't want you to know anything before I could be here to keep an eye on what you were doing." He turned to Eve. "I did get Dobran killed. As I said, there was as much bad as good that happened at Asarti." He spent the next minutes filling her in on the events of the last twenty-four hours, and ended with, "And I don't give a damn about Dobran's death, we can work around it. What I'm worried about is that whoever staged those explosions and the sniper attack will probably know in a matter of hours who was taking Dobran out of that château tonight."

"What?"

"Dobran had to be the target. We were careful, and no one knew we were in the château. It had to be a random accident that we were there at the same time as the attack. But I killed that sniper, and once they find him, they'll look for more answers."

"And who are 'they'?" Jill asked.

Joe's gaze returned to the reconstruction. "You tell me. Someone who wanted to eliminate Dobran as a witness but also wanted something Dobran had in his possession that could be plucked from his gallery in the confusion of the fire."

"But why will they know you were there?" Eve asked.

"Sebak said there was video surveillance in the gallery. Gideon was able to eliminate the cameras everywhere else but not in the gallery. And we were in too much of a hurry to get out of there with Dobran to stop and disable them."

"Amateurs," Novak said sourly.

"Walk in our shoes," Joe said curtly. "I needed Dobran. You'd do the same."

Novak was silent. "Maybe."

Joe turned back to Eve. "And once I'm identified, it will only be a short time before they'll make the connection to you. The first thing we've got to do is get you out of here."

"Do we?" Eve had known this was coming. It was Joe's protective instinct at work again. "I don't think so. Not the first thing, Joe. The first thing we have to do is figure out what happened and why. I'm not going to run away and hide from being arrested by the U.N., or whoever killed Dobran, until I know what I'm facing."

"I can take care of that once I know you're safe."

"No, Joe," she said quietly.

"Dammit, Eve." His eyes were blazing. "Dobran was a witness, and he's dead. Tonight, you proved with that reconstruction that Varak's death was a big lie. Do you think they'll let you live?"

"I haven't proved anything as long as the courts believe in the DNA. Dobran is dead, and I'd bet any lab evidence has been destroyed by now." She held up her hand as he opened his lips. "I'm just saying that we might have time to figure this out because they'll have to figure out what we know, too. I have no intention of getting myself killed." She smiled at him. "So back off and stop pushing. Now show me that statue. That could be very interesting." She looked at Gideon. "You really think it had to belong to Zahra Kiyani?"

He nodded. "Everything Dobran said indicated that it had to be her." His lips twisted. "Particularly the part where he called her a bitch. That definitely struck home." He watched as Joe dug into his backpack and pulled out the gold statue. "And it's the statue of the first Kiya. Who else would have it?"

"Who, indeed?" Jill came closer as Eve took the statue from Joe. Her gaze was lit with eagerness and curiosity as she stared down at it. "And why would she have it?" she murmured. "It's beautiful, isn't it? It must have nearly killed Zahra to have to give it up." She reached down and traced the script. "Great Beloved Wife . . . " She glanced at Gideon. "She never mentioned this statue to you?"

"There were things that she didn't confide. I imagine a multimillion-dollar artifact might be included in that range since she wasn't sure I was totally besotted with her." He glanced at the statue. "She should have told me about it. The fact that she had it would have definitely sparked my interest."

"She told Dobran that she had a lot of other artifacts. That it wasn't going to be the only payment," Joe said.

"I remember you said that." Eve was still looking down at the statue. Exquisite. And the idea that it might have been created in the court of Cleopatra VII added to the mystique. "Which leads us to the distinct possibility that the treasure that Kiya mentioned in her journal did exist, might still exist, and Zahra has it in her possession." She frowned. "And she still gave him this one artifact, which must have meant a good deal to her, to get him to falsify that Varak DNA."

"And in the end, that's the only thing of real importance," Novak said curtly. "All this talk of artifacts and Zahra Kiyani's obsession with them is bullshit. If Zahra is guilty of being an accomplice to Varak, then it doesn't matter whether she did a payoff at a bank in the Grand Caymans or with these artifacts. It means she's as guilty as that son of a bitch, and we have to go after her."

"No one is denying that," Jill said. "I just find it interesting as a storyteller that the story appears to be growing in scope." She met his eyes. "And I don't agree that it's not important. The fact that Zahra has a secret treasure cache worth millions, possibly billions, that she can tap at any time, automatically furnishes her with weapons. For one thing, it could have lured Varak into her camp. And since everything to do with Kiya is important to Zahra, it has also somehow become woven into this terrible connection to Varak. That makes it very important, Novak. You're just still pissed off that I didn't let you know the reconstruction was finished."

Silence. "Yes, I am." He turned to Joe. "When Gideon called me from the plane, I arranged for a couple agents to go to Asarti and blend in and see what was going on out there." He paused. "And how we can manage to cover your tracks. I should get a report soon."

"It better be very soon. Or everything may come crashing down on us." He looked at the reconstruction. "Do we agree that Zahra Kiyani has to be working hand in glove with Varak to maintain the lie that he's dead? The question is why, and how far it goes." He paused. "And how far it went while the war was still going on. If Varak was allowing her to use him as a double agent to defeat Botzan, it would make sense why her casualties were so slim."

Gideon gave a low whistle. "Oh, I can see that happening."

"But where is Varak right now?" Jill asked quietly. "Would he run the risk of staying in Maldara?"

"Questions," Eve said wearily. "So many questions." She looked at Joe. "But we still have time to get the *answers*. Let's just take a deep breath, then go after them."

"We'll see," Joe said. "As long as I don't see any sign of your becoming a target while you're doing deep-breathing exercises." He glanced at Novak. "And as long as I get that report from your people at Asarti right away."

"You'll get it," Novak said. "And now I'm going to go interrogate Sebak. I'll let you know if I find out anything more from him. It's not professional to hide information from people with the same goals." He turned and headed for the door. "You might keep that in mind, Quinn."

"I will," Joe said. "As long as you set the example." He turned to Gideon as Novak left the room. "One more thing. I want to know everything Zahra Kiyani does from now on. I need to know it all. You're familiar with the palace and know her routine better than anyone else, so you're the best one to do it."

"Lucky me. You do realize that my face is also on those videotapes? It's only a matter of time before Zahra realizes I'm not only an inconvenience but a threat." He shrugged. "So I guess I'd better get busy doing the advance prep work we need before she decides to target me." He strolled toward the door. "But you're right, I still have a few contacts in her personal entourage, and I'm very familiar with the gardens and every room in that overdone monstrosity of a presidential palace."

"Not only the bedroom?" Jill asked dryly.

"You underestimate me. I never limit myself when it comes to keeping a relationship fresh." He paused at the door, and said soberly, "Zahra's very complicated, but you can count on her striking fast and hard when she decides she's being threatened." His gaze went to the statue in Eve's hands. "And that's a threat, Eve."

The next moment, he was gone.

Eve drew a shaky breath as she shook her head. "Well,

that appears clear enough." Her hands tightened on the statue for an instant before she handed it back to Joe. Why was her hand shaking? The statue wasn't that heavy. But it seemed heavy. "But I can't let myself worry about Zahra Kiyani. I created that reconstruction for only one reason, and that was to find out if Varak was still out there." She wearily rubbed her temple. "And he's alive, Joe. I haven't been able to really comprehend that yet. He's out there . . . waiting."

"Because you're so exhausted that you can scarcely sit on that stool," Joe said roughly, his gaze raking her face. "You've pushed yourself until you're ready to collapse." He turned to Jill. "Get out of here. Leave us alone."

"Joe, she didn't do anything," Eve said quickly.

"I know that. Not this time," Joe said. "And no one would have been able to stop you. I've been there. But now all the adrenaline is gone, and you're crashing." He glanced at Jill. "You did as good as you could under the circumstances. I just want you out so that she can draw a breath without looking or thinking about Varak for the next few hours." He stepped toward Eve and pulled her to her feet. "Come on. I promise you that we're on our way to getting the son of a bitch." He slipped his arm around her waist. "We'll just take a little time together now, okay?"

"Do I have a choice?" His arm felt strong and warm around her, and she felt secure for the first time since he'd left her so many hours ago. "I guess I do, and I choose you, Joe." He was leading her toward her cot. "I'll always choose you."

"Because you're very smart." His lips brushed her temple. "Smarter than Varak or Zahra and sometimes even me. That's why you're going to rest now." He glanced over his shoulder at Jill, who was on her way out the door. "See to it. You understand?"

Jill nodded, gazing thoughtfully at Joe, then Eve. "I believe I'm beginning to understand quite a bit." She turned back and opened the door. "Don't worry. She won't be disturbed. I'll take care of it."

———◆———

KIYANI PRESIDENTIAL PALACE

He wasn't answering her!

Zahra gazed furiously down at her blank screen. She'd texted him twice, and he was ignoring her. Arrogant bastard.

She texted again.

DID YOU GET IT? WHEN CAN I PICK IT UP?

No answer.

YOU SAID I COULD HAVE IT BACK TONIGHT. WHERE IS IT?

At last an answer.

THERE'S A PROBLEM. I'LL TEXT YOU LATER.

She stiffened. No, this couldn't be happening. He had promised her!

I WON'T TOLERATE THIS. I'VE BEEN WAITING TOO LONG. I WANT IT NOW.

The answer came with swift brutality.

YOU'LL GET WHAT I CHOOSE TO GIVE YOU WHEN I CHOOSE TO DO IT.

The screen went blank.

Rage.

She closed her eyes, trying to subdue the anger. This was her fault, she had allowed him to intimidate her until he thought she was just another one of his cowed whores. And it had come down to this indignity.

It was over. She would not let it go on!

"Dalai!" She got to her feet as the maid came running out of the anteroom. "Come with me. We're going out."

———

Over an hour later, Dalai was driving Zahra off the main road and through the thick foliage of the jungle that surrounded and hid the armed compound and large house.

Zahra phoned as she got closer. "I'll be there in a few minutes. Call off your men, Varak."

"I've known exactly where you were since you got off the road. What a fool you are. I'm tempted to sit here and watch them blow you to bits."

"You won't do that. I'm too valuable to you. I'm not afraid of you." That was a lie. There were moments when she was afraid, but not of physical abuse. She was afraid of his reckless egotism and his power to send all her plans toppling. "So threaten all those idiots around you who can't see through you. I'm done with bowing down at your altar to feed that ego." She hung up.

Five minutes later, Dalai drove her up to the gates of the stockade, where Lon Markel was standing guard. Zahra leaned forward and nodded curtly at him. "Open those gates. I have to see him, Markel."

"Did he give you permission?" Markel asked with the hint of a sneer. "You know that he—"

"Open those gates!" Markel was *her* agent, only on loan to Varak, and he was daring to question her! It just showed how much respect had been stolen from her by that son of a bitch. "Now!"

He shrugged, opened the gates, and stood aside.

Two minutes later, Dalai screeched to a stop before the long porch of the house.

"Do you wish me to come in, madam?" Dalai asked. She was tense with nervousness as she watched the door open and Varak come out on the porch.

She was actually trembling, Zahra noticed impatiently. You'd think she'd have learned to control herself by now. But just one glimpse of Varak, and she was falling apart. "I haven't decided." She got out of the car. "Stay here, I'll let you know." She strode up the steps, her gaze on Varak. He was staring straight at her, and she could see why a weakling like Dalai might be afraid of him. The expensive plastic surgery for which Zahra had paid an enormous fee might disguise his features, but those dark eyes were piercing, and the power and ferocity were unmistakable. His black hair had been dyed to a pale sandy shade and allowed to grow longer than his usual cropped cut because she had thought it might soften his appearance. Perhaps it did at first glance, but that was also a failure in Zahra's opinion. All these temporary measures were only safe as long as everyone was certain Varak was dead.

"What do you think you're doing?" Varak said harshly. "I told you not to come here again. You could have led them right to me. People are always watching you."

"And I'm supposed to pay any attention to what you tell me to do?" She stopped before him, glaring. "And I'm no fool. I went out the secret panel, and I leave a car parked in a garage down the street. No one saw me."

"I know they didn't, or I wouldn't have let you come near here. Do you think I didn't know you'd do something like this?" He turned and walked back into the house. "Come in. I don't want my men seeing your tantrum." His lips twisted. "Or I'd have to either beat you or cut your throat. I don't allow myself to show weakness to them as I've demonstrated to you on many occasions." He poured himself a drink from the bar just inside the door. "You like that about me, don't you, Zahra?"

"I like to see power at work. It amused me to watch them grovel." She added through set teeth, "But I'm not amused now, Varak, and I won't grovel to you. What are you trying to do? Give me my statue."

"I'm trying to give it to you, bitch," he said. "I told you that there was a problem. I'm not playing mind games with you." He drank down his whiskey. "And I have more to worry about than your fancy statue. Something weird happened at Asarti last night that might be more important to both of us."

"Nothing is more important. Give me my statue."

"I'd have to find it first. Because it wasn't at Asarti."

She went still. "What?"

"Interested now?" Varak asked. "You weren't interested in anything about the way I was going to get the statue back. You just snapped your fingers and said you wanted it."

"You said you'd get it back from Dobran a few days after the skull was identified as you. You *promised* me. But he still has it."

"He has nothing. Dobran is dead. I had a sniper set up to take him out last night."

"Good. Then why don't I have my statue?"

"You were going to have it," he said harshly. "I was tired of hearing you nag me. I thought I'd get you off my back about the statue in case I had to go to Robaku and take out that Duncan woman in the next couple days. I knew I couldn't trust you to do it."

"My statue," she reminded him.

"I was going to eliminate Dobran as a witness and take the statue at the same time. I sent in a team to bomb the place and start fires that would block all the entrances and force them to use the one through the gallery. Dobran liked that statue, too, and I knew he and Sebak would go after it and out the gallery exit if they were forced to run. Then all I had to do was put several of my men with the fire and police departments who answered the alarm. They'd only have to break into the gallery and find a way to grab the statue and smuggle it out of the château. Not a difficult job in all the confusion that would be going on." He poured himself another drink. "It should have worked. I should have rid myself of Dobran, and you would have had your statue."

"Should?"

"I got Dobran." He lifted his glass to his lips. "Unfortunately, Nolan, my sniper, was also taken out by someone equally efficient." He sipped his whiskey. "And I just heard from the team who went into the gallery to get your damn statue that it had already been stolen. No sign of other thefts, just that one artifact. Unless Dobran decided to sell it."

"Not *my* statue." Her eyes were blazing. "Stolen? What really happened to it? Dobran loved it, he wouldn't have let it be stolen, and certainly not purchased."

"Maybe not. I'm leaning toward agreeing with you. We have the murder of my very talented sniper to consider. As I said, something weird happened up there last night. We might not have been the only ones who were after Dobran, and that's much more threatening than anyone's taking your statue."

"Then you should have gotten all this taken care of before anyone else had a chance to go after Dobran or my statue. I told you enough times that I wanted it done."

"Forget the statue!" He suddenly hurled his glass across the room to crash against the wall. Then his hands were around her throat. "You listen to me," he hissed. "You're not stupid. I wouldn't have gotten on your merry-go-round if I'd thought you were. Now stop acting as if you're an imbecile. I might have saved us both by taking out Dobran last night, but it might be too late if someone is onto us and got to him first. We've got to think about saving our asses."

His grip was bruising her throat. For an instant, she was feeling panic mixed with her fury. He always liked to hurt her. She knew how brutal he could be. "Let me go, Varak. How dare you speak to me this way. Stupid? I'm the one who had you brought to me when you were only one of Botzan's dirty mercenaries. I gave you the chance to come out of this war alive and richer than you ever dreamed." She stared him in the eye. "I've protected you, hidden you. I've done everything for you, and I've only asked you to do a few small things to keep our heads above water during a difficult time."

"A few 'small' things?" His thumbs pressed harder into her neck. "Play a double game and attack when and where you told me? Help you to set up your fancy image with the U.N., so they'd choose you to run this son of a bitch of a country?" He bent his head and his tongue touched the hollow of her throat. He whispered, "And make certain that papa dearest was killed in a timely manner so that you could take over the presidency?"

She inhaled sharply. "I did what was necessary. He wouldn't listen to me. He wanted to negotiate peace with them. You made no objection at the time." She went on the attack. "And as long as you continue to cooperate, I'll protect you...provided you protect me. But I won't let you destroy what I'm building. I'll get you out of Maldara as soon as it's safe. Then all you'll have to do is arrange to move my treasure safely out of Maldara for me, and I'll give you the share I promised."

"If it even exists; you've never let me see it." His fingers pressed harder. "I'm beginning to doubt you, Zahra. You don't want that to happen."

"Don't be foolish. It would be dangerous to take you there. I showed you the Great Beloved Wife, didn't I? Dobran jumped at getting it. You could see how valuable it is." She met his eyes. "I promise that as soon as I have the treasure secure, I'll buy you an island somewhere, and you can set up your own little kingdom."

"You have it all planned." He dropped his hands from around her throat. "But it's my decision, and an island sounds boring. I liked the life I was living before you dropped into my world. When we split that treasure, I'll look at my options."

That was what she was beginning to fear. She reached up and massaged the bruised flesh of her throat. The prick had hurt her this time. "I just want to keep you safe."

"I'm touched, Zahra." His lips twisted. "But you'd do better to think about keeping us both safe by helping me find out what happened at Asarti."

"You said you'd take care of that." She paused. "You really think that it might be more than just a theft? That someone knew that Dobran did the DNA?" She was getting more nervous as she thought about it. "It might not be so bad. No one could trace the statue to me. I took it from the treasure."

"You're back to covering your ass."

She made an impatient gesture. "What are you going to do?"

"My team at Asarti who slipped in with the firemen haven't been able to get the security videotapes of the gallery yet. They'll go back later and try again. That might tell us something. But that's not all. Hassan Sebak has disappeared. We need to track him down."

"Sebak didn't know about you. I made it a condition that the DNA remain absolutely confidential." She shrugged. "But, by all means, go after him. He might have stolen my statue, and all this worry might be for nothing. Besides, we have to remain safe."

"I notice which one you put first," he said sarcastically. "How nice of you to give me permission. But I've already set it in motion." He turned away and stripped off his shirt. "Now take off your clothes and lie down on that couch."

She had half expected it. Her resistance always aroused a sexual response in Varak. On occasion, she had actually used it to stir the passion hotter. But that was when she had attempted to use sex to bind them tighter together, when she'd had hopes that Varak might be someone she could control as she hadn't been able to control Gideon. But lately she had realized that Varak would not be controlled either, and the sex was only to subdue her.

He snapped his fingers and repeated mockingly, "Take off your clothes, Zahra."

Arrogant bastard. She shook her head. "I have to get back to the palace."

"But our agreement is that I'm never to be without amusement out here in the wilds. Have you forgotten?"

"I send you women to amuse you all the time."

"But I'm bored with them. They're whores, and nothing is new or exciting. No matter what I do to them, they just accept it." He smiled. "While you accept nothing without a battle. I want you to scream for me."

For a minute, she was tempted to pit her skill against his. But it was a struggle she was never sure she could win with him. She couldn't afford to lose when so much was at stake. "Not now." She turned to go. "But you enjoyed Dalai the last few times you had her. Fear is also exciting for you. I brought her with me in case I needed to negotiate." She looked at him over her shoulder. "I imagine you have no trouble making *her* scream?"

He smiled. "No trouble at all. She's like a startled doe most of the time. But you've trained her well, she never says no. Though I always prefer your services."

"She'll have to do. Don't damage her too badly. She's valuable to me. And I'll need her back by tomorrow."

She opened the door and motioned for Dalai to come into the house.

The girl was already tensing as she got out of the car, Zahra noticed. She had gone pale and was looking beyond Zahra at the open door.

Panic.

No, Varak would have no problem making her scream.

———————

ROBAKU

Jill called Novak the moment she walked out of the museum.

He didn't answer.

She called again.

No answer.

And then again.

He answered curtly, "What do you want, Jill?"

"I need to talk to you. Quinn just kicked me out of the museum, and I can't just sit and do nothing. Where are you?"

"In the village. Hajif set me up with a vacant hut to use as an office, and I'm trying to coordinate the men I sent to Asarti to gather information."

"Can I help?"

"No."

Time to eat crow. "I realize you're pissed off at me, and you have a right to be."

"Damn straight."

"Quinn doesn't trust you. Not me either, but I'm working on it." She paused. "And I knew it would only be a couple hours delay. It didn't seem too bad. What can I do to make it right with you?"

He didn't answer.

"What can I do?" she repeated.

"The eternal question with you." He was suddenly walking toward her out of the brush and turning off his phone. "You should have stuck with Quinn. As you said, I'm more pissed off with you than he is right now."

"It wasn't really Quinn, it was Eve. I had to balance what she—" He had put his fingers over her lips, and she looked up at him, startled.

"Hush," he said. "I'm trying very hard not to confuse this anger with anything more emotional or sexual. But since it's always there, it's a factor. Along with the fact that I find myself oddly hurt that you didn't trust me to handle this situation. That's very weird in itself. But it will help if you don't make excuses or tell me you owe me anything." He took his fingers away. "Now why did Quinn kick you out?"

Her lips still felt warm and tingling even though his touch was gone. "He wanted her to rest." She moistened her lips. "I was just another disturbance."

"Yes, you are." His lips twisted. "So he tossed you to me?"

"No, he wouldn't care where I went. She's the only thing important to him. It's kind of nice. Warm…" She met his gaze. "It was my choice to come to you, Novak. Because I do trust you." She added simply, "How could I do anything else after what you've done for me? No matter how much you want your own way, you'd never do anything to hurt me. I'll always come to you if you'll let me."

He was silent. "Oh, shit." He took a step toward her. Then he stopped abruptly. "You leave yourself wide open, dammit. You haven't been paying any attention to what I've been saying to you, have you?"

"Sure I have." She smiled with an effort. "Some of it sort of scared me. I'm really not the kind of person anyone would obsess about. I don't know what I'd do with you if I didn't believe you'd probably change your mind before all this is over."

"I can offer suggestions," he said thickly. "And you must be wrong because the obsession is definitely there." He paused. "But there's nothing I'd do to you that should scare you."

"You're back to walking wounded again?" She shook her head in exasperation. "For Pete's sake, it's not about sex." Though that was patently untrue. She couldn't get near him without this feeling of heat and electricity. She drew a deep breath. "Is it okay if we don't talk about this? I just wanted you to know that I do trust you. And it's important that you not shut me out of anything when everything seems to be exploding around us."

"Heaven forbid that you miss one single minute of any combustion coming our way," he said dryly.

She nodded. "Heaven forbid," she echoed quietly. "It's my story, my responsibility, and if I don't tell it, then it might not get told. And I brought Eve into this, and now Quinn is involved." She made a face. "You might say I even brought you into this, Novak."

"The hell you did."

"I came to you. Just as I'm coming to you now. You turned me down then. Don't turn me down this time."

He swore under his breath. "Low blow, Jill."

She nodded. "Yes. But I speak fluent Egyptian and Arabic. Can't you use me to find out what's happening in Cairo?"

"Possibly."

"Novak."

"Hell, yes, I'll use you," he said roughly. "Haven't I done that from the beginning? Quinn's right, we've got to either eliminate or delay anyone's finding out who killed that sniper and was in the château tonight. And we need time to get a plan together. Which means we have to get our hands on those gallery videotapes. I'll see if I can patch you into the local Cairo police from the Museum of Egyptian Antiquities, and you can express concern that some of the antiquities on loan to Dobran might have also been stolen. In short, lie through your teeth and work your magic."

She nodded, frowning thoughtfully. "I can do that. But it might be better if I contact a friend of mine, Matt Kimbro, who's a reporter for the *Cairo Messenger* and also does freelance. He knows most of the players in the government and police department. I worked with him during the nine months when I was covering riots in Cairo. He's been there for years, and he knows where all the bodies are buried." She grimaced. "And believe me, in Cairo, that's a hell of a lot of bodies. He owes me a favor, and I could ask him to call a few people and maybe follow up with the police and security company." She shrugged. "Or I could do both."

"Yes, you could." His lips were quirking. "And probably will." His smile faded. "And I'm glad there's someone who owes you a favor instead of your being obsessed with payback."

"I'm not obsessed, there just has to be a code, or nothing makes sense." She was taking out her phone and checking the directory. "And in my profession, I've found it's always more valuable to have someone owe me. It just didn't turn out that way with you."

"And why does this Kimbro owe you?"

"I'll never tell." She grinned as she started to punch in Kimbro's number. "Because that would be breaking the code."

"I'll find out, you know," he said softly. "I can always find out whatever I need to find out. And there's nothing I'm not going to know about you, Jill."

"The CIA showing all its black hat–white hat power. You have a tendency to surround and conquer." She met his eyes. "Did it occur to you that might be why you scare me? Who wants anyone to know everything about them? I'd feel smothered. Stay out of my private life, Novak."

He was silent. "I don't know if I can." He paused. "I'll have to see how it works out." He turned and headed back toward the village. "When you finish setting up Kimbro, come and let me know, and I'll give you something else to do. I wouldn't want to waste your talents."

———————◄——————

The long facial bones...

Not right. But so close.

Eve could see them before her even though her eyes were still shut. She moved restlessly on the cot as she realized how close...Just like the shape of those orbital cavities...

Too close.

It seemed impossible that all those details could be that identical and not actually be Varak. It didn't make sense, Eve thought frantically. Had she done something wrong? They all thought she was perfect. But she wasn't perfect, she could make mistakes. And what if Varak was the biggest mistake of her life? She had told them the reconstruction wasn't Varak, but the resemblance was too close. It didn't make sense. But what had she done wrong? Why had she made that mistake? Why were those orbital cavities—

"The brother!" Eve's lids flew open, and she sat bolt upright on the cot. "He has to be the brother."

"Shh, go back to sleep," Joe said. "Nightmare?"

"Only the same one that I've been living with while I've been doing this reconstruction. And I can't go back to sleep. The minute I woke up, I started to worry about the shape of his damn eyes." She threw aside the sheet and swung her feet to the floor. "When I was first looking at the photo of Varak, I thought that the reconstruction I had made had to be him. There were so many similarities. It was only when I actually compared them that I realized that I hadn't been working on Varak's skull." She was moving across the museum to her worktable. "But I got caught up in the computer verification; and then Jill was upset with what you were forcing her to do about Novak. Things kept getting in my way." She was dropping down on her stool and looking at the reconstruction. "And I didn't make the connection. I should have made the connection, Joe. It was stupid of me not to realize who he was."

"And it only took five hours of sleep to send the stupidity packing." Joe was on his feet and strolling toward her. "Before you start working again, don't you think you should put on some clothes?"

"I'm not going to work," she said absently. "I just wanted to take one more look at him. I was so scared, I'd made a mistake. There was all that darkness and anger...And the bone-structure similarities. If you compare it with the photo, you can see it."

"I'll accept your word for it." He put his hands on her shoulders as he stood behind her, gazing down at the reconstruction. "The brother? You think this was Varak's brother? He's never been mentioned. I don't remember his even having a brother."

"I didn't know either until Jill told me about him. He had no part in Varak's life after he was a teenager. He was Varak's younger brother, Oscar, and, as far as I know, they hadn't seen each other for years. He was afraid of him because he'd been bullied all his life." She shivered as she gazed at the reconstruction. "He had good reason to be afraid. There's nothing more cold-blooded than choosing your own brother to die in your place." She reached out and touched the orbital bone of the left eye with her finger. "But it was a clever choice. Not only was the bone structure similar, but even the DNA would have been similar if the minutest trace was found outside of Dobran's work. Insurance, Joe."

"You're fairly certain?"

"It's a very good bet." She looked up at him. "And that's going to help us, isn't it? We needed to find out who he was before we could claim he wasn't Varak. He was a murder victim, Joe. There's a chance that there might have been a witness to it. Or at least someone might have seen Varak with Oscar during the period right before his supposed death." She was trying to think of everything Jill had told her. "Johannesburg. His brother was supposed to have gone back home to Johannesburg after he split with Nils Varak. Can we trace him that way?"

"I'll trace him, you'll stay out of it." Joe held up his hand. "Look, you've done what you set out to do. No one is more dangerous than you to Varak now. You've shot holes in the fancy scenario he rigged up with Zahra Kiyani." He shook his head as she started to speak. "And don't tell me it doesn't mean anything if the courts accept the DNA over your work. It does mean something because you're so well respected. Why do you think Novak wanted you on his team? Jill might have wanted your expertise, but Novak knew that you could influence people and change minds. You'll stir up a hornet's nest, and Varak will come out and try to squash you before you do damage."

"But that's a good thing," she said quietly. "We want to bring him out, don't we? It will be easier for us."

"To use you as bait?" Joe shook his head. "Forget it. I want you out of Maldara. I'm going to send you to London and pull strings to surround you with every man from the Yard that I can beg or steal."

"I notice you say you're going to send me, not take me. Because you told me this had to be finished, didn't you? There's no way you're going to let Varak get away now that you know he's alive. You'll stay here and do what I should be doing while I'm palling around with all your buddies from Scotland Yard."

"It's the reasonable thing to do. You don't have to be here, Eve."

"No? I don't see it that way. I brought you here, Joe." She looked back at the reconstruction. "And *he* brought me. Jill thinks she's responsible for involving everyone in this nightmare, but it was Varak. Because he's alive, we're all swirling around him, drowning in what he is and what he's done. I won't go away and take a chance on letting him pull anyone else into that whirlpool." She smiled with an effort. "But you've convinced me how important I am, so I'll stay here at Robaku, where Novak and you can protect me." She paused. "Unless we can think of a way to use me with more efficiency."

"Eve."

"No, it's not done. *I'm* not done. I can't stir up any hornet's nest right now because if Varak doesn't go after me, he'll go on the run. We can't afford to have him do that, Joe. So I'll stay here and work on Mila, be a thorn in both Varak's and Zahra's asses, and we'll try to think of a better way to build a rat trap to catch them." She drew a deep breath and had to stop. This had been too painful. She always hated conflict with Joe when she knew it was pain and worry driving him. She had to get away from him and recover. She got to her feet. "And now I'll go get dressed. You're right, nudity lacks a certain dignity when I'll probably have to argue about this with Jill and Novak, too."

A muscle jerked in Joe's cheek. "Not Novak."

"We'll see." She headed for the bathroom. "I've been getting a different viewpoint about him lately. Jill trusts him."

"Eve," Joe said. "Don't do this."

She stopped at the door of the bathroom. "I know you're unhappy about it. But I can't do anything else." She opened the door, and added simply, "Because whenever I close my eyes, I see that schoolroom, Joe."

CHAPTER

13

Jill was waiting when Eve came out of the bathroom forty-five minutes later. She was staring at the reconstruction and looked up as Eve crossed the room toward her. "You really think it's the brother?"

"I do. I'm surprised you didn't think of it before I did. You're the storyteller. It's definitely a macabre twist on the story of Varak."

"It probably would have come to me eventually. I was just upset and a bit scattered at the time. But it does make sense."

"Now we have to find proof that Varak murdered his brother or try to discover when and where he disappeared. Hopefully, it will be about the time that helicopter exploded in the mountains."

"Quinn and Novak are already working on it. Dobran took a flight somewhere the day after he accepted that statue. It would be logical if it was to Johannesburg to examine and accept the body of Oscar Varak and prepare it for the DNA implant," Jill said. "Why do you think I'm here? Quinn came storming down to the village and told Novak that he had to put a trace on Varak's brother and determine if this is really him." She nodded at the reconstruction. "He wants all the puzzle pieces we have to be in place before anyone discovers that the skull is gone from that U.N. headquarters." She grimaced. "I got the impression he was trying desperately to stave off having you tossed in jail. I told him I wouldn't allow that to happen."

"If I remember correctly, you didn't give me the same promise," Eve said dryly. "You just said you'd be in the cell next to mine."

"Well, I didn't think that would go over well with him. He's still very tentative with me. Instead, I decided I'd come here and let Novak deal with him and see if you need any help."

"Only with information. What's been happening? It seems as if I slept for a long time."

"Not for a normal person." She shrugged. "I managed to get a reporter friend, Matt Kimbro, to go and squeeze information out of the local Cairo police. The police did collect all the security videos in the château, but they hadn't gotten around to viewing them yet. They're still in the evidence room."

Eve stiffened. "But they will view them. It's only a matter of time. And they'll find out it was Joe in that gallery."

"Maybe." She paused. "I told Kimbro it was important to me that I get hold of those gallery tapes. The evidence room might not be a problem for him if his contact is on duty. It's like the rest of the police department in Cairo. Bad and good. It's not that unusual for things to go missing . . . if the price is right. He said he'd let me know."

"A very good friend," Eve said. "To risk getting arrested."

"Yes. But he's smart, and I told him if it gets down to taking any serious chances, he's to call me, and I'll get him help. I'll go myself if necessary. Together, we'll be able to do it."

"And get yourself arrested, too?"

"We have to get those security tapes. It could hurt Quinn *and* you."

"Then let Novak go help your friend Kimbro."

"I will if it's more efficient. But Kimbro trusts me, and he was more likely to be accommodating if I was in the background. He's *my* friend, and he owes *me,* not Novak." She smiled. "And Kimbro might not need help. I told you, he's smart." She changed the subject. "Now, what other information do you need? Oh, Gideon has already gone to the presidential palace in Jokan to see what information he can gather about Zahra Kiyani. That's all I know right now. Sorry, more later."

"Nothing to be sorry about. It's fairly substantial." She was rifling through her cabinet and pulling out the reconstruction she'd begun on Mila. She carefully put the Varak reconstruction in the cabinet in its place. "And certainly more productive than what I'll be doing."

"I can't believe that."

"Believe it," Eve said curtly. "Sitting here and working is the only way I'll be able to keep Joe from going ballistic. He wanted me to fly back to London to cozy up with Scotland Yard."

"He told us." She hesitated. "Not a bad idea, Eve."

"You should have thought of that when you brought me here," she said curtly. "There's no way I can go back and forget everything I've seen and learned in Robaku." She glanced at her. "And you knew that would happen, so don't let me hear that again from you."

"Just a comment," Jill said. "Maybe because I wish I could take it all back."

"I know you do." She began to put in the depth markers. "Too late." She added, "So make amends and work with me to find that son of a bitch who killed these kids."

"You know I will." She turned away. "I'll go down to the village and get you something to eat. You've lit a fire under Quinn, and I doubt if he'll be here anytime soon. Maybe by the time I come back, I'll be able to give you another report. Anything else I can do?"

"Not unless you've taken up forensic sculpting." Eve waved her hand. "Out with you. Let me get into Mila."

"On my way." Jill headed for the door. "I guess I'm used to staying close and watching out for you. No need of that now. Quinn and Novak have arranged a virtual army to guard you."

I don't doubt that, Eve thought. The knowledge tended to smother her. But she shouldn't complain, it was all part of the surveillance which she'd told Joe she'd accept.

And she wasn't complaining; it was just difficult.

Mila. This little girl deserved her attention. Think of Mila.

———

"Fruit. And a salad creation that Leta made for you from Hajif's garden. The dressing is spicy but good," Jill said as she came back into the museum two hours later. She set the tray down on Eve's worktable. "No protein. But I'll work on that for your supper." She glanced at Mila as she went to the cooler to get Eve a water. "How's it coming?"

"Fine." She pushed back and started to eat the salad. "You're right, this dressing is good. What's Joe doing? I take it not making salad. Did he find out anything from Scotland Yard?"

"Only the brother's background. After Oscar went back to Johannesburg, he was into everything from petty thievery to gunrunning. No connection with his big brother during that time. It's pretty clear he wanted the break to be permanent. For the last seven years, he was involved with piracy in the Indian Ocean. He was first mate on a schooner that raided corporate ships and held executives for ransom. At least two of the prisoners were executed during those years. Oscar definitely was not a pleasant man. He learned a lot from big brother."

"But he was an amateur compared to Varak," Eve said. "And the last lesson he learned evidently was a horror story. Was he definitely back in Johannesburg at the time Dobran flew down for a visit?"

"Novak is checking that out." She shook her head. "It seems Quinn and Novak are working in tandem. Pretty scary, huh?"

"Intimidating. But it probably won't—"

Jill's phone was ringing. "Hold that thought." She glanced at the ID. "Cairo. It's Kimbro." She answered. "What's the word, Kimbro? Can you get the tapes?"

He sighed. "I'm afraid not. It's impossible." Then he chuckled. "Because I've already got them. You persist in underestimating me, Jill. They're tucked in my camera bag right now. Piece of cake."

Jill breathed a sigh of relief. "No trouble?"

"Just a return of favors. I slipped in and slipped out of that evidence room with my customary grace and style, leaving a hefty bribe behind. Which you will return to me with interest."

"Why should I? You owed me." She added teasingly, "And it was a piece of cake."

"So that I won't consider you in my debt now. I know you, Jill." He paused. "But to make sure, I'll accept another bribe. I want to know why you were ready to let me run that risk to get these tapes. You're usually boringly protective." He added, "And I want in on the story."

Jill's smile faded. "No, you don't. Not this story. Not now, Kimbro."

"It must be one hell of a scoop," he said softly. "If not now, when?"

"Soon. Don't push me, Kimbro. I won't shut you out. I promised you that you'd get the story of a lifetime. Just don't go probing into anything concerning Asarti. Okay?"

He sighed. "Okay. I guess you want these tapes right away? Where can I drop them off?"

"Where are you now?"

"Having breakfast at a sidewalk café about six blocks from the police station."

"Cocky."

"Why not? I told you it was a piece of cake. No problem at all. Really simple. You'd have been proud of me."

"Yeah." But she was beginning to be distinctly uneasy. "But sometimes things can be too simple. We've both gotten in hot water when we least expected it. Look around you, is there anyone there in the restaurant who looks familiar?"

"Not really. You're too suspicious." Silence. "Maybe that guy in the gray suit with no tie who's reading the newspaper. But I can't be sure."

"Then pretend you *are* sure and do me a favor. Get up and walk out of that restaurant. Don't look as if you're in a hurry. Stroll, don't run. Take a taxi and go back to your apartment and lock the door. I'll send someone to meet you and pick up those tapes."

Silence. "What is this, Jill?"

"Just do it, okay? I'm not sure if it's necessary. But it will make me feel better. Don't play games. Be careful. Call me when you get to your apartment." She hesitated. "And I think perhaps it might be a good idea if you go with the person who comes to get the tapes. I'll let you know when you call me."

Silence. "You're nervous about me. This must be nasty."

"Very nasty. I told you that in the beginning."

"You're going to feel very foolish about this if you're wrong. I'll rub it in, you know."

"I can take it. Are you leaving the restaurant?"

"I just threw some cash down on the table. I'm strolling, not running. There's a taxi down the street. You'll owe me for cab fare, too."

"Fine. Has the man in the gray suit moved?"

"No, he's still reading his newspaper. Looks like you're wrong."

"Good. Thanks, Kimbro. Call me as soon as you get to your apartment."

"You can bet I will. I didn't finish my breakfast. I'll use it as a guilt trip to make you tell me why you wanted these tapes. See you, Jill." He cut the connection.

"What's happening?" Eve asked.

"Maybe nothing." Jill was dialing Novak. "But Kimbro managed to get hold of those tapes, and I'd really like Novak to have them picked up right away."

"And your friend, Kimbro, too?"

"It might be a good idea to have Novak's men look over the situation and see if it's a good idea." She was biting her lower lip. "I don't have a good reason. I guess I'm allergic to having everything go just as it should. It's not been happening much since I came to Maldara. It makes me nervous." Novak picked up, and she said quickly, "We've got the se-

curity tapes. Kimbro is on his way to his apartment now."
She rattled off the address. "Send someone to pick them up
right away." She paused. "And make certain whoever you
send knows what he's doing. Okay?"

"Why?"

"Because Kimbro is my friend, and I'm not taking
chances. Don't argue with me, Novak. I've got what we
needed. Now you do your part."

He was silent. "Orders? I'll send Nassem." He hung up
the phone.

"Mission accomplished?" Eve asked as she watched Jill slip
her phone in her pocket. "You were pretty sharp. You don't
usually speak to Novak like that."

"He'll survive. I wanted him to get off the phone and do
what I needed." She shrugged. "I know it was overkill, and
he'll make me pay for it later. It seemed the thing to do at
the time." She looked at the food on the tray in front of Eve.
"You've scarcely touched your salad. Can I get you anything
else?"

"No, I'll finish this. I've been a little busy listening to
you." She made a face. "Stop hovering over me. I know you
want to go back down to the village and make sure Novak is
doing what you want him to do. Go!"

Jill smiled. "As you command." She headed for the door.
"It's ridiculous, you know. I'm overreacting."

"Or it might be instinct," Eve said soberly as she gazed
back at her Mila reconstruction. "I believe in instinct. I hope
that you *are* overreacting. Let me know when Novak's agent
actually has those security tapes in his hands."

"You'll be the first to know."

"I'd better be," she said wryly. "It appears that I'm the
only one who is out of the loop."

Five minutes later, Jill had reached the hut where Joe and

Novak had set up shop. Joe was no longer there, but Novak appeared to be just as busy as when she'd left. She hesitated at the door.

"Stop dithering," Novak said without looking up from his computer. "Yes, I did contact Nassem, and he'll be at Kimbro's apartment in thirty minutes. Satisfied?"

"Yes, you did the best you could." She came into the hut. Hajif had only managed to produce the one small bench where Novak was sitting for the makeshift office, but there were colorful blankets placed around the hut against the walls. Jill dropped down on one of the blankets and leaned back against the wall. "And it might not even be necessary. He was pretty sure he wasn't followed."

"But he's your friend." Novak's voice was without expression. "And with you, that means commitment and, therefore, possible inconvenience for me. I'm beginning to become accustomed to it."

"Poor you." She grinned. "Where's Quinn?"

"He received a call from his son. He wanted privacy."

"And probably to ensure that he not reveal a softer side to you," she said. "That's reserved for Eve and company." She took out her phone. "What other calls do you want me to make now that we've nailed down the security tapes?"

"You can call Gideon and see if he's made any contacts in Zahra Kiyani's august household yet."

"Busywork?"

"Maybe. You seem to be a little edgy. But useful busywork. Gideon sometimes gets carried away and goes in depth with any project. He needs structure."

"He's brilliant. You're lucky to have him."

"But I don't have him, that's my point. No one has him. He might go off in any direction if it pleases him. But he might be less likely to stray from the path if you're around."

"I'm not his guardian." She added slyly, "If that's what you want, then I should have gone with him."

"That's not what I want," he said flatly. "And you know it. Stay away from Zahra. Just check on Gideon. If nothing else, it will keep your mind off Kimbro."

"Busywork," she repeated. But she still dialed Gideon's number. No answer. She tried it again. In the middle of the ring, she got another call.

Kimbro.

She quickly pressed accept. "Are you in your apartment?"

"Locking the door now. Happy?"

"Moderately. Herb Nassem, a CIA operative, will be picking up the security tapes in about twenty minutes. Don't give them to anyone else."

"Can I ply him with liquor and see if I can talk him into telling me why those tapes are so important?"

"No, he has no idea. You weren't followed?"

"No. Not even that guy in the restaurant. He never stirred from that table when I got in the cab." He paused. "All kidding aside, you're not getting into anything over your head? I'm here for you if you are. Iron Man is my middle name. You don't need to get involved with these CIA guys. They can be trouble."

"Tell me about it," she said dryly. He might still want the story, but she was touched anyway. "I'll call you if I need to ditch them. But I hear Nassem is reliable. If he wants to pull you out of there, go with him."

"If you insist . . . and promise to keep in touch."

"Absolutely. When Nassem gets there, let me know. Thanks, Kimbro." She cut the connection and looked up to see Novak gazing at her. "He says he wasn't followed and that CIA can be trouble. I agree. But I'll give them the benefit of the doubt if this Nassem comes through." She grinned. "Probably not you. You're too far gone."

"Definitely." He tilted his head. "You're relieved."

"So far. I'll feel better once Kimbro gives the tapes to your guy. He should be there in another twenty minutes. I want this over."

Novak nodded and turned back to his calls. "It sounds as if you've got it covered."

"I hope I do." She started to dial Gideon again. "I couldn't reach Gideon before. While I'm waiting for Kimbro's call, I'll try him again..."

———————

But it wasn't over in twenty minutes.

No call from Kimbro.

It didn't mean anything, Jill told herself. Nassem could have been stuck in traffic or something. Cairo was always a traffic nightmare...

Another fifteen minutes.

No call.

She started to dial Kimbro.

It went to voice mail.

Shit.

Her hand was shaking as she started to punch in the number again.

"I've already tried him twice," Novak said quietly.

She went still. "What?"

"Nassem always has orders to call his superior, Karim Absar, when he makes contact with the subject. He was on his way up in the elevator after he reached the apartment building when he checked in twenty minutes ago. But he didn't call back after contacting Kimbro." He paused. "And he didn't answer when Absar called."

"So you called Kimbro," she said shakily.

"Twice."

"You said that." She moistened her lips. "Something must have happened. We should call the police or an emergency number." She rubbed her temple. "No, not the police. Stupid. We just robbed the damn police. The medical-emergency number. I think it's 123 in Cairo."

"My people will be faster. When they couldn't contact Nassem, I told them to get over to Kimbro's apartment right away. They should be arriving any minute."

"Efficient. You're always so efficient, Novak." She was having trouble concentrating on what she was saying. All she could think about was Kimbro. "You called him. Why didn't you tell me?"

"You were already worried. There was no use making it worse until I was sure that it was necessary. It could have been anything. It didn't have to be—" He stopped. "We're still not sure what problem they might have run into. We won't know until Absar's team gets there."

"But you have an idea, don't you?" She drew a deep breath. "Of course, we both do. But he didn't think he was followed, Novak."

"And he might not have been. If they had an ID on him after he took the tapes, they might have just gotten his address and been there waiting for him to show. Or his tail might have been very, very good."

"He might not have had to be that good. Kimbro was cocky. Piece of cake." She could feel her eyes stinging. "He said it was a piece of cake."

He muttered a curse. "We don't *know*, Jill."

She nodded. "We have to wait. You're right, we should find out soon." *Keep control.* Novak was being his usual professional self, and she had to follow his lead. But it was so hard. She linked her arms around her drawn-up knees and held them tight. "I told him to hold off, and I'd get him help, but he thought he could do it without any help. Cocky. He's always so cocky. And he had the deal made before I even knew it. I should have known he'd do something like that. I should have expected it."

"Shut up," he said roughly. "I can see where this is going, and I'm not letting you take either one of us there. It could be okay, Jill. I'll get a report from Nassem or Absar any minute, and we'll—"

His phone rang. "It's Absar."

She stiffened, her eyes flying to Novak's face as he answered the call. Whoever Absar was, he was spitting out words as soon as Novak answered, not giving him a chance to reply. Her gaze was focused desperately on Novak's face as he listened, but his expression told her nothing. "The tapes?" he asked once.

Still no expression.

Then, evidently, he was asked a question because he did answer. "No, don't wait. Take care of it. It has to be clean." He cut the connection.

She sat up straight, her gaze on his face. "Not good," she said jerkily. "Though I don't know how I can tell. I never know what you're thinking. Kimbro?"

"Dead."

She couldn't breathe. She felt as if she'd been kicked in the stomach.

"Dammit!" Suddenly Novak was on his knees beside her. His face contorted, his hands grasping her shoulders. "I had to say it fast and hard and get it over with. I *know* you. I couldn't play around with it when you knew it was coming."

"Yes, I knew it was coming," she said stiltedly. "I was just hoping I was wrong."

"Well, you weren't wrong." She was suddenly pulled into

his arms, his hand on the back of her head, her face buried in his chest. "Kimbro's dead. Nassem's dead. Both found in Kimbro's apartment. Stop shaking. I can't take it."

Jill couldn't take it either. She was clutching desperately at him. He seemed to be the only warmth in her world right now. "How?"

"Will you let me tell you later?"

"No. Now."

"The attack was probably made when Kimbro opened the door for Nassem. It appeared to be an assault from the rear. Absar thinks they might have been waiting in a vacant apartment down the hall for their chance to go after Kimbro. Nassem was almost decapitated by a knife blow to the back of his neck." He paused. "Or possibly a machete."

Machete . . .

"Kimbro?"

"Same weapon. Two blows to the chest and abdomen, one kill blow to the throat. It had to be fast, he would have bled out very quickly."

She closed her eyes tightly. "Is that supposed to be comforting?"

"The only comfort I can give you."

"It sucks, Novak." But she was still holding tightly to him. "The tapes?"

"Gone."

"And machetes are a strange weapon of choice for a thug in Cairo." She added unsteadily, "But it was Varak's favorite weapon."

"Varak wouldn't have been the one who did this, Jill."

"But he had an entire troop of machete killers in his personal army. Who knows what kind of force he has now? He could have sent one of them to take care of this small job. Nothing much, just killing a reporter who got in his way.

A reporter who *I* put in his way." She couldn't stop talking, couldn't stop the tears from flowing down her cheeks as she lifted her head to look up at him. "That's why I was afraid. All those deaths...I thought: What if Varak is still alive and comes back to do it again? And he *is* back, Novak. I brought him back. I set out bait for the tiger."

"The hell you did." His hands were cupping her face as he glared down at her. He said fiercely, "You know that's not true. Stop feeling sorry for yourself. I won't *have* it."

"I don't feel sorry for myself. I feel sorry for Kimbro, dammit. And I have to accept responsibility for the—"

"I gave you the assignment. You didn't even realize that anyone but you knew what Kimbro was up to. And you told me yourself he not only wanted to repay a debt, he wanted the story. If he hadn't moved too quickly, we could have had someone to protect him from the moment he left that police station. He was careless and overconfident, and it got him killed."

"It's not that easy. I drew him into the web because I was worried about what those tapes would do to Eve and Quinn. You can't absolve me of blame, Novak."

"Then let me share it. Because I sure as hell can't take watching you like this."

He meant it. All the fierceness and the almost brutal intensity that electrified him were naked in his face. It shocked her. She instinctively pushed him away. "You can't do that, Novak. You have your own problems." She shook her head to clear it. "And you shouldn't have to deal with all this angst I'm going through either. You had a man killed today also. Did you know Nassem?"

For an instant, his face still retained that shockingly fierce intensity. Then it was gone, and he said without expression, "I'd met Nassem a couple times. He was a good operator and supposed to be a good guy."

"Very vague. Is your life usually that vague?"

"It's safer to keep it that way in my job."

But there had been nothing safe or vague about him only a moment ago. Forget it. She shouldn't have even asked the question. Keep away from anything personal with Novak. "I can't do that." She got to her feet. "I used to try, but it doesn't work for me. People pop up, and suddenly there's a Kimbro or a Hajif or a Gideon." She was wiping her cheeks with the sleeve of her shirt. "Or even a Novak."

"And you get hurt."

"It depends on how the story goes. Sometimes I can make it come out right. I'm not sure about this one. I'm beginning to doubt it." She said unsteadily, "I suppose I should take care of arrangements for Kimbro. He doesn't have a wife or kid, but he used to talk about his mother in Toronto."

"Later perhaps. Not now."

Her gaze flew to his face. "Why not?"

"It's better if the bodies just disappear for a while. We don't want the police or Egyptian government involved in this yet. I told Absar to do a cleanup."

"What about the evidence? I don't want it cleaned up. I want the people who killed Kimbro to be caught."

"We'll send in a forensic team. Absar's already on the job. We'll find the murderers and take care of it. I promise you."

"He was my *friend*."

"Then be a friend to him. Don't go after the errand boy, go after Varak. They have those tapes now, and all hell may break loose." He met her eyes. "It's starting, Jill."

She stared at him for a long moment.

It was starting.

It had already started when Eve completed that reconstruction. But Kimbro's death had marked the beginning of the battle to come. There was no turning their backs on the struggle now. Those security tapes would light a fire that could cause a gigantic bonfire.

Accept it. Stop this clinging and weeping and wailing that wasn't going to help.

But Kimbro...

"All right. Then let's find Varak." She turned and headed for the door. She added fiercely, "But you keep your promise, Novak. I'm holding you to it." She paused at the door. "How quickly can we expect those tapes to explode in our faces?"

"Not long. I wouldn't say that either Zahra or Varak have a great degree of patience, and their underlings will know it. It's possible they could be seeing them in the next few hours."

"And then we wait for the explosion."

"Or attempt to cause one of our own." His gaze was scanning her face. "Are you okay now?"

Her lips indented in a ghost of a smile. "No, but I'll be better when we figure out how to cause that explosion. I don't like to feel this defeated. It's got to change."

———————

"Michael just called, Eve," Joe said grimly when he came into the museum. "He was phoning from the dig site in the middle of the day. I believe that constitutes big-time worry on his part." He shook his head. "Though I managed to stave off any action, Jane might have to face problems later."

"Dammit." Eve frowned as she turned to face him. "How did he sound?"

"Calm. Reasonable. Just trying to talk me into bringing him here to see you. He's worried, not panicking. Being Michael."

"And even when he panics, we wouldn't know it," Eve murmured. "He'd just do what he thinks he should do. Which scares me to death." Her lips twisted. "And he has perfect timing, doesn't he? You want me to go to London. He's putting pressure from his end. I'm caught in the middle."

"No conspiracy, Eve."

"I know." She sighed. "I'll call him back and try to reassure him. But he can read me like a book. Honesty is great except when you have to deal with someone like Michael."

"It will help if he just hears your voice," Joe said. "The vibes are always there between you, but just talk to him." He moved over to stand beside her. "It always helps me." His hand reached out to caress her cheek. "Even if you say the wrong thing."

"And even the times when you turn a deaf ear." She held his hand to her cheek for a moment. "But you must be more concerned about him than you're letting on if you ran here right after you talked to him." She looked up at him. "Or did you consider it an opportunity?"

He shook his head. "I wouldn't use Michael as a pawn, no matter how much I want my own way."

"I didn't think you would, but you really wanted me to get out of Dodge." Her gaze was searching his face. "What else, Joe? How bad?"

"Not good. Right after I hung up from Michael, I got a call from Jill. It seems that her friend Kimbro is dead, and the gallery tapes were taken."

"She must feel terrible," Eve said, sick. "I know she was worried."

"She should be worried," he said. "We should all be worried about those tapes."

"Are you blaming Jill?"

"Why should I blame her?" he said impatiently. "She was only trying to help. I'm the one who left those tapes in the gallery. I should have found a way to get them out of there myself."

"Sure, you had so much time, and nothing at all was happening around you," Eve said. Joe's first instinct was always to shoulder the burdens. "Forget it. How can we make it right?"

"It might be too late. As soon as they view those tapes, they'll go after me, and that will lead to you. The only thing we can do is brace ourselves for the impact. We're already doing all that's possible to go after Varak at top speed."

Brace for the impact. Eve shuddered at the words. Brace for Varak's striking out at them like a vicious rattler. Brace for Zahra's moving forward, sleek and dangerous and totally without conscience. "At the moment, it doesn't seem like top speed to me."

Varak wielding his glittering machete in that schoolroom.

Varak striking out at those helpless children.

He likes to kill the children.

She inhaled sharply as she remembered Jill's words.

"No!" Her hands closed into fists. "I don't have to wonder what else the son of a bitch might do. He uses children, Joe. That's why he staged the massacre at the schoolroom. He wanted to lure their parents to the school from the village, so he attacked the children. He knew it would be the one sure way to trap them." She met his eyes. "Because there's nothing a parent wouldn't do for their child." She paused. "There's nothing we wouldn't do for Michael. We have to be prepared that one of Varak's moves might be to go after our child." Even as she said the words, she could feel the fear and panic rising. "You were so worried about me, Joe. But forget about me. We should be worried about Michael. We should concentrate on keeping him safe."

"Slow down. You or Michael? That's no choice at all."

"But it's always been the right choice for us." She drew a shaky breath. "First, we have to keep Michael away from Maldara and away from me. We don't want to draw Varak's attention to him. Particularly not in connection to me. But we can't be sure he's safe at the dig either. Varak probably has all Zahra's power behind him, and judging by the appearance of that sniper at Asarti and Kimbro's death in Cairo, he must still have his own scumbags at his command. He could send someone to find him."

"I'll tell Jane to disappear with him until this is over."

"You know that would only make Michael more determined to go his own way. It's better to keep him busy. Besides, Jane should be protected, too. And while we're at it, even Cara's probably not safe. You'll have to make sure he can't touch anyone in the family. But I'm most worried about Michael and Jane. I'll call Jane and tell her what we're facing." She got to her feet and went into his arms. "I believe it's time for you to call those buddies of yours at Scotland Yard and persuade them to assign him that army of detectives you were going to surround me with." She laid her head on his shoulder, and said softly, "It was a good idea, just not the right person."

"Exactly the right person." His arms tightened around her. "I don't suppose I can talk you into going to be with Michael?"

She shook her head. "I have to stay away from him. Haven't you been paying attention?"

"I wish I could tell you that you're all wrong about this." He paused. "I might, if I hadn't gone down and looked at that schoolroom for myself." Joe's lips twisted. "Okay, then I suppose I'd better get on the phone again with the Yard. I just spent half the morning harassing them about Oscar

Varak." He gave her a quick kiss before he turned away. "We'd better get ready to defend the gates."

"And brace for the impact," she repeated somberly as she reached for her phone to call Jane.

———

"Why didn't you tell me all this before?" Jane asked quietly. "All Joe has been saying is that I should keep an eye on Michael because he might decide to take off and go to see you. That was worry enough, but now you're telling me that he might actually be in danger on this dig? Not fair, Eve."

"I know it wasn't. I was so grateful to you for giving Michael such a great time, and I guess I was hoping that what was happening here wouldn't get in the way. I just wanted to keep you out of it as long as I could. That time just ran out."

"I'd say it did," she said dryly. "And you had no business keeping me out of it. I'm supposed to be merrily playing in the dirt with Michael while you're being hunted down by this Varak. I should be with you."

"No, you shouldn't," Eve said firmly. "You should be exactly where you are right now. Joe has arranged to give you and Michael all kinds of protection, but those Scotland Yard people don't know Michael as you do." She paused. "And Michael would never be anything but honest with you even if he thought you were getting in his way. We both know he wouldn't be quite as honest with anyone else. This might be a bad time for him. He's going to need you."

"Now you're scaring me."

"I just mean he's going to be worried about me, and there aren't many people who can handle a kid like Michael when he's determined to do something." She made a face. "I wish I had ten of you at that dig."

"Do you?" Jane shook her head. "I can see why you're concerned, but I still want to come there and—" She stopped. "Okay, I'll do what you want. But no more trying to keep me out of this. Be honest with me. And be honest with Michael. Though he probably knows what's going on anyway. But it might be making him uneasy for you not to be perfectly open with him."

"You could be right," Eve said. "Sometimes it's hard to know what to do. First instinct is always to protect. Very well, honesty all the way. Thanks, Jane."

"And that's not all. If I'm responsible for taking care of Michael, then I'll do it my way." She added, "You're right, Joe's friends at the Yard might not cut it as far as Michael's concerned. And I can't furnish ten of me who could handle him. But I'll make a call, and I'll have at least one person who's capable of doing it here at the dig tomorrow."

"Who?"

"Seth Caleb's at his estate in Scotland." Her lips twisted. "I don't think you'd argue that Michael would be no problem for him. Michael adores him, and they're soul mates. Half the time, I don't even understand what's going on between them."

Jane was talking about Michael's relationship with Caleb, but she wasn't mentioning the off and on, tumultuous and passionate relationship she'd had with Caleb in the past. Eve hesitated. "The last thing I heard from you was that you weren't seeing Seth Caleb any longer. Has that changed?"

"No, I'm not seeing him, but Caleb has no qualms about dropping in on me whenever he pleases. And it will please him that I need him to come and guard Michael."

"I don't want to make things difficult for you, Jane."

"Things are always difficult when Caleb is around. We might as well make use of him. You and Joe will feel safer that Caleb is with Michael, won't you?"

Eve couldn't deny it. "He's totally remarkable."

"And that's all that's important." Jane smiled. "If I can't be with you, then you'll know that you've nothing to worry about as far as Michael is concerned." Her smile faded. "But you'll have me to worry about if you don't call me every day to tell me what's happening. This can't happen again, Eve."

"It won't. Never again. Good-bye, Jane." She ended the call. She knew Jane too well not to realize that having Caleb at that dig might be a strain considering the volatility of her relationship with him, but she also knew she wouldn't be able to talk her out of it. Jane would make any sacrifice, do everything she could to safeguard Michael and the entire family. It was her nature.

"Everything all right?" Joe was studying her expression.

"Great." She smiled with an effort. "Jane is in fine form. Michael couldn't be in safer hands. And that dig will definitely be braced for impact."

———◆———

"Get over here!" Varak's voice was crackling with fury as Zahra picked up the phone. "Right now, Zahra. Or I'll come to that fancy palace of yours." His disconnect was a crash in her ear.

He was clearly in a rage, Zahra thought, but he had no right to speak to her like this. She had already been out there to see him earlier today, and she wouldn't be at his beck and call. Then she stifled her own anger. She couldn't take a chance with Varak's volatile temperament right now.

And he must not come here. How many times had she told him that they must not take any chances? She would have to go, but he would hear from her about this when she got to his damn compound.

She tore out of the palace and, a little over an hour later, screeched to a stop in front of his house. She jumped out of the car and was climbing the steps when the door flew open and Varak came out on the porch.

"I won't take your rudeness, Varak," she said. "Next time, I'll tell you to go to hell."

"You'll take whatever I give you." He grabbed her wrist and was pulling her inside the house. "You've put me at risk for the last time. You promised me that you'd make certain I'd be safe if I played your game. Now everything is falling apart, and it's your fault."

"Nothing is falling apart except that I don't have my statue."

"The hell it's not." Varak's face was livid, twisted with anger. "I told you that you had to get rid of Duncan. But you were so frightened that all those diplomats who suck up to you would turn their backs and walk away. Now look what you've done."

"I *tried* to get rid of her. I even had Bogani drown that chef to protect us. I haven't done anything else but put up with your arrogance and insults." She glared at him. "And I've reached the end of my patience with you. What's supposed to be my fault, Varak?"

"It *is* your fault." He strode across the room toward the desk. "Do you want to see why you don't have your precious statue? I just got the security tapes from the gallery at Asarti." He pressed the button on his computer. "And guess who was dragging Dobran through that gallery."

She was looking over his shoulder at the computer screen. "How should I know who—" She stopped. "Gideon? It was Gideon at Asarti?"

"You told me he was once your lover. He seems to have forgotten old loyalties and formed others. He wasn't alone."

He fast-forwarded the tape. "Do you recognize this man, Zahra?"

"No, I've never seen him before."

"Neither have I. So I ran a check through a database I use. Actually, he's very well known in some circles. He's Joe Quinn, a detective with the Atlanta Police Department." He took a step closer to her, his eyes glittering. "And he's married to Eve Duncan. Now what would he be doing at Asarti, Zahra?"

She inhaled sharply. "How should I know? None of this is my fault."

"And it's not your fault that he was obviously trying to extract Dobran from that château when my sniper shot him? Not your fault that the one man who could tell the world that I'm still alive was being snatched away by the husband of the woman who is the premier forensic sculptor in the world? You don't see the connection?"

Zahra was afraid that she did, but she'd have to be wary about admitting it to Varak while he was in this foul mood. "Perhaps. But I don't know how the connection would be made. Duncan was working on reconstructions of those children. I saw them when I went to the museum for the press conference. Nothing to do with you. There was no threat."

"And was there no threat from bringing an expert forensic sculptor within a stone's throw of the U.N. headquarters where the skull was placed? Why do you think Quinn wanted Dobran? He already knew that Eve Duncan had been working on that skull and was certain it wasn't me. She fooled you. Can't you see it? Gideon brought her to Maldara, and everyone knows he and Jill Cassidy are friends. They all fooled you."

"I asked Wyatt, and he told me that Cassidy had no connection with the Children for Peace charity that contacted the London office."

"Just as she had nothing to do with trying to skewer me by paying Hadfeld for that story about my still being alive? I wanted to kill her then, but you persuaded me that I should only hurt and scare her. You should have realized that she wouldn't give up. She just went in another direction. So don't tell me that she had nothing to do with Eve Duncan's coming here." His voice was low and thick with rage. "Or that Duncan wasn't pretty damn sure of what Quinn would find at Asarti. Joe Quinn wouldn't have risked his reputation if Duncan hadn't thought she had proof that the skull in the U.N. vault wasn't mine."

"How could she know that?"

"That's what we're going to find out." He whirled to face her. "And I know you're ready and willing to help, aren't you?"

"Of course, I gave you my word." *Keep him calm. And this might affect both of us.* "Tell me what I can do."

He reached in her handbag and took out her phone. "You're going to call Edward Wyatt and tell him that you're in the mood for something different and are coming to see him at the U.N. residence tonight for your fun and games. You'll tell him to send everyone away so that no one will recognize you. You'll make it sound erotic enough that he'll be panting to do anything you want him to do."

He grinned. "But then he does that anyway. Right?"

She ignored the question. "What are you planning, Varak?"

"You'll get me and my men into that vault room, where I can check out that skull. Wyatt's already given you the code ID imprinted on it. If that code's not on that skull at the U.N. vault, then we'll know what Eve Duncan has been working on at that museum at Robaku."

"And what good will that do?"

"Then we start covering our bases and nullifying any gains Duncan and those others might believe they've made. The minute I know for sure that she has the skull, the game changes." His eyes were flickering, blazing with intensity. "I have a plan ready. Do you think I spent all these months cooped up in this compound without thinking of ways to protect myself and end up back on top, where I belong?" He nodded at the phone. "Make that call."

She was still glancing down at the video. "They do have my statue."

"I don't want to hear about that statue again," Varak said between clenched teeth. "*Listen* to me. You're going to do as I wish, or I'll blow all your plans to hell and take what I want in my own way. I'm sick of your stalling about giving me my share of that gold. Do you understand? I'm done with taking orders from you. From now on, you'll do what I tell you to do. Make the call."

"You will hear about it again," she said fiercely. "Because I will get it back. Don't give me orders, Varak." She was thinking, trying to figure out which way to go. She couldn't let him see that he'd intimidated her, but she could tell he was ready to do exactly what he threatened. The blowup she'd feared all these months was very close. Play along. Give him what he wanted now and see how she could turn it around. "I'll do this because it seems the best way to be certain that we're in as bad a situation as you're telling me. You do have your uses, and you might even be able to point a way out of it." She had a sudden thought. "But Wyatt is accustomed to having Dalai join us. I'll need her to come with us tonight, and I gave her to you earlier today. I have to have her back. Where is she?"

"Bedroom." He shrugged. "If she'll be any good to you."

She didn't like the sound of that. "I told you not to damage her." She was heading for the bedroom. "Now what have you done?"

"I enjoyed myself." He followed her into the bedroom. "You promised me more time than just these few hours, but I made them count. But you can have her now. If you think that it won't turn him off."

Zahra was gazing critically at the young girl. Dalai's wrists and ankles were tied to the four posts of the bed. Her naked body was bruised, her nipples bloody. Tears were running down her cheeks, her eyes were desperate, pleading, as she looked at Zahra. "Please..."

"She's not too bad," Zahra decided. "I'll tell Wyatt I did it, and it might even excite him." She went over to the bed and untied the ropes. "Though if I'd left her with you until tomorrow, it would have taken me weeks to repair her." She tossed a sheet to Dalai. "Wrap up and go get in the car. And stop crying, it's not as if it hasn't happened to you before. You should be accustomed to it by now. You're making me angry."

"I'm...sorry." The girl was frantically trying to get to her feet. "Don't leave me, madam. I'll do anything you want me to do."

"Yes, don't leave her, madam," Varak said mockingly. "She was a complete bore."

Zahra ignored him. "Just get out of here, Dalai. You'll have to make yourself presentable when I get you back to the palace." Zahra heard Varak laugh behind her as she began punching in Wyatt's number.

She drew a deep breath when Wyatt picked up the call. "I've been thinking about you. I've been amusing myself with Dalai today, but she's not enough for me right now. I'm coming to you tonight, and I want you to send everyone away and be prepared to entertain me..."

CHAPTER

14

Now what had Zahra been up to? Gideon wondered.

He drew farther back in the shadows of the old coach house as he watched Zahra drag Dalai out of the maze bordering the street and into the far end of the coach house.

He knew exactly where they were going. He had used the secret passage hidden in that last stall many times to get into Zahra's quarters during the summer when their affair had been red-hot.

Whatever it was that was causing Zahra to have reason to creep around in the dark and use those passages at a time like this was probably worth exploring...

What the hell? More than probably. He hadn't had much luck so far today.

He had spent most of the day moving around the exterior of the palace and refreshing himself on any changes that might have occurred in the years since he'd broken with

Zahra. Most of the new guards were unknown to him, but there was one he remembered who might be willing to deal if the money was high enough. He'd been holding off going inside the palace to explore and had only just verified that the secret passage leading to Zahra's wing was still available and intact. Then, when he'd seen Zahra and Dalai moving from the maze into the coach house, his curiosity had flared.

Dalai... The girl was draped only in a sheet, and she looked very much the worse for wear. Not good for her, but it might be an opportunity...

What a bastard I am, he thought bitterly. The girl was like a frightened rabbit around Zahra, and he was thinking about using her? Rabbit... He vaguely remembered Zahra scornfully calling her that in those days when she'd first come to the palace all those years ago. He scarcely remembered Dalai Sadar from the old days. She had been a new servant in Zahra's entourage then and not even into her teens, still a child. She had been brought from one of the Kiyani farms in the north when Zahra had said she needed a new maidservant. He only recalled Zahra's being impatient with her and telling him that she scurried around like a frightened rabbit and that it was going to be boring having to train her.

He recalled feeling sorry for the girl at the time and had often tried to ease the sting of Zahra's scathing words. But he had already been trying to edge away from Zahra, and a few months later, he'd made the break and was on his way to London.

And Dalai had grown up under Zahra's less than tender care and become the pretty, well-trained rabbit that Zahra had intended.

Had there been blood on that sheet?

His phone was vibrating in his pocket.

Jill. He took the call.

"I've been trying to call you for the last few hours, Gideon," Jill said in exasperation. "Why didn't you pick up?"

"I was busy. Granted, I'm very familiar with this palace, but when your aim is to spy on the enemy, you don't want to draw attention to yourself by chatting on the phone as you stroll around the property. It defeats the purpose. You caught me this time in the old coach house, where I could talk."

"Coach house? Zahra has a coach—Never mind. I've reached you now. Have you talked to Novak?"

"Would I answer his calls when I refused to answer yours? That would be rude."

"Stop it, Gideon. I have to tell you something." She paused. "We weren't able to get the security tapes back. Novak's agent, Nassem, was killed, and so was my friend, Kimbro. Kimbro actually had the tapes in his possession, but we have to assume that when he was killed, the tapes were taken by one of Varak's men."

"Shit. Nassem?" Gideon repeated. "He was a good guy, Jill."

"That's what Novak said." She cleared her throat. "So was Kimbro. But the reason I was trying desperately to get in touch with you is those tapes. If Zahra and Varak don't know that you were involved in that break-in already, they will soon. You shouldn't be there, Gideon. We don't know what they'll do if they think we might be getting close."

"I'm careful." He added grimly, "And all the more reason why we should find out what's going on with Zahra. I remember she has an office that adjoins her suite. I thought that I might rifle through her desk and see what I can find out. There are too many blanks that need to be filled in."

"It sounds too risky to do it alone. Come back here, and we'll find a way to work on it together. Haven't you been there long enough?"

"Maybe. I spent most of the time finding out that I knew practically none of Zahra's personal guards any longer. There's one I might approach if necessary." He paused. "But I did have what you might call an encounter with Dalai Sadar this evening. Do you remember her?"

"The young girl that runs around at Zahra's beck and call? There's not much to remember. She obviously tries to fade into the background. I feel sorry for her, and Eve was really irritated at the way Zahra treated her. Was she around when you were playing your sex games with Zahra?"

"Barely. She was just a kid, not even in her teens yet. I remember trying to get Zahra to be easier on her. But I wasn't around that long. Our ship had sailed."

"But you met Dalai this evening?"

"As I said, more of an encounter." He changed the subject. "I'm going to stick around for a little while. Quinn would say that would be a waste of time coming back to Robaku for help when I'm already here at the palace. He's all for conquering by combining tasks." He paused. "I'll see how I feel about that office when I get within striking distance. If I decide against going for it, I still have one other path I can try before I come back to Robaku."

"What?"

"Never mind. It's a long shot, but you can never tell what will work. I'll call you when I leave here. Don't phone me again. I won't be able to answer you." He ended the call.

A long shot. He stood for a moment in the darkness, staring at the wall passage into which Zahra and Dalai had disappeared. He had to admit he was curious . . . So go for the long shot?

And perhaps . . . reparation?

Gideon had no trouble remembering the layout of the rooms once he reached Zahra's wing. The maid's room was two doors down from Zahra's suite. She always wanted privacy but also to have instant service when she required it.

He moved silently down the hall, listening for activity from Zahra's suite or the guards on the floor below. He had waited almost an hour before he'd entered the passage. If it had been blood on that sheet, Zahra would probably have needed time to take care of Dalai's wounds.

He hesitated. Time to make the decision. Go to Zahra's office? Or go to Dalai?

Either would be a risk.

He stopped outside the maid's room.

No decision. That blood...He'd known this would be the choice.

He listened.

No sound of activity.

He silently opened the door and slipped into the bedroom. The room was so plain and without color, it appeared almost sterile. A bed. A pine washstand. A chair against the far wall.

He could see Dalai sitting on the edge of the bed, still wrapped in the sheet, her eyes fixed dully on the floor.

"Dalai," he said gently.

She stiffened, her gaze wide with alarm as she saw him.

Oh, shit. She was going to scream.

This was turning out to be a stupid idea, he thought. "Shh. Please don't scream. I'm Sam Gideon. Do you remember me? I'm not going to hurt you."

She didn't scream. She just sat on the bed, panting, looking at him with those wide, dark eyes. "Of course...I know you. What do you want with me? Did Madam Zahra send you? I wouldn't think she'd choose to permit you to have me."

"All I want is to talk to you. Zahra didn't send me." He grimaced. "In fact, she would be very angry with me if she knew I was here. I'm surprised you remember me. You'd just come to the palace when I first met you, and I didn't stay around for long. Your Madam Zahra and I were once what you might term an item, but that was long ago. She can't stand me now."

"I remember everything about you." She was still stiff and unrelaxed. "But you're right, now Madam feels differently. You have to leave here. I didn't think she'd send you to me. But she'll still punish me if she finds you here." Her voice was trembling. "She does hate you. I can tell every time she sees you or talks about you. You make her angry. She *must* not get angry."

"Because she'll punish you?" He came toward her, his gaze on the sheet. "You're bleeding. Did she do that to you? And those bruises on your shoulders?"

"Go away."

"I thought I knew what a bitch she was, but I might have been way off." His lips tightened. "You don't have to take this, Dalai."

"Go *away*."

"Did she do it?"

"No. Yes. Go away. You'll make things worse if she comes in and sees you."

"Then we'll keep our voices down, and she won't come in. Unless she decides to come in and clean you up. I was thinking I'd given her time to have done that already."

"Take care of me?" She gazed at him in bewilderment. "Why would she do that? She told me to take care of it myself because she had to take me out again later tonight." Her hands clenched on the sheet. "You have to leave. She'll be angry with me. She'll think it's my fault. She'll give me to him again."

"Him?"

She was shaking her head. "You have to go. She'll hurt you, too." She was beginning to tremble. "And I can't take any more right now."

"I'll leave soon." He was having trouble keeping his temper. She might be a rabbit, but she had clearly been mistreated, and she was displaying a courage that touched him. "Maybe you shouldn't have to put up with any more of this. That's what I want to talk about. But first things first; it annoys me that Zahra didn't take care of you." He went to the washstand and poured water in the basin. "So I believe I'll do it myself." He grabbed a towel and washcloth and came back to the bed. "You looked like you could use a little help when I came into the room. You were just sitting, frozen."

"I'm just . . . tired. I was . . . resting." Her hand clutched at the sheet. "Go away. I'll do it."

"But I'm not in the mood for Zahra to get her own way right now. I'm very irritated with her. So sit very still." He was pulling the sheet down as he spoke. "And I'll take care of—" He went still, staring at her breasts. "You look as if you've been savaged by a wild animal."

She had gone still. "It doesn't hurt much anymore. I don't believe she'd like you to see it."

"No?" The anger and pity were growing more by the second. "Who did this?"

She didn't answer.

"Maybe later?" He dipped the washcloth in the water. "Sit still. I'll try not to hurt you." His lips tightened. "Though I don't know how I'm going to do that. You look . . . raw." He was dabbing carefully at her breasts. "You should probably go to a doctor. I'm tempted to take you with me when I go."

"No!" She was frantically shaking her head. "I'm fine.

She'd be angry. It won't matter. She said it wouldn't. Some men aren't like you. Some men like to see—" She broke off. "Why don't you just go away?"

"Easy." He lifted his eyes to her face. "I went away a long time ago and that's why I don't want to do it now. I was thinking about that when I saw you downstairs. I was such a selfish bastard, just out of college, and I didn't care about anyone but myself. I thought you'd be okay, but what did I know? I broke with her and went my merry way. Hell, I've hardly thought of you all these years."

"Why should you?" She was looking at him with bewilderment again.

"That's right, you don't expect anyone to think about you or watch out for you." He held up his hand as she opened her lips. "But I'm not going to make it difficult for you. I can see this isn't the time. Do you have any salves you can use on these wounds?"

She nodded jerkily.

"Why doesn't that surprise me?" His lips twisted. "Then I'll let you do it so that Zahra won't be angry with you. Just let me finish this bit to make sure you won't get rabies from the son of a bitch."

She nodded slowly, her gaze fixed on his face. She sat very still while he finished washing and drying her upper body. Then, when he sat back on his heels, she asked quietly, "Is that all? I can see you're angry. Have you changed your mind? Do you wish anything else of me?"

It was clear what she meant, and he felt another ripple of rage mixed with pity. He shook his head. "Just get your damn salve."

He watched as she dropped the sheet, got to her feet, and walked naked across the room to a drawer beneath the washstand. Her body was exquisitely fragile, and he realized that there were more bruises than he had thought. That delicate gold skin had to have been brutally beaten. She took a small round tube of salve from a drawer and rubbed it over her wounds. Then she turned to face him. "It's done. But it might be a waste if she wishes me to bathe later to prepare myself again."

"Prepare for what?"

She didn't answer.

"Or should I say whom?"

She didn't answer. "What do you want with me? Why did you come?" She moistened her lips. "I'm very confused, and I'm so tired. I'm forbidden to complain. But, if it pleases you, I would like you to go so that I can rest."

"What would please me is if I knew what else you were going to have to face tonight from Zahra." He took a cotton throw from her bed and wrapped it around her. "Sit down. Rest. I'll be out of here soon. I didn't mean to stay this long. You threw me a curveball I didn't expect. I just have a few things to say, and I'll be gone."

Where to start? She was looking at him with those doe eyes that were making him feel as if he were aiming a rifle at her. *Start at the beginning. Start with honesty.*

"I didn't come here to cause you any trouble. But I'm going to ask you to help me. There's no reason why you should because it's clear no one has helped you all these years. Certainly not me." He shook his head. "And it might even be dangerous for you. If Zahra can treat you like this, there's no telling what else she'll do to you." He paused. "But I have to ask it because it's very important, and you may be our only hope."

"Help you?" She was frowning. "I don't understand. I can do *nothing*. She hates you and wouldn't permit me to help you. She would punish me."

"Permit? Punish?" He paused. "You're not a slave, Dalai. Even in Maldara, slavery is forbidden. I won't tell you that there wouldn't be danger, but I will tell you that I'll protect you if you help me." He added, "And I promise Zahra will never be able to punish you again."

"You lie to me." She shook her head. "I belong to her. My father sent me to her and told me I must always do as she commands."

"You belong to no one but yourself. He was mistaken." He wasn't getting through to her. How could he expect to overcome the brainwashing Zahra had been giving her all these years? But every word she spoke was tearing him apart, and he had to keep trying. "You've lived here in the palace and heard all the speeches the diplomats made about freedom. You know that Zahra wasn't telling you the truth. You're free to do as you wish."

She shook her head. "I've heard all that, but I'm different. She said that I belong to her, like the slaves that Kiya brought from Egypt on the Great Journey belonged to Kiya. That I have to do everything she wants me to do." She added wearily, "And she *can* punish me. So that's another lie, too. Will you go now?"

"Not yet. I have to tell you what I need. Then I'll let you kick me out."

"Kick you out?" she asked in horror. "I could not do that."

He smiled. "Yes, you could. You just need the practice, and it would come naturally to you. But you might need my friend, Jill, to help you get over the first hesitation."

"Jill," she repeated tentatively. Then she said slowly after a moment's thought, "Jill Cassidy. I've heard Madam speak of her. She does not like her either."

"No, Jill has gotten in her way, and she doesn't like it." His eyes narrowed on Dalai's face. "But you probably knew that, didn't you? That's why I need your help, Dalai. You know everything that goes on with Zahra. You've been with her for years, and she obviously treats you like wallpaper when she's not mistreating you. You see and hear everything. She'd never think that you'd betray her."

"Because I would not. You do not know what she would do to me."

His lips tightened. "I can imagine, judging by what I've seen tonight. But I'm asking you anyway. Terrible things have happened here in Maldara, and Zahra is part of a plan to start it all again. There were so many deaths. My friends and I are trying to keep it from happening, but we're working in the dark. We need names and faces." He paused. "Particularly the name and face of one man who Zahra might be protecting. I believe you probably have information that might shine a light on that darkness. Information that can save lives. I *need* it, Dalai." He paused. "And in return, I'll promise to take care of you, and protect you, and give you a life that will give you all the choices you could wish. Is it a deal? Will you trust me?"

"You want *me*?" She was gazing at him in horror. "She would kill me. She would let him hurt me."

"If you helped us, we'd keep you safe. Just furnish us with what we need to stop Zahra . . . and anyone else with whom she's dealing. We'd protect you and even send you far away if you wish."

"I cannot answer questions." Her voice was shaking. "She said she would treat me as Kiya would someone who betrayed her. She even showed me the place with no air."

"What place?"

"Go away!"

"I'm going." He moved quickly to the door. "I understand why you're upset. But I had to do it. If you help us, it could save lives. I know you think of me as an enemy, I've never done anything for you. But getting rid of Zahra might even save your life someday."

"You don't understand *anything*." Her eyes were glittering, blazing. "I don't want to die like a Kiya slave. I don't want to die at all." Her voice was no longer shaking but very strong and hard with determination. "I won't let you or her or anyone do that to me."

That sudden change of demeanor from meekness to ferocity had startled him. "I'm trying to understand, Dalai." Gideon looked over his shoulder as he reached the door. Ferocity? He must have just frightened her. Except for those huge, blazing eyes, she looked infinitely fragile, and he couldn't leave her like that. "Don't let anyone else hurt you the way you were hurt tonight. Do you have a phone?"

"Of course, Madam might need me. I must always be available to her."

"Of course," he repeated. He strode back across the room and threw his card on the bed. "I'll leave. But if you change your mind or get in trouble, call me, and I'll come and get you. And you won't have to tell me anything if you're afraid to do it."

Her eyes widened. "Why would you do that?"

"I told you. Because I didn't do it when I should have done it all those years ago. When I got bored with her, I just took off. I didn't give a thought to you."

Her eyes were still bewildered. "Of course, you didn't. Why should you?"

"I can't explain it if you don't know. Anyway, deal or no deal, call me if you need help."

"I cannot do that," Dalai said jerkily. She was silent another moment. "I think you are trying to be kind to me. But if I'm not very good, she said he will punish me again, and I can't risk it." Her voice was shaking again. "I could not *stand* it."

His eyes narrowed. "Zahra's not always truthful. She might not keep her word. If she changes her mind, you might remember that I'm offering you your own choices." He added with sudden urgency, "No strings, dammit. Just use the card and call me."

"I'm going to tear it up and throw it away. She might find it," she said unsteadily. "But I'll remember your number. I have a very good memory. But don't expect me to use it."

It was a small victory, but he'd take it. "I never expect anything. I hope for everything." But she was still so damn defenseless. He impulsively reached into his pocket and pulled out his pearl-handled switchblade knife and threw it on the bed beside the card. "Take this in case you need it. My father gave it to me when I came home from Oxford. I think he'd want you to have it." He smiled. "Now you can't tear that to pieces. It's a keepsake."

"No, but I can never use it." She reached down and gingerly touched the pearl handle. "I'll have to hide it away so that no one will ever see it." She shook her head. "Why don't you understand? I can't resist, or it makes it a thousand times worse for me."

"No, I don't understand. Because if you'd let me help, we could beat this." He turned and moved back toward the door. "Just trust me." He carefully opened the door and cautiously looked up and down the hall. "Take care of yourself, Dalai," he said. "Since you won't let me do it. And no one else seems—"

"I've never thought of you as my enemy."

He stiffened at the words and looked over his shoulder. "What?"

"I never blamed you for leaving me," she burst out suddenly. "Why should I? Everybody leaves. And I never
thought I was important enough for you to worry about."
She stared him in the eye. "And I liked it when you were
with her. You smiled at me and joked. It was different than
it was later. You were nice to me."

He was silent. "You have a very limited experience in that
area. And that makes me feel like even more of a bastard than
I did before. But *call* me. Let me help you."

She shook her head. "Go away."

He had to go, he thought in frustration. But she was sitting there, fragile, helpless, and he wanted to scoop her up
and take her somewhere safe. Another casualty in this damn
war that had taken so much from so many. But a casualty that
he thought he might have prevented.

"Call me!" He closed the door and moved swiftly down
the hall.

<hr />

ROBAKU

"It's about time you got here." Jill came down the path toward Gideon when he arrived at Robaku an hour later.
"Would it have hurt to have phoned me as soon as you
could? Did you find out anything when you were going
through Zahra's personal quarters?"

"I didn't get that far," Gideon said. "I was checking out
something else, and I got involved." He held up his hand.
"Don't ask. I came up with zeros all around."

"And you're upset." Jill was reading his expression. "You
didn't by any chance run into Zahra while you were 'involved.'"

"If I had, I would have probably broken her neck," he said grimly. "I was ready to do it tonight."

"Why?"

"A poisonous combination of personal guilt and a few revelations that were particularly infuriating." He stopped, then said, "Okay, I was thinking about using her maid, Dalai, to help us. I thought she could be a fount of information. But I blew it. And besides, she's been used enough." He made a face. "At one point, I believe I even offered your services, Jill. Be prepared if I drop her on your lap if I change my mind. Why should I be any different? Do you know Zahra even used the Kiya card on Dalai to convince her that she was only a slave and didn't have any right to argue about how she was treated?"

"Kiya," Jill repeated. "It doesn't surprise me. After all, a queen must have her slaves. It was clear she seemed to consider Dalai her special property."

"Exactly."

"That sounded bitter." She was thinking. "I did feel sorry for her. And I remember that Eve was angry about the way she was treated." She nodded suddenly, and said recklessly, "Go ahead. By all means, hand her over to us. We're so frustrated that we'll be glad to find a way to get some of our own back."

"Easier said than done. I'd have to fight Dalai as well as Zahra." He changed the subject. "No word about whether the security tapes were delivered to Zahra or Varak yet?"

"Not as far as we've heard. I was hoping you'd know something when you got back from the palace."

"Well, Zahra was definitely on the move this evening, and she had plans for later tonight." His lips twisted. "I was tempted to follow them, but it sounded as if it might concern Dalai more than any connection to Asarti."

"Novak is monitoring the chatter, but nothing yet," Jill said. "Other than that, we're just trying to think of a way to make certain Eve's safe and find proof that it's Oscar's skull that we have in that museum. We'll probably hear about what Varak plans to do about those tapes soon enough." She shrugged. "But I don't think anyone is going to sleep well tonight."

"Then I might as well go have a drink with Novak and confess that I had an utterly worthless day. I don't dare go to Quinn. He won't accept any report that won't contribute to keeping Eve safe and out of jail."

"By all means go get a drink. You look like you need it. I might join both of you later before I go to Hajif's to turn in. He offered me a mat in his hut, and I'm trying to give Eve and Quinn their privacy." She turned and strolled toward the museum. "But first I'll go tell Eve that you're back and that we might have to adopt Dalai before this is over…"

———

U.N. HEADQUARTERS
10:32 P.M.

"You look beautiful tonight." Edward Wyatt stood at the top of the grand staircase and watched Zahra walk up the curving stairs toward him. Her dark hair shone as she passed beneath the huge crystal chandelier. His eyes lingered on her breasts, spilling out of the low neckline of her nude-colored silk gown. "Fantastic. Do you know how many times I've imagined you walking up to my bedroom toward me here in my own place? This is my domain, everyone has to kowtow and fawn to me. But all I could do was wonder what you would do to me if I could ever get you here."

"But I'm the one who arranged this. I'm always the one in charge," Zahra said coldly. "And if you didn't do as I told you to do, I will not stay. You've sent everyone away? I mustn't be seen here or I'll be known as your whore when I go to New York for my speech, and all those diplomats will not give me the respect I deserve. I'll be angry if you've made this visit difficult for me, Wyatt. I've been looking forward to it since I called you."

"Do you think I haven't?" he asked hoarsely. "I couldn't think of anything else. Of course I sent them away. I told my private secretary that I was having a confidential meeting with a member of the Botzan secret service who wanted to speak to me about a possible terrorist threat he might need our help to solve. That's what you wanted, right?"

"That's exactly what I wanted. We'll see if you can please me in other ways tonight." She had to get Wyatt out of the hall and into his bedroom right away. Varak had said he wanted the way clear to bring his men down to the vault ten minutes after she and Dalai arrived. She turned and said to Dalai behind her, "Come along. I want to see him perform. He's sure to be better than you were today. Where's your bedroom, Wyatt?"

"Third door." He gestured as she swept by him but paused to watch Dalai hurry after Zahra. "Hello, Dalai." He smiled maliciously. "How are you? You appear to be moving a bit stiffly. I hear she gave you a hard time today. I hope you're not going to spoil things for me tonight."

She quickly shook her head. "I'm fine, sir."

"You wouldn't lie to me?"

"Of course she wouldn't lie," Zahra said impatiently. "I'll allow you to strip her down so that you can see the bruises. I thought you might enjoy it. Providing you don't waste my time with this chatter."

"I'm sorry." Wyatt moved down the hall and flung open the door for her. "I promise I won't waste your time."

"We'll see. Dalai, come and help him undress. I find I'm eager to see just how much he's been anticipating this." She gave him a catlike glance over her shoulder. "And judge what kind of torment it will take to make it worth my while to have come here tonight."

———

Varak carefully drew the heavy bronze box out of the vault and laid it on the desk. "Get me the liquid, Markel."

Markel had it ready. "You're sure this will work?"

"Don't question me." Varak flipped open the lid and stared down at the blackened skull. "Hello, Oscar. How nice to see you again," he murmured. "It seems okay, Markel. He's as ugly a son of a bitch as the day I burned him to a crisp." He took the skull out of the container and turned it over. "Did I tell you that I'd been wanting to do that since the prick took off and ran back to Johannesburg, Markel? Well, actually since he annoyed me when he was a kid. I just hadn't gotten around to it yet."

"You told me," Markel said nervously. "Why don't you check the number so that we can get out of here?"

"There's no hurry now. Zahra will keep Wyatt busy." He was opening the vial. "And who knows, this might actually be Oscar. It could be that Duncan didn't go this route. If she did, then I'll act accordingly. I've got my plan in place." He put a drop of liquid on the bone near the ear. "And I'm actually looking forward to showing that bitch, Duncan, there's no way she can beat me." He added with sudden harshness, "I'm tired of hiding away when all I want to do is break out and let them all see what I can do."

"You said that the gold would be worth it." Markel's gaze was focused on the skull. "Did you make a mistake?"

Varak's head swung around like a striking cobra. "I don't make mistakes."

Markel backed away. "I only thought maybe circumstances had changed," he said quickly. "Is there anything I can do to help you with that skull?"

Varak didn't speak for a moment, and Markel tensed. Then Varak said, "No, I've got it." He looked back down at the skull. "Just be still and let me see how this is going to play out. Whatever goes down, I'll get what I want." He added, "Because I don't make mistakes, Markel."

He waited as the liquid did its work.

"Anything?" Markel asked.

Varak didn't answer. His eyes were on the skull.

Son of a bitch!

No numbers appeared. Nothing.

It was *not* Oscar.

And the rage was beginning to sear through Varak.

It was an insult that Eve Duncan had thought she could do this to him. Of course, she was only a woman, and Joe Quinn might have manipulated her. But she had to have been the one to do the actual reconstruction to prove that skull wasn't Varak's. He was suddenly furious with everyone connected to this defeat. Gideon, Joe Quinn, Eve Duncan, Jill Cassidy. He wanted them all *dead*.

No, he wouldn't accept that they had defeated him.

"Varak?" Markel said tentatively.

"Shut up," Varak hissed. He took the skull and hurled it across the room to smash against the wall. "The bitch thinks she fooled me." His hands clenched into fists as the white-hot rage tore through him. "Let's show them how wrong they are. Set the C-4."

"Where?"

"Everywhere, you fool. Everywhere."

Markel hurried out of the vault room.

Varak strode across the room and jammed an explosive in the empty eye socket of the skull lying on the floor.

Markel was back in the room and setting the charges.

"When you finish, get the other charges set throughout the house," Varak said. "Then tell the men to do the other blocks. Be ready to detonate when I call you." Then Varak was running out of the vault, down the hall, and up the staircase. Where the hell was she? Then he heard voices behind a door down the hall. A second later, he was throwing open the door of Wyatt's suite.

Wyatt was naked and kneeling before an equally naked Zahra. His head swiveled, and he stared in shock at Varak. "No one is supposed to be here. What are you—doing—"

"Blowing your brains out." Varak shot him directly between the eyes.

Then he glared at Zahra as Wyatt fell to the floor. "It's the wrong damn skull. It had to have been switched by that bitch, Duncan. You should have gotten rid of her. You should have gotten rid of all of them." His eyes were blazing. "That's why she sent Quinn to Asarti. You're to blame for this. Now I have to protect myself."

"And you call killing a U.N. diplomat protecting yourself?" She was staring in horror at Wyatt's shattered head. "How am I supposed to handle this?"

"I don't give a damn. I've already made plans to get rid of all the evidence. You just find a way to keep them from coming after me. Fix it. Put your clothes on and get out of here. This place is going to blow in another seven minutes. I won't wait for you."

"You're blowing it up?" She shook her head dazedly.

"You are insane. Do you know what kind of nightmare you're going to—" She was gasping, choking as his hands closed on her throat.

"Listen to me," he hissed. "And keep listening. From now on, you're going to do exactly as I say. I'm done playing with you. Do you know how much I want to squeeze just a little harder and break your damn neck? I won't tolerate your ordering me about. I'm in charge now. Do you understand?"

She couldn't speak, so she nodded.

He released her, and she backed away, holding her throat. His smile was savage. "Yes, you do understand. Now get out of here and do what I told you. You're always telling me how clever you are. Now prove it. It's my game now, my orders, Zahra." He whirled and strode toward the door. "Fix it!"

Zahra gazed after Varak for an instant as anger and shock struggled within her. Fix it? How was she supposed to fix this catastrophe? She looked down at the blood spattered over her naked body. It was like him to barge in and make things as difficult and horrible as possible for her, she thought bitterly. And this time it had been far worse. She was trying to swallow. She reached up and touched her bruised throat. This time she'd thought he was going to kill her. She knew he'd been very close.

"What do we do?" Dalai whispered from the bed across the room as she scrambled to sit up. "Do we have to do what he says?"

Zahra had forgotten she was there. She whirled on her as she grabbed her gown. "You do what you always do. You obey my orders." She slipped the gown over her head. "And my orders are that you do whatever he says until I tell you differently. I don't want you causing me any trouble while I work this out. I might have to do some delicate negotiations with him before I get what I want." She headed for the door. "Now get dressed and go down and get in the car."

"Negotiations," Dalai repeated numbly as she threw on her top and sarong skirt. "Then I'll have to do what he wants. That's what you mean?"

"That's what I said, isn't it? Hurry. We have to get out of here. He's a little crazy right now. He *hurt* me. The bastard almost killed me. I have no idea what he's going to do next."

"Yes." Dalai's voice was trembling as she hurriedly stumbled after Zahra down the grand staircase. "He's very angry. I can see there's no telling what he'll decide to do now . . ."

———

ROBAKU

"Wake up, Jill!"

Novak, she realized sleepily. He was shaking her, and he sounded really—

Then she was wide-awake. Her eyes flew open.

Darkness, but Novak was kneeling above her with a flashlight. "What's wrong? What are you doing here?" She sat bolt upright on her mat. "Is Eve—"

"Eve is fine as far as I know," he said roughly. "You can check yourself as soon as we get to the museum. I've called Quinn, and they're waiting for us. Put on your shoes, and we'll get over there." He pulled her to her feet. "Because there's a hell of a lot wrong. I just got a call from my agent, Palmon, in Jokan to tell me to check my computer."

"Jokan?" She was slipping on her tennis shoes. "What happened in Jokan?"

"What didn't happen in Jokan?" He was pulling her toward the door of the hut. "I don't believe there's any doubt now that Zahra and Varak believe they know why Eve sent Quinn to Asarti to get corroborating evidence from Dobran."

"Stop talking in riddles. Just tell me." She tried to stop at the door of the hut. "And give me just a second to tell Hajif and his wife I'm leaving. I don't want to frighten them."

"I'll send someone." He was pulling her down the path toward the museum. "As for telling you, it's not really necessary. That should give you a hint." He gestured to the night sky to the north. "What do you think, Jill?"

She halted, frozen, her gaze on the baleful red glow that lit the entire horizon.

"Screw your hints," she whispered. "What happened, Novak?"

"The entire block that the U.N. occupied was blown to kingdom come. Along with two of the side streets on either side. Pretty clear that whoever set those charges didn't give a damn if they blew up the entire city to make certain of that U.N. building."

"Casualties?"

He shook his head. "It only happened forty-five minutes ago. But my agent says that no one could have lived through the primary explosions at the U.N. site. Initial information from Wyatt's staff is that he was the only one there tonight. But it's a total inferno, and the soldiers and police can't even get near it to try to recover bodies. The neighboring streets are even worse. There were definitely multiple deaths in those shops and houses. I'll be given updates as soon as they're available."

"Why?" she asked dazedly. She swallowed to ease the tightness of her throat. "Why would they do it? An attack on a U.N. facility would cause an uproar. Zahra wouldn't want to be associated with anything like that."

"Unless it wasn't her call," Novak said grimly. "Unless she's lost control of the agenda. We'll probably know soon enough. This is her city, she'll have to be involved in explaining and mopping up this disaster."

"And soon," Jill murmured. She couldn't take her eyes off that glowing red horror in the distance. "I don't see how she could possibly talk her way out of this holocaust."

They had reached the museum, and Jill saw that it was ablaze with lights. Joe was throwing open the door. "What the hell?" His eyes were glittering, his lips tight. "What's happening there, Novak? You've got to know something."

"You know as much as I do right now," Novak said curtly. "I'll find out all I can when I get to Jokan. I sent Gideon on ahead when I got word, and I'm on my way. I only wanted to bring Jill to you before I left." He turned away. "Take care of her. There's no telling what's going to happen next."

"You're leaving?" Jill asked, startled. Then she recovered. "Of course you are. This is a disaster, and you're CIA. I should be going also. I have contacts, I might be able to—"

"No," Novak said. "You'd get in my way. I don't want you seen there. Eve may be the prime target, but you've got to be high on their list by now. It's not as if I won't let you know right away. For once, just do as I say for—" His phone rang. "Gideon." He answered and listened for another minute. "When?" he asked. "Find out and get back to me. I'll be there as soon as I can."

"What is it?" Eve asked as she joined them at the door.

"President Zahra Kiyani has just requested TV time to address the nation in response to this national disaster. Gideon believes that she'll be speaking in the next hour or so. He'll give me a definite time in the next fifteen minutes." His lips twisted. "It probably won't be immediately. She'll want to give every news agency on the planet time to chime in and give her maximum exposure. I imagine the palace newsroom is already packed."

"Of course, it is," Jill said. "It's a great story. I should be there." She stared him in the eye. "I *will* be there, Novak."

"You'll have to pass," he said coolly. "You have another story to cover. Anything Zahra has to say will almost certainly have a direct influence on Eve. You're the one who chose Eve to be the one to put her neck on the line. Hell, you've been in agony about your responsibility for getting her poisoned." His voice became crisp and cold. "So suck it up and forget about that story luring you to the palace. You haven't finished this one yet. Stay here and make sure she lives to read it." He turned and strode down the path.

Jill stared after him, stricken.

"Pretty rough," Eve said quietly. "He probably didn't mean it all."

"Yes, he did." She shivered. "He always means what he says. You can always count on that." She drew a deep breath. "And the bastard is so damn smart that he's usually right. He sees right through you and cuts out all the bullshit like he has a scalpel." She turned to Joe. "You can see that, can't you? You know he's right about my being to blame for Eve's being in this position."

He nodded. "He's right. You had plenty of help, but you're the one who worked and made it happen."

"And yet I was ready to run back to Jokan as soon as I saw another story beckoning, another way to go after Zahra and Varak. It was fresh and new, and all I could think about was that maybe this was the direction I should go."

He was silent. Then he said, "Do you think that wasn't my first thought?" He made a face. "I've been frustrated as hell, and I don't respond well to it. But it's second thoughts that matter, and I knew it was impossible."

"But I had to have that second thought drummed into me." She turned to Eve. "Forgive me. It won't happen again."

"Stop talking as if this is all about me," Eve said, disgusted. "Joe is bad enough. But I have to put up with him." She turned and went over to the computer on her worktable. "I'll stand only so much from you, Jill." She turned on the computer. "Now let's see if we can find out what's happening in Jokan."

CHAPTER

15

The local Jokan television station switched from the shots of the U.N. disaster to the newsroom at the presidential palace two hours later.

Zahra Kiyani walked slowly up to the stage from a carved door opened by two uniformed soldiers. She was wearing an elegant white suit, and every glossy hair in her chignon was in place. She looked absolutely stunning as she turned to face the audience.

But her expression was tense and sober, and she paused a moment before she started to speak. "I grieve with you, both my own people and the loved ones of those friends from foreign lands who died tonight in that terrible massacre." Her voice was shaking, and her eyes were suddenly shining with tears. "You will notice I wear white instead of black for mourning. For those who are not familiar with Kiyanis, this is the custom of my family to honor our dead." Her voice broke. "And everyone who died tonight I regard as a member of my own family." She stopped a moment, struggling. "This is a monstrous thing that happened, and there are no words I can say that will explain or give comfort to you. All I can do is give what answers I can and grieve with you. First, I have to express my heartfelt condolences to the family of the Honorable Edward Wyatt, whom I've been told almost certainly perished in that explosion tonight. We had become friends during these last months. His Herculean efforts to help me bring health and happiness back to my countrymen after the devastation they had suffered will live in my heart and memory forever." Another emotional pause. "Unfortunately, that bravery and dedication very likely caused him to be targeted. The police are still investigating, but we suspect Botzan terrorism. They have informed me after questioning the wife of Edward's private secretary, Peter Greville, that Edward had scheduled a confidential meeting tonight with a Botzan secret agent who was attempting to capture a radical, terrorist group who were trying to revive the terrible war that killed so many of us." She swallowed. "Including my own father. I had received reports and threats to my life from this group for the last few months, but my own secret service had not succeeded in apprehending them. I can only believe that Edward thought the force of the U.N. might bring them to justice and risked his own life in order that the peace would not be broken." She cleared her throat. "Because that was the kind of noble, giving man the Honorable Edward Wyatt has been since the moment I first met him. May God bless his family and my eternal thanks to Great Britain for sending him to my country so that I could learn from him." She lowered her head and was silent a long moment, struggling. "Forgive me. This is as difficult for me as it is for you all. I know I promised you information, and I will give it.

Naturally, because this hideous disaster has just occurred, that information may be sketchy, and I beg you to understand. I can only tell you what I've been told. The consensus of those around me is that the terrorist group got wind of the meeting with Edward and wished to set an example. It was easy for them because he had sent all of his guards and employees away for the night in order to satisfy the demands of the Botzan secret agent. That was like the Edward I have come to know, risking everything..." She went on: "But in the last hour we've found out that he was not the only target. The terrorists weren't satisfied with only killing him. His private secretary, Peter Greville, and several of the guards were attacked and shot in their residences in the early hours of the morning. The police told me that there's reason to believe that they wanted to make certain everyone connected with the death of Nils Varak paid the same price. You might remember that Varak's skull was being held at the U.N. headquarters." She shuddered. "It shouldn't surprise us that the monster who almost destroyed my country should be worshipped by those murdering terrorists." The tears that had been brimming were suddenly running down her cheeks. "But it does surprise me. I can't understand anything about people like this. Shouldn't the deaths stop sometime?" She looked directly in the camera. "But we all have to understand it because we have to stop it. It can't go on any longer. Together we *can* stop it. Help me, and I will help you. I will let you know whatever I find out about this atrocity so that we can share knowledge as well as our sorrow. I will set my own agencies and soldiers to seek out those answers. I'm going to cancel my trip to New York to speak at the U.N. in order to devote myself to keeping those beasts from devouring my country." Her voice was suddenly ringing with resolve. "That is my duty, and I will give every minute of every day to it. I ask for your prayers and your support." She stepped back. "Good night and God bless."

She turned and walked away.

———————

Jill gave a low whistle as she looked up from the computer screen. "She aced it. I bet every reporter in that room is giving her a standing ovation. Hell, I'd probably do it, too, if I didn't know she was lying through her teeth."

"But you do know," Eve said. "Gideon told me once that she was magnificent in a number of ways. This is apparently one of them." She leaned back, and added thoughtfully, "Do you know what I was thinking about when she speaking? She was totally beautiful, totally persuasive, and able to move everyone with whom she came in contact. Mesmerizing. She reminded me of her favorite ancestress."

"Kiya?" Joe asked.

"No, she tolerated Kiya, but she identified with Cleopatra. Cleopatra had the power, and Zahra adores power. Pity. Because Kiya was probably more intelligent." She shook her head. "But Zahra definitely covered all the bases with that speech. She produced a logical villain based on recent history. She glorified Wyatt and Great Britain and the entire civilized world. She even gave a reason why those guards were killed when they weren't even at the U.N. headquarters tonight and why the place was chosen to be targeted. You can bet that Swanson and anyone connected to that skull was on the hit list. All very logical and acceptable." She grimaced. "And then she sealed the deal by setting herself up as a combination Joan of Arc and Mother Teresa with all the glamour of Cleopatra. That YouTube video is going to get millions of hits, and the Zahra Kiyani legend is going to grow and grow."

Jill nodded. "Hell, she might decide to bypass using Egypt as a stepping-stone and go straight to Washington. After that speech, it's going to be nearly impossible to make her out to be anything but a heroine. It's like Jackie Kennedy in that bloody pink suit."

"That's what she intended," Joe said harshly. "What they both intended. What the world believes to be Varak's skull is now totally destroyed, and if we brought up the skull on which Eve just did the reconstruction, it would be an uphill battle to prove it wasn't a complete forgery. It throws everything into confusion. Very smart. Zahra and Varak make a formidable team."

"Murderers," Eve said with a shiver. "Another massacre, and she managed to sugarcoat it."

"Yes." Joe met her eyes. "It just goes to show how determined they are to protect themselves. They assassinated Dobran and killed your friend Kimbro, Jill. That explosion tonight was just another safety measure. They're going down the list and checking off the hazards to eliminate." He paused. "And you're probably next on the list, Eve. You have a spotless reputation, and that's dangerous to them." His tone was suddenly urgent. "The game's changed. *Now* will you let me take you out of here?"

"Do it, Eve," Jill said. "As he said, it's going to be an uphill battle from now on. If you stay, you'll be vulnerable to anything they decide to do to you."

"What am I supposed to do? Let Joe bury me in the mountains somewhere and hope Varak won't dig me up?" Eve shook her head. "I won't live like that. I won't let Varak believe he can roam the earth and get away with all this slaughter. There has to be a better way to handle this. We just have to find it." She was thinking, trying to see some way out. "We have to take advantage of any weakness they might have. Zahra has to have a different agenda than Varak. Jill says she's always been cautious, and she must feel as if she has a tiger by the tail."

"This is all guesswork," Joe said impatiently. "And all it means is that I'm not getting what I want and that Eve is still in danger as long as she's here." He drew a deep breath. "Because who's to know if Zahra won't think of some clever reason to blow up this village as well? I wouldn't put it past her." He strode toward the door. "I need some air. Then I'm going to call Novak. I'm having problems with your 'logic,' and I want solutions."

———◆———

OUTSIDE U.N. HEADQUARTERS
JOKAN

Gideon's eyes were stinging from smoke as he closed his computer after watching Zahra's speech. "Interesting. She's either amazingly improved from the time when we were an item or she was inspired. What do you think?"

"I have no idea." Novak added, "But Jill would say she told the story with incredible conviction and that she came across as a combination of Angelina Jolie and Mother Teresa."

"I believe she was inspired...maybe by Varak," Gideon said absently as he gazed at the ambulances still racing from the homes and shops on the streets surrounding the U.N. toward the hospital. He was realizing that some of the smoke he was breathing was carrying the scent of the burnt flesh of those victims caught in the flames. It was too damn familiar. "But I don't think even Mother Teresa could inspire any mercy for the people who did this. What's the count?"

"More than fifty. If the staff of the U.N. hadn't been sent home, it would have almost doubled."

"She mentioned that some of the guards who took care of the vault had also been assassinated. Swanson?"

Novak nodded. "They wanted to get anyone connected to the skull. It was a well-planned raid."

"Varak can be brilliant." Gideon's lips twisted. "The smell of this smoke reminds me of the day I came back home to bury my parents. He was very thorough. Everything stank for weeks of smoke and flesh. He burned every living soul on the property."

"You never told me that."

"It was over," he said. "Until it wasn't." He looked away from the ambulances. "Do you need me any more tonight? I think I should—" His phone rang, and he glanced down at the ID. Presidential palace. No designated name.

He quickly turned away from Novak. "Excuse me. I've got to take this."

Novak's brows rose. "Confidential?"

Gideon didn't answer as he moved a few more steps away. He punched the access key. "Gideon."

"I've got to see you right away." Dalai's voice was shaking. "You said you'd help me. Will you still do it?"

He stiffened. "Yes. But I'm a little busy right now. I'm sure you can hear the sirens."

"I've been hearing them ever since I got back to the palace. I think I'll hear them forever."

"Then I imagine you heard more than the sirens. How close were you to the explosion?"

She didn't answer. "I need to see you. I'll be at the coach house in thirty minutes. Please come."

"How can you get away? I'm standing here watching the U.N. headquarters burn to ashes. And I just heard Zahra give a speech to rock the ages."

"She's surrounded by all those reporters. She doesn't want

me around to get in her way. She told me to stay in my quarters."

"She never did like to share the spotlight."

"Will you come?"

"I'll come." He cut the connection. He turned back to Novak. "I'll see you later. I have something to do."

"Curious. Or someone to see?"

He smiled. "Perhaps."

Novak's narrowed eyes were studying his face. "It's that young maid of Zahra Kiyani."

Gideon's smile never wavered. "Perhaps."

"Be careful. It could be a trap. It's odd that you'd hear from her after Zahra probably blew up a good bit of the city. She could be dangerous. Are you sure it's worth it?"

"No. But it's promising." He lifted his hand. "I'll call you later and let you know."

Dalai wasn't in the coach house when Gideon slipped inside the back entrance twenty minutes later. But the entire palace seemed to be teeming with activity, he noticed. He'd been lucky not to be seen coming here.

It could be a trap.

Yes, it could. He was taking a chance that Dalai had not gone to Zahra and told her that he had been to see her. Or more likely, she might have lost her nerve and was still cowering in her bedroom.

Then, suddenly, the door of the passage opened, and she was there, running toward him. "I was afraid you'd leave. Madam called me down to the press office to redo her hair. She said it wouldn't photograph well if she—" She broke off and drew a deep breath. "But you didn't leave. So it's all right."

"Yes, it's all right," he said gently. "Why did you call me? Did someone hurt you again?"

"No, not like that. Usually it's only him. It was the blood...he shot Mr. Wyatt in the head. There was so much blood." She was biting her lower lip. "But he *will* hurt me again. I know it. She's too afraid of him. She'll do anything to keep him from hurting her. But I don't matter to her. She'll use me again and again to please him." She was gazing desperately up at him. "But I can't *bear* it. I can stand most things, but not that. I'll tell you whatever you want to know. It's a kind of bargain, isn't it? But you don't have to promise to keep me safe, or send me away somewhere. Just keep me away from him."

"Hush." He reached out to stroke her hair. "I will promise to keep you safe. But I can't do that unless you help yourself. You're still not telling me names. Give me his name, Dalai."

She was silent. "It's very...hard. She said no one is supposed to know it. She said she would send me to—" She swallowed. "Varak. His name is Nils Varak." She was looking searchingly at his face. "But I think you knew it, didn't you?"

"But I had to be absolutely certain. Now I am." He added grimly, "I believe you're aware that Varak's presence here in Maldara is a huge secret. There aren't many people who would be brave enough to say his name."

"Yes, I knew it was a secret. That's why Madam spent all that money for that plastic surgeon to change his face. And I'm *not* brave. I had to do it. After I came back tonight, I was lying in bed and shaking. Because I knew I was going to have to do it. I knew I had to ask you to help." She braced herself, and, suddenly, she was no longer trembling. "Because I'm not strong enough. I don't know any of the ways that you would. I'll have to learn them. You were always so strong when you were with her. You were never afraid. You even laughed at her when she tried to order you about. If I do what you wish, you'll keep her from giving me to him again." She paused, then said quietly, "Or because I believe you hate him, you will kill him. That would be much better."

Gideon felt a ripple of shock. He had not expected those last words. Dalai had spoken with no passion, only simplicity and determination. But who could blame her after all she had been through? "I'll never let you go back to him." He smiled grimly. "And, if you can tell me where to find the bastard, I have friends who will be glad to go with me and see that Varak will never live to see another day."

She closed her eyes for a moment. "I'm sorry to make you do this. I know it should be me." She opened her eyes. "But I will repay you."

"Just tell me where I can find him."

She nodded. "He has a compound deep in the rain forest over an hour from here. It's off Nagali Highway, and the roads going to and from the property are patrolled by Madam's soldiers. And he has his own soldiers at the compound. Many soldiers. I don't know how many." She paused, thinking. "He likes explosives. I've seen them in the warehouse there."

"Yes, I'm aware that he likes explosives," Gideon said harshly. "Anything else?"

She shook her head. "I'm sorry. I was always in the bedroom."

He felt another bolt of rage and pity. "Nothing to be sorry about. You've told me a great deal. We don't have to talk about him anymore. Let's talk about Zahra. She's very important, too."

"She can't help you get to the compound," Dalai said quickly. "Varak doesn't like her to come there. He's afraid she'll be followed."

"No, forget about the compound for a moment. I need to know everything about her relationship with Varak. We might be able to use it. Are they lovers?"

She shook her head. "She used to sleep with him. But she doesn't anymore. She sends him whores... or me."

"That doesn't surprise me. Well, why does she put up with him? What binds them together?"

"I don't know what you mean." She was backing away from him. "I have to go now. I've been here too long."

She was suddenly on edge, he realized. She had started to shake again. The minute he had started to question her about Zahra... He was thinking back to the conversation in her room. "You're frightened. You said something about Zahra's sending you to the place where there was no air. What did you mean?"

"It's not important to you. I've told you about Varak. He's the only one you have to worry about." She started to back toward the stable.

"Wait. I could try to take you out of here now."

"No, you couldn't. Not while Varak is still alive. You might not be able to do it if you did." She glanced back over her shoulder. "And then she would know. It would be worse for me."

"I'll make sure that we're very careful when we go after him, so that won't happen. But I can't just leave you here." He reached in his pocket and scrawled numbers on a card. "This is my friend Jill's phone number." He came toward her and put the card in her hand. "If you don't hear from me, if something happens, call her, and she'll take care of you."

"No," she said fiercely. "Nothing is going to happen to you. You're strong. No one can hurt you. Do you think I'd send you to him if I thought—" She broke off and whirled away from him. "I will call you if I hear of something that might hurt you."

Then she was gone.

Gideon gazed helplessly after her for a moment before he turned toward the maze that led to the street. After this night of fire and death, he hadn't dreamed that Dalai would furnish them with the weapon that might bring Varak down. He should be happy and full of hope. But that vulnerable young girl who had been a victim all her life was still here, and he had no real grasp of what she was facing.

Stop thinking about her. He could only help Dalai by eliminating the threat that was terrifying her the most. So they'd have to go over what she had said about the compound and start planning.

He reached for his phone to call Novak.

ROBAKU

"Varak," Jill murmured. "It seems too good to be true. I thought everything was going down the tubes when Zahra came out with that save earlier tonight." She was gazing at the night sky over Jokan, which was still glowing malevolently. "I was afraid to hope."

"And it might be too good to be true," Novak said. "We won't know until we check out that compound where Dalai said we could find Varak." He looked at Gideon. "I told you it could be a trap. You said the girl seemed almost as terrified of Zahra Kiyani as she was of Varak. Zahra has been brainwashing her since childhood."

"It wasn't the same," Gideon said. "She's scared of Zahra. But she thinks she'll only be safe from Varak if he's dead. There's a distinction."

"One of which I approve," Joe Quinn said, turning to

Eve, Jill, Novak, and Gideon, who were standing in front of the museum. "It's the first break we've had. Let's go for it. You can check out the terrain and make sure it's as safe as it can be for us, Novak."

"I appreciate your faith in me," Novak said dryly. "I definitely want to check out everything connected with the girl. Gideon is being a little too trusting."

"Only because he's feeling guilty about not having helped Dalai when he had the chance," Eve said. "He was trying to persuade us to adopt her."

"Maybe," Gideon said. "But now we might owe her." He turned back to Novak. "How do we verify the information?"

"I'll send a team to the property to take a good look as soon as it gets light. In the meantime, I'll order a couple infrared drones to scan the area." He cocked a brow as he glanced at Joe. "Providing that meets with your approval?"

"It does." He added, "As long as I'm heading the team that goes in at daybreak."

"No!" Gideon was adamantly shaking his head. "You head the team, Novak. Keep Quinn out of it."

"That's not going to happen," Joe said curtly. "What the hell is wrong with you, Gideon?"

"I've seen how you operate," Gideon said. "It's half instinct and half intellect and all exactly how you want it to go. It might be effective, but I don't want to rely on your decisions when I promised Dalai that we'd be careful not to tip our hand and get her in trouble with Zahra. I wouldn't want Zahra to cut her throat if she thinks she's been betrayed."

"You shouldn't have made her promises," Novak said slowly.

"Well, I did." He met Novak's eyes. "I knew there was a possibility you'd want to move fast. But we've known each other a long time, and I didn't believe that you'd let her get killed if there was any way to keep it from happening. I don't care if you send me or someone else to pull her out of that palace if you make a decision to go for it. I just don't want any action taken without warning." He paused. "And I trust you not to do it."

Novak stared at him for a moment. Then he shrugged and turned away. "I'll do whatever is possible. No promises." He glanced at Joe. "It appears that I'll be heading that team. No offense. I'd trust you implicitly. You're just a little too volatile for Gideon at present." His gaze shifted to Eve. "I wonder why?"

"Joe wouldn't let anything happen to Dalai," Eve said quietly.

"Unless he thought there was reason to think your safety was on the line," Novak said. "Then no one else would have a chance. But hopefully that won't happen today." He looked back at Joe. "Right, Quinn?"

"Hopefully." Joe added impatiently, "It doesn't matter. I'd rather be checking the area for land mines anyway. The girl mentioned explosives."

"Whew." Gideon smiled. "That was close. Defusing land mines seems an ideal job for you. Sorry, Quinn."

"You might be very sorry if you pull that shit again." He turned to Novak. "What time do we leave?"

"Six."

"Then we'd better get some sleep." Joe took Eve's arm. "If you don't mind sharing a bed with a callous bastard like me."

"Ouch," Gideon murmured as he watched them leave. "I knew that was a mistake. But I wasn't able to do anything else for that poor kid."

"I knew it was a mistake, too," Novak said. "You're lucky

you didn't piss him off." He turned and headed down the path. "And now I'll go back to the village and do a check to see if Dalai is telling us the truth about the location of Varak's compound and find out everything I can about it. I'll encode and send out two of the X-4 drones. Gideon, I want you to go to the airport and see that there's no slip-up. Got it?"

"Got it."

"Make sure they're functioning properly with the codes I enter. I want accurate information before we start out. In the past, Varak's hideouts have always been almost impregnable. I have to know what to expect, or I'll have to make adjustments." He added, "And try to get a couple hours sleep."

"All those goals might not coincide," Gideon said dryly as he disappeared down the path.

Jill stood hesitantly, gazing after him. She felt totally useless, when she should have had a hand in helping to make this plan work.

"What are you waiting for?" Novak was looking over his shoulder. "An invitation?"

She went still. Then she was running after him. "I'm glad you remembered your manners," she said lightly as she fell into step with him. "I was wondering if I was going to have to barge in on you."

"I knew that would be your next step. You wouldn't have been able to go back to Hajif's hut and try to go back to sleep. That would have been far too sensible and normal."

Yes, Novak had developed an almost paranormal ability to read her, Jill thought. It should have made her uneasy, but she was finding it oddly comforting to have him there, understanding who and what she was. Not always approving, often frustrated, volatile, and disturbing, but an undeniable part of the fabric of her life.

"I wouldn't have been able to sleep," she said. "I'm excited. Can I do something to help you get those drones programmed?"

"Perhaps." He saw her frown and grinned. "Okay, I'll put you to work. Why not?"

"Right." She nodded. "You can never tell when I'll run across a time when I'll need information like that. Drones seem to be an essential part of my life these days." She ducked through the opening of the hut. "How long will it take?"

"Not that long if all goes well. We have Gideon on the other end double-checking." He lit the lantern. "He'll be very careful about not making any mistakes. He knows I'm not pleased with him."

"He was doing what he thought was right," she said quietly. "And you must have thought he was right, too, or you wouldn't have let him talk you into doing what he wanted."

"I hadn't decided one way or the other when Quinn stepped in. It would have been more diplomatic to let him take the reins." He shrugged. "But Gideon didn't allow me the choice. I don't like to be put in that position."

"Joe Quinn is almost a stranger to Gideon, he had to go with the man he trusted. It was important to him." She stared him in the eyes. "I'd be the same. I trust you. If it was important, I'd go to you, Novak."

He went still. "Don't trust me too much, Jill. That's what I told Gideon. I only do what I can." His lips twisted. "And since I'm such a selfish bastard, what I can do sometimes alters from minute to minute."

She shook her head. "I don't believe you."

"No?" He gazed at her for a long moment. Heat. It came lightning fast out of nowhere. Taking her breath away. She couldn't look away from him. "Well, I did warn you," he said as he took out his computer. "Let's get to work. I'll show you how to look up the address and directions and coordinate it into the drone's memory."

She was relieved that electric moment had passed. Or was she? She was feeling a strange sense of loss. Of course she was. "It sounds complicated." She came closer to look down at the screen. Then she was beginning to get excited again at the challenge before her. "You're sure it won't take more than an hour or so?"

———————

It took an hour and five minutes to program the two drones.

It was not nearly as complicated as she had thought to learn the codes and keep them straight. She had followed Novak's lead, and it was like learning a new game that was as absorbing as it was exciting. She found she was disappointed when she had put in the last equation. "Is that all?"

Novak was grinning. "Unless you want to teach it something else. We're supposed to be gathering information, but I suppose we could rig up a bomb or two to drop on that compound."

"No, that would be breaking your word to Gideon." She was still looking at the computer screen. "It's very sophisticated, isn't it?"

"State of the art." He held up his hand. "But I can see you already creating a story about it. Don't do it. Drones are constantly being upgraded, but this one is very special."

"Okay." She sighed. "But it was great fun. Thank you for letting me play with it."

"My pleasure. It was fun watching you. Your cheeks are still flushed, and your eyes are shining like those of a kid opening a Christmas present." He chuckled. "Next time I'll show you how to set the bomb capability."

"It was fascinating." Her smile suddenly faded. "And dangerous. Bombs and all those technical spy devices...I shouldn't be this excited. I just got caught up in the moment. It's not a game."

"It's whatever you make it." He signed out of the program. "And for you it was a game and a story unfolding and excitement."

"But not for you."

"No. Much darker," he said. "But it was good stepping into your world for a little while." He turned to look at her. "Maybe I'll remember it when it gets a little too dark in mine." He reached down and pulled her to her feet. "Now go to Hajif's and get to sleep. You should still have a few hours."

Heat, again. Out of nowhere. Tingling through her body, causing her breasts to swell. She quickly pulled her hand away. "Hardly seems worth it."

"I don't suppose I could talk you into not getting up when we take off? There's no reason why you should."

Other than the fact that she should be going with him. The darkness of which he'd spoken was suddenly overwhelming her. This was her fight as well as his, and now he was going to face the monster while she was supposed to stay here and snooze. "There's a reason," she said tightly. "You know there's a reason." She turned on her heel. "I'll see you at six."

A few minutes later, she had reached Hajif's hut. She stood outside the door, breathing hard. She couldn't go in right now, she was too upset. She sank down on the ground and leaned back against the wall. Her hands clenched into fists.

She *hated* it. She felt helpless, and it shouldn't be like this. She was the one who had gone to Novak in the beginning and asked him to help her go after Varak. Now he was going to leave her behind when she was responsible for everything that had happened since that night? Reason told her that she would not be an asset if she insisted on going with Novak. She had no military experience and might even be a danger to the team. He had a right to expect her to stay out of it.

But she wanted to go. She *needed* to go with him. Varak was a devil from the depths of hell. He had reached out and killed thousands of people. Who knew what kind of force he still had at his command? It might be intended to be an exploratory foray into that jungle, but that didn't mean it would stay that way. The panic was rising as the thought stabbed through her. How many stories had she written about good plans gone wrong?

They could all die.

Novak could die.

No!

She jumped to her feet. She tore across the short distance that separated her from Novak's hut in seconds. The next instant she was inside. "This is all wrong!" she said fiercely. "I can't have it like this."

He whirled to face her. "What's wrong?" He was instantly on the attack. "What happened?"

"I won't be cheated." She hurled herself at him. She was in his arms. She was kissing him. "I won't have *you* cheated. Varak has already taken too much. Take off your clothes."

"What?" He pushed her away from him to look down at her. "What the hell are you doing, Jill?"

"Nothing that's in the least thought-out, or probably even sane. And you have a perfect right to say you've changed your mind and don't want me. But I think it's still there, or I wouldn't be feeling—"

"Shut up," he said hoarsely. "You're damn right it's not

sane. And every word is making me rock-hard. Get out of here."

She shook her head. "You want it. You want me. You've told me you do." She broke free of him and pulled her tee shirt over her head and threw it aside. "And I wish you'd take your clothes off so that I won't feel as if I'm some kind of sex maniac. I'm not very good at this seduction bullshit. I've always thought that kind of thing was phony." She was trying to undo her bra. "But if that's what you want, then I'll try to—"

"Stop it." He grabbed her wrists and held her still. "You're killing me." He drew a deep breath. "Talk to me. Tell me what brought this on before I throw you out."

"That's just like you. You tell me what you want, then all of a sudden you're worrying and pushing me away because you think that I'm so damn vulnerable." She glared up at him. "I'm not weak. Sometimes bad things happen to me, but I can handle them. I'll always be able to handle them without you taking care of me. So back off, Novak."

"You're not answering me."

"Because when you come into the room I tense up because I know your just being here will change everything. It shouldn't be that way. I write my own story, dammit. But not when you're around. Why do you think I've been fighting you? But now Gideon pulls this thing with Varak out of his hat, and suddenly it doesn't matter." She repeated through set teeth, "It doesn't *matter*. So take off your clothes, Novak."

"Not quite yet." His gaze was narrowed on her face. "Why did it make a difference?"

"Don't be stupid. I can't go with you, dammit. I'd be a liability. What if something happens to you? What if you die? Then Varak would win because we'd both be cheated by him. We wouldn't be able to have this." She was trying to steady her voice. "I won't have that, Novak. I want you to have everything you want. And I want to have everything I want. And we both know what we've wanted since the day we met." She swallowed. "So will you please let go of my wrists and take me down on those blankets over there and do something about it?"

"So I'm to thank that bastard, Varak, for you?" His hands tightened on her wrists. "I don't think so, Jill. I don't find that prospect appealing." His lips twisted. "What am I saying? I'm going crazy at the thought of dragging you down on those blankets. I just can't stomach the idea that he'd have anything to do with it." He suddenly smiled recklessly. "So I'll have to make sure that it's only between you and me. Because I'm not going to be fool enough to walk away from you no matter what brought you here." He dropped her wrists and started to unbutton his shirt. "Though I admit I had a crazy idea that I should be noble and all that crap. But I'm way past that. I've been wanting you too long."

"I never asked you to be noble. You're the one who called me walking wounded." She watched him drop his shirt on the floor. His body was so lean and sleek and muscular, like a panther's. She couldn't take her eyes off the corded muscles of his stomach. "And I just didn't want you to think I wasn't strong. I've never shown anyone as much weakness as I've shown you."

"That's supposed to be weakness?" Two movements, and he pulled her into his arms. He was rocking her gently back and forth. "Just be quiet, will you? You're making me crazy. I don't want to feel like this about you right now. All I want to think about is how much I *need* you." Then she realized her bra was gone and he was rubbing her breasts back and forth against his chest. She gasped as she felt the warmth of his flesh against her, the faint abrasiveness of his chest hair against her nipples, which was causing her to tighten and swell.

"That's right," he murmured. "This is what I want...But it's not enough. I want my mouth on you."

And the next moment, his mouth closed on her nipple.

Suction.

His tongue...

His teeth...

Her back arched as she felt the pressure.

"Wait," she gasped. She was wildly shedding her clothes as his mouth never left her. "I can't take—"

"Yes, you can. You can take everything. This is how strong you are." He pulled her down on the blankets. "So don't tell me you're not strong." He was shedding his clothes as he spoke. "I'll show you what you can take." He stopped suddenly as he looked down at her. "I'm going wild. I'll try to let you set the pace, but I can't promise. The last thing I want to do is hurt you. Don't let me do that. Just tell me."

She was panting, moving against him. The feel of his hips against her... "Will you stop worrying? I *know* you, Novak. Just *touch* me." Then she suddenly lunged upward and took him instead. "Yes!"

He froze. His face contorting. "Well. That ends that, doesn't it?" he said hoarsely. "It's up to you from now on. I'm gone..." He started to move.

Fast.

Hard.

Heat.

Hot. So hot.

She heard herself gasping, crying, as she met him, tried to take more of him.

Crazy.

It went on and on. He was moving her, positioning her, so many positions...until she thought she couldn't take any more; and then she found there were no limits.

His face over her, tense, almost in pain.

Then it was going faster, harder.

"Novak..."

Darkness.

Light.

Pressure.

Impossible that it could go on.

But it had to go on, she couldn't let him leave her...

Then he was gathering her close, lifting her. "Jill?"

But he wasn't leaving her she realized out of the haze of madness. He was taking her with him.

Her fingers dug into his shoulders.

She thought she screamed. But there was no sound, she realized. Because she had no breath and was clinging helplessly to him as wave after wave was overwhelming her.

"Okay?" His chest was moving in and out with the force of his breathing. "I didn't do—"

"Don't you dare," she gasped. "I'm quite sure you wouldn't ask that of any other woman at a time like this. I'm fine, better than fine."

"You're not any other woman." His voice was low against her throat. "I'm not sure I'll ever be able to compare you to other women." He lifted his head to look down at her. "So don't expect it."

She met his gaze. She wanted to pull him down and return to the hot, erotic intimacy that had gone before. She couldn't read his expression and it was making her uneasy. Sensuality. Intensity. Something else...

"That's fine with me." She smiled with an effort. "I don't mind being unique. As long as you understand who I am and realize you can't change me."

"Ah, yes, I mustn't try to influence your story." His lips twisted. "I'll try to keep that in mind." He kissed the hollow of her throat. "But you evidently don't mind me taking action on this level. You came to me."

"Yes."

He licked her lower lip. "And you didn't once think of Varak, did you?"

He knew she hadn't. She still wasn't sure what he was thinking. "Novak, what are you doing?" She paused. "Are you angry?"

"I wouldn't be so ungrateful. I don't really know what I am at this moment. I'm having problems sorting out what I'm feeling about this particular chapter in your story." His lips moved down to her breast, and his tongue flicked lazily at her nipple. "But I do know that we're both in complete agreement that this was entirely successful." He moved over her. "And we want more. You're ready for me. Am I wrong?"

She was more than ready. It had been such a short time, but she was burning. Dangerous. It was so dangerous to feel that sexual intensity for him. She wasn't even certain that it was only sex. She had always been confused about her emotions regarding him. Admiration, respect, gratitude were all mixed with that wariness. It would be even more dangerous if it was more than sex.

Worry about it later. She bit her lower lip as the waves of heat moved through her. She couldn't think now that his hands were moving, teasing, entering. Just take what he was offering. "No, you're not wrong." She pulled him down to her, and whispered, "There's nothing I want more than this now, Novak."

◆———

Voices.

Novak was on the phone, Jill realized drowsily.

Then she was wide-awake. Her eyes flew open, and she saw Novak sitting at the bench across the hut. He was fully dressed and gazing at his computer.

"What is it?" Then she shook her head as she realized what it must be. "What time is it? Did you get the drone results?"

He nodded. "About ten minutes ago. They came in a little after five. I've been going over the results with Gideon."

"What were they?" She was quickly throwing on her clothes. "Why didn't you wake me?"

"No need. You didn't get much sleep," he said absently, his gaze on the computer. "It's not as if you could do anything about it."

That was true enough, Jill thought. She had probably drifted off to sleep only minutes before he'd received those results. And it only heightened her frustration that he was perfectly right about her not being able to help him in any way. That was what had started the sexual marathon that had caused her to still be here when those results had come in. "You're probably right," she said curtly. "Call it curiosity. I'd like to know."

He turned to face her. "I'm sorry. I didn't think." He tapped the screen. "Very heavy foliage and tree cover. Glimpses of what could be a residence and four bunkhouses. Several possible vehicles. Farther back on the property, a concrete pad that could be used for a helicopter." He looked up at her. "And the infrared showed at least forty or fifty figures under that heavy canopy of foliage."

"Then it could be true." She inhaled sharply as excitement gripped her. "Dalai must have told Gideon the truth. It could be Varak."

"It could be Varak," he agreed. "Particularly since the drone also detected the presence of explosives throughout the area. Varak has always been fond of his land mines. But that foliage is like a thick blanket, we won't know until we get there. And several of those figures were probably sentries moving around the property. One false step, and we could get ourselves killed, or tip Varak off that we're on the property. We've got to be careful."

"Then you won't be able to go in and get him right away." She tried not to sound as relieved as she felt. "You'll have to mount surveillance until you're certain?"

"Probably. I want to know everything about the place, and I want a visual on Varak."

"Dalai told Gideon that Zahra had paid for plastic surgery."

"I've been on the hunt for Varak ever since he showed up in Maldara. I studied him for years after he started his killing sprees here. He might change his face, but he's a big bastard, and he won't have been able to change the way he moves. I'll know him." His lips tightened. "And then I'll find a way to go in and get him."

"Unless you find an opportunity to get your hands on him today," she said bitterly.

He nodded. "Maybe."

"That's what I thought." She turned and headed for the door. "Do let me know when you make a decision."

"Jill."

"Look, I know you have to do this," she said jerkily. "But next time, I want to be there when it happens, so you find a way to not get yourself killed today."

"I'm not going to get myself killed," he said quietly. "What happened between us blew my mind. I have no intention of cutting what we have short. Will you come back here tonight, and we'll do it all over again? Plus more erotic embellishments?" He added mockingly, "Provided that Varak doesn't kill me."

He was actually joking? "You bastard."

"I admit I'm a little raw about your having to use such a sleazy excuse as Varak to come to me. Particularly since I've discovered that you've become an obsession." He added softly, "I'll come to you with no excuse at all. From now on, I won't be able to leave you alone. Expect me."

"The hell I will." She left the hut and strode toward Hajif's place. She'd wanted to *hit* Novak. The news that the possible strike on Varak might be temporarily averted had thrown her from despair to relief, then to anger. He was annoyed that it was Varak that had been the impetus to bring her to him? Screw him. She had been in a turmoil of emotion all night. Scared to death that he might get killed, then having probably the most erotic sexual encounter she'd ever experienced.

She had reached Hajif's hut, and she stopped to get a breath and calm down. It wasn't sunrise yet, but she knew that it was almost time for Novak to go to the museum to meet with Joe Quinn. She couldn't hide away here. She would wash, change her clothes, and be on her way there, too. Eve would expect her, and it wasn't professional to do anything else. Though she knew Novak would have made certain Eve was guarded, if Joe was going with Novak, Jill should be there to protect and support Eve.

Screw Novak.

But please keep him safe today, dammit, she added quickly.

CHAPTER

16

I'll call you as soon as we know anything," Joe said. He kissed Eve and headed for the door, where Novak was waiting. "Don't worry. I checked Novak's security arrangements, and you'll be fine."

"Yes, I'm really worried about that," Eve said dryly. "I'm not the one who's going to be checking out land mines."

"I know what I'm doing, Eve," he said quietly as he glanced over his shoulder. "You know that's true."

"I know, but that doesn't help much." She gestured impatiently. "Get out of here. The sooner you leave, the sooner you'll get back. Keep safe."

He nodded, and his glance shifted to Jill. "Make yourself useful. Watch over her."

"I will," Jill said. "Why do you think I'm here? I realize she's my responsibility." She was trying not to look at Novak. The anger she had felt was dissipating, lost in the panic, and she tried to hold on to it. "Good luck." Her gaze shifted to Novak. "You, too, Novak. Don't do anything stupid. You promised Gideon."

He smiled mockingly. "I'll keep that in mind. I'll definitely see you later, Jill."

Then they were both gone.

And Jill found herself going to the door to watch them go down the path. Her hands clenched into fists. "Look at them. They can't wait to get out there and play their war games. They could get themselves blown up."

"Yes, they could." Eve came over to stand beside her. "And it's really getting to you." Her eyes were on Jill's face. "Maybe more than I would have thought."

"And it's not bothering you?" Jill shook her head. "I know better than that. I've never seen anyone as crazy about a man as you are about Joe Quinn. I didn't expect you to be this controlled."

"I have to be controlled," Eve said quietly. "Joe is a detective, and he's in danger every day. I face this too often to let myself fall apart every time he walks out the door in the morning. It's his job, and it wouldn't be fair to him. And he's fantastically efficient at that job, and that helps."

"Is he really that good with land mines?"

"Yes, trained by the SEALs, and he kept up with advances. He's done work on cases where he had to defuse them. And once when we were in Scotland, he got rid of a number of them planted on the road bordering a lake we were exploring. He knows what he's doing. So I trust him with those damn bombs as well as everything else." Her lips twisted. "Even though at times like this it nearly kills me. Particularly since this time I'm to blame for his being here."

"No, you aren't. I am," Jill said in frustration. "Joe knows that, everyone knows that. Which is why I should be going with them today." She raised her hand. "Mistake. You don't have to tell me it would be a mistake. I know it would be a mistake. I'd be a liability. I don't have the training." She added gloomily, "I think I should get Novak to send me to that same CIA training camp in Afghanistan where he sent Gideon."

"What? I don't believe you'd stand a chance in persuading him," Eve said. "And he'd probably be right. That's not where you make a real difference in life. You don't shoot people. You use your brain and figure out how to change the way they think so that they'll do what you want. It's part of your ability as a storyteller. That's where you make the difference. That's your talent, and who should know better than I how good you are at it?" She grimaced. "Though considering the kind of situations in which you become embroiled, it might not be a bad idea to keep that training camp on the back burner as an alternate plan. But I'd find another way to reach the same goal."

"Easy to say. Right now I feel like one of those medieval women who were left home to tend the castle while the men rode off to save the world. It's driving me crazy." Her gaze suddenly narrowed on Eve's face. "And I bet it's driving you crazy, too. You'd hate it as much as I do. How do you cope?"

"Like you, I try to be reasonable about the greater good. I have a son to think about, and that has a tremendous influence." She suddenly smiled recklessly. "And when I can't stand it any longer, I go for it, get on my trusty steed, and ride hell for leather and leave that safe, boring castle behind."

Jill smiled back at her. "I thought as much." Her smile faded. "But what are you going to do today?"

"I'm going to work on Mila." Eve went over to her worktable. "Because that's where *my* expertise lies. And I'll try to get lost in my work and forget that Varak might have a more sophisticated land mine than we've seen yet. I'm going to trust Joe and Gideon and Novak. I'm going to wait for Joe's call. If I have to stay in the castle, I'll be as productive and inventive as I possibly can. So that next time, I might be the one to save the world." She glanced over her shoulder. "Sound like a plan?"

"It sounds like you," Jill said. She turned away. "I'll have to think about it. I'm having trouble adjusting at the moment. Thanks for letting me vent. I needed it."

"I could see that. No problem." She smiled. "It was good talking just to remind myself of all the things I knew were important. Sometimes emotions get in the way." She paused. "I'm scared, too, Jill. Varak seems like the ultimate bogeyman. He's escaped so many times during these last years. No one has been able to touch him. And now he's got Zahra Kiyani in his corner. When Gideon told us about the compound, I thought that it was going to be okay. But what if it isn't? Novak's drones uncovered some nasty surprises."

"They'll find a way to get around them. It might just take a little while."

"Yeah, I know." Eve forced her gaze to shift back to her reconstruction. "Definitely time for me to get to work."

Jill watched Eve's hands flying over the clay. Eve was focusing, her determination unquestionable as usual. It was a quality Jill envied at this moment.

Then do something about it, she thought impatiently. She turned and went out the door. The morning sunlight was getting stronger, and it was warm on her arms as she sat down beside the door. She had promised to watch over Eve, but she needed a little distance now.

Because Eve's words had struck a strong, resounding chord. She had to think about them, examine them, let them begin to come alive. She knew about words. They were a part of her mind, part of who she was. And these words might be some of the most important of her life.

You don't shoot people. You use your brain to figure out how to change the way they think so that they'll do what you want. It's part of your ability as a storyteller.

That's where you make the difference.

That was true. All her life that was what had made the difference. Yet from the time she had brought Eve to Maldara, she had stepped back because of guilt and uncertainty. She had relied on Novak, Gideon, Joe Quinn, and Eve herself to make most of the moves forward. She'd been content to merely sit on the sidelines and watch over Eve.

And Kimbro had died. Eve had been poisoned. There was no telling how much blame Jill had to shoulder about the bombing of that U.N. building because she hadn't been more aggressive.

She had to close her eyes for an instant. She couldn't be sure that everything would have been different if she'd been more true to herself. But what if it had been? When you wrote a story, every chapter, every paragraph, every plot point made a difference.

She opened her eyes and drew a long breath. Okay, don't look back. Look forward. Do what Eve said she could do, use her primary talent. Figure out a way to change the way the story would go. Pray that trip to Varak's encampment would yield dividends but don't count on it. Rely only on yourself.

Look at the principal characters and how they would behave. Explore weakness, strength.

Varak was a sociopath, almost impossible to judge.

But Zahra...

What had Eve said about Zahra?

And now he's got Zahra Kiyani in his corner.

But did he really have her in his corner? Could her character be moved, shifted?

Think about that . . .

And who else had moved into the spotlight?

Dalai.

Strange to think of that slender, vulnerable girl in anything as bold as a spotlight. She had fluttered in and out around Gideon, then had run away. But there had been no doubt that she had been honest and helpful about Varak. Jill hadn't realized until now that something about her encounter with Gideon had made her uneasy . . .

Put the thought aside. Let it simmer.

Go back to the beginning, when she'd first gotten that offer from Hadfeld.

That was really the start of the story . . .

NAGALI RAIN FOREST
2:35 P.M.

"Quinn's not back yet?" Gideon murmured to Novak as he crawled back from checking on the other men on the team. "It's been almost an hour. I don't like it. He stopped us four times before we got half a mile into the property to disarm land mines. I have an idea this whole jungle is one big time bomb."

"So does Quinn," Novak said grimly. "That's why he wanted to explore ahead to make sure that it would be minimally safe for us to go forward without blowing ourselves up. The sentries are the least of our worries."

"Well, they may not be the least of Quinn's worries. I didn't hear any explosions, but one of the sentries might have gotten him." Then he shook his head. "No, Quinn's too sharp. Forget I said that. I just want to get moving. So do the rest of your team, Novak."

"Do you think I don't?" He paused, struggling with his own impatience. "Quinn knows what he's doing." He added, "I hope."

"That didn't appear to be a sincere vote of confidence." Joe Quinn was suddenly moving out of the palmetto bushes next to them. "But I can see why. I thought I'd be back before this."

"Why weren't you?"

"I knew after a half hour that I wasn't going to be able to bring any of the team much farther than this point. I've never seen an area so heavily seeded with land mines. Varak must be truly paranoid. I watched one of his sentries, who obviously had a defined path, and he was very careful about not going off that path. He probably didn't know where all those land mines were either."

"And that surprises you?" Novak asked. "Varak would have been amused if one of his men was careless enough to get himself blown up." He asked, "Where were you for the rest of that hour?"

"Taking photos. Trying to determine sentry placement. I found the helicopter pad." He looked at Novak. "And I located the main house and bunkhouses."

Novak tensed. "Varak?"

"I didn't see him. And that area is so heavily fortified, there's no way we'd be able to get into his house or get a shot at Varak without being blown away ourselves." His lips twisted. "I thought I'd better get back instead of staking him out. After all, you are heading this team."

"Not so that anyone would notice," he said. "You said that the team wouldn't be able to go any farther, but you managed to flit all around the damn encampment."

"I knew what I was doing. One man with experience. An entire team tramping through there would end up in pieces. The odds are someone would make a mistake." He looked at Gideon. "And that young girl you were so concerned about would pay for it when Varak got spooked. Do you want that?"

"No. But I *do* want Varak." He turned to Novak. "What do we do?"

Novak thought about it. Dammit, he couldn't see any options at the moment. He muttered a curse, then said to Gideon, "Go back to the men and get them out of here and back to Robaku." He whirled back to Quinn. "You said one man could do it. How about two? Can you take me back to that house so that I can verify that bastard is Nils Varak?"

Quinn gazed thoughtfully at him. "Maybe. You want to stake him out?"

"I want to see him *move*. And maybe there's some way we can get in that house for DNA. If we can't, I want to get a video to send to our lab for facial analysis and verification. They'd be able to determine if his basic facial structure would support that plastic surgery Zahra paid for. It's not much, but I don't want this all to be for nothing. Can you do it?"

Quinn was thinking about it. "You do know that it gets dark very early in rain forests like these. Those tree canopies block out all light. You'd have only a limited amount of time to stake him out. We'd have maybe three or four hours." He added grimly, "And it's hard as hell to avoid those land mines when I can see. Even at dusk, it would be a risk. I can't use a flashlight because of the sentries."

"Stop telling me about the problems. Will you do it?"

"Shit," Gideon said. "Novak!"

"Answer me, Quinn." Novak held his eyes. "Can you get me there?"

Quinn suddenly smiled. "Sure, no problem. I know the way now. Providing you can follow in my steps without a single deviation. Not even an inch." He added dryly, "That would be nearly impossible for you considering that you don't like to go any way but your own."

"But not quite impossible," he said curtly. "I'd have the comfort of knowing you'd be blown up before I would." He turned away. "Let's go, Quinn."

Quinn nodded. "By all means. I was pissed off about having to stop and come back to you anyway." He moved back into the palmetto bushes. "Stay close, Novak. I'm going to be moving very fast."

———————

ROBAKU
5:50 P.M.

"What do you mean they went back into that jungle?" Jill stared at Gideon in horror. "Gideon. Why did you just leave them there?"

"I had orders, dammit," Gideon said. "I couldn't go with them, but I could get the team safely back. That's what I did."

"Since when did you ever obey orders?" Jill's voice was shaking. "You do what you like."

"Not when it comes down to sacrificing thirty-two men by not obeying two men who have a hell of a lot more experience than I do."

"No, you'd rather sacrifice—"

"Easy, Jill," Eve said. "It's not his fault. Would you like to go up against Novak or Joe?"

"Yes, I'd like to knock their heads together." But she realized Eve was right. It was just the shock that had caused her to attack Gideon. Shock and sickening fear. But she had to control it. Eve was just as frightened as she was, and she mustn't make it worse for her. She forced herself to nod at Gideon. "You did what you could. I'm just scared."

"Me too." He made a face. "I nearly flipped when Novak wanted to go back with Quinn to stake out Varak. I would have done anything I could to stop them. I was worried about Quinn's being a wild card, but Novak was just as bad today."

"Or just as good," Eve said quietly. "They're both professionals, and they wanted to get the job done. What can we do to help them, Gideon?"

He shook his head. "Not much of anything. Just wait. I left two men on the road that borders the property to send me word if anything...unusual occurred."

"You mean if one of those land mines blew up," Jill said.

Gideon nodded. "That was what Quinn was worried about. I told you that he told Novak he wanted to get out of that jungle before it got dark."

"Yes, you did." Eve was looking out the window at the fading light. "It should be dark soon."

Gideon didn't say anything.

Jill's gaze flew to his face. "Gideon?"

"Not in that rain forest," he said. "It's probably been pitch-dark for the last thirty minutes."

She inhaled sharply. She felt as if she'd been kicked in the stomach.

Gideon said quickly, "You know they'll call as soon as they get to a safe area."

"Whenever that is," Eve said numbly. She straightened her shoulders. "Yes, Joe will call me as soon as he can. I know that."

"Of course you do. Let's go outside and get some air." Jill

strode toward the door and opened it for Eve. "Like you said, they're both professionals."

She watched Eve go out the door before she turned to Gideon. "How bad was it out there?"

"Deadly. What you'd expect from Varak," he said soberly. "It's set up to be a killing field, between the land mines and the multiple snipers. If the team had gone in, the chances are we'd have never come out. Novak knew that, but he was desperate."

"So he took the chance himself." Her lips twisted. "And he'll do it again." She started out the door toward Eve. "If Varak didn't kill them both this time." Her hands clenched into fists at her sides. "We'll have to see if Eve gets that call."

———

The call didn't come until almost an hour later.

Jill's heart jumped, and she whirled to face Eve.

Eve nodded and quickly checked the ID. "Joe."

Relief so great it made Jill dizzy. "Thank God."

Eve answered the phone. "You're an idiot, Joe," she said huskily. "Are you both all right?" She nodded at Jill at his answer. "You don't deserve it. When will you be here so that I can tell you in person?" A moment later she hung up the phone. "Another forty-five minutes. They didn't leave the stakeout until it was almost fully dark, and it took them longer to get back through the jungle."

"I would think it would. Was the risk worth it? Did they get what they needed?"

Eve made a face. "Joe said partially successful. But partially is never enough for Joe."

"Nor for Novak." Jill tried to keep her voice steady. "I'll go inside and tell Gideon that they evidently didn't get blown up. Coming?"

Eve shook her head. "I'll wait out here. I'm too edgy to be cooped up right now."

"And you want to see Joe the minute he walks down that path."

"You might say that," she said lightly. She leaned back against the wall. "Though I do intend to be very stern with him."

"Yeah, sure." Jill opened the door and went into the museum.

Gideon immediately looked up. "Eve heard?"

Jill nodded. "Both okay. They'll be here in about forty-five minutes. You'll probably hear from Novak soon."

Gideon gave a low whistle. "I'll call the airport and let the team know."

"Do that." She was silent a moment. "They didn't get everything they needed. They'll probably go back, won't they?"

He hesitated. "It depends on how successful they were."

"The only results they'd consider successful enough to stop them from going after Varak would be if they'd managed to kill him or had gotten some scrap of DNA material that would prove his identity. Neither of those things was likely to happen according to Joe. Right?"

"That's what he said," Gideon said warily.

"Then no way should they run the risk of going after him again," she said flatly. "We need to leave him alone and try another direction."

"It's Varak, Jill," he said gently. "He's out there waiting for us to scoop him up."

"It's the wrong thing to do. I sat here all day, going over everything that has happened since I got that first message from Hadfeld, until the moment you showed up with the location of that compound from Dalai. It's like a story with huge gaps missing, but nothing I thought of or tried to put together made going after Varak in that jungle the right thing to do." She held up her hand as he started to protest. "And I'm not going to argue with you. I know where you're coming from. I'll talk to you later." She turned and headed for the door. "Will you stay here with Eve until Joe and Novak get here? I'm tired, and I think I'll go down to Hajif's hut and rest for a while."

His eyes widened in surprise. "You don't want to wait until they get here?"

She shook her head. "So I can hear about how they avoided the killing fields? Maybe later. Right now, it doesn't appeal to me. It makes me feel sick to my stomach." She headed down the hill toward the village.

She needed to be alone. She didn't know what her attitude would be when she saw Novak again. The day had been fraught with tension and worry and attempts to forget that he might not be coming back. That first moment when she had realized he was safe had been dizzy and shocking and put her on an emotional roller coaster. What they had between them was only sex and passion and the strange bond of fascination that had formed these past months, she told herself. Last night, she had been swept away, and today had been so emotional that she couldn't regain her equilibrium. It was better if she took a step back until she was more cool and able to analyze her responses.

And there was no way that would have been true if she'd been there when he'd walked into the museum tonight. No, she needed to go to see Hajif and Leta, have a light meal, then go to bed.

She would deal with Novak tomorrow.

———

Her phone rang three hours later.

She tensed, then rolled over on her sleeping mat and reached for it.

Novak.

Bite the bullet. He wouldn't stop calling until she answered. "Hello, Novak."

"Get out of there and come to me. I need to see you."

"I'm already in bed."

"I don't care. Come to me, or I'll come and get you. You don't want Hajif and Leta to be upset." He cut the connection.

No, she didn't want Hajif to be drawn into this. She rolled off the mat and threw on her clothes. A moment later, she'd stalked out of Hajif's hut. She saw Novak in the doorway of his hut, framed against the lantern light behind him, and strode toward him. "What do you want, Novak? That was completely rude, and I don't appreciate you—"

"Shut up." He pulled her into the hut and jerked her into his arms. "I'm having a very bad day." He kissed her. "And I didn't need to have you hiding out and avoiding me at the end of it. Particularly after Gideon was telling me how weird and stiff you were being." He kissed her again. "That's not going to happen. If you don't want to screw me, that's your decision, but you're going to be with me. I need you." He pushed her down on the blankets. "Do you want a drink? I could use one right now. A glass of wine?"

"How polite." She sat up, trying to get her breath. What had started out as anger was transforming into that same electricity she had felt last night. Her breasts were swelling, her lower body tingling, readying. "And you can't force me to be here. What's wrong with you, dammit?"

"Wine," he answered himself. "You like wine." He poured a merlot from a bottle into a glass. He poured himself a whiskey and sat down cross-legged in front of her. He handed her the goblet. "No force. I merely made a suggestion."

"Bullshit."

He grinned. "Okay, I wanted to catch your attention."

"I almost decked you."

"And I wanted a little sympathy after a hard day."

"Not the way to get it. And since when have you ever come to anyone after something goes wrong? I've never seen anyone so self-sufficient."

"It's a new era." He took a sip of his whiskey. "Maybe I've never found anyone with whom I wanted to share my very rare failures. Or maybe I just wanted to see you sitting here and know that there was someone I cared about whom Varak hadn't been able to touch. Anyway, I was frustrated as hell when you weren't there when I got back to that museum. I needed you."

He had said that before, and suddenly Jill's impatience was dwindling before it disappeared entirely. It would take a lot for a self-assured man like Novak to admit to needing anyone. "Gideon said that it was bad out there." She took a sip of her wine. "A setup for a killing field." She added with sudden fierceness, "So why did you go back with Quinn and try to get yourself slaughtered? Varak's killed close to six hundred thousand people in that war, and he clearly built that compound as a trap. You knew it, and you still talked Joe Quinn into staking out that house."

"I didn't have to talk very hard. Quinn wanted him as much as I did. I only had to let him control how he got me through that land-mine tangle. Quinn likes control."

"And you don't?" She shook her head in frustration. "The two of you together are a complete disaster."

"Actually, I found we worked very well together today."

"And that could be an even bigger disaster." She drew a deep breath. "Would you like to tell me why you waited until after dark to start trying to get back out of that jungle when Quinn told you how dangerous it would be?"

He shrugged. "It wasn't that bad. Quinn had the route pretty well memorized, including land-mine placement. And we had no choice. We didn't get even a glimpse of Varak until almost twilight. I was afraid we might have to give it up for the day." His lips twisted. "But then Varak's true nature came to the rescue. He evidently hadn't had his quota of blood recently. He had one of his soldiers dragged to that dirt yard before the front porch to be punished for some infraction at the attack on the U.N. headquarters. At least that was the excuse. I think he probably just wanted his men to witness how all-powerful he was." He paused. "He used a machete. He took a long time. I had no problem getting the videos."

Jill felt sick. "You said that you'd know him just by the way he moved. Was it really Varak?"

He nodded. "I'd swear to it. But that wouldn't be enough, of course. Not now that Zahra has convinced everyone that Varak's skull was destroyed at the U.N. headquarters. Probably the videos won't be enough either, but we can send them through our photo techno unit at Langley to establish what he could have looked like before surgery. But we'll have to go back and break into that house in the compound and get a DNA specimen so that I can get the director to let me stage a raid powerful enough to bring Varak down."

"That means you're determined to go back there," Jill said tightly.

"It's our only option if we want to grab the bastard before he decides to leave the country. We're lucky to get the chance."

"I don't believe there's any luck connected to Varak unless it's bad luck. He definitely couldn't be recognized?"

He shook his head. "His face has been changed, his hair is sandy-blond, not black. The only thing that's the same is that muscular, powerful body and the way he walks. The arrogant bastard strides around as if he owns the world..."

Muscular and powerful... As arrogant as if he owned the world.

Jill went still. "His hair is dyed blond now? I only remember Dalai telling Gideon that he'd had plastic surgery."

"Very good plastic surgery. But his hair is kind of dirty blond now."

Fair hair. Suddenly, her chest was tight, and she was having trouble breathing. It couldn't be the same man, could it? Varak wouldn't take the risk of exposing himself just to inflict that act of terror on her. And she hadn't been able to see what shade her attacker's hair was in the darkness, only that it was light, fair. But she had felt the straw-like texture beneath her fingers when she'd been fighting him.

But it had done her no good to fight him, she remembered in a panic. She'd felt so weak, and he'd been brutally strong...

As if he'd owned the world.

"Jill?" Novak's gaze was narrowed on her face.

"You said you took a video." She moistened her lips as she put her glass of wine carefully on the floor beside her. "I want to see it."

"No, you don't," he said flatly. "You don't want to ever see that bloodbath."

"You took it. I want to see it."

"Why?" he asked roughly. "So that you can add it to your collection of nightmares? There's no need for you to see it."

"That's up to me, isn't it?" She had to keep her voice steady. "You thought it important enough to risk getting yourself killed. Show it to me."

"I tell you, it's the stuff of nightmares. You don't want

to—" He suddenly broke off. "Nightmares..." His gaze was searching her face. "Don't make me show you this, Jill."

"I want to see it."

He muttered a curse. "And it seems I'm going to let you see it." He got to his feet, went to the phone lying on the bench, and brought it to her. "Do me a favor and don't watch more than the first five minutes. He does a lot of strutting during that period and doesn't get into the carnage until you see him take his machete."

She was bracing herself to press the PLAY button. "He loves that machete." She swallowed. "That's how he killed those children."

"Press the button," he said roughly. "Just watch it and get it over with."

She pressed the button.

Fair hair. Eyes glittering as Varak strode out on the porch and looked down at the man kneeling in the yard.

Ferocity.

His lips pulled away from his teeth like that of a feral animal.

Malicious pleasure.

Anticipating the pain to come.

He was speaking, hurling threats at the man on his knees.

Then he was walking down the steps.

Power. Arrogance. As if he owned the world...

She couldn't take her eyes off him. She was staring in helpless fascination.

Even when one of Varak's men handed him his machete.

"No, dammit!" Novak was there beside Jill, jerking his phone away from her. "No more."

"No more," she repeated dully. She didn't need any more. She'd seen enough. "Thank you. I...couldn't seem to stop. He was like a snake that was weaving back and forth and hypnotizing me. Not letting me move." She hadn't been able to move that night in the jungle either. "I couldn't move at all. Only snakes aren't that strong..."

"Shh." She was suddenly in his arms. "No, they're not that strong. And I'll be chopping the head off this particular snake very soon. He's just jumped even higher on my kill list." His hand cupped the back of her head, his lips at her temple. "It was him?" he asked softly. "He was one of those sons of bitches who raped you that night?"

She shook her head. "No, he was the one who was telling the rest of them how to do it." Her voice was shaking. "He kept saying they weren't hurting me enough. That it wouldn't do any good unless they broke me. He seemed angry about it. He was the one who kept beating me and beating me..." She had to take a deep breath. "It was him. I recognized the eyes." She added, "And the voice. I didn't realize I'd remember so much. It was such a hideous blur. Or maybe I just tried to block him out." She recalled something else. "And that laugh. I'll always remember him laughing when he leaned over me and asked how I liked it—" Her fingers bit into his shoulders. "But he never actually raped me, and I didn't get a chance to scratch him. He must have been very careful about DNA. He'd know how dangerous it was to him...Maybe that was why he was so angry. He'd hate it that he couldn't make me suffer as much as he wanted." She buried her face in his chest. "But you were right—arrogant. As if he owned the world."

"He won't own more than six feet of it when I get my hands on him," Novak said harshly. "I knew you thought he was one of them when you kept insisting on seeing the video. I couldn't stop you when you had a right to know." His lips tightened. "And I had a right to know, too. I've been wanting to kill those bastards from the night it happened."

"It never occurred to me it could be him," Jill said. "I just thought it was a few thugs hired by the people who killed Hadfeld to make certain I left Maldara. Why would Varak become involved in . . . that . . . when it would automatically put him in danger?"

"Why would he use a machete on that man today? The idea probably amused him. I'll have to ask him before I gut him."

His voice was colder than she'd ever heard it, and Jill was beginning to be afraid she'd made a terrible mistake. Novak had already been determined enough to go after Varak in that hellish jungle, and she might have tipped the scales even more. She rushed to repair the damage. "Don't use me as an excuse. I've told you time after time that none of that was your fault. I wasn't your responsibility. Do you hear me?"

He didn't answer.

"And what if you're wrong about making another run at Varak?" she said harshly. "I've been thinking about it today, and it seems too dangerous. He's sitting there with his land mines and his damn machete ready to strike. I know you believe it's the logical way to go, but it could get you—"

"Hush." He pulled her down and fitted her spoon fashion against him. "Just lie here and let me hold you. We'll talk later. You're upset, and I didn't handle any of this right."

"No, you didn't. You should believe me when I tell you something. I know it's partly my fault. I got upset when I realized Varak—" She stopped and started again: "How can I persuade you not to go back into that jungle after Varak?"

"You can't." His lips were brushing her ear. "I can make this work, Jill. All I have to do is figure out the best way to do it."

"You mean to keep him from using that machete on you. It's the *wrong* thing to do," she said passionately. "We can go at it another way."

He didn't answer.

And he wouldn't answer, she thought. "Stubborn jackass."

"Only when I know I'm right. Relax. We'll talk later."

But he wouldn't listen then either. "No, we won't. You're already making plans, and they don't include me. You're scared that I'll break apart. It's been like that from the beginning." She added, "So you shouldn't be upset if I make plans that don't include you."

He stiffened against her. "What's that supposed to mean?"

"It means that this is *my* story, and I'll do anything I can to make it come out right. You're about to mess it up."

"I don't like the sound of that."

"Ditto. Do you want it more clear? It seems I'm going to have to take events into my own hands." She tried to relax her muscles and took a deep breath. "So I'm going to do as you suggest and lie here and take a little while to pull myself together. Because you were right, that video shook me up. But it probably shook you more than it did me because I promised myself that I'd never let any of those men hurt me again. They're no more than a passing memory to me now, and soon, they won't even be that. And it doesn't change anything that one of them was Varak. It will just take a little longer to forget him." She closed her eyes. "I'm going to try to sleep. When I wake up, I hope you'll make love to me because I found it wonderful, and I'm not at all sure that we'll ever do it again."

"Are you finished?" Novak kissed her ear again. "I don't know what's happening with you, but I'm very good at working through problems. That all sounded very final. But I assure you it is not." He held her closer. "By all means rest. Because once we start, we'll be doing it again and again and again . . ."

CHAPTER

17

Jill moved silently across the dimness of the hut.

"Come back," Novak murmured, as she reached the door. "There's still plenty of time."

She glanced over her shoulder. Novak was only a glimmer of strength and sensuality in the half darkness, but she still felt a hot tingle of sensation run through her. Ignore it. The hours with him that had gone before had made her body too accustomed to the sheer sexual eroticism of what they were together. Her breasts still felt heavy. Her skin felt satin-smooth and pliant. "You're wrong. We're out of time. Maybe I'll see you later, Novak."

The next moment, she was out of the hut. She drew a deep breath of the moist, humid air and started up the path toward the museum. It was only a little after six, and she'd been tempted to go to Hajif's, but she'd be too close and available to Novak there. Last night, he had shown her that he would have no qualms about bursting into Hajif's home if he wished.

And she did not wish to see Novak anytime soon. The sex had been too hot, and there had been that element of domination of which she was always aware with Novak. He hadn't liked it that she'd refused to communicate with him in any other way than the one that had driven both of them to the edge and beyond. If she'd stayed any longer, she would not have been able to fend off either arguments or conversation.

Conversation? They were so far apart, it was a totally foreign concept. He just wanted her to say that he was right, and he wasn't listening to her. And she was so frightened that Varak would kill him that she was desperate to try anything that would leave Varak out of the equation.

And that meant leaving Novak out of the equation as far as she was concerned.

Okay, then, start as she intended to continue.

Check in with Eve, then explore the path that had been beckoning to her since yesterday afternoon...

———————

"You've been very restless this morning." Eve looked up from her Mila reconstruction as Jill put coffee in front of her. "Everything okay?"

"As okay as it can be." Then Jill was silent. But she couldn't leave it at that. "Did Joe mention when they'd be going back to Varak's compound?"

Eve shook her head. "Just that they want it to be right. They were frustrated as hell yesterday." She added soberly, "I don't like it either, Jill. But I can't convince him that we have any other option. Joe doesn't like it that they found that helicopter pad. It would be too easy for Varak to get a helicopter pickup and fly out of there if he took the notion."

"And that means they probably won't wait longer than tomorrow or the next day." Jill forced a smile. "And that's not long to come up with another solution. But miracles happen, don't they?" She tilted her head. "Now I should let you get back to work. Is there anything else I can get for you?"

"No. How many times do I have to tell you that you don't have to wait on me, Jill?"

"It's no trouble. I don't have anything else to do now that Joe is here. He's eliminated my primary job of making sure that you're safe. He's so good at it that I feel useless. You don't really need me any longer." She lifted her hand as she headed for the door. "If you think of anything you want, give me a call. Till then, I'll stay out of your way."

"You've made sure never to be in my way," Eve said quietly. "And no one could ever call you useless."

"That's good to hear." She smiled as she opened the door. "See you later."

Jill moved quickly down the path and into the jungle several yards from the museum. She wanted complete privacy, and this area had seemed the best way to ensure it.

She sat down beneath a kapok tree and took out her phone. She paused, looking down at it. She could still change her mind. She might be wrong. But she had to go with her instincts. She drew a deep breath, took out the slip of paper with the phone number Gideon had given her when he'd come back from the palace the night before last.

This is how you make a difference.

She hesitated, then dialed the telephone number.

It rang once.

No answer.

It rang again.

Nothing.

On the third ring, it was quickly picked up.

"This is Jill Cassidy, Dalai," she said quickly. "Is it safe for you to talk? If it isn't, hang up on me."

Silence. "Is he dead?" Dalai's voice was a mere agonized breath of sound. "Gideon said you would only come to help me if he couldn't. Did I kill him?"

"No," Jill said quickly. "He's still alive. Can you talk? Where is Zahra?"

"The British prime minister is here. She took them to the hospital to visit the victims." She brushed the question aside. "Tell me. Is Gideon *hurt*?"

"No." Jill added deliberately, "But he could have been. It was very close."

Dalai struggled to get control. "Thank God. How I prayed that he would be safe."

"That's very kind." The girl was obviously sincere, but Jill had to harden her heart against the impulse to soften. Difficult to do since all she could think about was how much Dalai must have gone through over the years. "But you still sent him out to that compound."

"He *wanted* to go. You all wanted to go. You all knew how evil Varak is. I told you everything I could to help you."

"We realize that. It wasn't enough. Though Gideon was still grateful. And he did what he could to protect you before he went into that jungle to go after Varak." She added, "But that compound was one huge trap. It was a miracle they got out alive." She paused. "And they're going to go back if you don't stop them. Help me to stop them, Dalai."

Dalai was silent. "You know *nothing*. How can I do that?" She paused, her voice edged with panic. "Varak has to die, and I cannot do it. Do you think I haven't thought about it? But when I'm with him, it's as if he devours me."

"It's the fear that devours you," Jill said. "Do you think I don't know how that feels?" But she couldn't be too sympathetic or Dalai wouldn't take that final step they needed her to take. The girl had come so far against tremendous odds. Just from listening to Gideon about their encounters, Jill could read between the lines. Dalai was clearly a fighter but not a trusting one. She had even been afraid to trust Gideon. So give her something to fight against, someone to fight beside. "But don't expect me to let you cover your head and send people I care about to do what you should be doing. This is your battle, too. What you gave us didn't work. As I said, every step at that compound is a trap. We need more from you." She paused. "Gideon told me about the way you handed him Varak on a platter but dodged talking about Zahra. He accepted it because he felt sorry for you." Her voice became flat and uncompromising. "I don't feel sorry for you. I can't afford to do that. It's too dangerous for all of us. I won't pity you, but I'll respect you and work with you. Because I believe you can do anything you have to do to help us, Dalai. I thought a long time about how you fit into the picture, everything that you'd discussed with Gideon, your background, what you must have felt, what you wanted out of life. What your story really was...And then I realized that Gideon was letting his guilty feelings blind him to the fact that you aren't quite the victim he thinks you to be. Yes, you've been mistreated and threatened and terrorized. Who could deny that's true?" She paused. "But I believe you've managed to survive it because you're very, very strong. You had to be strong to live with Zahra Kiyani since you were a child. She's a powerhouse and as evil as they come. Gideon believes you've been brainwashed, but I think you've just done and said the things you had to in order to survive. I did the same thing when I was living in all those foster homes when I was a kid. But you had it even rougher than me. It took someone very smart and patient to fight that silent battle with Zahra all these years. I imagine most of the time she doesn't realize you're doing it. You're still fighting, but I'd bet somewhere down deep you've been waiting for your chance to get away from her. You might even have a plan? I think that first night that Gideon came to you, the reason you were so upset was that you were afraid he'd get in the way of any plan you might have to free yourself from Zahra. Is that true?"

Dalai didn't reply.

It was pure guesswork and instinct, but Jill had to go with it once she'd started. "But then Varak showed up on the scene, and it was a horrible scenario that you couldn't tolerate. You had to do something, anything, to get rid of him. You're frightened of Zahra, but in the end you didn't see her as the prime immediate threat. You thought you'd have time later to find a way to escape from her. So you distracted Gideon from discussing anything about her so that he'd concentrate on Nils Varak. Varak had hurt you terribly and would hurt you again if given the opportunity. It was to your advantage to have us go after him with full force right away and prevent him from doing that." She smiled sadly. "So you called Gideon and delivered the message you wanted to send. When you left him, Gideon had a mission."

Dalai was silent. Then she finally said, "You're . . . very clever. Madam said you were." Another silence. "That's the reason she hated you. She tried to get that Wyatt man from the U.N. to stop you. But he couldn't do it, so she had to go to Varak."

It wasn't that frank admission that surprised Jill but the fact that Dalai's voice and manner had altered in the space of that silence. Both were no longer trembling or fearful, only troubled.

"Gideon is clever, too," Jill said quietly. "He would have realized what you were doing if he hadn't been so conscience-stricken about how he treated you when you first came to the palace. He has a great heart, and it tends to get in his way."

"There's no reason for him to feel badly," she said jerkily. "He treated me very well. Everyone else was afraid of her." Then the words tumbled out. "I didn't *want* to do this. But he was always so smart and strong. It's what I most remembered about him. I thought he'd be all right. I didn't mean not to tell him the whole truth." Then she stopped. "No, I guess I did. But I gave him Varak, someone I knew he wanted very much. And, yes, I knew it would also keep me from being hurt again. There's nothing wrong with that. I thought I could tell him all the rest about Madam later, when it would be safer for me."

"No, there's nothing wrong with that," Jill said. "I can understand how you might feel you had to protect yourself any way you could." She paused. "As long as it didn't hurt anyone. Because I realize what you went through. We're alike in many ways. We've both been victims." She added, "I believe you know that, don't you? You said Zahra had to go to Varak to help her. You heard exactly what Zahra asked Varak to do to me when she couldn't get what she wanted from Wyatt."

Silence. "She was very angry with you. He told her it would be better to kill you, but she said that would be . . . awkward, and that they should just hurt you." Another silence. "I knew what that meant. I was very sad. You should have done what she wanted."

"No, that would have been the wrong thing to do." Jill hesitated, then said deliberately, "Because that would have made me the slave she's tried to make you, Dalai. You know that if you don't fight, that's what happens. I was hurt, but I healed, got to my feet, and started to fight again. I'm fighting now. And that's what you've got to do."

"Do I? Even though she said she's like Kiya, and I was meant to be her slave?" Jill realized there was actually a trace of sarcasm in Dalai's words, and it only showed how far they had come toward honesty in these last minutes.

"Bullshit. How do you know that you're not the one who's like Kiya? You can be whatever you want to be. Look at you. You've already started to fight." She added dryly, "Though definitely in a manipulative manner. I'm afraid we're also alike in that quality, and lately, I've become very aware how destructive it can be. I've sworn off it myself unless it's an emergency." She changed the subject. "But it's time to admit that the only way you're going to get rid of Varak is through using everything you know about Zahra. Zahra's the key. It's too deadly going after Varak. There are too many traps. So you'll have to give me a way to use Zahra to bring Varak to us."

"There's no way to do that," she said quickly.

"I believe we'll think of a way. We'll talk, and something will come to us. It probably won't be as slick and efficient as what you were planning to have Gideon do. But we'll get there."

"You don't *know* her." Her voice was suddenly harsh. "Stay out of this. Let me handle her. I know how she thinks, how she reacts. You could spoil everything. You don't know what she'd do."

"No, but you do. You know everything about her." It was time to stop pushing. She had to step back and let the decision come from Dalai. "If you're ready to help us, then find a way to call me. I don't want to put you at risk again. Let me know, and I'll somehow find a way to get you out of there so that we can talk more freely." Her voice took on an urgency that could not have been more genuine. "But we don't have much time. People will die." Now add the single plea that might change the story. "Gideon will die."

She cut the connection.

Jill drew a deep breath. It was done.

Now all she could do was sit here and wait for a call that might not come.

———

The call came three hours later, when the sun had just started to go down.

Her heart jumped as she saw the presidential palace ID on her phone. *Yes.*

"I will help you." Dalai's voice was intense and angry when she came on the phone. "I have no choice. Though you'll probably be like all the rest of them who care only about themselves. But you mustn't be stupid or careless. Do you hear me? I won't be put in that...place again."

"Hopefully, I won't be either of those things," Jill said. "How can I help you? Should I send someone to the palace to get you?"

"You're already being stupid. You'd spoil everything if you did that." Dalai drew a deep breath. "Besides, I'm already here."

Jill stiffened in shock. "What? Where?"

"Robaku. I knew that's where you were. Madam was angry enough about it. I decided there was no sense my trying to tell you anything on the phone. I'd have to come there anyway."

Jill was stunned. "Just like that? You walked out of the palace and just decided to come here to see me. How?"

"Madam leaves a car in a garage two blocks from the

palace that we use when she goes to see Varak. Most of the time, she likes me to drive, so I have the keys."

Jill shook her head in bewilderment. "Then you could have escaped whenever you chose."

"No, I couldn't. She would have chased me down and caught me. It wasn't the right time. Neither is this, and you keep on asking questions," she said, exasperated. "I only have a few hours before she'll be back from that meeting with the British prime minister. I've parked down by this brook with the boulders. I've come this far. Now you come to me."

"I'll be right there." Jill was jarred out of the shock as she realized what the consequences were of Dalai's decision. "How long have you been here? No, you had to have just gotten here, or they would have been all over you. Look, you might have visitors before I get there. Don't run away. Just wait for me."

"Visitors?" Dalai repeated, alarmed. "Not Gideon. I don't want to see Gideon. I came to see you."

"Fine. Just wait for me." She hung up and called Novak. "Did you get the drone intruder report?"

"It just came in. How the hell did you know?"

"She's no threat. Don't do anything. Don't tell anyone you got it." Dalai had mentioned Gideon, she remembered. "Don't tell Gideon. She particularly doesn't want Gideon."

"Who is no threat?" he said sharply. "What are you doing, Jill?"

"Dalai. And I'm trying to get off this phone so that she won't run away." She was already striding down the path toward the brook. "But I can see that's not going to happen unless I let you come. Okay, meet me at the brook. And don't you let anyone hurt her." She cut the connection as she rounded the bend and saw Dalai standing beside the brook. She was wearing a black cloak over her top and sarong skirt, and she looked as if she were going to fly away any minute. Jill drew a breath of relief. "I was afraid you'd be gone. It would have been wise of you to give me a little warning." Jill skidded to a stop before her. "I'm sure you must have picked up information from Zahra and Varak that this place is a virtual armed camp."

"No, they've never mentioned it." She was frowning. "Varak doesn't like having Eve Duncan here, but Madam told him to stay away from Robaku. She didn't want to cause an incident if—" Dalai broke off, then said impatiently, "And I wasn't sure I was coming here, so how could I give you warning? I didn't know if I'd change my mind. But no one saw me."

"Except the spy in the sky. Which means Novak saw you." She looked down the path. "Don't get spooked. Here he comes. It was easier to bring him here than argue."

Dalai froze, her gaze on Novak. "I have to go."

"No, you don't. This is Jed Novak. I trust him. Gideon trusts him." She turned to Novak. "Don't you do anything intimidating. She's here to help us. She's already literally gone the extra mile. So let me handle it."

Novak stopped, staring at Dalai. "She doesn't appear to be a threat. Though her coming here automatically makes her suspect." He took a step closer. "And she doesn't seem to be intimidated, only wary." He smiled at Dalai. "Maybe we should have a truce to see if either one of us has cause for concern." His smile faded. "Though I didn't like it that she didn't want Gideon here."

"I was . . . ashamed," Dalai said. "He was kind, and I knew he pitied me." She looked him straight in the eye. "I used it."

"Not good." He glanced at Jill. "Why is she here?"

"Because I don't want to see anyone get blown up by that homicidal maniac. She might be able to tell us how to work around it. She knows Zahra, inside and out."

Dalai was still holding Novak's eyes. "And she says Zahra is the key. Do you believe that, too?"

"Jill and I are at odds on that score. But I'm always willing to listen to differing opinions." He was gazing at her searchingly. "Do you think she's right?"

"She might be. That's why I'm here." She shivered. "Though I don't want to be. I *hate* this place."

"Because of the children," Jill said. "I understand."

"Yes. No." She shook her head. "It always frightens me. I want to leave here." She said impatiently, "But I'm here, so what do you want to know?"

"Everything," Jill said. "But you told me when you first got here that you couldn't tell me anything on the phone. You said you would have had to come here anyway. Why?"

"Because you think you understand, but you can't. I knew I'd have to show you." She whirled on her heel and strode along the bank toward the tall boulders that bordered the north side of the brook. "Let's get it over with."

Jill was running after her. "Where are you going?"

"The boulders." Dalai was hurrying down the path. "Now don't talk to me. I'm nervous about this, and I'm afraid I'm doing the wrong thing. I've never trusted anyone but myself before. I still don't." A moment later, they'd reached the edge of the creek, and she was skirting around it until she reached a group of tall boulders that bordered it to the south. "The third one . . ."

Then she fell to her knees and was digging at the dirt at the base of the boulder. *"Yes."* She had revealed a nine-inch-square keypad. Then she froze, gazing down at it. "Give me a minute. I'll be all right in just a minute."

"What the hell is this?" Jill fell to her knees beside her. The girl was clearly terrified. She reached out to take her hand. "What's wrong? Let me help you, Dalai."

"No one can help me." Dalai was staring down at the key-pad. "That's what she said. No one can help you, Dalai."

"Zahra?" Jill was frowning in confusion. "She was the one who said that to you?" Then she stiffened. "Zahra was *here*?"

Dalai drew a deep breath. "Of course she was here. She's always been here. She regards Robaku as her special place. She brought me here several times a year from the time my father sent me to her. Usually at night, when she considered it safe." She pulled her hand away from Jill's. "And she hated it when you got in her way."

"You mean when she built the museum?"

"No, she thought that was a triumph. It was all your stories and keeping those villagers from being moved." She was looking down at the panel, bracing herself. "There's a code." She was punching in a four-letter code. "She gave it to me when she first started training me to help her take care of this place. She waited almost a year before she trusted me with it." Her lips twisted. "When she thought that I'd been taught to obey every rule she'd set out for me as a slave should." She paused. "And the consequences if I failed in any way."

"Dalai, what are you talking about?" Jill asked quietly.

"You wanted to know about Zahra Kiyani. I'm telling you about her." She met Jill's eyes as she punched in the final letter. "This is who she is. Shall I tell you what the four letters of the code are?"

Jill was beginning to make a wild guess.

Then she heard a click, and the rocky ground around the boulder appeared to shift. The next instant, it slid open to reveal a trapdoor with a metal ladder.

She heard Novak mutter a soft oath behind her.

"The ladder is very sturdy and safe," Dalai said. "So is the cavern below. It was built by Zahra Kiyani's great-grandfather, but the Kiyani family kept it updated and repaired through the years. You can understand why she didn't want the village disturbed in any way."

Jill was gazing down into that darkness. "You've known about this for years?"

"She needed someone to come with her to check and make certain all was in order. She trusted me. She made certain I could be trusted." She reached in her cloak and pulled out a flashlight and thrust it at Jill. She made an impatient gesture toward the ladder. "Go and see for yourself. I can't go down there yet."

"Stay here, Jill," Novak said. "It could be a trap."

"She's still shaking. Just look at her," Jill said. "For heaven's sake, it's no trap. I'm going down, Novak." She turned on the flashlight. "You can keep an eye on her if you want—" Novak was already climbing down the ladder. "It's okay, Dalai. You can wait for us here." Jill headed for the trapdoor and started down the ladder.

There were over twenty steps, and she saw Novak standing on the ground beside the ladder. She jumped from the fourth rung and caught hold of him to steady herself. The earth was soft and mushy beneath her feet, and the smell was a blend of earth scents and rotten vegetation. And something else that was causing Jill's stomach to tense. She moved the beam of the flashlight to pierce the darkness. Stone walls, a path leading south, away from the creek.

"I think we know what that code is." Novak had pulled out his pen flashlight and was looking around at the stone walls. "She gave us enough clues."

And he'd already figured it out, she thought. He'd probably done it before she had. That intelligence and the amazing ability to put puzzles together…"I need to be sure." Jill started down the narrow, rocky path.

"I don't suppose you'll let me go ahead, Jill," Novak said.

"No. My story." She gave him a smile over her shoulder as she moved faster. "I brought you here. Are you trying to cheat me?"

"Perish the thought. I just wanted to be sure there weren't any snakes down here."

"Keep an eye out. But I don't think Zahra would permit that. I'm sure she always sent Dalai down to check it out."

Then she made the turn in the stone path.

She stopped and inhaled sharply.

"It's true . . ." She had to gather her composure before she glanced over her shoulder at Novak again. "Now you can tell me what four-letter code Dalai punched in at that boulder."

"Kiya," he said softly. His gaze was traveling around the sizeable room and all the treasures it held.

"Too easy." She was dazzled as the beam of her flashlight fell on wonderful vases, trunks overflowing with gold and precious jewelry. And several truly superb gold statues. "If Zahra hadn't been so arrogant, any security expert would have told her that was the least safe password she could have chosen." She crossed the room and touched one of the statues. "Well, we found where Zahra grabbed that wonderful statue she gave to Dobran. But none of those statues are as fantastic as the Great Beloved Wife."

"Amazing." Novak was examining one of the engraved gold coffers. "There's so much here. I know that it was supposed to be a wagonload of treasure. But that was a long time ago. You would have thought the family would have gradually let some of it go."

"Family tradition," Jill said. "Gideon said that Zahra was an absolute fanatic about family history and tradition. Evidently, it was a trait passed down through the ages." She drew a deep breath, then wished she hadn't. That sickeningly familiar scent . . .

"Jill?" Novak's gaze was on her face.

"I'm fine. I just want to get out of here. We should get back to Dalai."

"I'm here." Dalai was standing behind them. Her face was chalk pale. "I told you I'd only be a minute." She pulled the cloak closer about her as if to ward off a chill. "Have you seen enough?" She was gazing searchingly at Jill's face. "Maybe more than enough. You're very clever, Jill. I believe you see things that others wouldn't see."

"I see that you look ill." Jill moistened her lips. "And frightened. Why are you so frightened to be down here?" She was thinking back, trying to put together everything she knew about Dalai. "Gideon said that you were terribly afraid of Zahra." She was trying to remember. "He said you said something about the place with no air." Her gaze flew to Dalai's face. "Is that this place, Dalai?"

Dalai nodded. "I can't breathe down here." She swallowed. "I know it's my imagination, but it doesn't make any difference. My heart starts to pound, and I want to scream."

"Just being underground?"

"What?" Dalai looked at her as if she were crazy. "No, it's the cage." She moved jerkily across the room to a row of large, gold, bejeweled chests against the far wall. "That's what Madam called it, the night she made me get into it." She paused beside an elaborate gold chest whose top was thickly patterned with a beautiful, closely woven, openwork design. She threw open the chest, and Jill saw that it was empty. "It was that first year she brought me here, and she had to make sure I was broken enough that I'd never betray her." Her voice was trembling. "So one night she made me climb into this chest, and she locked it. It wasn't quite airtight, but I thought it was. It was dark and I couldn't breathe and I thought my heart was going to jump out of my chest. I screamed, and I couldn't stop screaming. I heard her laughing. She said she was sure Kiya had punished her slaves this way, and I had to learn that every time I failed her, she would put me in this cage. If I was lucky, she'd remember to take me out." She was looking down at the coffin-like interior. "She remembered in thirty-two hours."

Dalai couldn't have been much more than a child, Jill thought in horror. An experience like that would have scarred anyone, much less a vulnerable girl totally dependent on that monster. It was a wonder that she had not been totally crushed. "I don't know what to say," she said gently. "You'll never be able to keep from remembering that time, and I can't help what happened to you." She added with sudden harshness, "But I'll be there to lend a hand when you're ready to throw that bitch into her own cage."

Dalai looked at her in surprise. "I didn't tell you that to make you feel sorry for me. I just had to make you understand." She turned away from the chest. "She only put me in that chest one more time, and I knew what to expect, so it wasn't as bad. But I couldn't stop remembering that first night whenever she made me come down here."

"I can understand why," Novak said grimly. "But I don't understand why you even came down today. We saw what you wanted us to see. You were right, we had to experience it for ourselves."

Dalai shook her head and turned to Jill. "No, I had to make sure that you knew everything that happened here." Her gaze was searching Jill's face. "I think you do. You figured it all out. When I first saw your expression after I came down, I could tell." She met her eyes. "Do you want me to put it into words?"

Jill couldn't look away from her. That scent was surrounding her... The panic was rising. "No." She whirled away from her. She couldn't go yet, she knew there was one more thing to check. "I'll be right back, Novak. Take care of her."

Then she was out of the treasure room and stumbling down another short path. The pungent scent was stronger now, and she could see broken boards on the ceiling up ahead. She had to stop as she saw the dim light piercing the cracks in that wood.

Sickness.

Horror.

"Jill." Novak was holding her. "Come on. Let's go back."

"I had to be sure," she said numbly. "I couldn't believe what Dalai was trying to tell me." She was clinging to him. "That's the schoolroom, Novak. It's only a few yards away from Kiya's treasure. The Kiyanis allowed that schoolroom to be built practically on top of their precious treasury. Dalai said Zahra's great-grandfather moved the treasury here, and that was very smart, wasn't it? I'm surprised it wasn't Zahra. Because no one would disturb a village school or suspect what was below it." She swallowed. "But I could smell the scent of that schoolroom the minute I came down here. The chalk, the burnt walls and floorboards... All that death... I know it so well."

"I know you do." He'd turned her and was leading her back toward the treasure room. "And it's going to hit you harder any minute, so I want to get you out of here. That's why I left your Dalai and ran after you."

"She's not my Dalai, she doesn't belong to anyone. But someone should help—" She stopped and closed her eyes. "There's more... She was trying to tell me, but I didn't want to listen. I didn't want to hear the end of the story." Her eyes opened. "But I have to hear it now." She pulled away from him and strode back into the treasure room. Dalai was still standing where she'd left her beside the golden cage. Jill crossed the room toward her. "The schoolroom." Her hands clenched into fists at her sides. "It was all coming together before, but I need the words now. It wasn't just a random attack, was it? Tell me."

Dalai shook her head and said unevenly, "Zahra didn't have enough cash to keep paying Varak, and she was afraid the Botzan army might take Robaku."

"Go on," Jill said.

Dalai was shivering. "So she told Varak about the treasure and promised him a share if he stayed, kept working for her, and found a way to keep her treasure safe until the war ended."

"And he took the deal," Jill said hoarsely.

"Yes, he wants that gold. It's still all he talks about."

"The gold," Jill repeated jerkily. She had to get the words out. "And his solution to get it was to stage a massacre that killed all those children and half their parents and made that schoolroom a memorial site that no one would want to desecrate."

Dalai nodded.

"One more question. Did Zahra approve of his 'solution'?"

"Not right away. She said that it appeared to be a practical plan, but he would have to lower his fee since she was going to have to do a good deal of the publicity and diplomatic work herself."

"Yes, that would enter into any negotiations," Jill said unsteadily. "Couldn't you tell someone?"

"I wanted to live," Dalai said simply. "I was afraid. I'd only heard bits and pieces of the plan, and I didn't know about the schoolroom. But I know that I will go to hell forever for being such a coward." Her voice broke. "When I heard about the children..."

"Yes, the children..." Jill said dully. The children who had died only yards from where she was standing. She couldn't stand here, thinking about it. She had to get out of here. She turned and headed for the ladder.

A few minutes later, they had all surfaced by the boulders. It was only twilight, Jill realized. It had seemed a very long time ago that she had descended that ladder. She looked at Dalai as she got to her feet. "Yes, you're sorry," she said jerkily. "I can see it. But now you have a chance to change your story. To not let a massacre like that ever happen again. Can we count on you?"

Dalai looked away from her. "I'm here, aren't I? I've told you things that would get me killed...or worse." She lifted her chin as she turned to face her. "I'll do whatever I can. But I'm still a coward. Don't expect me to be something I'm not."

"All I want now is for you to listen and call us if there's anything we should know." She added, "And I'll do the same. We'll do the rest together, Dalai."

Dalai gazed at her for a moment before she turned and went toward her car. Then she suddenly looked back at them. "You're going to do it, aren't you? You're actually going to take them both down?"

Jill nodded. "I promise you. And you're going to be there when we do it. No one deserves it more."

"I...believe you." Her dark eyes were filled with wonder. "And I think I might be able to...trust you."

"Good." Then Jill had a sudden thought. "Have you been here too long? What if Zahra's missed you?"

"Then I'll lie to her. I've learned how to do that very well. I'll make her believe me." She shrugged. "Then Madam will beat me, and I'll weep and be very contrite and afraid. She's too busy right now to do anything else to me."

"I wish you wouldn't call her Madam," Jill said bitterly. "It sounds so subservient. It reminds me of the way she's treated you all these years."

"It's what she wants me to call her. If I stopped, she would think it odd and punish me. But someday I will not care what she thinks." She got into the car. "Because she won't be able to use her fine, golden cage if Robaku is no longer available to her. Isn't that sad?" She didn't wait for an answer but drove away from the brook area and headed for the road.

"She's certainly not the rabbit Gideon said Zahra called her." Novak's thoughtful gaze was following her. "And she might say she's a coward, but I don't see that either. It's as if she was opening, changing, revealing new facets, every moment she was here."

"She's a survivor," Jill said. She turned and headed for the museum. "And what she's done today may make us survivors, too." She glanced at Novak, and said fiercely, "Because we know how to fight Zahra and Varak now. We know what holds them together. You know damn well we have a weapon if we use it right. And it's got nothing to do with Varak's compound. So don't tell me that you're going back there."

"I wouldn't dare," he said dryly. "You're so savage, you might throw me in that golden cage."

She shuddered. "Don't even talk about it. I don't understand how Dalai was able to go through what she did." She looked back at the tall boulders, which suddenly appeared threatening in the gathering darkness. "I made her a promise, Novak. Now you have to call everyone up to the museum and get a plan together to make sure that I didn't lie to her."

CHAPTER

18

"Kiya?" Gideon shook his head. "It seems impossible that treasure has been here in Robaku all this time. You'd think Hajif or someone else would have stumbled over it at some time or other."

"Dalai said Zahra was careful," Jill said. "And who would believe that it was right under their feet for all those decades." She smiled bitterly. "And after the massacre, no one wanted to go near that schoolroom. Just what Varak thought would happen." She turned to Eve, who had been very quiet since Jill and Novak had returned to the museum over an hour ago. "I couldn't believe it when I saw it. Don't go down there, Eve. It...hurts."

"I have no intention of looking at that treasure," Eve said. "It would make me ill." She leaned back against the cabinet. "All I want to do is find a way to use it to get our hands on Varak." She crossed her arms tightly across her chest. "Soon."

Joe nodded. "That's the aim," he told her quietly. "If Varak has been sitting there in that compound waiting to get his hands on that gold, all he'll need is a push. He set up his compound as a trap, and we can do the same thing with Robaku. Dalai said that they had no idea how we were fortified. We can just make sure that it appears to be a simple, sleepy village with only a minimum number of guards to give Varak trouble. And we'll have to find a way to get the villagers out of the line of fire. We just have to make sure it's all handled right."

"So that no one gets a machete in their throat," Eve said wryly.

Jill had heard enough. "But first we have to get him here." She was on edge. Yes, both Joe and Novak had plans that would probably work once Varak was lured to Robaku. They were already thinking of strategy, and that was fine. But that wasn't her priority. "Zahra." She got to her feet. "We have to make her be the one to spur him to leave that compound. That's what I told Dalai, and that hasn't changed. And I should be the one who does it." She smiled faintly. "I'll weave her a fine story and make her believe it's her own. As Eve said, it's what I do well. The rest of you can think and scheme and spend your time making Robaku the most splendid trap on the planet. Just let me get him within your range."

Novak was shaking his head. "And let yourself be within the range of a woman who would have no compunction about tossing you into the deepest dungeon if she can get away with it. Even Dalai said she hates your guts."

"Then as Joe said, it's my job to handle it right. I'm going to call my publisher when I get back to Hajif's hut and ask him to set up an interview for me tomorrow with Zahra Kiyani. That's the first foot in the door." She met his eyes. "I'm going to do it, Novak. Don't get in my way."

"No promises," he said curtly.

"If you do, I'll just work around you. I'm going to do what I do best." She headed for the door. "Now you all do what you do best, so mine won't be for nothing."

Then she was out the door and moving down the path toward the village. She carefully didn't look at the path that led to the sparkling brook and those tall boulders. The horror and sadness were still too close to her. She just wanted to get away from them for these next few moments.

"Jill."

She stopped and looked behind her.

Eve was coming down the path after her.

"It's going to be okay, Eve," Jill said quickly. "Don't try to talk me out of it. It's the only way that makes—"

"Hush," Eve said, still coming toward her. "Stop talking and start listening. I have something I have to say to you."

———————————

THE NEXT DAY
10:40 A.M.
KIYANI PRESIDENTIAL PALACE

"What a pleasure to see you, Ms. Cassidy." Zahra's tone was almost a purr as Jill walked into the small, elegant office where she'd been escorted by both a uniformed soldier and a bespectacled young clerk. Zahra was sitting in an elaborately carved chair behind an equally graceful desk. She was dressed in a deep teal-colored maxidress and looked stunning as usual. "But then it's always a delight to have you visit the palace. We have such a long-standing relationship. Of course, it's not always been harmonious, but I believe we'll be able to iron that out now. I'm sorry you weren't among the journalists here the other evening to hear my speech. I was truly spectacular."

"I was a little busy, but that's what I understand." Jill paused. "It was superbly done. But then, you're always ingenious." She glanced around the office. "I assume this office is totally secure? You wouldn't have had me brought here if it wasn't. And your clerk gave me the equivalent of a strip search before they let me in to see you." She smiled. "As you said, you can't count on my being either reasonable or harmonious. You've always considered me a troublemaker."

"And so you are." The purr had suddenly vanished. "I thought I could discourage you, but you were too stupid. You kept insisting and getting in my way. Robaku is *mine*. You had no business writing all those stories objecting to my moving those peasant families out of the village."

"Actually, I *was* stupid," Jill said. "I agree with you on that score. Because I thought our battle was entirely about Robaku and those children. I had no idea you had another agenda entirely on the back burner." She paused. "Or that you'd gotten yourself involved in something that was more ugly than I could ever dream. Not until Joe Quinn went to Asarti that night and came back with this." She pulled a photograph out of her bag and pushed it across the desk at Zahra. "She's very beautiful, but you should have known that Gideon would recognize it as the first Kiya."

Zahra stiffened, her hand clenching the photo. "I don't know what you mean." But her gaze was almost hungry as she stared at the statue. "I've never seen it before."

Bingo. Jill realized she had hit a nerve. Move the needle a little farther. "What a pity. It's extraordinary. Joe Quinn gave it to his wife as soon as he got back from that fishing expedition. Because she's an artist, too, he thought Eve would appreciate it."

"He gave it to *her*?" Zahra couldn't seem to take her gaze from the photo, and her lips were tightening viciously. Then she forced herself to look away. "It doesn't make any difference. It's just a statue. It has nothing to do with me."

"But the fact that that crook, Dobran, had it in his possession, and did the DNA falsification on Nils Varak, might be very awkward for you if it came to light."

"No proof," Zahra said. "I know nothing about Nils Varak other than he's a monster who almost destroyed my country. We've taken whatever weapon you thought you had away from you." Her eyes narrowed on Jill's face. "See what response you'll get if you take that nonsense to the media or anyone else. You should have seen how that British prime minister was bowing and scraping to me yesterday. I'm a heroine, haven't you heard?"

"Yes, and you won't be easy to topple," Jill said. "But you've made me very angry, Madam President. I'm going to try exceptionally hard to see that happen. I've found political figures aren't that difficult to bring down once you find their Achilles heel. I won a Pulitzer doing that a few years ago."

Zahra's lips curled. "Threats?"

"Not yet. First, I'll tell you what I'd do to win another Pulitzer. I won that first one totally on my own. This time I'd have help. I'll bring Eve Duncan in to give interviews and tell her story. It won't have quite as much weight after you and Varak destroyed the skull at the U.N., but she has an amazing amount of respect and credibility. It would stir up a good deal of talk and cause people to start asking questions." She smiled. "And I'd be there to answer those questions. You thought my stories were troublesome before? I'd never stop. Eve has already been speaking to the U.S. embassy and asking them to intercede with the U.N. to grant extended permission to continue her work at Robaku. She can be very persuasive."

She leaned forward across the desk, her eyes shining, her words firing like bullets. "We're planning to set up permanently at Robaku, and you'll never get rid of us. Before we're through, you'll never say that Robaku is yours again. It will be *mine* and Eve Duncan's. We've already drafted plans for tearing down that hideous schoolroom and building a fine chapel where families can come and pray for their slain children. I'll be taking pictures of the schoolroom and showing what it could be with public support. I'll spend a lot of time describing the children who died there. You'll remember how much sympathy my stories have aroused in the past year? Well, before we're through, anyone who reads those stories about Robaku will want to get in there with a jackhammer and tear that schoolroom down themselves." Jill could see the shock in Zahra's face at the picture she'd drawn. Okay, hit her with another one from a different direction. "And you might be interested to know that in another fifteen minutes, Eve Duncan will make an announcement on your local television station that she's invited several top news agencies to Robaku for a press interview tomorrow afternoon. She's promised to divulge a startling revelation regarding the tragedy." She added mockingly, "They were all very eager to accept the invitation. I'm afraid you're old news now, Zahra. And Eve Duncan gives so few interviews."

Her eyes were suddenly wary. "Revelation?"

"It's a good way to intrigue and start the buzz going, don't you think?"

"That sounds like a threat to me," Zahra hissed. "You'd both blow your credibility. No one would believe you. You wouldn't take the chance."

"I admit I hesitated, but Eve is an idealist. Once she finished the reconstruction of that skull, she said she couldn't live with herself if she kept silent. What could I do but throw my support behind her?" Jill paused. "And it's not a threat but a warning. Or perhaps an opportunity. I don't really want you if I can have Varak. He's the big story. You're small potatoes."

"What?" Jill could see her eyes flash. She'd thought that bruising Zahra's vanity would be the way to hit home. Then Zahra recovered quickly. "Varak is *dead*. There is no story where he's concerned."

"I think there might be. I've studied Varak for years, and I know what a complete sociopath he is." She tilted her head. "I have no idea why you're doing this, Zahra. I wonder if you realize what you've gotten yourself into by dealing with him. You're a strong, dominant woman, and he won't put up with it. It's only a matter of time before he kills you." She smiled faintly. "You've probably already had to talk yourself out of situations you found dangerous."

"I don't know what you're talking about," Zahra said through set teeth. "Varak is dead."

"No, he isn't. Not yet. But you'd be much better off if he was." Jill added bluntly, "Because I'll never stop going after him, and you'll be caught in the cross fire. Pity, since you've been doing so well lately. But they'll burn you at the stake once they find out how you've been coddling Nils Varak." She paused. "But if you find a way to deliver him to me, I won't care if he's accidentally shot by you or one of your soldiers. Maybe you could set it up so that you'll truly be a heroine. All I want is the monster dead and the story finished. I might even be able to persuade Eve that Varak dead is the primary goal, and we don't want to spend years in courts just to tangle with your lawyers. As I said, you're ingenious, and I'm sure you could figure out how to come out of a scenario like that in fantastic shape. Consider it a challenge."

"I consider this insanity." Zahra got to her feet, her cheeks flushed. "And I'll have to ask you to go." Then she suddenly burst out, "You think you can do this to me? You'll lose. I always win." Her eyes were glittering with malice. "Just as I won from you before." She took a step toward her. "Did what they did to you hurt, bitch? I told them it had to hurt."

"Then they did what you told them to do," Jill said steadily. "I've already figured out that had to be Varak. Why do you think I want him so much? Give him to me, and he'll never bother either of us again. Take the challenge, Zahra."

She turned and strode out of the office.

Her phone. Jill had to have her phone.

She quickly stopped at the clerk's desk and picked up her belongings from the security basket.

Don't look to see if anyone is following.

Just hope that Zahra was now turning on the TV in that office to watch Eve Duncan and make sure Jill hadn't lied to her.

Eyes straight ahead.

Jill called Gideon as she walked out of the palace. "The Kiya statue. It has to be in full view, somewhere close to Eve, while the TV broadcast is going on."

Gideon cursed. "We don't have time, Jill."

"Make time."

———◆———

Bitch! Bitch! Bitch!

Zahra's hands clenched into fists as she watched Eve Duncan's face on the TV across the office. Eve was sitting at her worktable, and Zahra's statue of Kiya was resting on the dais like a favorite ornament. Like it belonged to her. Zahra wanted to throw something at that image, which had no hint of the glamour or fascination that Zahra possessed. The only thing she could see in that woman was boring sincerity.

Maybe no one was watching her damned announcement.

But they probably were, and they'd probably watch her TV interview tomorrow, too. Jill Cassidy was right. Those news reporters were like hungry vultures.

She felt a rush of panic. Things had been going so well. She'd thought she had everything under control. Now she had to deal with the scandal that might come if Eve Duncan came forward, with Jill Cassidy standing beside her. That was going to be a media and diplomatic nightmare to straighten out. How was she going to handle it?

Her phone was ringing.

Varak. She hoped he hadn't seen that TV announcement. But the bastard always knew what was going on.

She answered the phone. "Don't blame me for this. It's not my fault. I just found out about it."

"It *is* your fault. I told you to fix it. What's that announcement the whore is going to make tomorrow?"

"What do you think? According to Cassidy, they're going to cause big-time trouble. I told her that no one would believe them, but she was raving about setting up permanent shop at Robaku to call attention to Eve Duncan and her reconstruction work." She added the one threat that had frightened her the most: "And getting permission from the U.N. to tear down the schoolroom and build some kind of chapel. There's no doubt that they'd find the treasure."

Varak was cursing. "If you'd gotten rid of them earlier, this would never have happened. You've stalled me and stalled me until we're down to this. I can't afford for even one person to believe them. It's my neck on the line, you stupid cunt."

Zahra felt the fury surge through her. It was too much. He was talking to her as if she were one of the whores she provided for him. As if she didn't have enough to worry about without these insults. "Then if you think I've done so badly, why don't you take care of it yourself?" she spat out. "Maybe I was wrong to keep you from being reckless enough to take us both down. Get rid of all of them for all I care. Do what you like!"

She cut the connection.

She was breathing hard, panting, as her anger continued to rise. She should probably call him back and try to pacify him, but she couldn't do it. It had gone on too long. The son of a bitch had actually almost strangled her the last time she'd seen him. Hadn't Jill Cassidy said something about how dangerous it was to deal with him? As if she didn't know that for herself. But she was smarter than Cassidy ever dreamed of being, and she could handle him.

If she wanted to do it.

Think. She slowly leaned back in her chair. The situation had turned critical. She could either face a nightmare of explanations and suspicions if Eve Duncan gave her interview tomorrow, or she could accept that in the end, Varak's solution was best. Eliminate those troublesome people at Robaku who were a threat to her and Varak. And who'd had the nerve to steal *her* Kiya statue, she thought angrily.

Or she could handle the problem in a way that was infinitely more pleasing and satisfying in her eyes. A little more difficult, but it would eliminate giving that son of a bitch anything he wanted.

Take the challenge, Jill Cassidy had said.

Zahra could meet any challenge.

She just had to decide which way she wanted to meet it.

But regardless, it would have to involve Varak. She reached for her phone to call him back.

"I was angry," she said the moment he answered the phone. "I'm still angry. But it's clear something has to be done. You've been nagging me about your share of the treasure? Well, I'm ready to talk about it. But not until you give me everything I need before you fly out of here."

———————

ROBAKU

"You could have called me when you were on your way back here," Novak said curtly when he met Jill as she parked her car. "Would that have been too much bother?"

"No, but I knew that you'd have someone monitoring the front gates of the palace and would know when I left." She was walking quickly toward the museum. "And I didn't know what kind of high-tech listening devices Zahra's people might have. I took a risk even calling Gideon. I didn't want her listening in when I chatted with anyone."

"It wouldn't have been a 'chat,'" Novak said. "And they don't have anything that high-tech. Strictly low-grade stuff."

"I didn't know." She added wearily, "And I didn't want to talk to you anyway. Zahra is never easy, and she was particularly difficult today. I had to concentrate on doing what I had to do." She glanced at him, and said deliberately, "What I told you that I could do. Pressure, Novak."

"And did you do it?"

"I believe I did. I won't know until I see signs later. I lined up choices for her. I suggested she could kill Varak, which I'm sure she'd like to do. And I told her that schoolroom would be threatened by Eve and me, so she might order Varak out of his rat hole to attack us. She'll be terrified that her precious treasury might be discovered. Or there's the possibility she's so besotted with the statue that she might get careless and go after it herself. But even then, she'd probably pull Varak into it in some way. Zahra might take one choice or none at all. But it might lead her to make her own choices, which might suit us as well. All we care about is getting Varak here." They had reached the museum, and she put her hand on his arm. "How did Eve's TV announcement go?"

"Fine. She was warm, concerned, businesslike, appealing." He grimaced. "And hating every minute of it. She doesn't care for the media."

"I know. But this time it wasn't my fault. It was her idea to get Gideon to set it up." She paused. "I did everything I could to talk her out of it. It paints a big bull's-eye on her chest."

"And you don't have one? Be serious."

He was right. After that conversation with Zahra, she'd put everyone here at Robaku at risk. "We knew what we were getting into from the beginning. Eve didn't."

"She knows now. She thinks you're doing the right thing. She's right." He was standing looking at her. "Though I hate to admit it." He suddenly kissed her, hard. "And I know you pulled it off with Zahra. We're going to find out before this day is over that you changed the story to suit yourself." Then he was releasing her and turning away. "I've got to get back to the village and make sure we've made Robaku look like a peaceful, helpless place that Attila the Hun would lust to get his hands on."

"Not too helpless," she called after him.

"Be quiet, Jill," he said over his shoulder. "You told us to do our job and let you do yours. You're officially on the side-lines now." He disappeared around the curve of the path.

But she didn't want to be on the sidelines. She was still on edge and needed to know what was happening. She opened the door and went into the museum to see Eve.

"I'm glad you're back." Eve looked up from working on

the Mila reconstruction. "I wanted to get rid of Novak. He was pacing the floor in here after I threw out that TV crew. That was the last thing I needed."

"But he said you did very well."

She shrugged. "As good as can be expected." She smiled. "We had to scramble to get that Kiya statue displayed. Why did you want us to do it?"

"I'm not sure. Instinct. The sight of it might be the final thing that pushes her over the edge. It seemed right."

"And your instincts have proved to be very good as far as getting people to make that final commitment. I'm evidence of that." Her eyes narrowed on Jill's face. "How did you do this time?"

She smiled. "As well as can be expected." No, Eve deserved more than that. "I wish I knew. It might have worked. Everything seemed solid. I appeared to be striking the right notes. We'll have to see." She looked around the museum. "All those skulls in their pretty boxes are gone. Where are they?"

"I thought it would be better if we hid them somewhere in the jungle. Zahra knows they're here and wanted to get rid of them. She could have Varak target them."

"Target," Jill repeated. "That's what I told Novak you were now."

"Of course I am. Now stop talking about it." She looked back at Mila. "I want to finish this bit, then I want to call Michael and talk to him for a while. It will relax both of us."

"You told me that he...knew things. Won't he realize that something is wrong?"

"More than likely. But he'd realize it anyway. I'm not going to cheat either one of us today because I want to pretend everything is fine. I'll just tell him I don't want to discuss it, and he'll accept it."

"That's good." The bond between mother and son must be as intricate as it was strong, but Jill knew that this call might not have been made if Eve hadn't been aware how precarious was their position. "He's a wonderful boy."

"Yes, he is." Eve looked up and made a face. "Now stop fretting about us. I have no intention of dying today. I just don't want Michael not to have heard my voice when he's going to be worrying. Joe can't call him right now, so it's up to me."

"Where is Joe?"

"Varak," she said simply. "He went to keep an eye on the compound to see if there's any indication that Varak might be going to take action. He promised to report back to Novak as soon as he saw any signs." She met Jill's eyes. "And that should tell us if your talk with Zahra worked. I really hope it did because Joe was not at all pleased about my little TV show today."

"I hope so, too." That was a massive understatement. Jill dropped down in a chair and tried to relax her tense muscles. "I guess all we can do is wait to hear from Joe."

The call came from Joe two hours later.

Jill straightened in her chair as Eve took the call. Her gaze flew to Eve's face, trying desperately to read her expression.

But Eve was listening and only said one sentence before she ended the call. "Then I'll expect you."

She put down the phone, and her eyes met Jill's. "Joe's on his way back. You did it, Jill." Her eyes were shining, and the excitement and triumph were all there in her face. "Varak's on the move!"

———————

KIYANI PRESIDENTIAL PALACE
10:40 P.M.

Where the hell was Dalai?

Zahra strode into her quarters and tore off her dress and threw it on the bench. "Dalai, get in here. I need you!"

Dalai was suddenly in the room, her eyes wide with alarm. "I'm sorry, madam. I thought you'd be downstairs longer."

"You're not supposed to think. Just be here when I want you here. I need to change and be ready to get out of this place. Get me that scarlet pantsuit and the black boots."

"Right away, madam." Dalai flew toward the closet room.

This wasn't the time for the idiot girl to be this careless, Zahra thought. Everything tonight had to go precisely as she had planned. Dalai must not hesitate with performing even one order.

And Dalai wasn't the only one who had to perform faultlessly to Zahra's orders. She dropped down on her vanity stool, reached for her phone, and punched in Varak's number.

"I don't have time to talk to you now," Varak said impatiently when he picked up. "The team I sent to reconnoiter Robaku just got back. I've been getting their report."

"What was it?"

"It's going to be a snap. We'll be in and out in a heartbeat."

"Then you'll take time to talk to me. I agreed to this madness, but I won't go into an attack on Robaku blindly. I have to know what I have to deal with when all the smoke clears. It's got to look like the attack was made by the same terrorist group that blew up the U.N. headquarters. You can't be careless or messy, or I'll never be able to justify the deaths. Duncan is too famous."

"I thought that you'd agreed never to give me orders," he said softly. "When this is over, you might need another lesson."

Bastard. He couldn't resist the threat even in a situation where he might be getting everything he wanted. Zahra instinctively raised her hand to her throat. "When this is over, I'm never going to see you again. You can take your share of the gold and go straight to hell."

"So brave now that you're back in that fine palace. Perhaps I'll get a palace of my own now that you're doing the smart thing and giving me what you promised." His voice lowered. "But how do I know that your Kiya's treasure is worth my time? Maybe you've been lying to me. You've never actually let me go down there to see it."

And she wouldn't this time if there was any other choice. "I told you that I'll let you go down there tonight before you attack Robaku. You can check it out yourself."

"I wouldn't have it any other way. It had better live up to expectations."

"You said you were in a hurry. I'm trying to give you an update on what I've done to protect us. Do you want to hear it, or would you rather threaten me?"

"Both. But I'll listen as long as it includes the release of that damn gold you've been promising me all this time."

"I have no choice. I can't be careful any longer. And I have to get rid of you before someone finds out that Duncan is telling the truth at that press conference."

"How awkward. It would be a disaster for me, bitch."

"Don't worry, I'll get you safely out of the country. I've arranged to have an army transport truck be driven to Robaku and parked a few miles down the highway. You can have your men drive the truck to pick up your share of the treasure after you've eliminated the problem at the village. And I want you out of Robaku and on your way to the airport within an hour."

"But you claim there's such a lot of gold," he said mockingly. "And it would go faster if I didn't have to divide it. Perhaps I'll arrange to get a second truck."

She stiffened. "Don't even think about it. I have a private jet waiting at Jokan airport for you to get out of the country. If the pilot sees more than one truck driving up to be unloaded, then he has orders to take off and leave you to find your way through the jungle and out of Maldara on your own."

Silence. "You wouldn't do that. I'd still be a risk for you."

"I won't let you steal my share of Kiya's treasure," she said fiercely. "You caused me to lose the Great Beloved Wife statue. I won't be cheated of anything else. You deliver my Kiya statue back to me and clean up that village. Then you get out of my country."

Another silence. "I'll let it go for now. I can always come back."

"That would be madness. Even you wouldn't run that risk again."

"Wouldn't I? But I run through money so quickly, and the idea of your looking over your shoulder is so pleasant. I can just see—" He broke off, and said impatiently, "But I have no more time. I have to make certain I'll have no problem with Robaku tonight. Give me the code to that treasure room."

"So you can steal it all and go on the run? You'll get the treasure when I know that you've given me what I need."

"And how will you know that?" he asked sarcastically. "I can't see you risking your neck and dodging bullets to come and check."

"Of course not. I'll send Dalai to report back to me and open it for you. You've always found her accommodating." She saw that Dalai had come back in the room and was frozen in place at the door. "And if you do everything I've told you to do, then I might allow you a bonus. You can take her with you." She smiled maliciously as she saw the young girl go pale. "Plane flights can be so boring."

"I'll decide later. Just have her there ready to open that door when I'll need her."

"At two in the morning?"

"Two. If everything goes as planned." He cut the connection.

She set her phone on the vanity and looked at Dalai. "You kept me waiting. How many times have I told you that mistakes have consequences?"

"It won't happen again, madam." Her voice was trembling. "Please don't send me to him."

"What you wish isn't important. But you might be lucky. I'm not certain how things will work out tonight."

"But you're sending me to Robaku alone? You told him you aren't going with me."

"But I seldom tell the truth to Varak. That would be the height of foolishness. Eve Duncan still has Kiya's Great Beloved Wife. I saw it on that television broadcast. Varak knows how valuable it is. He said he'd get it back for me as part of our deal." Her lips twisted. "Oh, he'll go after it, but he'll also try to steal it from me. How could I trust a little rabbit like you to keep him from doing it? No, I'll have to be there in case he tries to steal it after he rids me of Duncan. That statue is *mine*." She met Dalai's eyes in the vanity mirror. "And you'd better not make any mistakes tonight, Dalai," she said coldly. "I won't tolerate them."

"I promise I won't make any mistakes." Dalai nodded at the clothes on the bed. "May I help you dress? Is that what you're wearing?"

"Why else would I tell you to bring them?" She gazed at her image in the mirror and was abruptly dissatisfied. "I have to look spectacular tonight. Do you understand? I have to look like the queen I am. Whenever anyone looks at me, they have to be impressed. It's going to be a special night."

She could see that Dalai was staring at her, puzzled. But she wasn't about to make explanations. She was the only one who counted, and everyone would realize that after this was all over. Whichever choice she made, she would make it a success. "Hurry. It's almost eleven. Do my hair . . . " She added, "And I want to use the ruby comb in it tonight."

Dalai's gaze flew to her face.

Zahra caught the glance. "That always alarms you, doesn't it? Why? You've never seen me actually use it in the way it should be used."

"It doesn't alarm me. Whatever you wish." She was heading for the closet room again. "I'll go get the comb out of its special container. I'll be right back."

* * *

Dalai had to steady her hands as she dialed Jill. She had to hurry. Zahra seldom followed her into the closet room for any reason, but this was a strange night. She kept her voice to almost a whisper when Jill answered. "It will be two or shortly before. They're going after Kiya's treasure."

"It's been taken care of," Jill said. "Anything else?"

"Only to watch Eve Duncan. Zahra's angry about the statue. She won't stop until she gets it." She cut the connection and thrust her phone in her pocket. Don't stop. Keep moving. Nothing must look suspicious. Every motion, every word, must seem totally natural. She knelt at the mahogany jewelry box that held the special container and drew out the jeweled comb. So beautiful. But Zahra had never cared about the beauty. She had just wanted to play her deadly game when she had taught Dalai to make the poisonous liquid with which the prongs were usually coated.

She put the shimmering ruby comb on its tray and took a deep breath. Then she started for the closet door to go back into the bedroom.

Be natural. Don't let her see anything.

She could do this.

But Zahra was right.

This was going to be a very special night.

"Two," Jill said as she turned back to Eve and Joe. "And we might have gone overboard about luring Zahra with that statue. Dalai is worried about Eve." She looked at Joe. "Can you persuade her to get out of here? If the statue is the bait for the trap, I could take her place here."

"It's not only the statue," Joe said grimly. "The two of you set Eve up, and now they want her dead." He turned to Eve. "Are you happy now?"

"No, but I will be if you stop growling and get out of here," Eve said. "You've arranged all kind of surveillance around this museum, Joe. You said Varak will reconnoiter before he strikes and will know exactly where I am. But he won't risk coming after me if he thinks it's a trap. He's got to feel as if he's in charge." She looked him in the eye. "Well, if I'm a target, let them come and try to take me. That way we'll know Varak won't skip out on us. That's what this is all about. Then you can whisk down and save me like Superman."

"Get out, Eve," Jill urged. "Sometimes things don't turn out as planned. He's right, we did this together. But you wouldn't have even been on this continent if it wasn't for me. Do you think I could stand the thought of—"

"Out." She turned her back on them and went to her worktable. "I don't care about what you think you can stand, Jill. I won't let Varak have even a chance of escaping tonight." She looked down at the half-finished reconstruction of Mila staring up at her from the dais. "He's never going to be able to do this to a child again." She sat down on her stool and began to smooth the clay beneath Mila's cheekbone. "So both of you clear out, and do whatever you have to do to make that bastard think that I'm as helpless as those kids were when he took his machete to them. Let's get this over with."

———

"I'm going to stay here." Jill stopped abruptly only a short distance from the museum. "It's not as if I can do anything down at the village, Joe."

"You can keep me from pissing off Novak," Joe said curtly. "Not that I'd ordinarily care, but most of the action will probably be aimed at the village, and I'm leaving him in the lurch. He knows that there's no way I'll be anywhere but with Eve."

"And you shouldn't be. What does that have to do with keeping Novak from being pissed off?"

"He asked me to send you down to Hajif at the caves, where the villagers are sheltering. He wants the old man to keep his eye on you." His lips twisted wryly. "Which he knew would be a near-impossible task. If Eve hadn't wanted to get rid of you also, I wouldn't have even been able to get you out of that museum."

"You didn't get me out. There's no reason why I can't stay here. I might be needed."

"No, you won't," he said bluntly. "You'd probably only get in my way. I have no desire to watch over anyone but

Eve, and you might distract me. Go down and let Hajif find you something to do."

She silently shook her head.

He muttered a curse. "I can take care of her myself. I don't need you. Shall I show you?" He took her wrist and pulled her off the path and into the jungle. He pointed at a large banyan tree a few feet away. "That's where I'll be situated. From the second branch I'll have a clear shot at anyone approaching the front of the museum. No one could get past me." His tone was low, intense. "And I'm a dead shot, Jill. Do you want to hear about my qualifications in the SEALs? What's more, I wouldn't hesitate for a second. All Varak has to do is show himself, and he's history."

"I know that."

"And there are two more of Novak's men who have sharpshooter credentials who will be stationed within signaling distance. You're not needed here, Jill. We can take him down."

She might not be needed, but she desperately wanted to be here.

Joe nodded slowly as he read her expression. "But it's not smart, you could get in our way."

She gave one last glance at the museum, then turned on her heel. "Heaven forbid I do that. By all means, go climb up your damn banyan tree and do all that SEAL stuff. Just don't let her get hurt while you're flexing your muscles."

She took off down the hill toward the village.

CHAPTER

19

"Hurry, Dalai!" Zahra was running past the brook toward the tall boulders. "Can't you see that I don't need to have him angry with me right now? Tonight is going to be difficult enough for me."

"I'm right behind you," Dalai said. "I don't see him. He hasn't gotten here yet. You don't have to—" She inhaled sharply as Varak stepped from behind the boulders. He was dressed in camouflage and had an ammunition belt across his body, a gun on his shoulder, and a holstered machete at his waist. He was carrying a large backpack. He looked angry and impatient, and Dalai could feel the fear tighten her throat. No matter how often she told herself that she must not be afraid of him, it didn't help.

He barely glanced at her as he turned to Zahra. "I thought you weren't going to be here." He smiled mockingly. "Don't you trust me?"

"No." Zahra took a step toward him. "I want my statue. Dalai is nothing. I decided you'd have no trouble refusing to give it to her after you took it from Duncan." She met his gaze. "But you'll have a lot of trouble if you try to cheat me."

"You flatter yourself." His lips twisted. "The only problem I've ever had with you was surviving your vanity and stupidity. Now show me how to get into that treasury room, then get out of here. The only thing I want to do is take a look down there and make sure you aren't cheating me. After that, I don't have much time. I've got to give Markel the signal to start the attack on the village while I take care of the museum."

"By yourself?" She frowned. "I told you not to be careless."

"There are half a dozen men here on the hill who will be on hand if I need them. But I won't need them. I have a few special surprises that I've planned for her, including the one you offered me." His gaze went to the museum in the distance. "Duncan's like you, a stupid woman who doesn't realize who she's dealing with. It will be a pleasure to teach her."

"I don't care how you do it as long as I get everything you promised me." She knelt before the third boulder and quickly entered the code. "Go down, take a look around to make sure that I didn't lie to you. Then come up and get rid of every single trace of anyone who might be a difficulty to me."

He started to move toward the ladder, then stopped. "I think you'd better come with me." He gestured down into the darkness. "I don't like the idea that you've changed your mind about sending pretty little Dalai here alone. I don't care for abrupt changes of plans."

She shrugged. "I'll go if you like. Do you think I have

someone down there ready to knock you out and toss you in a trunk as I did Dalai one time?" She laughed. "You would have been amused. But I'd never try that with you." She'd pulled out her flashlight and was climbing down the ladder as she spoke. "Come along, Dalai, he's afraid of us."

Dalai turned on her own flashlight, took a deep breath, and followed her. It was worse than it had ever been, she thought. This place of horror and Varak, who was the giver of pain and terror. It would be all right. She could get through this. No one was really paying attention to her. Be the rabbit Zahra thought she was.

Varak stood and watched them both go down before he turned on his flashlight and ran down the ladder.

The beam of his flashlight illuminated the hallway; and then he was striding down the hall and into the treasury.

He stopped short. "Holy shit!"

"I told you I didn't lie." Zahra was behind him. "This is *mine*. Kiya meant it for someone like me, who was strong enough to use it as it should be used."

"You mean by giving it to me?" His beam was going from treasure to treasure, examining the jewels and the gold. "Yes, I'm sure she knew exactly what she was doing." He turned back to Zahra. "And there's so much. No wonder you were willing to give me half. But it would be very hard to choose." He paused. "Almost impossible."

She stiffened. "Then I'll make it easy. I'll stay down here with Dalai, and I'll choose the items I want while I'm waiting for you to bring me the Great Beloved Wife. You will come back, have your men quickly load the treasure I will give you, and get out. I will keep my share safely here at Robaku as I've always done." Her voice hardened. "And you will not betray me. Did I forget to mention that I told my Minister of Police that I feared for my life from those terrible terrorists? He insisted on having me monitored so that I would be able to be immediately traced in an emergency. If I don't call in every hour, they'll come after me," she said fiercely. "You said you'd have no trouble with an attack on this sleepy little village. You won't find my personal guard quite as easy to handle. You might end up with nothing."

He was silent. Then he shrugged. "Just commenting." He smiled. "I believe I can tolerate our arrangement." He suddenly turned to look at Dalai. "Did you really toss her in a trunk down here?" He watched as Dalai froze, her gaze fixed on him. "I believe you did," he said softly. "When you start choosing your half, save the trunk for me."

"If I get my statue," Zahra said. "And you make sure I'll have no more trouble with Robaku. Then you'll get everything I promised."

"I've already paid my dues to you. I did it the day I destroyed that schoolroom for you. Consider everything else as a bonus." He met her eyes. "And you know I'll do it well. You've watched me do it before. There won't be anyone left alive when I've finished here."

"And how you enjoy it." She chuckled. "You should pay me."

"Not amusing." He glanced around the room overflowing with treasure. "And if I don't get what I consider my fair share, I'll have to take it. Now show me how I get to that tunnel you said would take me to the museum from here."

The tunnel! Dalai froze. Why was he asking that? Dalai's eyes widened in panic as she whirled to Zahra. "The tunnel you had started when you had the museum built? But remember, you decided not to finish it. You said you liked the idea of linking them to have a way to get the treasure out, but then you realized thieves could also get into the treasure room through the museum."

"Of course, I remember," Zahra said coldly. "But necessities change. Varak said he needed a way to get into the museum undetected. The tunnel was over two-thirds done, and Varak said that he'll have no problem setting off an explosion that will allow him to blow the rest of it. He said one blast, and he'd be inside the museum." She smiled. "Won't that be an interesting surprise for Eve Duncan?" She turned to Varak. "I don't mind your blowing her up, but you bring me my statue intact. I'm making it easy enough for you."

"You forget that there's more than this little surprise to think about," Varak said sarcastically. "It's only a way to get in without being seen. I also have to worry about what happens once I hit that area with the second round of explosives. Where's that tunnel?"

"Behind that granite rock to the left of the ladder. Show him, Dalai."

Dalai was already moving toward the ladder. This was all going wrong, she thought desperately. Who would have thought Zahra would remember this old tunnel? But Dalai should have thought about it. Eve Duncan might die because she hadn't considered the possibility it might be used.

"Get out of my way." Varak was striding out of the treasure room and heading toward the ladder. "You're shaking. Why are you scared? It's no wonder I find you such a bore." He was working at loosening the rock behind the ladder with the pick he'd yanked from his backpack. "Maybe I should take you with me and show you something to be really afraid about." The rock came free, and he rolled it aside and peered into the damp darkness. "Stinking mess." He put on his backpack. "I'm going to have to crawl most of the way. You'd better not have lied to me, Zahra." He disappeared into the darkness.

Dalai watched for a moment before she whirled around

and turned back to Zahra. "Did you lie to him? Can he get through?"

She shrugged. "He thinks he can. I wouldn't lie when it means my statue. I want him to get to the museum."

"But you lied to him about the Minister of Police. I wasn't sure he'd believe you."

"Neither was I. But it worked, didn't it? Not bad for a 'stupid' woman."

"Do you think that he'll actually get you the statue?"

She shrugged. "I believe he'll kill Duncan and take the statue from her. Whether he intends to give it to me won't be clear until it happens. But at least he will have done what I needed him to do as far as Duncan is concerned. Once he gets back here, I'll know what I need to do about him." She tilted her head as she gazed critically around the treasure room. "Pity. I might actually have to give him some of Kiya's treasures if he does everything he promised he'd do here. As he said, he's quite lethal, and he could succeed." She added cheerfully, "But I can always arrange to get all of them back later. All I'd have to do would be to hire someone like Varak to help me. As long as Varak stays away from Maldara and isn't causing me any problems, I could live with his having a moderate share . . . for a short time."

"There's no one 'like' Varak. He would take more than a moderate share."

Zahra's smile deepened. "Then I would have to make an adjustment."

"You mean, you would kill him," Dalai said quietly. "That's why you wore the ruby comb tonight."

She shrugged. "It's another alternative, another way to get rid of him. It would be easy enough. The bastard is so big and strong. Yet all I'd have to do would be to get close enough to him to just run those prongs over his throat." She reached out and stroked a gold-rimmed vase next to her. "Not quite as safe, but I could use this attack on Robaku to my political advantage. I've been considering—" She broke off, frowning as something struck her. "You don't sound like yourself, Dalai. Why are you asking me all these questions?" She started to turn to face her. "Haven't I told you that—" She stopped as she saw that Dalai had crossed the room and was staring down at the golden trunk. "What are you doing?" Then she thought she realized what was happening. "He frightened you." She shrugged. "It might not happen. The idea just intrigued him."

"As it intrigued you." Dalai's gaze hadn't shifted from the trunk. "It must have made you feel very strong and powerful." She lifted the lid and gazed down inside it. "Because being that afraid made me even weaker and more dependent on you than ever."

"You had to be taught your place." Zahra was frowning again. "And you're sounding very disrespectful. I won't permit that, Dalai. You know what I'll do to you."

"My place," Dalai repeated. "I've let you tell me what that is all these years. I believe I've learned it very well." She paused. "But not from what you told me. It was because I had to teach myself who I really am to survive you."

"What's *wrong* with you?" Zahra hissed. "I won't take this from you. Have you forgotten who I am? I'm the leader of this country. Your father sent you to serve me. I let you live in my palace. You're nothing, Dalai."

"So you tell me," Dalai said. "Nothing. Or rabbit." She paused. "Or slave. But I'm none of those things, Zahra."

"Zahra?" Her lips tightened, her expression incredulous. "Insolence. You do not address me in that fashion."

"No, I won't address you at all," Dalai said. "After I've finished with you, I will go away and not see you again. I will try not to ever think of you." She met her eyes. "And I believe I will succeed because I'm stronger than you think I am."

"Go away? Do you think I'd let you leave me?" Zahra's dark eyes were glittering, her lips curled. "Perhaps I will, but only to go to Varak. I'll let him teach you manners, you little slut. You shake when he looks at you."

"Yes, I do. But how will you send me to him when you said you might kill him? You must make up your mind, Zahra." Her smile had a tinge of mockery. "Because threats won't work anymore. I'm afraid of Varak, but I'm not afraid of you. I haven't been afraid of you for a long time."

"Of course, you are. You know what I can do to you. You jump when I snap my fingers."

"Because I knew it pleased you, and it kept me safe. Pretense. Only a game. You had to believe I would never betray you. You had all the power, and I had to wait until it was my time." She met her eyes. "I realized when I was lying in that trunk that I wasn't going to live if I didn't change and become as strong as you are. I'm afraid your punishment backfired, Zahra."

"And you think this is your time?" She laughed. "What a fool you are. I've never been more strong."

"And I've never had a time when I wasn't alone. It makes a difference." She shined the beam of her flashlight around the room. "Kiya's treasure. I've always hated it. But only because of what you did to me here. You said she was like you, but I think she stood on her own."

"Not alone?" Zahra's voice was suddenly suspicious. "Why aren't you alone? Why are you saying all this now?"

"Because you're not going to get your statue. You're not going to get to make a choice of alternatives. Varak is going to die, and everyone is going to know what you've done."

She was looking down at the trunk again. "I could tell them, couldn't I? You've shared so much with me."

"You? No one will believe you," Zahra burst out. "Why would anyone pay attention to a little servant girl when she's muttering lies against me?"

"Perhaps when they hear from your own lips that they're not lies." She reached down into the trunk and pulled out a disk lodged against the ornate side of the gold interior. "Your voice is very well-known, Zahra. Jill Cassidy thought that there would be no problem having it identified by experts." Her smile was bittersweet. "It was her idea to put the recording device in this golden trunk. I wouldn't have chosen it because the fear is still with me. But she's kind, and she was upset when she heard about my hours in this cage."

"You and that bitch *bugged* my conversation with Varak?" Zahra's eyes were blazing. "It won't do you any good." She was moving toward Dalai, every step sleek, catlike. "Because you're going to give it to me. Who knows? I might forgive this madness if you don't make me more angry."

"No, you won't." Dalai was backing away, slipping the disk into her jacket pocket. "I've gone too far. We both know it. You'll have to stop me any way you can."

"I want that disk," Zahra said between clenched teeth. "Give it to me."

Zahra jumped toward her.

Dalai threw her flashlight at her, and it hit Zahra in the mouth. Then Dalai dived behind a huge urn as the flashlight rolled across the floor.

"Hiding, little rabbit?" Zahra was half kneeling as she moved across the dim room. "How stupid to throw that flashlight at me. How are you going to see me? But I still have my flashlight, and I'm catching glimpses of you. Frightened? Look at you, dodging behind all those trunks and statues in the dark. I'm closer to you now. I can hear you breathing. And you said you weren't afraid of me. Liar."

Dalai froze behind a carved chaise. She could hear Zahra breathing. But Zahra sounded excited, and Dalai realized that she was excited, too. She wasn't frightened as Zahra assumed. The blood was pumping through her veins, and there was no fear, only the rush of adrenaline. She felt... eager, her gaze on every move Zahra made.

She could see Zahra's shadow behind the glare of her flashlight. She was reaching up to her chignon.

The ruby comb, Dalai thought. She had been expecting it.

She watched in fascination. Zahra was loosening the comb in her hair, getting it ready for the strike. "You're right. You've gone too far," Zahra said softly. "You went too far the moment you thought you could stand up and be anything but the slave you are. Slaves should always kneel, Dalai. You should have remembered that."

Then she leaped. She was on top of Dalai. She hit Dalai's head with the flashlight. Then she struck Dalai again.

Dalai rolled away from her, grasping the flashlight and using all her strength to pull it away from Zahra. Then she was frantically searching in her jacket pocket as she watched Zahra pull the ruby comb from her hair.

She was aiming the prongs at Dalai's face! Dalai felt the prongs break the skin at her chin as she fought to push Zahra's hand aside. Strong. Zahra had always been so strong...

"Yes," Zahra said fiercely. Her eyes were gleaming down at Dalai. "That should be enough. You'll feel the poison any second. You're *dead*, Dalai. We both know it." But the comb was moving again, raking Dalai's throat, she could feel the blood flow... "But this is pure pleasure..." Zahra whispered: "I want more. I want to see you suffer. You thought you could hurt *me*? You betrayed me!"

Zahra was enjoying this too much, Dalai thought. If Dalai didn't move quickly, Zahra might decide to cut her throat. Dalai's hand closed on the switchblade knife in her pocket. Distract her. She gazed at Zahra frantically, pleadingly. "Please, don't do—"

She rolled to the side, taking Zahra by surprise. The switchblade was out and open.

Dalai reached out and plunged the pearl-handled knife into the hand holding the comb.

Zahra screamed.

"What are you doing?" Zahra was staring at her hand in disbelief. "Why did you—You fool! It's too late. You'll be dead in—"

"That's what you said." Dalai's heart was beating hard as she carefully edged away from the knife she'd plunged into Zahra's hand. She swallowed. Everything had gone so quickly, she was having trouble believing what she'd done. "And you might be right if you hadn't always let me prepare the poisons for the comb. But I couldn't take a chance that you would use the poison on Eve Duncan instead of Varak. I had to be in control." She stared into Zahra's eyes, then her glance shifted to the knife sticking upright in the hand clutching the comb. "You understand control, Zahra."

Zahra's eyes widened in horror as she realized what Dalai meant. "The comb had no poison? You switched the poison to that knife?"

"I had to be prepared. That's what I told myself. But it might have been a lie." She said wearily, "Maybe this was always how I intended it to end. I could have run. I could have hit you on the head. I could have just pretended that nothing had changed. But I let the words come. I let you go after me." She was slowly sitting up. "Because something *had* changed, and I couldn't ignore it."

"It *hurts*." Zahra was staring dazedly down at the wound in her hand. "It's burning, you bitch. You did it. It's really the poison." She was suddenly trying to move toward her. "I'll *kill* you."

Dalai shook her head. "You're already too weak. Remember how you described what the poison would do to frighten me? All you can do is lie there and hate me. It won't be long now."

"I *won't* die," Zahra panted. "Weak people like you die. I'll live through this. I'm like Kiya and Cleopatra, queens who ruled the world." Zahra's voice was frantic with fear and anger as she felt the poison sear inside her. "But I would have been greater than them. I have to be greater. I won't let you take that from me. I won't let anyone take—"

Dalai shook her head. "You're not great, Zahra." She leaned closer and looked into her eyes. "You're nothing. You should recognize that word. *Nothing*. And soon you'll be less than nothing."

Zahra's eyes were filled with outrage and horror. Her mouth fell open, and her eyes glazed. "*No!* Not me. I won't have it! This can't happen to—"

She was dead.

Dalai stared at her for a long moment. So many years of fear and torment... She should feel something, shouldn't she? She felt nothing but flatness and bewilderment. She got wearily to her feet. It didn't matter what she was feeling. Maybe she'd know later.

Now she had to do something to help Jill or Eve Duncan. Varak had seemed so confident that he could get through that tunnel. Dalai had to call Jill and let her know. She was helping no one staying down in this splendid golden treasury that Zahra had worshipped.

Hurry!

She reached for her phone as she started to run up the ladder.

She heard the explosions before she'd gone more than two rungs.

She climbed the rest of the rungs, panicked.

Then she was outside, staring desperately in the direction of the museum. But she couldn't see it! It had disappeared.

All she could see was the thick layer of rolling black smoke reaching for the sky.

———

"Come back inside." Hajif was trying to draw Jill back into the cave. "You're not supposed to be out here. All is going well. Mr. Novak said that it should be over soon."

She could see that it was going well as she gazed down at the streets of the village. Varak's men had been sitting ducks for Novak's team waiting for them. But there was still violence and blood and all the hideous signs of war to which Jill had become accustomed.

The acrid scent of tear gas . . .

Gunshots.

Men running . . .

Explosions.

Men firing automatic rifles . . .

And men with machetes . . .

How she hated those machetes.

"Come back inside," Hajif said again. "Mr. Novak will not be—"

Kaboom.

The ground shook, throwing her to the ground.

Then another explosion.

Her eyes flew toward the hill.

Smoke. The entire hill was wreathed in thick, black, smoke.

"What is that smoke?" Hajif's gaze had followed Jill's to the top of the hill. "Was it a bomb? I don't see a fire."

Neither did Jill though she thought she could see a dull glow beyond those thick clouds of smoke. "I think...it's a military-grade smoke grenade. I've seen them before, in Pakistan. Varak must have launched it with a chemical explosive of some sort to keep feeding the smoke." She was struggling to get to her feet. "Probably oil or carbon base...I don't know why he—" She broke off as the reason came to her. "No one can see through that smoke. You'd be almost blind."

Smoke. Black. Impenetrable. Curling like thick shadow serpents into the sky from the hill.

From the museum.

That thick black smoke would completely obscure vision from only a few yards away.

And Joe's position in that banyan tree was more than twenty yards from the museum. He wouldn't be able to see anything.

Panic iced through her. "No!"

Then she was ripping off her tee shirt. "Keep everyone in the caves, Hajif." She wrapped the tee shirt over her mouth and nose as she tore away from him. She heard Hajif shouting behind her as she ran through the jungle and streaked up the path.

Through that impossibly thick smoke, she couldn't even see the banyan tree where, only hours earlier, Joe had shown her he'd set up to take his shot. She didn't know if he was still there in the jungle or heading toward that museum as she was doing.

She didn't care. She only knew what she had to do.

Get to Eve.

She reached the museum. The door had been thrown wide.

No fire. But smoke in every corner and pouring out the door.

And there was a gaping black hole where the back windows had been. A hole big enough for Varak to have been able to take Eve out of the museum and avoid that front entrance.

And no Eve.

Maybe Joe had already gotten her out...

But Mila's reconstruction was still on the worktable. Eve would never have left her there to be destroyed.

She grabbed the skull and took it with her as she tore back out of the museum.

Her eyes were stinging as she ran out into that thick cloud of smoke again. She shouted, "Eve!"

"Here she is!" It was a man's voice in the distance. "Come and get her, Jill. It *is* Jill Cassidy, isn't it? How could I ever forget your voice? I was hoping to see you here."

And how could she ever forget Varak's voice? Laughing as she struggled beneath the weight of his body as he beat her. Don't think of that moment of weakness. Make him speak again so she could locate him.

And so Joe could locate Eve.

"Say something, Eve," she called. "Has he hurt you? He's a coward and very good at hurting helpless women...or children." Her hand tightened on her gun. "Isn't that right, Varak?"

"Yes, because they're of no importance. Except when they're being stubborn. Your friend Duncan is proving to be very obstinate. She won't tell me where the Great Beloved Wife statue is hidden. Come and help me persuade her."

"Stay where you are, Jill," Eve called. "You know you can't do anything. Don't give him what he wants."

Jill was almost sure Eve's voice was coming from the dense jungle behind the museum. She started toward it. "You're alive. That means there has to be something we can do."

Are you listening, Joe? Do you hear us? All that training, all that intensity and boundless passion. Track him. Find him.

She was struggling to breathe. Her throat felt raw. But there was less smoke as she rounded the curve in the trail that led to the rear of the museum. She thought she could see darker figures among the haze. Eve?

"I see you, Jill," Varak said. "You're just a shadow in all this smoke, but I can make you out. And I don't see the gun in your hand, but I know it's there. Because you had one when we had our little party with you. It didn't do you any good then. It won't do you any good now. Because your friend, Eve, also had a gun, and I was forced to smash a few fingers and take it away from her. I admit I was tempted to use my machete on them. But perhaps later... right now all you have to know is that the barrel of the gun is pressed to her temple. That means you're going to come forward and toss your gun to me, or I'll press the trigger. I'll give you to the count of three. I want that statue, and I don't have time to play games. Unfortunately, I've had a call from Markel, and he says things aren't going as we hoped in the village. So it seems I've got to get out of here." His tone was suddenly harsh. "But I'm not going before I get that statue. It appears as if I'm going to need money. But I'd do it even if it weren't worth a fortune, just to keep it away from that bitch, Zahra. She worships it." He started the count. "One... Two..."

"Stop." She knew that the crazy bastard would do it. "I'm coming toward you. We can work this out. Don't hurt her."

Where are you, Joe?

He had to be close. He was a much better tracker than she was. There had to be a reason why he hadn't made his move, and it was probably that threat Varak had made.

She stopped a few yards from Varak. The smoke was still thick here, but she could see him. He had a scarf covering his mouth and nose, and it brought back the chilling memory of that night in the jungle. Forget it. Fear was her enemy, and it would only weaken her. She flinched as she saw that he hadn't been lying about the gun pressed to Eve's temple. She quickly tossed her gun on the ground beside him. "If things aren't going your way, you should let her go and run. If Eve Duncan dies, they'll never stop hunting you."

"I've been hunted for most of my life. I haven't been caught yet." He cocked his gun. "The statue, Eve," he said softly. "I know you have it. I saw it when you were bragging about that press conference on TV. Where is it?"

"I'm listening. I want to live," Eve said. "I have a family. I did hide that statue. But Jill might be right. Maybe we can make a deal."

She was playing for time, Jill knew. Banking on the belief that Joe was close. But Joe couldn't do anything as long as that gun was pressed to Eve's temple.

So get the barrel away from her.

Give Joe his chance. Give Eve her chance.

How?

Then, as she looked down at the reconstruction of Mila that she was still carrying, she realized she knew.

"But maybe we shouldn't give in to him, Eve. He's bound to be lying to us." Jill's voice deliberately rose hysterically. "I told you what he did to me. I can't let—" In midsentence, she hurled Mila's skull with full force at the hand in which Varak was holding the weapon and knocked his gun up in the air. The next instant, she dived to the ground next to him, reaching for the gun she'd just tossed to him.

She heard Varak swearing as he stomped on her hand and instinctively swung the weapon in his hand toward her to fire it.

Pain.

She gasped as the hot wave of agony spread through her side.

But he was turning away from her toward Eve again.

No!

But Eve was tearing away from him and dropping to the ground. "Now, Joe!"

A single shot from a Remington 700.

Varak's body whiplashed as the bullet struck him in the throat. His eyes bulged as he saw the blood spurting. "What the—" Then he started to fall to the ground.

But Joe's second bullet tore into Varak's left eye, jerking him backward.

And then the third bullet struck him in the center of his forehead, and his head exploded.

Jill saw him collapse a few yards away, the blood pouring from the wounds. So much blood . . .

Dead. Is that how monsters died?

Eve was kneeling beside Jill, her face pale. "Lie still." Her voice was shaking. "Why couldn't you have just waited? I could have stalled him. You're bleeding, dammit."

"Mila . . . I'm sorry about Mila. I couldn't think of anything else to do. All that . . . work . . ."

"What? Mila? Where did that come from? For heaven's sake, I think that she'd forgive you. I know I do." Her voice was suddenly fierce. "Providing you don't die on us. I won't have that, Jill."

"Of course, I . . . won't die." Jill's voice sounded strange, slurred, even to herself. "I'm just a little . . . tired . . ."

Darkness.

———

EMBASSY HOSPITAL

There was light streaming through that window, Jill realized as her eyes opened. Strange. It had been dark only minutes ago, but now it was light...

She saw Novak's face above her. And that hospital smell...

"Nairobi?" she whispered drowsily.

"No, we're done with Nairobi." He leaned forward. "Embassy hospital. But we do keep meeting this way. It's got to stop, Jill. I don't think I can take much more."

Then she was wide-awake. "Eve!"

"She's fine," he said. "You took the bullet. But you're fine. It was a flesh wound in your left side, and you have a cracked rib." He grimaced. "Well, maybe Eve's not so fine. She was with you most of the night after the doctors patched you up. She wouldn't let anyone else get near you. She only left when Quinn said that her son was on the phone and needed to talk to her. Then she graciously allowed me to sit with you."

"No one needs to sit with me. You shouldn't be here anyway. I know you've got stuff you need to do." She had a vague memory of smoke and explosives and men running... "Your team probably needs you. It must be a major disaster scene at Robaku."

"It is, but we've got it under control. I've been back and forth to Robaku all night." He paused. "And I *should* be here." His hand covered hers on the bed. "Stop giving me orders. This isn't your story anymore until you get out of that hospital bed. It's mine."

His hand was warm and safe, and she didn't want to move it. "You said I was fine." She had a sudden thought. "Dalai. Is she okay?"

"Other than trying to fight everyone in the emergency room to make them release her. They insisted on keeping her overnight to make sure those cuts on her face and throat didn't contain the same poison that killed Zahra. Her room is down at the end of the hall." He shook his head as she tried to sit up. "No, you don't get out of that bed until the doctor says that you can. I'd say she's proved she can take of herself."

"That doesn't matter. I brought her into this. She deserves my support."

"And I can see that you're already planning on how to get down that hall as soon as I leave this room. Relax, Jill. It's not going to happen."

He wasn't going to budge. He was being his usual domineering self. She fell back against the pillows. It wasn't worth fighting him right now. Her throat still felt raw, her side was throbbing, and she had to figure things out anyway. "You'll have to leave here soon. You've programmed everyone not to be able to do without you. You said you had it under control. What does that mean? What did you do?"

"As soon as Varak's men were subdued, I had photos taken of the scene and Varak's body removed and flown to Nairobi for complete DNA and lab work. Then I brought U.S. Ambassador Sandow and his staff to Robaku and started the real battle." His lips twisted. "To keep us all from getting arrested. I had to call in my director to use all his political connections to try to smooth the way until I could get those DNA results. I'm lucky he didn't cut me loose. He still may decide to do it."

"Not likely. You're the golden boy, and he'll know that if anyone can clean up this mess, it will be you." She smiled. "And I might be persuaded to write a story or two to sanitize your spotty image."

"I'll pass. You're right, as long as I can manage to make this appear as a triumph for democracy and keep a civil war from erupting, I'll dodge the flak." He paused. "That's going to be the prime danger, Jill. The Kiyani legislature is already in an uproar about their president's being murdered. We gave them no details, but we're going to have to do it soon. They're making threats to everyone in Maldara, and Botzan is the main target. It doesn't help that Zahra had recently turned herself into a heroine." He met her eyes. "We're exploring options to keep them from turning this into a disaster."

It was clear there was meaning behind that last sentence. Options? What would keep this from becoming—

No! She immediately rejected the thought that had occurred to her. But she knew that it had occurred to Novak, too. She was silent a moment, trying to think of any other possible way to avoid it. But there wasn't any other option at this moment, dammit. "You know what you have to do," she said jerkily. "No more deaths. No more war. There can be no confusion or infighting. Zahra has to stay a heroine. She has to be the one who helped take down Varak in revenge for his attack on the U.N." Her lips twisted bitterly. "Varak killed her, and she died a martyr. You can stage that beautifully, Novak. You'll have to get a reputable journalist to break the story as soon as possible." She added fiercely, "But it won't be *me*. I won't lie and make Zahra Kiyani out to be anything but who she is. And when all this craziness is done, I'm going to be the one who discovers that disk that proves that a mistake has been made, and Zahra is actually a murdering bitch. Is that understood?"

"Understood," he said quietly. "It will save lives, Jill."

"Stop trying to soothe me. I know it's necessary. We can't let our trying to keep Varak from starting his slaughter all over again begin a war of its own. But it's a lie, and I hate it. So go away and do what you have to do. I'll look at it as one of those dark Grimms' fairy tales instead of a story that I can be proud of. I'll block it out and be fine with it in a few days."

"No, you won't," he said. "And I'm not fine about any of this. I don't want you to send me packing. You scared me to death," he said hoarsely. "I just want to sit here and make sure you're not going to fade away."

"Well, now you've had your time to do that," Eve said brusquely from where she was standing in the doorway. "Now get back to work, Novak. Joe said you know all those diplomats and politicians better than he does, and he needs you to keep them at bay until we get the results back on Varak's DNA. The situation is getting explosive. Right now, no one is sure that we didn't perform our very own coup."

"Maybe we did." He got to his feet. "My director said that it was only a question of semantics. However, you'll be comforted to know that Jill and I discussed a way we might avoid a civil war." He was heading for the door. "But there are a few more things that might be helpful. I think I'll give Gideon a call." He looked back at Jill, and said sharply, "Stay in that bed until you see the doctor."

Before she could answer, he was gone.

"If anyone can stop the tanks from rolling, he can," Eve said with a grin. "He might just roll back over them." She came across the room and dropped down in the chair Novak had vacated. "Joe says he's watched him, and he's incredible at pulling strings and manipulating situations. Rather like someone else I know."

Jill flinched. "Mine was a onetime effort. And I've tried to make up for it."

Eve's smile ebbed. "I'd say throwing yourself in front of a bullet for me might qualify. But it wasn't only a onetime effort. You pulled the strings that brought Varak to Robaku."

"And almost got you killed." She looked at Eve's bandaged hand. "Varak said he hurt your hand. Are you okay?"

"Just bruised. And don't be ridiculous. We all knew what

the stakes were. We were all ready to pay them." She leaned forward. "I'm not going to thank you. That goes without saying. I just need to tell you that, in spite of the way we started out, I've been thinking of you as my friend for a long time now. I *keep* my friends, Jill. I have no intention of letting you slip away because you're still having guilt feelings. So get a grip and realize that we're in it for the long haul."

"I'll try to oblige." She found her throat tightening with emotion. "Though I'm not sure Joe wouldn't agree that the guilt is justified."

"You still have a cracked rib from the bullet you took for me. Joe might just think you walk on water right now."

Jill chuckled. "That won't last."

"You can never tell. Life has been nothing but surprises since I got to Maldara."

"But you'll be very glad to leave."

Eve nodded. "I want to go home." She paused. "But not quite yet. I'm going to take a quick trip to see Michael and Jane while Joe and Novak settle all the furor that happened at Robaku. Then I'm coming back to finish the reconstructions of those children. It shouldn't take me more than a few months, and I want to finish what I started."

"What *I* started."

"Whatever. You're doing it again, Jill. Stop it." She got to her feet. "Now I'm going to tell your doctor that you're awake. And then I'm going down the hall to see Dalai. I tried before, but she wasn't talking to me. She's kind of shut down. She seems very much alone."

"As soon as they let me up, I'll go and see what I can do," Jill said. Then she changed her mind and reached for her phone on the bedside table. "No, it's not me she needs."

CHAPTER

20

Y ou're putting me to a lot of trouble, Dalai." Gideon sighed as he opened the door of her hospital room. "Particularly since it seems I'm a busy man today, very much in demand. You could be a little more accommodating."

She stiffened, her gaze flying to his face. "I didn't mean to cause you trouble. I didn't ask to see you. Go away."

"That appears to be your theme song where I'm concerned." He came into the room and strolled over to the bed. "But I can't go away because Jill thinks that I have to make things right with you." He shook his head. "Which is unreasonable because you've told her that I was the injured party. But Jill has to make her stories end the way she wants them to, so I guess we'll have to go along with her." He gently touched her cut chin. "Zahra hurt you. I told you to let me know if that happened again. You persist in not listening to me."

She moved her head away from his touch. "It's nothing," she said jerkily. "And it shouldn't matter to you anyway."

"Ah, yes, because you used me." He shook his head. "I'm an incredibly rich man, Dalai. Do you realize how many times I've been used since that first time I saw you when you came to Zahra? The two seem to go together. You become accustomed to it after a while. Sometimes it's even amusing watching the process."

"Amusing?" She looked at him in disbelief. "This was different. I could have killed you."

"Only if I was too stupid to protect myself."

"I could have killed you," she repeated.

"You appear to be stuck on that thought." He frowned. "So I guess I'm going to have to go at this from another angle. Yes, there was a slight possibility that you might have been to blame for getting me killed if everything had gone wrong. So you'll just have to do something to make up for it."

She tensed, her hands clenching on the sheet. Her eyes lifted to meet his own.

"No," he said quietly. "How could I do that to you when all I can see when I look at you is that big-eyed young girl who could have been my sister." He shrugged. "But I have no sister, and Varak killed my parents. We're both alone. But I believe we could manage to be friends. So I think we should stick together for a while until you become accustomed to life without Zahra."

She frowned suspiciously. "Are you pitying me again?"

"Perish the thought. I'm going to put you to work." He smiled. "Because it appears I'm going to be used again. This time by Novak, and I can't talk him out of it. He thinks he can quiet down all the uproar in the Kiyani government by arranging with the generals and bureaucrats to accept me as interim president until they can scramble and set up an election." His eyes were suddenly twinkling. "Since everyone would find me acceptable due to my charm, wit, and fat wallet. I told Novak to get me out of there fast, or they'd draft me for the duration."

"President..." She was looking at him in bewilderment. "Like Zahra?"

"Interim," he repeated. "And definitely not like Zahra. So will you come back to that place you must have hated, and we'll make the best of it for the time we have to be there? Then I think you might be ready to go to school or start a new life. Whatever you like."

"I have no money to start a new life. I have *nothing*."

"Not true. You have Kiya, the Great Beloved Wife. Novak is pulling strings to donate the Kiya treasury to the Kiyani people, but I bought the Great Beloved Wife in a separate deal at an enormous fee."

"And you think I would take that from you?"

"No, I'm not offering. I know better. But the interest on what the statue will bring in from tours and exhibits will be a tidy sum. You can consider it part of your salary."

"And what am I supposed to do for this salary?" she asked warily.

"Jill says that you've been very inventive surviving Zahra. I'm sure you'll find ways to make that hellish period in the palace bearable for me. You've listened and know everything that's going on in that government. You know where all the political bodies are buried. Maybe you'll even be able to get me out of that interim position sooner. Now that would earn a gigantic bonus."

"No, it would not," Dalai said flatly. But her eyes were shining with sudden interest. "No pity. But I could do this. I know these people. I've watched them all for Zahra and reported back to her. And I know their servants and every flaw in their lives." She frowned. "But it would be easier if you could make them accept me with respect. It made it more difficult for me when they saw the way Zahra treated me."

His lips tightened. "You mean as a slave."

"She did not say that word around anyone but me."

"But the implication was there."

"Always."

And it was incredible that she'd managed to rise above that stigma as well as all the other abuse Zahra had inflicted on her, Gideon thought. *But don't show sympathy or I'll never get her to accept help.*

He said lightly, "Then I guess we'll have to give you a fancy official title and your own staff to overcome it. What do you think?"

She stared at him for a long moment. "I think you're still trying to be kind to me." She was gazing directly into his eyes. "You cannot help yourself. It is your way, your character. And I need that kindness right now. But I will not need it for long." She lifted her chin. "Give me a little time, and you will see that I will get stronger and stronger. I don't know anything about this being friends. But you will learn to rely on me. It will be me who helps and lends *you* strength when you need it, Gideon."

Gideon nodded solemnly. "I don't have the slightest doubt that will be true." He turned to leave. "I'm already anticipating being deep in your debt."

"Wait." She moistened her lips. "I'm sorry I can't return your knife to you. You said it was a keepsake. Eve told me that Novak probably won't give it back because he thought Zahra's death shouldn't be connected to me."

"It was *your* knife, Dalai. I told you that I thought my father would want you to have it." He smiled. "I know he'd think it couldn't have been used for a better purpose. Neither do I."

She stared at him defiantly. "And neither do I."

He chuckled. "Then we won't worry about it, will we? Now I have to go and see Jill and tell her that we've come to an agreement. If that's all right with you?"

She nodded. "Yes, go talk to Jill." She suddenly smiled. "Because you're not at all sure about any of this except that you wish me to be safe and happy. But she will understand. When I told her that Zahra had told me once that she was like Kiya and I was only her slave, she said bullshit. She asked me how I didn't know that I wasn't the one who was like Kiya." She straightened, and her smile vanished. "Tell Jill that I've decided that she was right. I *am* like Kiya." She added quickly, "But I won't let that hurt you or anyone I care about. I just have to learn who she really was and how to control it."

"I'll tell Jill." He added gently, "And being like Kiya isn't all that bad. She changed the world for herself and generations after her. I'm looking forward to seeing what you can do." He lifted his hand. "I'll see you tomorrow, Dalai."

———————◆———————

"She *is* like Kiya, Gideon," Jill said thoughtfully. "She's a survivor. Her story has been a nightmare so far, yet here she is on the road to her own Great Journey." She tilted her head. "But I didn't mean for you to practically adopt her, Gideon. I just wanted you to do something to make her feel better."

"And I did it," he said lightly. "But I'm warning you that she'd be insulted if you mention adopting her. She's having enough trouble understanding the friendship concept. If there's any adoption going on, I have an idea that she'd be the one in control." He leaned forward and brushed a kiss on Jill's forehead. "Don't worry about it, this is right. It's what

I should have done a long time ago. We'll work it out together. Maybe I should be grateful that Novak is pulling me into that mess in the Kiyani government. It will give Dalai something to challenge her." He straightened and turned to leave. "What's next for you? Are you going to be at that news conference tomorrow? I need a friend in the media to glorify all my good points."

"The media loves you. That's another reason why Novak is bulldozing you through the legislative session. You're perfect, Gideon."

"True." His brows rose. "Does that mean you're deserting me?"

She shook her head. "It means I'm tired and need to move on," she said wearily. "It means I don't want to be around when all of Maldara is fawning over Zahra's memory. It means I've been fighting this battle for two years, and now that we're ending the story, I'm ready to skip the epilogue. I feel flat. I need something fresh and new to spark me."

"I'm fresh. I'm new. Just watch what I do to those stale old bureaucrats once I get my foot in the door." He added coaxingly, "It will be fun, Jill."

"I've been doing some research in my spare time on a project that will be fun, too. And you'll be too busy to miss me, Gideon. Maybe I'll come back for the coronation."

"Coronation was Zahra. I have no royal aspirations. Just a little fun for the shortest possible time, then I'm back in my plane and heading for the wild blue yonder." He grinned. "Don't lose touch, and I'll head your way."

She watched him walk out of the room before she turned and started packing up the few belongings Eve had brought to her. She was going to miss Gideon. He had been her friend and ally since this had begun. But it wasn't as if she was losing him entirely. People moved constantly in and out

of her life. It was how she lived, how she worked. It didn't
alter how she felt about them.

It wouldn't change how she felt about Novak.

Don't think about Novak right now.

It was hurting, and it wasn't as if she hadn't known that it was
going to end like this. It was why she'd fought to keep it from
beginning. It was too intense. He was too dominant. They'd
both do far better alone.

Alone.

She wasn't really alone, she told herself. She had friends,
she had her work, she didn't need a man like Novak, who
would be a constant disturbance.

She didn't need Novak.

She would finish packing, check out of this hospital, and
go say good-bye to Eve. Eve had said that their friendship
was for the long haul, and she owed her that courtesy.

Then she would give Novak a call on her way to the airport. That would be the best way to handle it.

No, Novak would be furious. He would recognize it for
the escape it was. She didn't care. It would be too easy to
let herself delay the inevitable. She would take any way she
could to avoid the pain of what had to be done.

She needed that escape, she thought wearily.

———

"You're not going to get away with it," Eve said flatly when Jill
walked into the museum two hours later. "Gideon blew the
whistle on you with me. I squealed to Novak. He should be
here any moment."

"So much for enduring friendship," Jill said. "I was going
to call him. He's just . . . busy."

"Absolutely. Novak is doing a hell of a lot to keep this

country stable. He doesn't deserve having to face you running out on him right now. Don't be a coward. It's not like you. At least you should stick around until he has a chance to get his breath." She crossed the room and gave her a quick hug. "Ordinarily, I'd stay out of your business. But you've never made it a practice to stay out of mine, so why should I worry? We've gone way past that." She smiled. "Whatever you choose is fine with me. But you never ran out on me, and it's not fair to do it with Novak."

"You're damn right it's not," Novak said grimly from the doorway. "But that doesn't mean you didn't try to do it." He was across the room and pulling Jill toward the door. "And I could see it coming when you woke up in that hospital room." They were outside now, and he slammed the door shut behind him. "You were worried and concerned and wanting to set everything in order."

"Of course I was. I'd just returned to consciousness, and I wanted to make sure everyone was alive and well, dammit."

"No, there was more to it than that. I know you very well now, Jill. There was an edge. You were relieved when I was called away by Quinn. If Eve hadn't phoned me today, I would still have been here with you anyway. I would have tracked you down. I wasn't about to let you walk away."

"It seemed to be a good time to do it." She moistened her lips. "We have our own lives to lead, and they would interfere with each other. We both know that what we had was purely sex, sparked by the adrenaline from what we were going through."

"Do we?" He jerked her into his arms and kissed her. "I don't know anything of the sort. I don't know what's happening with us, but I'm not afraid to stay around to find out. But it's clear that you *are* afraid." His hands closed on her shoulders. "Not that I blame you. You haven't had the most stable life since your father tossed you out into the world. But it still makes me mad as hell."

"I can tell." She tried to shrug away from him. "I'm not afraid. I'm just being reasonable."

"And keeping your own personal story close to you, private and untouched. I know you don't want to let anyone come in and add anything to your life. But I'm not going to let you get away with that." His eyes were boring into hers. "Because I'm too selfish, and I won't let you go. And I won't let you lie to yourself and cheat us both. Remember the night you were so afraid Varak was going to cheat us? It's the same thing, Jill." His grasp tightened. "You're smart, recognize it. You don't have to commit. Just admit to yourself what you're doing."

She couldn't look away from him. Was it true? She wouldn't be questioning herself if there wasn't an element of truth in his words. And she'd thought she knew herself so well. She smiled with an effort. "And admit you're right?"

He went still. "That would also help a hell of a lot."

"I won't do it." She paused. "But I might admit that I was running away, and that's neither honest nor intelligent. That would also mean I thought there was a reason to be afraid of you. But you've never done anything to make me afraid. You never will." She suddenly kissed him. "So that means this is my problem, and I refuse to be afraid of it. I'll have to examine why it exists and face it."

His arms tightened around her. "*Yes.*"

She smiled and shook her head. "Not that easy, Novak. I told Gideon the truth about being ready for something new and fresh. I'm still going to leave Maldara. You're going to be busy here for a long time straightening out Varak's identity and preventing those bureaucrats in Botzan and Kiyani from starting another civil war. After you finish, if you still think there's something besides sex between us, come and see me. And who knows, maybe the sex will be enough."

"I don't believe that will be true." His eyes were narrowed on her face. "And just where am I supposed to find you?"

"I'll let you know. My first stop is Cairo to do more research." She found herself drawing closer to him. She wanted to touch him. The excitement was growing. Why be afraid to take a chance? Why not have it all? Novak was the most exhilarating man she had ever met. Share the sex. Share that wonderful mind. There was time enough to see what else might be waiting for them. "After that, I could let you know where I'll go from there."

"Research?" He tilted his head. "Just what are you doing, Jill?"

"I've been thinking about Kiya. I thought I'd try to find out her story. Or at least where she was buried."

"In Egypt?" He shook his head. "She died in Maldara according to the journal."

Jill shook her head. "No, not Cleopatra's daughter. We already know a good deal about her. The *first* Kiya. Akhenaten's Great Beloved Wife from the Eighteenth Dynasty. She had such a powerful influence, yet no one knows that much about her. Her life is surrounded by mystery, and we're not even certain where her remains can be found."

"You've found yourself a deeper mystery to dig into?" He shook his head ruefully. "And you can't resist the story."

"No, why should I?" It was all clear to her now, all hesitation gone. "The world is filled with millions of incredible, wonderful stories. And each one is an adventure to explore. But I'm inviting you along on this one, Novak. Do you know why?" Her brilliant smile lit her face as she went back into his arms. "Because I'm beginning to believe that if we're lucky, if we don't screw this up, in the end, you might be my very favorite story of all time."

AUTHOR'S NOTE

Kiya, daughter of Cleopatra VII, never existed except in my imagination. However, Queen Kiya, the Great Beloved Wife of the Pharaoh Akhenaten, was real and one of the most mysterious and intriguing figures in Egyptian history. No one is sure where she came from before arriving at his court, though some scholars believe she might have been a Mitanni princess. But once she was established in Cairo, Kiya was evidently a source of boundless controversy and excitement. From the richness of her monuments, there was no doubt she had an exalted status, and, at one time, Egyptologists thought she might have even been the mother of Tutankhamun. This proved to be unlikely, but her title of Great Beloved Wife certainly must have made her position at court very competitive with Akhenaten's beautiful chief wife, Nefertiti.

But Kiya disappeared from history during the last third of Akhenaten's reign. Her name and images were erased from monuments and replaced by those of Akhenaten's daughters. Why?

Exile? Death? Disgrace?

Or did Kiya just become bored with the court and go away on her own Great Journey to a far land?

You know which one I would choose.

But it's a mystery . . .

ABOUT THE AUTHOR

Iris Johansen is the #1 *New York Times* bestselling author of more than 30 consecutive bestsellers. Her series featuring forensic sculptor Eve Duncan has sold over 20 million copies and counting and was the subject of the acclaimed Lifetime movie *The Killing Game*. Along with her son, Roy, Iris has also co-authored the *New York Times* bestselling series featuring Kendra Michaels. Iris Johansen lives near Atlanta, Georgia.

Don't miss the next page-turning thrillers
from Iris Johansen!

Available now

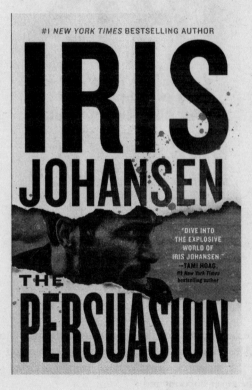

#1 NEW YORK TIMES BESTSELLING AUTHOR

IRIS
JOHANSEN

"DIVE INTO
THE EXPLOSIVE
WORLD OF
IRIS JOHANSEN."
—TAMI HOAG,
#1 New York Times
bestselling author

THE
PERSUASION

When Eve Duncan's daughter, Jane MacGuire, becomes a
killer's target, Jane must team up with longtime love interest
Seth Caleb in this action-packed novel.

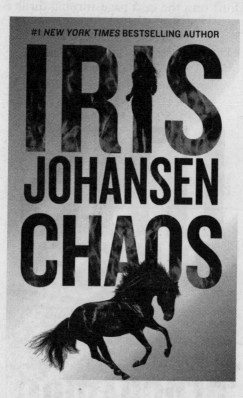

#1 *NEW YORK TIMES* BESTSELLING AUTHOR

IRIS
JOHANSEN
CHAOS

Iris Johansen introduces a compelling new female protagonist, Alisa Flynn, a CIA agent who may be willing to go rogue if it means catching the most heartless band of criminals she's ever encountered.

For a complete list of books by

IRIS JOHANSEN

VISIT
IrisJohansen.com

 Follow Iris Johansen on Facebook
Facebook.com/OfficialIrisJohansen

 Follow Iris Johansen on Twitter
@Iris_Johansen